Praise for *Paint and Nectar*

"With textured and captivating characterization, Ashley Clark sweeps us into an intriguing tale sure to entrance! Readers will be enchanted by Ashley's authentic portrayal of Charleston and its rich history and beautiful charm. A Southern fiction gem!"

—Amanda Dykes, author of *Yours Is the Night*
and the 2020 Christy Book of the Year

"Ashley Clark solidifies herself as a compelling voice in Southern fiction, with a promise to find stories between every brick and blossom. *Paint and Nectar* is infused with the history and romance of feuding families, seamlessly spanning generations through a love of art, architecture, and the city of Charleston, which beats as the heart between them."

—Allison Pittman, *The Lady in Residence*

"Ashley Clark has painted a story more vivid than any watercolor. Her characters are like sweet friends, real and imperfect and dearly loved. *Paint and Nectar* is as enchanting and charming as Charleston itself. What a delightful read—not to be missed!"

—Liz Johnson, bestselling author of *The Red Door Inn*

Praise for *The Dress Shop on King Street*

"*The Dress Shop on King Street* by Ashley Clark is so much more than your typical romance. It's a rich, complex, and uplifting story of family lost and found that I won't soon forget. If you loved *Before We Were Yours*, you will love *The Dress Shop on King Street* as much as I did. Highly recommended!"

—Colleen Coble, USA Today bestselling author
of the Lavender Tide series and *One Little Lie*

"*The Dress Shop on King Street* is a novel that will sweetly tug you into a story line that flows seamlessly between two times, only to intertwine in beautiful ways. Page by page, secret by secret, moment by moment, a story is woven of love lost and found, and hopes and dreams restored. And each page was a gift I did not want to walk away from. Enter these pages only if you want to feel Millie and Harper's stories deeply, and in the process, be reminded of how gentle God is as He guides us through dreams lost and found. You might just fall in love with a new-to-you author's writing. I know I have."

—Cara Putman, bestselling and award-winning author
of *Delayed Justice* and *Shadowed by Grace*

Paint
and
Nectar

HEIRLOOM
SECRETS

Paint and Nectar

A NOVEL

ASHLEY CLARK

BETHANYHOUSE
a division of Baker Publishing Group
Minneapolis, Minnesota

© 2021 by Ashley Clark

Published by Bethany House Publishers
11400 Hampshire Avenue South
Bloomington, Minnesota 55438
www.bethanyhouse.com

Bethany House Publishers is a division of
Baker Publishing Group, Grand Rapids, Michigan

Printed in the United States of America

Library of Congress Cataloging-in-Publication Data
Names: Clark, Ashley, author.
Title: Paint and nectar / Ashley Clark.
Description: Minneapolis, Minnesota : Bethany House, a division of Baker
    Publishing Group, [2021] | Series: Heirloom secrets
Identifiers: LCCN 2020052771 | ISBN 9780764237614 (trade paper) | ISBN
    9780764239229 (casebound) | ISBN 9781493431489 (e-book)
Classification: LCC PS3603.L35546 P35 2021 | DDC 813/.6—dc23
LC record available at https://lccn.loc.gov/2020052771

This is a work of historical reconstruction; the appearance of certain historical figures are therefore inevitable. All other characters, however, are products of the authors' imagination, and any resemblance to actual persons, living or dead, is coincidental.

Cover design by Kathleen Lynch / Black Kat Design

Cover photograph of woman by Malgorzata Maj / Arcangel

Author is represented by Spencerhill Associates

21 22 23 24 25 26 27   7 6 5 4 3 2 1

In memory of my Grandpaw Jim,
who loved bluebirds and gardens.
And from whom I got my knack for embellishment.

And to my other grandparents—Dolores, Melody, and Ernie—
for giving me the gift of family and all it means.

I am grateful for the heritage of faith
the four of you have given me.

The question is not what you look at,
but what you see.

—Henry David Thoreau

PROLOGUE

December 1861
Longitude Lane, Charleston, South Carolina

Not a day went by she didn't think about her daughter.

Where she may be, if she was safe . . . who'd bought her.

At first, Rose didn't sleep at all. Then she wasn't fit for work so they sold her too. That's how she ended up working as a house slave for Clara.

Clara was a girl herself back then.

Clara wasn't a girl no more. Rose had a plan, see. She'd been a real hard worker and real kind, too, with the hope of getting information about her daughter. Rose always'd known Clara wasn't too keen on slavery like her daddy was, but she never expected this. Never expected Clara was capable of what she'd just done.

They had to be careful. For Rose herself, for Ashley, and also for Clara. She didn't want Clara getting in trouble, and if Clara's father caught them . . .

But he wouldn't, so long as they stayed focused.

Rose reminded herself of yesterday's nightmare. How her jaw hurt real bad from clenching it in the night. Started off beautiful— Ashley skipping around in innocence, just a grinnin' at her mama—

and then those men snatched her and took her away. And Rose felt she was gonna be sick when she peeled herself out of bed this mornin'. Was like she'd lived the nightmare in real life all over again.

She needed to get to her daughter. She may've already taken too long.

Everything hinged on Clara's help.

Missus Clara cradled the silver spoon in the palms of her hands now. The sky above them darkened with clouds, and the ground below them shook with the thunder of cannons. Rose and Clara huddled together near the carriage house at the end of the garden, a shovel in Rose's grasp.

Clara looked at her with fiery eyes, and the message passed clearly between them.

It has to be now.

"He's coming," Clara said. She closed her hands around the spoon. "I can't believe Father promised him my heirloom silver as a gift." She raised her chin and held on to Rose's gaze, a move that caught Rose by surprise every time. She wasn't used to white folks looking directly at her like that. "Dowries aren't even fashionable any longer. Suppose he bargained for one in exchange for taking this troublemaker off Father's hands." Clara shook her head, a humorless chuckle escaping her mouth. "Oh, Rose, I'm afraid." She fussed with her lacy gloves. "I shouldn't admit that. But can we really do this? Bury the silver before they find it? Leave everything behind?"

Yes. No hesitatin'—yes.

"Missus, you stronger than you know, and braver too. God'll give you the strength to do the right thing. Now you want me to get started diggin' before the rain comes?"

"Yes." Clara placed a hand to the well-defined waistline her corset provided and drew in a deep breath. She glanced up to the heavens. "But you'd better make it fast. I fear we don't have much time before he arrives."

ONE

1929
Longitude Lane, Charleston, South Carolina

William wasn't born a thief. Never had been the type to pocket a trinket from the market or get a rush from taking something that didn't belong to him.

But was *imitation* really stealing?

Scratch that. He needn't think too long for the answer, or guilt might overshadow his resolve. His sister needed him, and he didn't have any room for thinking beyond that right now.

Anyhow, because of all this, the average person might wonder how he ended up in this room with this man. Well, the thought of it never even occurred to him until recently. His mother would have a conniption if she knew everything he'd gotten himself into.

But his mother was the reason for this. She'd sent his sister away. Wouldn't acknowledge Hannah was in the family way, wouldn't even talk about the baby except to say there were places for handling these things discreetly. William's sister would go to no such place, and that led him to his current circumstances.

Namely how William was in this room, with this man.

Suffice to say, what William lacked in criminal experience, he made up for in artistic skill. He could paint a nearly identical Rembrandt and no one would be the wiser. He had diligently studied to play the piano like Gershwin. He would also like to think he had some people skills. Unfortunately, none of these things mattered to his mother, and they mattered even *less* to his father.

The arts were a feminine study, his father repeatedly insisted, and according to him, the family business was where William belonged. But William had no interest in securing and growing the family fortune.

Therefore, William was plumb out of options.

As he stepped deeper into the famed Mr. Cadigan's study, he felt an odd wave of calm wash over him. He took in the room full of silver, the paintings poised along the furniture and walls, as if they were people in a train terminal, waiting for their next destination. He recognized a good many of the pieces from the newspapers.

Cadigan would, of course, ship these treasures out of Charleston at the first opportunity. No one would be the wiser in Boston or New York. Buyers would assume the southern gems had come from looted houses during the Civil War—not that they were recent acquisitions.

"Pinckney, you understand why you're here?" Cadigan tapped his cigarette twice against the ashtray as a wild curl of smoke snaked upward from his nostrils. The study was dim, with only two Tiffany-style lamps to illuminate the wrinkled face of Mr. Cadigan and the moon-shaped scar above his lip. A souvenir of a recent job gone wrong. At least that's the story he told.

"Yes, sir." William crossed his arms over his chest. For the first time since approaching the house, his heart began to beat faster. The reality sank in. William only hoped his stance was strong enough to cover his hesitation before Cadigan would notice. "The watercolorist."

Cadigan nodded. "That's right. Her paintings are beginning to fetch a pretty sum around here, especially with the tourists. You study them, make copies, and I will do the rest of the work. If all goes well, she won't even know we've forged her little treasures. But if anything goes wrong . . . ." He puffed his cigarette once more.

"My policy is, new guy always takes the fall. Do a good job, and next time, you won't be the new guy."

William's stomach turned. "I'm not a criminal." It's what he kept telling himself anytime the thought *imitation is stealing* made its rounds in his mind. "This is just a onetime shindig to help my sister stay afloat."

Cadigan's wicked grin blurred the clarity William had felt just moments prior. "Whatever you need to tell yourself, pretty boy. Look, do the job well and it's your call if you need more work from us. But again—do it poorly, and you won't have that choice." He crossed his leg over his knee, and the tassels of his loafer shook. "Are we clear?"

William nodded once. "So, your guys will get me in this garden party, and then what? How do I find the paintings?"

"Patience, my boy. Your inexperience shows." Cadigan tapped his cigarette once more. "You'll befriend Eliza. The artist. Over the next few weeks, get her to trust you. Make her love you so much she would give you the originals if you asked her. In other words, make her love you so much that she practically robs herself."

William swallowed hard. "When I paint the fakes and you sell them, then I get my money?" His sister and nephew needed the money yesterday—as the saying goes—so he didn't have time to doubt the plan. At least it was something, and it'd keep her from riding the rails with that little boy in tow.

"Yes. When I do business, I never go back on my word." Cadigan held out his hand, and William reached to shake it.

But as William turned to go, Cadigan stopped him. "One more thing . . ."

"What's that?" William hoped this job wasn't about to become more complicated.

"Be careful with Eliza. She's . . . well, she's quite charming. The last man I put on this job fell for her, only to be left pining like a puppy for weeks. This time, I want my paintings."

William slid his hands into his pockets. "Charming or not, a romantic entanglement is the last thing I need right now." Without the financial means to support a wife, much less a family, he had no business falling in love—especially not with his sister counting on him. Lord knew how hard he had tried to find honest work before turning to this route.

Besides, William enjoyed the flirtations of a good many women and had yet to meet one he found interesting enough to commit his entire life to. Was that so wrong of him?

He was certain Eliza would be no different.

Eliza Jane had always been of the mind that enough lipstick could solve any problem. But when it came to making small talk with her father's associates, there wasn't enough lipstick in the world.

So imagine her pleasant surprise when a man who was tallish, with chestnut hair, a pleasant smile, and a sharp suit, came strolling through the gates of her garden. And imagine her further surprise at discovering he wasn't as boring as the rest of them, for he grinned at her as if they were the only two in the garden.

Maybe it was the twilight or the gumdrop color of the camellias against the trees, blurring against the sky. But there was something interesting about him.

He allowed the men accompanying him to take the lead, making the necessary introductions. An apprentice, it would seem, from their brief words with her father. None of the other men made eye contact with Eliza, except to look her way and murmur how beautiful she was, how proud her father must be, blah blah blah.

Oh, she didn't mean to be cruel. It was just that these businessmen could be *so dull* sometimes. It was almost as though they hadn't eyes to see the color of the day as it slipped into night, and the color of the night as it slipped into morning.

Grandma Clara always used to say Eliza had been born with a

paintbrush in her hand. Eliza sighed. What would Gran say if she could be here now?

Someone cleared his throat. Eliza glanced up out of her reverie to find the handsome one looking at her. The half grin on his lips seemed to suggest he was humored by her attention waltzing off, and she liked him already for having that reaction.

"William, ma'am." He dipped his chin as she took his hand, which he'd extended to her, as any good southern man worth his weight in salt ought to.

That is to say, too many men had lost all sense of common manners. You burn a few corsets, and the next thing you know, all sense of decorum goes out the window right along with those suffocating contraptions. Not all women were flappers, turning a blind eye to prohibition down at The Blind Tiger. Some of them still appreciated a man taking the effort to straighten his bow tie and look a woman in the eye.

Oh, times were hard, no doubt. While the rest of the country was roaring its way through the decade, Charleston was still reeling its way back from destruction. In many cases, by destroying itself. But there she went, getting lost in thought again.

"Eliza Jane," she said. She always loved the melody of her own name.

"Beautiful." William's half grin deepened.

Her cheeks warmed in a blush. Her cheeks never warmed in a blush. She meant to ask him whether he meant her name or herself, but her father and aunt were standing directly opposite them, just within earshot, and she knew better than to walk straight into that one.

So instead she simply smiled back, sure he would understand.

The gramophone rang out a jazzy tune from the camellia "room" of the garden—situated just past where the guests were mingling around the fountains.

"May I?" William asked. He never had let go of her hand.

This time, it was Eliza's turn to nod. And as she cozied closer toward this stranger—William—she let the magic of the camellias enclose them for a few fine moments.

She breathed in the coffee bean aroma of him, and smelled something else she recognized. Paint? Was he also an artist?

Eliza watched as a bluebird perched, twittering away from the flowering tree above. And then she closed her eyes, as she always did when she was memorizing a moment she would later paint.

There are times in life—sometimes, not always—when the water on paper drips with the color of just the perfect hue, until the effect is something so ethereal that the artist knows it must simply be experienced because she can never produce it again.

And the color shifts over time, shifts still over sunlight, until the watercolors fade completely back into the paper itself, and all that's left is the memory.

The February blossoms were Eliza's favorite. Always had been.

Well, maybe not always.

TWO

2020

Three days ago, Lucy met Declan at her sister's engagement party.

Two days ago, he called her to ask her on a date.

Last night, she spent the hour before midnight texting back and forth with him about favorite ice cream flavors, old movies, and beloved local spots around Charleston.

And in three minutes, Declan would be here to pick her up.

Lucy looked in the mirror, pinning, then unpinning, the silver headband in her hair, and then pinning it once more. *Humph.*

The extra-hold hairspray had been far too stiff, so she'd brushed it out in favor of a brand that promised lightly held waves. But now she had hair that was . . . well, confused. And she smelled like the beauty aisle at Walgreens.

She puckered her lips together, straightened her fitted skirt, and pushed the sleeves of her long sweater up to her elbows.

There.

At least her clothes looked the part. Her dear friend Harper would be proud of her.

She'd had an impossible time trying to come up with an outfit when he'd suggested Five Loaves—a personal favorite of hers— for their dinner. Normally, she wouldn't be so nervous and would show up to the eclectic local eatery in jeans and a T-shirt, but seeing as how this was a date, a whole lot more planning had gone into this outfit. She needed to accomplish that messy-bun-and-graphic-tee look that actually requires twice the effort of a fully formal ensemble.

That is to say, this guy was a catch.

Lucy hadn't been able to get Declan out of her mind since she first met him last week at the party. He and his cousin Peter had left quite the impression, albeit for different reasons. Peter was . . . well, more Harper's type. Whether Harper saw it yet or not, Lucy had noticed a spark between those two as Peter listened intently to Harper talk about the dress she'd made for the Senior Show at their school. Lucy was excited to see what would happen next for Harper.

But in the meantime, Declan.

Her heart skipped a beat just thinking about him. Their conversation had flowed so easily, and she was a bundle of nervous excitement thinking about where tonight's date may lead.

One minute to go—

The doorbell rang.

Lucy blew out a deep breath. So, he was punctual. She wouldn't hold it against him.

She reached for the door handle, and there he stood, with one hand casually in the pocket of his jeans and the other holding a small bouquet of little flowers out toward her.

Was this guy for real?

"Hello, Lucy." His tone was rich.

She took the bundle of flowers from him. "Hello, Declan."

Lucy hesitated a moment, inhaling the fragrance of the bouquet and truly appreciating the gift before she carried the flowers into the kitchen and arranged them in a vase. "Let me get these situated, and I'll be right back."

When she returned, he held open the door. She stepped back toward the entry, ducking under his arm. "Thank you," she said, feeling confident about her graceful move. Only she misjudged and stepped closer to him than she meant to, bumping awkwardly into him. The fragrance of his cologne and the warmth of his body swirled toward her as she looked up at him.

She bit her bottom lip. "Sorry." She smirked, trying to make light of the misstep.

His gaze drifted from her eyes to her nose to her lips, where it landed until she blinked. "That's okay."

She quickly put two feet between them and locked the door.

Her heart thumped against her chest, and the back of her neck tickled. She took a deep breath. She needed to get her head on straight. She needed to get to know the guy better, and she couldn't do that by tripping over him or babbling.

Declan glanced up toward the emergent stars as the streetlamps flickered on for the evening. "Nice weather tonight if you're up for the walk," he said. "Or I could drive us."

Lucy slung her purse over her shoulder. "Walking is good." She nodded. Yes, that would give her something to do with her nerves.

"That'll work well. Our reservation isn't for thirty minutes any-way." He looked over at her as they both stepped onto the side-walk. She considered whether he might try to hold her hand and whether she would let him.

"I remember you mentioning Five Loaves when we talked at your sister's party," he added.

"Wait." Lucy reached out to touch his elbow without thinking. She dropped her fingers from his soft sweater. Was that cashmere? "That's why you suggested it?" she asked. Kudos to him for not only listening to her that intently but also for remembering.

His eyes danced as his walking pace slowed. "Is that a problem?"

"No." Lucy drew out the word. "I just . . ." She shrugged. "I am pleasantly surprised at the attention to detail is all."

He gently reached for the small of her back to steer her around the corner. "Well, get used to it, because for better or worse, you've got my undivided attention for the rest of the evening."

Lucy laughed. She did wonder for a moment whether he was a

little *too* charming, just playing the Matthew McConaughey role of her dreams, but she was going to enjoy this while it lasted, before she had to get back to college next week. And then after that . . . well, if Declan could juggle getting to know her in a nearby-but-still-different city, who knew where things might lead.

A little bird fluttered from tree to tree along the sidewalk, and the two of them turned in tandem toward King Street, neither of them looking to the other for direction, both of them following memory and their feet—the well-worn patterns that come from years of having walked a certain way and a certain direction, the surety that comes from familiarity . . . in this case, the familiarity of what locals called the Holy City.

"Funny how our paths have never crossed before," Declan said. "Since we both grew up in Charleston."

"Who's to say they haven't?" Lucy adjusted the purse at her shoulder and looked up at him with a grin. "I mean, at any given time, we could've walked by each other on the street. On field trips as children, or visits to Blue Bicycle Books, or brunch at Hominy Grill. Do you remember that place?"

"Do I *remember* that place? Are you kidding? I still have dreams about their jalapeño hush puppies. It's a shame they closed down."

Lucy and Declan turned onto King Street as twilight deepened, and along with it, the magic of the city grew.

"Yeah, there was always such a long line to get in that restaurant, but the food was worth it, for sure. It was a real gem. I was sorry to see the city lose it." As they strolled past the storefronts, Lucy noticed a plaque honoring the Charleston Preservation Society's role in preserving one of the buildings. "I'm a big believer in preserving old things."

Declan rubbed his chin with his thumb. "Hmm."

"Hmm?" Lucy crossed her arms, turning to him. "What does that mean? You disagree?"

"Oh I wouldn't say I *disagree*, necessarily. Obviously we can all appreciate walking past the church George Washington attended during his time here or the remaining walls of the original colony of Charles Town."

"But?"

Declan hesitated, letting out a deep breath. "But I would also add that the city isn't a museum. There's a balance to be had to encourage progress." He shrugged. "Sometimes structures have to be torn down to make that happen." He shook his head. "But look, I see why you feel strongly about preservation, and I respect that. I do."

Lucy tilted her head to the side, trying to read in between the lines of his comment. At first, he had seemed apathetic toward the cause of preservation—and preservation was not a passive retreat—but on the other hand, his comments about the Revolutionary-era buildings all through the historical district suggested he both knew and cared.

She wouldn't press it for the time being. She had a whole lot more to learn about him before concerning herself with their respective thoughts on the future of the city.

As they approached the building where she and Declan had met last week, Lucy leaned closer to get another look through the windows. Harper had talked nonstop the entire drive back to Savannah about how perfect the storefront would be for a dress shop on King Street.

But as Lucy leaned closer, the silvery, leaf-patterned headband in her hair came loose from its pins and tumbled toward the sidewalk. Lucy tried to catch it but grasped only air.

Declan bent down to pick it up for her, and Lucy realized it'd broken in two.

"Well, that's disappointing," Declan said, holding up the headband where it'd snapped down the middle. "But you know what? I bet I can get this fixed for you. My mother has got an entire room full of crafting odds and ends. I'm sure she can do something."

Lucy smiled up at him. "Really?"

"Absolutely. No use in throwing away a perfectly good headband."

He held it up once more before slipping it into the pocket of his khakis. "Why, it's practically a crown."

Lucy's smile turned into a grin. His generous offer warmed her like a cup of hot cocoa on a chilly day.

They both picked up their pace down King Street, and Lucy enjoyed peering into the windows of the antique shops, boutiques, and bookstores they passed. Passersby were walking back and forth to restaurants, and the fact she was here on a date with Declan settled in, sending another flutter of butterflies within Lucy.

"Let's play a game," Declan said. "I'll give you a phrase, and we both say the first thing that comes to mind."

Lucy slid her hands into the pockets of her long sweater. "Okay."

"Best dessert in Charleston."

She didn't even have to think. "Christophe—"

"—Christophe Artisan Chocolatier," he said in tandem.

They both started laughing.

"That was easy," Lucy said. She clapped her hands together. "Oh, I have one! Favorite place to watch the sunset."

"Pineapple—"

"—Fountain." She nodded. "Because sometimes you can see dolphins from the pier."

"Exactly." Declan pointed toward her. "Most important meal of the week?"

"Sunday lunch," Lucy said and grinned, crossing her arms. "After church."

Declan nodded. "When I was a kid, we would walk home from church and catch up with the neighbors on their porches and in their yards gardening. Do people still do that?"

The streetlamp cast a glow upon them, and Lucy shuffled her feet. "I don't know. But they should. I did that as a kid too. Only I get the impression my walk home was a little longer. Sometimes we drove to church." She laughed. "Did you grow up South of Broad?"

"I did. Actually, I still live there. My parents live near the Battery, and I live a block up from Rainbow Row in one of those renovated historical properties."

"Wow," Lucy mouthed. "Living the dream. I bet you pinch yourself every morning, waking up to that view."

Declan studied her a long moment. "You know what? I work so much, I often forget to enjoy it. Thank you." He held her gaze. "For the reminder."

His brown eyes were more tempting than Christophe's chocolate.

Lucy's grin softened as the church bells chimed behind them. "You're welcome."

The sudden sound of Declan's phone startled her.

"I am so sorry." He pulled it from his pants pocket. "This is my mom. I need to take the call."

"Of course." Lucy waved her hand toward him.

Declan unlocked his phone, looking up at the old, two-story building beside them as he answered. "Hey, Mom—everything okay?" He froze. "*What? When?*" He shook his head. "And you're all right? Have the police arrived?" Long pause. "I'll be right there."

Declan pocketed his phone and looked toward Lucy. "I am so sorry. We're going to miss our dinner reservation. My parents have been robbed."

Lucy saw the flashing lights of the police vehicles lining the curb outside his parents' house long before she noticed the residence itself.

She covered her mouth with her hand. "Oh my word, Declan. I'm so sorry." She reached out to touch his arm, letting her fingers linger against the cashmere this time. "They're all okay though, right?"

"Yeah." He blew out a deep breath. "They don't even know when exactly they were robbed, because they've been on vacation in Europe and don't take out the family silver all that often. Could've been days, weeks, maybe even months."

Lucy frowned as they approached the property's wrought-iron gate. "I don't understand. Wouldn't they have noticed signs of forced entry?"

"Not necessarily." Declan shook his head. "It has all the markings of the work of a notorious silver thief. The guy just recently got out of jail. Took them two decades to find him the first time around. His whole shtick is slipping into homes undetected, then taking only the inheritance-quality silver. He leaves the imitation stuff and is meticulous to detail so he doesn't trigger any alarms. We're talking—he's willing to take hours to get inside and will replace any glass or fencing he may have to break for entry."

"Why go to all the trouble?"

Declan approached the gate of the home, Lucy following close behind. "That way, any trace of him will have vanished by the time the family notices and reports the theft." A man Lucy assumed to be his father, who was talking to two police officers, waved them closer. "I know all about this guy because he's robbed us before. Guess he didn't find what he was looking for, so he came back."

Lucy's eyes widened. "You mean he returned as soon as he was released?" What a bold move.

Declan shrugged. "Obviously I can't be sure, but that would be my guess." The two of them reached Declan's father and the officers.

"I'm sorry," one of the officers said. "This is a crime scene. You'll need to stay back."

"They're with me," his father said to the police. "This is my son."

The man nodded. "In that case, I'm sorry about the theft. We're going to do everything we can to hold the perpetrator accountable, but I do have to warn you, whoever did this was savvy." His expression was grim. "We're not optimistic we can get your heirlooms back to you."

Declan rubbed his face with his hands. Lucy didn't know what to do. She wanted to console him and seem supportive, but she also didn't know the extent of what had been stolen or what meaning it all might have to their family, and she didn't want to sound as though she were offering a pithy apology on their behalf. So she just stood there beside him.

"If that's all, sir, we're going to interview your wife now. Give us a call if you can think of anything else that may help with the case." At that, the officers moved across the lawn toward the entryway of what could only be called a mansion.

Lucy looked at it for the very first time, and that's when it hit her.

She was standing in front of the Pinckney mansion.

The Pinckney mansion.

Which meant Declan was one of *the* Pinckneys.

Not a second cousin of an ancestor who'd gone astray or a fancy-last-name-with-little-wealth situation like her own clan of Legares, but honest-to-goodness heirs to the fortune, Jane Austen style. We're talking Darcy level here, only southern.

Declan's father grew increasingly red in the face. "You and I both know what that thief was after." He spoke as though Lucy weren't even standing there.

Declan crossed his arms. "Careful, Dad . . . we don't know that for sure."

"Yes, we most certainly do." He huffed in anger. "That thief thinks *we* have it! The Revolutionary-era silver." The man threw up his hands. "But we know the truth. Those fools, those Legares, stole it from us generations ago, and now their selfish act haunts us still."

Declan's gaze grew stony. "You think he's going to keep robbing us until he finds it?"

"Of course I do. He clearly wants it for his private collection, rather than the pieces he melts down. The guy is brazen, and we know his MO from when he robbed us years ago. When he wants something for his private collection, he is relentless. The Paul Revere–signed heirloom silver is invaluable. It's the sort of thing you'd stop at nothing to get."

Declan clenched his jaw. "What's our move, then?"

"*We* stop at nothing to get it." The man's face grew even redder still. "From the Legares."

Declan said nothing. Only nodded, agreeing.

Lucy's heart began racing, like a spy with a secret. *Hold up a minute!* she wanted to yell. *My family doesn't have the silver either!* In the old anecdote she'd always heard, it was the Pinckneys who'd stolen it. So if Declan's father didn't have it, where could it be?

Was it lost forever?

She may never know. But she did know one thing.

The past fifteen minutes had brought out a different side of Declan.

And she didn't like what she saw.

Their earlier conversation on King Street echoed through her mind, in particular Declan's words: "*I see why you feel strongly about preservation, and I respect that. I do.*"

She couldn't believe he had the gall to say he respected preservation. Not when their family business was the largest modern development company in the city.

Some things, it seemed, were too good to be true.

Good-bye, Mr. Darcy.

THREE

1929

Eliza let herself be swept through the garden in William's arms until the music changed to "The Charleston" and he stopped dancing. With her hand still resting upon his arm, she looked up at him and raised an eyebrow. "Don't know how to dance the Charleston, do you, William?"

He shrugged, his suspenders tightening with the movement. He had a boyish charm about him that had lingered despite his rugged good looks.

Eliza slid her grip from his arm to his hand and stood beside him. The nearness of their bodies did a little trick to Eliza's heart, but she ignored that because, after all, it was only a dance. And though she loved to dance, and she believed dancing *could* be an expression of beauty like painting or writing or any other art, more often than not, dancing was theater and nothing else. Not that theater wasn't art, of course, but the point being you couldn't trust your feelings during a dance any more than you could trust an actor. In Eliza's own experience, that could be said of actors on *or* off the stage, but that was another story for another day.

"I'm going to show you the pattern, and once you get it, you simply exaggerate the kicks. All right?" She stepped back with her right foot, then kicked, kicked, tap, back-togethered her way through several measures of the music.

William was a fast learner, and in no time, Eliza was teaching him how to make their kicks cross over one another and how to add in the arm movements. William began to laugh, while several other party guests congregated behind them—their arms flailing and feet kicking in time with one another.

That's what Eliza loved so much about the Charleston. For a few moments, everyone danced together, whether with a partner or not. For a few moments, you could lose whatever troubled you as your feet sought the steady beat of the music.

She smiled, her heart thudding as she kicked higher.

When the song ended, everyone laughed and clapped. Then gradually, they returned to other places throughout the garden—some getting drinks, others talking business. But Eliza and William stayed put, making snippets of conversation as they danced.

"So you live here?" William asked. "You must dance in this garden every night."

Eliza laughed. "Well, the dancing's not quite the same by myself, but I do spend a lot of time out here among the camellias. I'm a painter." Their eyes locked, and her heart swirled faster than the tassels at her hemlines.

"Yes. I have to confess, I know who you are." William looked deeper into her eyes, his own gaze softening, and Eliza found herself increasingly smitten by him. "I should have admitted it upon introduction but didn't want to seem overly eager. That said, you've done quite a bit to reinvent Charleston with your watercolors."

Was she blushing? Because Eliza felt as though she was blushing for the second time this evening and worried lest William think this a common occurrence or—perhaps more horrifyingly—that he flatter himself. Neither alternative was a good one. Even if the man *was* the reason for the heat in her cheeks, he needn't know it, yes?

She moistened her lips and willed the color out of her cheeks, then ran her hand along the edge of her bob hairstyle. "You are too kind. I am but a small part of many artists who are working to help restore our beloved city, and consider myself fortunate to be among them. Do you know of the Preservationist movement? Susan Pringle Frost and a good number of other likeminded individuals? Perhaps you would be interested in that as well, since you seem to share my investment in the city . . . or at least in the city's art."

"Perhaps I would." William spun Eliza under his arm, and it was in that beautifully free moment that she caught her aunt's glare from across the lawn.

In no time, Aunt Margaret had squared in on them like a cat stalking a mouse, ready to pounce upon all the fun.

Eliza sighed. William frowned. "What's the matter, my dear Eliza?"

But she hadn't time to answer, nor he, to finish his thought.

"Eliza, I see you've found yourself a dance partner." Her aunt practically scowled. For a relatively young woman, she had so many wrinkles—probably from the severity of that very scowl, repeated frequently—at least by Eliza's observation. "Has he confessed to you yet that he is a scoundrel?"

"Aunt Margaret!" Eliza took her by the arm, sending an apologetic look toward William. His expression tightened with concern, and she couldn't say she blamed him. He was probably contemplating whether he wanted to associate with someone who clearly had volatile family relations.

Eliza led her aunt several feet away, out of William's earshot. "What are you thinking?" she hissed. Typically, she would use more care to express respect for her elders, but this was outright ridiculous.

"Do you even know who that man is?" Aunt Margaret asked, throwing another scowl toward William. "I'll tell you. William *Pinckney*. As in, the Pinckney family."

"Oh my heavens." Eliza placed one hand to her forehead, careful not to rub the cat-eye liner on her eyes. "Surely you do not blame that man for whatever indiscretion happened between our families."

Aunt Margaret lowered her voice but intensified her tone. "They're thieves, Eliza! The lot of them. Stole our family silver straight out of the ground. It's no wonder they've amassed such a fortune. I bet none of it's honest."

"First of all, we don't know for certain that they stole anything. It's not as though you saw them. These are assumptions and always have been. And second, you're talking about the man's *grandfather*!"

Aunt Margaret *harrumphed* her disgust as she crossed her arms over her chest. "Once a thief, always a thief if you ask me. And no niece of mine is going to associate herself with that family. It's an embarrassment to our own. I don't care if their riches and their station are greater than ours."

Eliza put her hand to her pearls. "Surely you aren't suggesting I so rudely dismiss Mr. William?"

"That's precisely what I'm suggesting." Aunt Margaret raised her chin. "And it's high time you learned a little respect, if you ask me. Why, just you dancing with that man is practically blasphemy to this family."

Eliza could not believe this was happening. She was practically a grown woman, for goodness' sake. Certainly old enough to wed, should the situation present itself. All Aunt Margaret's threats simply served to make William that much more attractive.

Yet Eliza knew her aunt well enough to realize the woman would make good on her promises if pushed to do so. She taught at a girls' school and was as strict as they come. Eliza need not provoke her wrath.

"Yes, ma'am." Eliza hated herself for saying the words.

One nod, and Aunt Margaret was gone. Poor William never stood a chance. Now Eliza must go to him—this stranger who she really wanted to be more than that—and explain her aunt forbade their friendship.

Her stomach turned sour at the thought, as William grinned at her in the absence of her aunt. But she saw no other way.

The next morning, William ran a towel over his damp hair and looked into the mirror. He wondered if the outside world could see how little sleep he'd gotten last night.

Everyone thought William was strong and capable. If you talked to his mother, he was the one on track to restore his family's ailing business. If you talked to his sister, he was the one who stepped up to be sure she and her baby had their basic needs met. But sometimes William worried about himself and everyone else unraveling, because William knew the truth.

Sometimes he was scared.

He knew everyone got scared sometimes and it was nothing to be ashamed of. Monsters under the bed and that sort of thing.

But William, see, was really, truly scared—namely that without him, his sister would have nowhere to turn. And she regarded him as so much more capable than he actually was.

He set down his razor, having finished shaving his five-o'clock shadow, then winced as the aftershave stung invisible cuts along his jawline.

He put some bread and fruit into a sack and tied it for easy carrying. The walk from downtown Charleston where he was living to the plantation where Hannah was working would not be easy. The plantation owners were giving her room and board in the old slave quarters for free in exchange for tending their sprawling gardens. But she was barely making ends meet. Not to mention, with his little nephew still waking in the night, she wasn't sleeping.

William locked up the room he was renting and started off on his journey. Several hours later, sweat dripped from under his shirt, and his hair fell askew. He stepped up toward Hannah's front door and knocked, but then heard the sound of a toddler's laughter behind him.

William laughed too, setting down the satchel and taking the child in his arms. "There you are, little Franklin. Making mischief, no doubt. What's next—are you going to start jumping the rails?" He ruffled the boy's hair.

Hannah came around the corner, rubbing her hands on her skirt apron. "Let's hope not," she said with a smirk. She touched the little dimple at the boy's cheek. "Your mama's going to move heaven and earth to keep that from happening." Her smile was sad. William chided himself for joking about the topic. He should've been more cognizant of its potential reality.

Hannah bent down to pick up the provisions he'd brought and opened up the little package. "Oh, brother, you spoil me. Let's get this fruit in the icebox."

William bounced little Franklin in his arms as they all stepped inside the home.

It was meager, to say the least. But Hannah had put fresh flowers in several vases, their cheery color offsetting the otherwise drab walls. She had set her old quilt over the bed and sewn patchwork drapes out of fabric, which he recognized as remnants of her faded dresses. She'd really cozied up the space—as best she could, at least.

They looked at each other. Hannah smiled.

"You met somebody." She rested her chin on her hand.

"I don't know what you're talking about." William made silly faces at Franklin, hoping that by his distracting the boy, Hannah would leave well enough alone.

"She another flapper? Let me guess. She works down at The Blind Tiger? Turning the proverbial blind eye to prohibition?" Hannah winked to soften her accusation.

William didn't give her any inclination it stung. Did she think so little of him? Instead, he worked hard to still the tapping of his loafers against the floor as he nervously shuffled his feet.

But Hannah's grin merely widened. "Oh, come on. You've got to tell me." She sat down on the bed and motioned for him to sit beside her. "You really like this gal, don't you?"

Franklin reached his chubby hands toward his mother, so William transferred the boy and then sat beside them both.

He cleared his throat, hoping the right words would follow. They did not.

Because the truth was, William had found himself quite smitten with Eliza last night. And he very much hoped this visit to his sister would prove to offer clarity and a restructuring of his priorities. In particular, that unless he took very desperate measures, Hannah and Franklin may not have enough to eat.

Yet that was Hannah for you. Making conversation about the very thing a person was trying hard to ignore.

And yes, Hannah was right. William could not get Eliza out of his mind all night long, no matter what he tried. Reading the papers didn't work any better than a glass of warm milk or a cup of tea. Every time he closed his eyes, he saw the depth, the mirth, of her own brown eyes looking back at him. He'd dozed a few times but kept dreaming they were dancing again, the beaded hem of her skirt flouncing as freely as he ever wished his own heart might be.

But alas, his heart was not his for the giving. At least not to Eliza. 'Twas a very humbling truth indeed.

Nevertheless, Hannah needn't know the whole story. She would sooner starve than steal so much as a cracker.

"Please. Just tell me." She crossed her arms over her chest, waiting for his response. The sleeves of her dress hung loosely—quite loosely—about her arms. She was working too hard and eating too little. It showed. "I could use a happy story. Lend me some of your eternal hope, would you, Brother?"

William pulled at his suspenders. Talk about a predicament. What had he gotten himself into? Unless . . .

Well, he didn't have to lie to his sister, did he? After all, he had indeed found Eliza to be enchanting. To put it mildly. She needn't know the other part of the story. Why he was at the party in the first place.

"All right, all right." William held up both hands and grinned. "I'll tell you. But just know it's nothing serious, okay?"

"It never is with you, is it, William?" Hannah teased.

William started to respond honestly, then thought better of it. So he swallowed back his words to keep from correcting his sister—not that she was wrong about the whole avoiding-commitment jab. But rather that, for the first time in his life, he had met someone who held his interest enough to continue pursuing.

If only his sister didn't need him.

If only *needing him* didn't mean fooling Eliza.

If only.

FOUR

Modern Day

One Year after the Date with Declan

Lucy Legare's family lived south-ish of Broad Street. And to one familiar with Charleston, that meant south-ish of everything Lucy's mother aspired for Lucy to be. South of the prominence her last name may imply. Daddy always joked he didn't tell her mother he was but a distant cousin of the famous family until after they said "*I do*."

A little bit south, it seemed, of all life's expectations.

So Lucy tried—she really tried—to remain upbeat while her mother bumbled through social media to find the photo of this new man Lucy was apparently set to go on a blind date with tomorrow. But the breeze blew on the steps outside the Charleston Museum of Art where the two of them stood, and Lucy found herself gripping her to-go cup of tea from Poogan's Smokehouse so tightly that the lid fell askew.

"Mom, I'm sorry to interrupt you, but I really do need to get inside. I'm several minutes late for my shift as it is." Yes, the job was just part-time work, but Lucy hoped it might soon turn into a full-time opportunity.

"Oh, it'll only take a second." Her mother tucked perfectly styled hair behind her ears, showing off her pearl earrings. She wore a navy pantsuit and cranberry lipstick deeper than her Charlestonian drawl. Mama got away with a whole lot by flashing that smile. Bless her. "Yes! Here he is." She tapped the photo.

Lucy squinted, trying to enlarge the image with her fingers. "Mom, there are six other guys in this picture. I can hardly see his face."

"He's in law, Lucy. You don't need to see his face."

"Mother!" Lucy closed her mom's hands around the phone, hoping she would take the cue Lucy was no longer interested in looking at the photo. "That's extremely insulting to the poor man."

But her mother simply waved her hand. "I'm only joking, dear. You're too uptight. Besides, he actually is very handsome. You'll see for yourself tomorrow."

Lucy stifled a groan. She slipped her free hand into the pocket of her long cardigan and enjoyed the last few sips of her tea. No drinks allowed inside the museum.

"Regardless, he doesn't really seem like my type." Lucy took several steps down to the sidewalk and dropped her cup in a trash can. When she returned to where her mother stood, she was met with a southern glare. Which was like an ordinary glare wearing too much floral perfume.

"Is it the handsome part or the rich part you find so off-putting?" Lucy's mother straightened the metal chain strap of the handbag she was wearing over her shoulder but otherwise made no move to leave.

Okay, Lucy did gasp this time with exasperation. "You are impossible."

She didn't dare tell her mother the other thought she was having: that every date in the past year had paled in comparison to that magical hour she'd spent with Declan.

You know, before the whole realizing-he-was-arrogant-and-elitist-about-her-ancestors thing destroyed any chance she had to pursue that magic further.

Oh, he'd called after their date. Two times, actually. Not enough to show desperation, but still, enough to show intention, and typically she would have liked that about him, but these circumstances were anything but typical, and ultimately, she had to tell him. *She* belonged to the family he and his father had disparaged the night their silver went missing.

They both recognized the hurdle for what it was—insurmountable—and had successfully avoided speaking ever since, even though she'd been back from Savannah for several months now.

Lucy's mother smiled, turning to take the steps back down. Clearly, she thought she'd won. "I just want you to be happy."

And to carry on the family line so our thirteen-generations-in-Charleston streak doesn't end with me. It was the truth, and they both knew it. Sure, Lucy's sister was to be married in a matter of weeks, but her sister was also insistent she didn't want children.

Which left Lucy. And the handsome lawyer, apparently. Her mother's newest attempt at matchmaking.

Oh, her mother meant well. Lucy knew that. But sometimes . . . well, if Lucy had a nickel for every time her mother put her into this situation . . .

"I'm off to get ready for a charity event tonight." Her mother waved. "Enjoy your afternoon."

Lucy waved back, forcing a smile to her face despite the entrapment she felt at the thought of dating the mysterious lawyer. It wasn't until she stepped inside the museum and the cool, open air of the lobby that she felt like she could breathe once more.

She climbed the four flights of stairs and had worked up a sweat by the time she made it to the collections area. Lucy pulled her access badge from her purse and scanned it to get in.

"Well, aren't you pretty as a peach." Ms. Beth stood beside an open file folder, cataloging every piece of art to ensure it was all right where it belonged. Her grey hair was bent into wavy curls, and her freckled complexion needed no makeup save the hint of mascara and berry lipstick she always wore. She smelled like flowers—not a heavy sort of smell, but the type of fragrance that might waft toward you from an actual bouquet in the room.

Lucy pulled her long blond curls into a ponytail. "And you are too kind. The humidity did a number to my hair on the walk over from lunch with my mom on Broad Street."

"Oh, that sounds nice! The lunch, not the hair—though I think that looks nice too." Ms. Beth set the art piece back inside the file and kept her finger on it to mark the space. "Where did you go? I've had a hankering for those biscuits they serve at High Cotton."

"Those are delicious." Lucy smiled. "We went to Poogan's Smokehouse. My mom had been saving up for S.N.O.B., but they were full." Lucy shrugged. "I like Poogan's better anyhow." She took several steps toward where Ms. Beth was working on the files. "How's the progress coming along?"

"Oh, you know. The usual."

Lucy *did* know. Because the two of them dealt with endless counting for hours on end in exchange for the opportunity to see some of these pieces up close. Lucy's personal favorites were those they were cataloging today from the Charleston Renaissance—a unique time when a group of artists and writers redefined the culture, and thereby the future, of this city as a place where tourists wanted to come.

In fact, several works from this very museum had prompted her love of early-twentieth-century watercolor, which later became a focus of her study at Savannah College of Art and Design. She'd done well in all of her classes, but now that graduation had come and gone, jobs in the art industry were hard to come by. She was fortunate to have this one, even though it was part-time.

Few people realized the amount of work that went into maintaining an art gallery's collection. Most of the pieces, in fact, were held in storage to be rotated for public viewing when the time was right. So in the meantime, someone had to make sure they were accounted for. Lucy and Ms. Beth, along with many volunteers, were happy to be those people.

Ms. Beth pointed to the larger pieces suspended from pulleys beside her. "You can start on those if you like. I know the watercolors are your favorite, and you haven't had a chance to see them up close yet."

Lucy's heart began to beat faster at the thought of being so near to these pieces she could breathe on them. Some of them she hadn't seen since they first caught her interest in high school, and some she had never been given the opportunity to view. Carefully, she slid out the first partition filled with framed art.

The entire partition held Eliza Ravenel watercolors. Lucy was starstruck. Soft tones blurred the Lowcountry landscapes, and her signature bluebirds and blushing pink camellias rounded out the earth tones.

No wonder people saw these and wanted to visit Charleston. If Lucy had lived back then, she would've been on the first train into the city. Each piece was not only visually striking but also carried with it a moment, a particular beauty that transcended time.

"How are your sister's wedding plans coming along?" Ms. Beth straightened the silk scarf tied at her neck.

"Oh, you know. She's in the final stages where she's made her last-minute decisions on cheese cubes and sparkling lemonade, and my good friend Harper has just finished steaming all the dresses." Lucy pressed away creases from her own pencil skirt. "Of course, that also means she's going to be moving out of the apartment we share, and I'll soon have nowhere to sleep. So there's that."

Well, not exactly *nowhere* . . . she could always go back to her parents' house. But Lucy didn't consider that a viable option at this point, given that her mother would probably try to set her up with eligible men for breakfast, lunch, and dinner.

"What type of rentals are you looking for? Or do you want to buy?" Ms. Beth added to her tally of art pieces, all perfectly in line—just as they should be.

"In my dreams, I would love to own a historic Charleston single house. Like the kind on Church Street and near South of Broad where the artists lived and worked during the Charleston Renaissance." Lucy took in the painting in front of her and sighed before turning to Ms. Beth. "But that's . . . wildly impractical. I've got some money set aside from graduation gifts, but if I'm being honest here, I could never afford that." Lucy clenched her teeth and made a face that said *yikes*.

Ms. Beth stepped closer and squeezed Lucy's shoulder. "You'll find something, sweetheart. I'm sure of it. What's meant to be will come. Sometimes life is like art. Trust the process."

Easy for Ms. Beth to say. She had a stunning home in the very area of town where Lucy dreamed of living. But still, Lucy nodded. Ms. Beth was right. Life *was* a process, was it not? And like watercolors, you never knew how things might blend together.

"Speaking of art, I'd better stop babbling or I'll never get these tallied. I appreciate your concern. I'm sure it'll be fine." Lucy turned back toward the next work of watercolor.

But wait a minute. This couldn't be right. . . .

Her eyes widened.

She reached for the magnifying glass, studying the painting from a different angle.

"Lucy? What's wrong?" Ms. Beth asked, concern evident in her tone.

Lucy's heart skipped. Surely she was incorrect. But the provenance of this artist's pieces . . . the works she'd studied in college . . . she knew what she was looking at.

And what she was not.

She met Ms. Beth's worried gaze. The woman had every right to be concerned.

"I think this painting . . ." Lucy gulped. "Has been forged."

FIVE

Eliza gathered up the treasures she'd salvaged with her Preservation Society friends this morning and lugged them into the carriage house at the back of the property, her arms full with old doorknobs and even a wrought-iron garden gate.

From over the fence, she could hear a ragtime tune from the neighbor's piano. Eliza smiled. She didn't recall having heard the neighbors ever play the piano before.

Curiosity got the best of her. Eliza set the items down inside the carriage house, then pulled a little metal stool from the space and shimmied it all the way toward the ivy-laced brick wall separating their property from the neighbor's.

Eliza clambered up the stool, careful to keep her balance despite her heels, and clinging as best she could to the bricks. Trying to be discreet, she made sure only the top of her freshly crimped waves, her eyes, and her nose showed above the wall.

That's when she saw the pianist through the window.

William.

Eliza gasped. She put one hand over her mouth, and just then, as if he could feel himself stared upon, he turned to look at her. They made eye contact for one electric second before she ducked back below the cover of the wall.

The music stopped.

She hurried off the stool and rushed back into the carriage house.

She held her breath, her heart racing, and debated between actually walking over there and speaking with him versus staying inside the carriage house indefinitely.

Me oh my, what had she gotten herself into?

After several minutes and a whole lot of deep breaths, she had regained her composure and decided to venture back out into the garden.

At the top of the wall, she immediately saw several camellia petals in a cluster that hadn't been there before. And beside them—a tiny note ripped from a larger pad, anchored down by a rock so as to keep it from floating away.

My dear Eliza,

I do hope your aunt won't object to this gesture, as after all, I did stay on my side of the wall. If by chance you may be here again tomorrow, you may find another song and another note waiting.

Yours,
W

Eliza pressed the paper to her chest. The one word, *yours*, seemed to warm her from the outside in. She would tuck the tiny note away in her diary in hopes it may anchor her, for she feared she herself may float off the ground with these sorts of gestures. And yet with the fluttering of excitement, of all the new possibilities, she knew one thing.

Under no circumstance could her aunt find out she and William had spoken. And what's more—Eliza could never prove her aunt right about William by allowing her heart to be broken.

The only way to keep a heart intact was to never give it in the first place.

She had learned this after her Grandma Clara died, and her mother too, of the flu in 1919. It wasn't rational—she *knew* it wasn't rational—but ever since the month they died she had felt as though they'd left her behind.

It wasn't a feeling she wished to repeat.

Still . . . Eliza ran her fingers gently along the edge of his signed *W*. It was only a note exchange, with the promise of another. How much harm could that really bring?

Sometimes painting didn't come easily.

Sometimes painting didn't come at all. Despite her best attempts, today was one such day. The memory of dancing with William was as of yet a little too perfect to put onto paper. Every time she tried to sweep the color onto the page, the vibrancy of it all created unexpected trouble as she attempted to blend the landscape.

Eliza Jane swept both hands beneath her chin-length bob as she sashayed toward the carriage house. She practiced the steps of the Charleston as she went, hopping from cobblestone to cobblestone of the backyard garden until she reached the third and final outdoor room.

Bluebirds fluttered all around the grass like daubs of rich indigo paint against a landscape, drawing attention to themselves, their wings on full display until they perched on the old oak tree. And Eliza thought to herself how funny it was that birds were always doing that, making a grand spectacle with their flying but landing on a firmly rooted tree at the end of the day.

She shivered as the breeze swept the falling leaves away, then rubbed her arms. Should've brought her shawl outdoors, but she hadn't thought of it until this moment.

Mother would say she was liable to catch cold . . . though she was always saying that back at the farmhouse where all the crops were dead or as good as it, and Eliza figured over here in the city the wind was less severe.

Eliza ran her thumbnail under her other fingernails, trying to clear away the evidence of an afternoon spent painting—or attempting to paint, anyway. But the sunlight had faded, and now she would enjoy the twilight-turned-evening from the beauty of the garden.

Her garden. Was it even possible that might be true? She still thought of the space as belonging to her mother. That she might now possess the place herself was at once an honor and an overwhelming responsibility: this place where red-and-pink-swirled camellia petals fluttered to the ground as though creating a carpet for fairies.

Oh, technically it all belonged to her father, but he never ventured out here except for his parties and would be perfectly happy with Eliza staking her claim to the place.

While organizing a few painting supplies and salvaged odds and ends she'd stored inside the carriage house, she'd be remiss if she didn't also check for a new note from William upon the adjacent brick wall, wouldn't she?

And if William happened to be playing the piano and she happened to hear him and invite him to climb over the bricks, well, certainly no one would fault her for it.

Eliza grinned. The very thought of it sent her heart fluttering.

She hadn't intended, of course, to so blatantly disregard her aunt's wishes, but she was in the greatest of moods, and all that Charleston hopping had landed her straight in front of the wooden door of the carriage house—rounded at the top and utterly charming. Besides, Eliza was all but certain she was alone among the roses that climbed up the brick structure of the small carriage house, so she leaned down to smell their fragrance. A young woman could dream, couldn't she?

That's when she heard the sound of the piano.

A tune by Cab Calloway that widened her smile and weakened her knees. She'd told William the song was one of her favorites.

Eliza took hold of her necklace lest it get caught on flowers or thorns or any other number of things that might catch a long string of pearls, and she stood up on her tiptoes as if a better sight of the brick wall between them might also afford her better hearing.

And despite herself—despite every rational notion of what she should be doing—Eliza swayed back and forth to the music, mouthing the lyrics to herself. But then an awful thing happened, just awful. The long swoosh of her necklace caused her to stumble upon the rose bush exactly as she feared. In all the commotion, she nearly turned her ankle and paused to rest one hand on her chest when she realized the wall had a little window, formed by several missing bricks.

And from that window, from inside his own house, William stared back at her. His fingers flew over the keys as his smile grew wider. Indeed, the pianist might be the handsomest man she had ever seen. Not only because he had such an interesting face—she could just stare at it for ages—but also because he carried an air of mystery, and she was dying to solve it.

And Eliza was quite glad that despite the advice of her aunt, she had not stayed away.

He took his time finishing the song, and Eliza took her time watching him. Though no one should bother her at least until supper, she still feared what might happen if her aunt in particular caught her staring at William through the wall.

It was silly, the whole of it—her passing little notes back and forth with him as though caught up in some forbidden romance, when in reality the messages were perfectly innocent and, if she were being forthright, altogether far too neighborly for Eliza's liking.

Except for his recurrent signature of *Yours, W,* the entirety of this love affair existed solely in Eliza's imagination. And yet she'd been hopelessly devoted from the moment she'd danced with him, for she fit so perfectly within his arms.

Eliza was so caught up in this memory that she didn't notice when the song stopped and William opened the door—that is, until

William himself peered back at her through the space in between the bricks and gave her such a startle that she jumped backward.

She brushed the dirt from her T-straps and whispered her disapproval, though she knew the impulse was silly because nobody could hear them out here, clear at the end of the garden. "How's that for a hello? You nearly caused me to break an ankle. Would that have satisfied you?"

"I'm tempted to say *quite* but get the impression you aren't up for the teasing." Even through the small gap in the bricks, Eliza could see his eyes dance with wit.

"You humor yourself, I see." Absentmindedly, Eliza pulled at the pearls around her neck.

A wicked grin lifted the corner of William's lips. "Eliza, could I be forthright with you?"

She set both hands to her hips and lifted her chin. "I would expect nothing less."

William glanced behind him, toward the house where he lived, then looked back at her. "I would very much like to be on your side of the wall."

His words caused her heart to do its own little jig. She bit down on her bottom lip and glanced at the house behind her. No sign of her aunt or father. Would it really be so awful to invite him over, only for a few minutes? It wasn't as though she planned to do anything scandalous. She could show him her new knickknacks in the carriage house, and maybe her new paintings too.

Sure, her aunt might not be happy with the arrangement, but her aunt did not need to know.

"Would you like to come over?" She asked the question quickly, before she had a chance to lose her nerve.

"You mean it?"

"Sure, but only for a short while. I don't want my aunt catching wind, or I'll never hear the end of it."

William grinned. "Understood."

Eliza heard him push something against the wall, and moments

46

later, he hopped down onto her side. Seeing him so near that she could smell his aftershave did something funny to her senses, and she couldn't think straight to initiate conversation.

So instead she just stood there, a couple feet away from him, which was entirely farther than she would have liked but entirely closer than her mind would apparently allow for clear thinking.

It would seem that in the past two weeks of swapping little notes back and forth above the wall, she had grown quite smitten. And frankly, she was altogether unsure how she felt about the prospect. No man had ever caused her to lose her wits like this before. And a little part of her had to wonder—was it all too good to be true?

"I've been painting." Eliza blurted out the words as she pointed toward the carriage house several steps away. "Would you like to come inside and see?"

"Absolutely." William followed her toward the curved doorway of the building. As the two stepped inside, Eliza shut the door behind them and felt as though she could breathe deeply once more now that her aunt wouldn't be able to spy them together.

William stepped toward one of the larger pieces she'd painted several weeks ago and whistled low. He wore a light blue shirt tucked halfway into pressed navy trousers, the other half untucked, a casualty to his jump over the wall. The look was so charming, she resisted the urge to tell him lest he fix it. He turned to face her. "Eliza, these paintings are really something."

"You think so?" She tucked her hair so it curled up behind her ears and took a half step closer.

"Oh, absolutely." He pointed to the horizon where it blended between fallen petals and camellia buds and leaves. "The blurring of flowers at the start and end of their bloom . . . it's really quite evocative. This one will fetch a high price, for sure."

Eliza fiddled aimlessly with her bracelets, running them up and down her wrist. "If you want it, you can have it."

William hesitated. "You don't mean that."

"Of course I do." Eliza shrugged. "Consider it a thank-you for livening up what was sure to be another one of my father's boring parties. I typically escape to my camellia garden in the midst of these soirees, but I didn't have to because of you."

William raised an eyebrow as he stepped closer. His nearness intoxicated her. "Hmm, so I'm entertainment for the guests, am I?"

Eliza allowed her eyes to twinkle back at him. "One could say that, sure."

"And do you offer such deep gratitude to all your party entertainment?"

Eliza lowered her voice. She knew no one could hear, and yet the moment felt like a secret all the same. "Only to those who know how to play Cab Calloway."

A curl of Eliza's hair fell across her forehead, and in the most wildly natural gesture, William reached to brush it away. His fingertips gently brushed against her eyebrows, and in that singular moment, Eliza was nearly sure he might kiss her.

She was even more sure she would let him.

SIX

Modern Day

The sound of her cell phone vibrating against the iPad on her nightstand woke Lucy with a start. It'd taken two reruns of *The Great British Baking Show* on her tablet before she could fall asleep last night, after all of yesterday's junior sleuthing about possibly forged artwork. She squinted and looked toward the window.

What time was it, anyway?

She reached for her turquoise reading glasses and settled them onto the bridge of her nose before looking at her phone. Quarter after eight. She hadn't meant to sleep so long. Today was supposed to be filled with apartment shopping and job searching, since the meager savings she had from her old college job was quickly dwindling. Her part-time job at the museum was not going to suffice for much longer.

She rubbed the sleep from her eyes and unlocked her phone to listen to her new voicemail. Probably just spam. Absentmindedly, she tapped to hear the recording.

"Hello, Miss Legare. My name is Trent Boone, calling from the law office of Boone and Boykin. I have a rather unusual matter to discuss with you that I think you'll find quite urgent. I'll be in the office all day."

The message went on to give specifics about the law firm on Meeting Street.

49

Lucy stared down at her phone. An unusual matter? What in the world? Was someone she knew involved in legal trouble?

Her sister's voice echoed from the other room. Lucy slipped a stretchy robe on over her fleece pajamas and stepped through the short hallway toward the kitchen they shared. What she saw there stopped her in her tracks.

"Heavens, Lucille! Quarter after eight and you're dressed as though the day is going to wait for you." Her mother sipped coffee and sat on a kitchen barstool across from Lucy's sister, Olivia.

Olivia pulled a pan of cinnamon rolls from the oven, then shot Lucy a smile that said *I'm sorry I didn't warn you*. The cinnamon rolls smelled amazing, but Lucy would have to eat hers faster than her mother would like. She had a law office to get to.

Olivia scooped out a roll for each of them as Lucy poured herself some coffee.

"Mom, what a surprise," Lucy said.

"Your sister and I are going shopping for wedding accessories. Since you didn't answer my texts last night, I just had to come over a little early and ask how your date went with that handsome lawyer."

"Umm . . ." Lucy looked straight into her coffee cup, swirling the liquid slightly. How did she put this? She willed herself to glance at her mother, who waited with an expectant smile. "Mom, I know this isn't what you want to hear, but the lawyer—"

Her mother held up one hand. "Say no more, sweetheart. I already know what you're going to say."

Lucy took a sip from her coffee cup, skeptical about the temperature . . . and what was coming next. "You do?"

"Yes, I do. And I think I've finally figured out the problem." Mom rubbed her mauve-lined lips together. "You're sabotaging your own happiness because you're concerned about living up to my expectations. Men like him come from families with certain societal expectations. Soirees and benefit parties and such. You feel like you're in over your head."

Oh, that was *so* not the problem.

Lucy took a huge bite out of her cinnamon roll, because if she was chewing it, that meant she didn't have to be talking. The woman was losing her marbles, and Lucy had to get out of here quickly because she had half a mind to tell her as much.

She took a swig of her coffee and looked her mother straight in the eyes. "Mom, I've been trying to be polite, but here's the truth. Austin is already in a relationship with his favorite person. And that is Austin. Now, if you cared a lick for what's going on in my life beyond your desire to see me married off, you would realize I may be on the brink of a huge breakthrough at the museum, but I haven't told you about that because I can't get a word in edgewise with you."

Her mother balked, placing her hand over her pearls. "Why, I . . . Lucy Legare, how dare you speak to your mother that way? Young lady, I raised you to respect your elders."

"Which is the entire reason I've been going along with these farfetched plans to date these pathetic men, but Mom—"

Olivia gave Lucy a *red-zone, red-zone* glare. But this was just too much. Her mother actually thought the problem was Lucy herself?

Mother puffed up like a peacock. "Well, excuse me for trying to teach my daughters to have high expectations of themselves."

Lucy rubbed her temples. She made herself take a deep breath. "Look. Mom, I'm sorry if I've hurt your feelings or if you feel I've spoken out of turn. But I just don't want to go on any more blind dates with your friends' sons, all right? I can manage my own dating life perfectly fine."

Like you "managed" it with Declan a year ago? Yeah, right. Look how well that ended up.

But she chided herself for being so negative. What happened with Declan was not her fault. She had liked him . . . *really* liked him, actually . . . until she realized his family blamed hers for the missing silver and still carried the grudge to this day. No matter that the authorities arrested the silver thief the week following

51

the robbery. No matter that it was all based on fiction. Her family didn't have that silver any more than his did. To this day, actually, the silver had never been found.

Maybe it never would be. And maybe that would be for the best.

Lucy tightened the belt of her robe and took one more bite of her cinnamon roll. The sugary glaze melted against her tongue, a warm comfort among the suddenly icy temperature of the room. She tapped her fingers against the kitchen bar, regret over her blunt words beginning to turn in her stomach.

She should've played nice and avoided the conflict. With so much else in the air right now, an argument with her mother—even a minor one—was the last thing she needed.

"I hope y'all enjoy shopping. I'm going to hop in the shower."

"You don't want to come with us?" Her mother smiled.

"Thanks, but I can't." Lucy took the last sip from her coffee. "I have a date with a lawyer." She was devious to tease this way, but she couldn't help herself.

Her mother's eyes grew wide.

Charleston was changing.

The landscape of the Holy City was changing too. The church steeples, known to be visible by boat or land, were becoming more difficult to spot between cranes and new development projects.

Not that Declan was complaining. Those development projects—*his* development projects—meant more clients, which meant better cash flow, which meant better business for everyone. He wasn't a fool. He knew his father expected him to take over the company in the next decade, so he was somewhat relieved to know the thing would be in good standing. At the rate things were going now, their company would remain the most profitable of its kind in town.

Declan crossed his Oxford loafers up on his desk, popped the tab on a can of flavored carbonated water, and looked out the long windows of his minimalistic office onto the city streets. His second-floor view provided plenty of opportunities to people watch whenever he was on a short break. And the breaks were always too short, weren't they?

Tourists crowded around a guide who pointed toward St. Michael's impressive steeple. A group that almost certainly was headed toward the famous Rainbow Row congregated just up the way. A few men in tailored suits hurried along the opposing sidewalk, probably late getting back to the office after their lunch break.

A woman with long blond curls and a flowing sweater caught his eye as she walked past, looking up toward the numbers on the building. She was beautiful.

And oddly familiar. She was . . .

Lucy?!

Recognition dawned as his pulse began to speed.

Declan pivoted his office chair in a hurry before she noticed him staring. What did he think she was going to do? It wasn't as if she would march up the stairs and scold him. She probably wanted to avoid him just as much, if not more, than he wanted to avoid her. What had begun as pure magic between them had quickly escalated the tension from their families' irreconcilable differences. Neither Declan nor Lucy needed the headache of their families practically despising one another.

And what was more—and particularly problematic—was Declan found himself inexplicably attracted to her despite his good sense. So his urgent reaction had come less from a fear of Lucy making some sort of move and more from the sinking realization he had been pining—very, very briefly, okay—over the blond stranger on the street.

Declan leaned forward slightly, careful that his silhouette would be hidden by the long curtains. Lucy had continued walking down the sidewalk. He told himself he wasn't disappointed. He didn't quite believe it.

He cleared his throat just as his father opened the door to his office. Declan sat up a little straighter and smoothed some hair that had fallen down on his forehead during his mad dash away from the window.

His father was the sort of man who always looked as though he were in a hurry. Declan wondered if he appeared the same way sometimes, though he'd do well to age like his father. The man's salt-and-pepper hair, trimmed perfectly above his ears, and a few wrinkles here and there were the only things that gave away his age. Well, that and the nervous tic he'd developed last year.

He took a seat in the chair across from Declan and crossed his arms over his chest. "I need you to make an acquisition."

"Sure." Declan rubbed his eyes with his hands, trying to concentrate on his father's words and erase the image of Lucy that was dancing through his mind.

"It's a property down on Longitude Lane."

"Yikes." Property so close to Church Street was a hard nut to crack. The laws protecting historic structures South of Broad proved consistently tricky to navigate for a development company like their own.

"I know. That's why I'm asking you. It's a very important acquisition, and you're the only one I can trust won't mess this up."

Thanks for the vote of confidence, Dad.

His father meant these types of things to sound encouraging. Declan was sure of it . . . well, pretty sure, at least. But sometimes he wondered if the man realized the pressure Declan felt, knowing his entire life was mapped out for him. There was never any question or any choice about working for the family business and someday taking it over. His father seemed to view the company as an heirloom Declan should be honored to receive. And maybe Declan would share that view a little more if his father would let him make his own decisions from time to time. Put his own spin on things.

His father stood. He didn't ask, *"Does that sound good?"* He never did. Declan was expected to nod respectfully and accept the challenge as an honor. He took a deep breath and tried to put on a good show of it.

"You can count on me." Declan reached for his flavored water and took another slurp.

"I know I can." His father stopped in the doorway and tapped his hand against the modern-style doorknob. "You're the only one who can effectively go to war with the Preservation Society."

"You're brutal." Declan laughed at him and shot a wadded-up piece of paper toward the doorway. His father gave a wicked grin and disappeared.

"I'm thinking about volunteering for the Preservation Society." Lucy pointed at a framed photograph of an old building that was prominently displayed in the lawyer's office, alongside a notation that the Preservation Society had saved the property from demolition at the hands of a development company. "I love reading these types of stories."

The lawyer across from her wore a seersucker suit with a baby blue bow tie. His white hair made his ruddy cheeks stand out all the more, and he looked as though he'd put on a good bit of weight in the time that had passed between the family photos on his desk and now. Not that Lucy was judging—the food around Charleston was so good, even a cycling instructor might find her jeans too tight.

The man smiled, looking up toward the photograph on the wall. "That was a gift from the Preservation Society after I helped them negotiate some legalese regarding the property you see in the photo. Very generous. A lot of good people there, and what a legacy the group has! Why, we wouldn't know Charleston as we do today were it not for the preservationists back in the 1920s."

"I agree. It's amazing to think about all they accomplished. Bet they never expected what houses like Rainbow Row would become all these years down the road."

"I bet they didn't." Mr. Boone chuckled. "As the saying goes, too poor to paint and too proud to whitewash."

Lucy smiled as she crossed her ankles. She liked that this man had an appreciation for history. It made her feel like she could trust him. "Wonder what the men and women from the Charleston Renaissance would say if they could see the city today? And all because they had the foresight and the grit to preserve history. It's wild to think so many of these structures date all the way back to the start of our country."

"Indeed, I do wonder what they would think." The man's eyes turned sad. "Though I must admit, I see so many cases of families selling ancestral homes because their neighbors are big-city transplants who honk their horns a little too quickly, or because property taxes have simply become too high. I do fear that we have made Charleston *such* a charming locale that we may be losing what makes it distinctly Charlestonian. The slow pace, the warm hospitality, the spunk."

"Interesting." Lucy had, of course, noted the ever-worsening traffic since she'd arrived back home from college in Savannah. But she'd assumed the quicker pace of the people on the streets was simply her imagination. Maybe she was wrong. "Perhaps what the city needs, then, is another sort of renaissance."

"A way to both preserve the city's historic culture *and* welcome new visitors to its gates and gardens. After all, as fascinating as Charleston's early history may be, we both know the years that followed were also traumatic for many. There is certainly room for development, even as we preserve the good parts of our history. A renaissance of a different sort sounds just like what we need." The man nodded and pointed toward Lucy. "I recognize a visionary when I see one." He grinned and straightened a pile of papers by tapping them on his desk. "Speaking of gates and gardens, you may have a chance to fulfill your own prophecy soon."

Lucy bit down on her bottom lip. "Come again?"

He set the papers down and leaned forward, his elbows on his desk. "I contacted you because you've come into an inheritance."

"An inheritance?" Lucy nervously tapped her shoe. Her mind rushed to keep up. Did someone die who she didn't know about? Mentally, she ran through the list of all her favorite great-aunts. No, she was certain they were all still living. Her mother would've reminded her to get a hair trim before the funeral. Lucy shook her head. "I don't understand."

"The proprietor wishes to remain anonymous, but I must say, our conversation today leaves me no doubt why my client would choose you of all people as the recipient of this property. Miss Legare, you are now the owner of a historic Charleston single house."

It was a good thing Lucy was sitting, because shock, and then joy, and then shock once more took her out of her body and then back into it with a sudden quickness in all her senses. She felt the same sort of hyperawareness one feels after scarcely avoiding a car crash. Her breath was quick, her fingers tingly. She opened her mouth, but no words would come.

The lawyer continued, clearly used to the signs a person was struggling to keep up, much less respond. "The house is near Church Street in the most charming alleyway, with brick walls overgrown with ivy. I'm very familiar with the area because my wife and I frequently take walks that way. I know you'll find it a delight."

Near Church Street? But that was just what she'd always dreamed about. Lucy felt as though, at any moment, an alarm would go off and abruptly wake her from this dream. Could this actually be happening in real life?

"What street is the house on?" Lucy asked.

"Longitude Lane." And the man smiled once more.

SEVEN

1929

Eliza adjusted her red cloche and tapped her foot against the ornate leg of the sofa to the beat of the gramophone's tune. The quick beat matched the skipping of her heart as she thought of William and the little notes they'd been passing across the brick wall.

Oh, the notes were perfectly cordial, perfectly innocent. Nothing that would raise a single eyebrow should anyone come across them.

Yes, indeed. Their platonic nature was abundantly anticlimactic. But something about the way the man scripted his letters . . . Eliza sighed. It was also abundantly romantic.

She set her copy of *Woman's Way* magazine down on the table beside her and snuck a peek through the windows, toward the length of the garden. Her gaze went over the fountain, past the camellias, all the way toward the brick wall and the carriage house at the back.

Then she stood abruptly, her attention darting around the room like a thief afraid of being caught in the act. This impulse was exceedingly silly, of course, for even if her aunt caught Eliza searching for William's note, what harm was there in piddling around one's own garden?

And yet Eliza's heart quickened further just at the thought of it. Perhaps something about the note exchange was not *quite* so platonic, after all. For in her heart of hearts, she knew her aunt would never approve of it.

Despite that, Eliza stepped outside as the sunlight played hide-and-go-seek with the shadows. She skipped over toward the bricks, but no new notes caught her eye, so she ran her fingers along the top of the wall just in case she'd missed something.

She hadn't.

Her heart and all its expectations fell.

Such a reaction was imprudent, she knew, and yet she felt it all the same. Two days had passed since William's last correspondence. The thought of him vanishing triggered one of her deepest fears: being left behind.

Though ridiculous to admit, she had lived in such a way that she had tried to guarantee no one would leave her again, as her grandma and mother had. In life, that meant pouring her heart into her art. In love, that meant never getting close enough to a man to be hurt. But now . . . well, now, William was beginning to change all that.

She cared for him. Did he not care for her in return?

Just as her stomach began to turn with the prospect, Eliza caught a glimpse of a piece of paper under a cluster of fallen camellia petals that had been pushed by the breeze behind the carriage house.

She knelt down and scooped the paper out with bare hands. Hope glittered like the dancing garden sunlight as she realized she had not been forgotten after all. She murmured the words aloud, hurrying into the carriage house, where she kept scraps of paper and a pen for her responses.

My dear Eliza,

I hope your afternoon is a smart one and that the bluebirds we share between our two lawns end your day with a fond farewell.

Yours,
William

Eliza scribbled out her response and left it in the usual spot, wondering if William, too, had felt the pull of disappointment from the two days of silence. Was it bad that she hoped he had?

Dear William,

I apologize for my delayed response. You see, I just found your last note in a pile of fallen camellia petals behind the carriage house. I must confess to missing our correspondence to such an extent that I rifled through the dirt without gloves.

Eliza

Dawn brought the promise of another note from William and the joy that came from its fulfillment when Eliza discovered his hand-written words tucked away on the wall behind the carriage house.

My dear Eliza,

To think of your delicate fingers raking through the dirt on my behalf! But I must make a confession of my own now—I am glad you did.

Yours,
William

Eliza grinned, glad he could not see the blush warming her cheeks. She traced her thumb over his scripted words as she thought of her own response—what would be the first of many exchanges in the days that followed.

William,

Perhaps this is a presumptuous idea, so forgive my forward thinking. But what if we used a bound notebook and simply passed it back and forth over the property line? That way, we might ensure a note will never go missing again.

Eliza

My dear Eliza,

Not only is that head of yours pretty, but you've got wits about you as well. I am leaving this final notation beside a notebook. Shall we call it a correspondence journal, perhaps?

Yours,
William

First Journal Correspondence

My dear Eliza,

Here's to you and all the beauty you bring into the world. Can you get away tomorrow at twilight? I thought we might go for a stroll.

Yours,
William

Dear William,

The truth is, lately I've been so preoccupied by our note writing that I haven't brought much beauty into the world. It's almost as though I've got the painter's version of writer's block. Is there a term for such a thing? I find my mind too accelerated to patiently allow the colors the time they need to blend on their own. I keep over-saturating the paints. Oh well. Perhaps tomorrow.

A stroll sounds lovely. I'll meet you on the corner of Church Street.

Eliza

It was probably the rain dripping down from the eave beside her bedroom window that awakened Eliza that night. Her heart thudded in her chest as she sat up in bed, clutching the quilt in her hands and trying to make sense of why she'd told herself in a half-slumbering state to fully awaken.

She slipped a shawl over her shoulders and slid her feet into her slippers as she hurried down the stairs and out the back door. She nearly fell along the slick grass, for she was not being careful, and as she always said, carelessness leads to accidents. But she didn't fall. She righted her balance and hurried on.

The rain was gentle yet, and she whispered a prayer as she came closer to the correspondence journal she shared with William. Had he, too, awakened during the rain? Had he come before her to get the journal back inside?

Eliza squinted, trying to get a clearer view of the bricks in the moonlight and finally finding the bound journal. She brushed several raindrops from its cover and tucked it protectively under her shawl.

She had gotten here just in time. What a travesty it might have been should the raindrops have soaked these promises. Not that they were promises, really—more so sentiments. In fact, they carried very little with regard to gestures toward the future. All the promises were bound up still within Eliza's own heart, which perhaps explained why she was having so much trouble painting these days, for everything was so tidy, so safe, so simple. So scary.

This cycle had happened many times in Eliza's life, again and again, but with joy and with grief. Always with the honesty of difficult emotion, so that sometimes she simply struggled to put herself on the paper, even though she knew she ought to. Because sometimes the ideal seemed too perfect to put on the page—to work through the nuances, to let the paints run. And other times, she didn't feel strong enough to be so very vulnerable, so very alive.

But perhaps she was overthinking, as usual. After all, it was so late in the night.

Eliza tucked the journal closer toward her heart and ducked her head as she hurried back inside.

Problem was, William's brush strokes were too harsh.

Eliza's masterpieces showed evidence her brush floated effortlessly over the paper, at the whim of the color and the water's blend. But you couldn't replicate that. You could try, of course, and William was trying. But imitation was nearly impossible when the originals so closely resembled real life.

He admired it, he admired *her*, and yet he was growing more frustrated by the moment.

William set his brush down at his easel, running his hand over his face in hopes of wiping the strain from his eyes.

He was a good painter. He knew that.

But Eliza Jane was an artist.

William shook his hand out, then reached for the paintbrush once more, dipping it in the water, then the paint, and then trying—really trying—to trail the strokes across the paper with grace.

These forgeries were giving him fits, as were his growing feelings for Eliza. He was in such turmoil that just yesterday he'd nearly called it quits on the whole thing.

But then he'd received a letter from Hannah saying her landlord was struggling financially and that she'd now be required to pay a small rental fee for her home. Even considering this sudden expenditure, Hannah would still find nowhere else that was nearly as safe and reasonable as her current dwelling.

And so William had no choice. And maybe that should have brought him closure, but instead, it only made the tug pull all the harder.

Three knocks sounded at the door.

William started up so fast, he knocked his paint and his water, splashing them both against his painting in progress. His heart thudded against his chest as he turned.

Eliza.

Upon registering who she was, his heart pounded even faster.

He fumbled to set the painting upright on the ground and out of eyesight, before she could recognize her own patterns beneath the messy splatters.

"Ready for our stroll?" she asked. She was radiant from head to toe. So radiant, sunbeams seemed to follow her from the light into the shadows, never dimming at all.

She was wearing what might be his favorite dress yet, and that was saying something, because she had quite the collection.

"Yes. Absolutely." William reminded himself to smile, wiping a remnant of muddled water from his shirt with the rag he kept beside his easel. "I thought I was meeting you on the corner," he said. "I apologize you've caught me in the middle of something. Very ungentlemanly of me, I'm afraid."

"I like to keep people on their toes. My aunt says it's very un-ladylike." She leaned slightly up onto the toes of her heels. "I sincerely hope you will disagree."

She gave her silk navy hat a gentle tug, securing it to her hairpins, and slipped a fragrant rose blossom behind her ear. It was the color of cream with tips of pink, matching the shade of her dress and her blush.

"Indeed I do." William reached for his hat from the coat rack and settled it on his head, then stepped toward Eliza. "Besides, a visit from you is welcome any time of day."

He dared touch the back of her dainty dress. He shouldn't. He really shouldn't. Because even her presence magnetized him, and guiding her gently through the door of his home and then his garden and then the gates by touching her was only going to make matters more complicated.

But he couldn't help himself.

Eliza looked up at him with a wide grin. She didn't seem to mind his hand on the small of her back at all.

Hmm.

Now that was going to be a problem.

Because, as he realized quite suddenly, he had—somewhere in

the depths of his mind, that is—believed he had no chance with a woman like Eliza.

And that had made this whole disastrous scheme a lot easier.

But now . . . well. Now he wondered if he'd been wrong.

"You look like you belong in that novel F. Scott Fitzgerald published," Eliza said.

The evening air held a hint of the breeze as Eliza stepped toward him on the city street. William held out his elbow toward her, and she took it gladly, her stomach fluttering.

"You're beautiful," William whispered into her hair, and Eliza grinned as they stepped out into the city. "I thought we could take in the waterfront while there's still some daylight to see it by. What do you think?"

Eliza nodded, looking up at him. "That sounds like a splendid idea to me."

He righted his cap. "Good of you to brave a walk with me despite your family's disapproval. And speaking of which, where is your aunt this evening?"

"She's off at some fancy dinner party. But you mustn't say such things about yourself." Eliza held tighter to his elbow. "After all, it's my opinion that matters."

William's eyes twinkled. "And what *is* your opinion, Miss Ravenel?"

She regarded him a long moment, smiling softly over her shoulder. "I'll let you know."

"Then I'll make good use of this evening." William winked.

Anticipation raised the hairs at the nape of her neck, though she wouldn't give him the pleasure of knowing it.

The two of them crossed the street and came to a home in severe disrepair. The ironwork had been pulled off the patio and all other valuable ornamental items stripped away so that the centuries-old home looked embarrassingly bare.

But Eliza stepped closer, undeterred by the disrepair. She began climbing through the little pile of rubble the homeowners had discarded by the street.

William's eyes widened. "What are you doing?" He seemed to be *truly* asking, as though he couldn't make heads or tails of it.

Eliza knelt to the sidewalk, hidden from view except for her head and shoulders, and she peeked behind the mountain of all that had been deemed broken and cast off. "Isn't it obvious?" She grinned. "This house was built during the Revolutionary War, William."

She tossed some items to the top of the stack and, using other pieces, made another small pile to the side. Those were items she would salvage. "I'm rescuing what I can, then I'll take these things to my friend Susan," she said. "Susan will use these pieces in homes she is preserving that were built during a similar architectural era. And that way, something of the original history can be salvaged."

William knelt down beside her. "What is it you *really* mean to accomplish, though?"

She admired him for asking it so directly. "Why, saving what is still good about the city. Charles Town's structures were built alongside the very beginnings of our country. If we do our job well, perhaps a hundred years from now someone may stroll down these streets and discover where the Founding Fathers once dined or attended church services. If we redefine the city through art, and music, and preservation—make this a place people want to come on their travels—wouldn't it be amazing? And while visiting, maybe they will purchase a book of stories or a painting, and then take it back home and share a little bit of Charleston all over the world, until our beauty grows famous and our struggles become lessons."

William fiddled with his suspenders. "You have a way with words, Eliza Jane. If anyone can accomplish such a feat, it's you."

"You mean it?" Eliza felt her cheeks warm from the flickers of interest in his eyes.

"I do."

A short time later, William and Eliza returned to their cozy corner of Longitude Lane. A passion vine grew between the empty spaces along the iron fence between their homes, and a few orange butterflies fluttered nearby.

Eliza marveled at the pattern of the veins on the leaves, of the leaves themselves along the branches of the tree—of their falling, then growing once more. Maybe that's one reason she loved her garden so dearly—for while she despised change, she took comfort that nature would always bring another season, another breath, another opportunity. Nature would keep going long after she ceased to be. While perhaps fatalistic, she found peace in remembering she was not at the center of everything nor was she the fulcrum upon which goodness and beauty hinged. Rather, she was, perhaps, their bloom—and bloom she would, gladly.

William scooped up her hand. "Want to come over to my side of the fence for a little while?"

Eliza nodded, smiling.

William swung open the half-moon-shaped gate, which creaked its resistance.

He led her toward a grassy area beneath an oak tree, then sat. She followed his lead, and the two of them both leaned back upon the ground with their hands as pillows against the dew of the coming evening.

From this angle, the tree was towering, and squirrels and all sorts of songbirds scurried among the branches, enjoying what remained of the day.

A bluebird fluttered past them with a striking sweep of its cobalt wings. Eliza sighed contentedly.

"What are you thinking?"

She turned her head toward him. "Just that a bird like that—a bluebird especially—may as well be a metaphor with wings."

William looked at her, his grin widening. "What do you mean?"

His gaze exhilarated her, and her heart began to skip along as she explained. "Why, they're a representation of beauty."

"Beauty?"

"Yes." She nodded softly, and only dared blink for a moment lest this magic vanish when she broke his gaze. "Beauty arrests our attention to look upward. It reminds us that there are things in life, such as love and the divine, that we long for so ardently we *know*—even if we only know it for a fleeting moment—that our yearnings are far deeper than our eyes can see. And that's what faith is, I think."

William situated his elbow against the ground and propped his fist against his cheek. "That's really profound."

"Thank you." Eliza smiled. "That's why I like to include bluebirds in my paintings. They're a reminder that while beauty may be fickle in its coming and going, there's a permanence in the impression it leaves on our hearts. There are roots growing within us that sustain its wings. And maybe *that*, really, makes beauty the greatest witness to glory there is."

William took her hand once more, and the two of them looked up into the tree. A mockingbird perched on a limb above them, singing a perfect melody.

And everything seemed to turn black and white, as the strong branches of the tree cast a deepening pattern against the still-lingering light of the day.

EIGHT

Modern Day

Lucy stood in front of the house at 86 Longitude Lane, looking up at its broken shingles and paint-stripped porch posts. Harper and Harper's boyfriend, Peter, stood close.

Peter—a historian accustomed to working with old things—often rescued antiques from condemned houses just before they went to the landfill. Harper was equally enamored with old stories, though she was far more interested in vintage clothes and accessories—an interest that served her well as she ran her thrift store, Second Story, alongside Peter's quirky grandma, Millie. Lucy knew she could trust anything the two of them had to say.

"Well, the foundation's solid. I'll give you that much." Peter repositioned his backward baseball cap and looked up at the Charleston single house.

Lucy twirled and continued to study the place, though she doubted Harper and Peter saw the same thing as she did. Sure, some shingles were missing. One of the windows had been boarded up. And Lord only knew if that chipped paint was full of lead.

But it was hers.

All hers.

This place was a dream, a mystery that God had put in Lucy's path right when she needed it. The scratched-up floors, the porch that ran along the side of the house, and the jasmine out front—all of it, every bit, was part of that dream.

So when Lucy looked up at the place she'd just inherited, she imagined the previous owners gardening. And Lucy could almost taste the biscuits and tea she could make fresh here every morning. Maybe having her own home would be like the secret ingredient she was missing . . . because try as she had to follow the family recipe, Lucy burned those darn biscuits every time.

She squinted and put her hand to her forehead to block the sun. Single houses were known for their breeze-catching design, but at midday, no feat of architecture could protect her from the sweltering heat.

"So your assessment is that it needs a lot of repairs?" Lucy adjusted one of the bobby pins holding up her long blond hair.

"Um, Lucy . . . I'm just going to be honest with you. This place is a money pit." Peter bit down on his bottom lip. His eyes flickered with hope, and she held tightly to it, however dim. "But you know how I feel. There's always something worth saving."

Someone had once seen the beauty in this place. Surely the structure had faced the threat of being torn down before. So Lucy would honor that legacy. She'd make the necessary repairs to the historical home, one way or another.

Lucy was about to say as much when she felt goosebumps. She heard the vehicle before she saw it for the first time. The squeal of tires blurred her attention from the house toward the driveway as she tried to make sense of what was happening and finally registered that a car had suddenly veered and another car, a sports car, was headed straight for her own—

Crash!

It happened so fast, she couldn't have done anything to stop it.

Lucy stood, mouth wide open. Had someone really just hit her *parked* car? The faithful old Accord she'd owned since learning to drive?

The troublemaker vehicle sped off, while the car that was forced to crash into hers slowly pulled over. She knew she should probably blame the first driver, but blaming the other was far easier because she recognized him.

He opened his fancy door and stepped out. His dark hair was perfectly groomed, his suit was perfectly tailored, and even his Oxfords were perfectly flawless. He ran one hand through his hair and stepped confidently toward them.

Lucy groaned. The fact he looked like a J.Crew model made this moment even more appalling. Now only a few feet away, he cleared his throat and pointed to the indiscretion. "Do any of you know who the Accord belongs to?" He said the words without looking at anyone, his focus still on the cars.

When it was clear he wasn't hurt, she adjusted her dangly earrings and squared her shoulders, preparing for battle. Lucy ran her tongue over her teeth to hold back the words she really wanted to say.

His gaze trailed from Peter, then to Harper, and then he seemed to notice her for the first time. A satisfying but all-too-momentary look of panic widened his eyes.

"Peter?" Surprise was evident in Declan's tone. You'd never know he and Peter were cousins with the way their lifestyles differed so greatly. Whereas Peter had managed to leave money-grabbing, elitist ideals behind, Declan was clearly still aspiring for a definition of success that would make even Mr. Darcy proud.

"Harper? Lucy? This is a strange coincidence . . . and even more embarrassing now." Declan gestured toward Lucy's Honda as he cleared his throat. "Does one of you own that car?"

"*Oh yes,*" Lucy hoped her glare said back to him. "*Someone owns it, all right.*"

Declan seemed to hear the unspoken words loud and clear. He pulled a cell phone from his pocket. "If you give me your number, I'll be glad to pay for any repairs."

"That car is eleven years old, Declan." She put her hand on her hip. "My insurance is probably going to consider it totaled."

He shrugged. "Then I'll pay whatever gap there is between the deductible and the cost to purchase another one. A newer one."

Lucy looked him square in his chocolate eyes. Anxiety began to push through her veins as she considered how she might afford this with her part-time salary. But that anxiety was soon forced out by frustration.

"You really don't get it, do you? I like my car. I don't want a new one."

"Who doesn't want a new car?" The man looked toward Peter for backup. Peter was smart enough to choose that moment to meander toward the garden. Declan turned back toward Lucy. "Look. I'm really sorry, okay? The other guy came flying into my lane. There was no time to react."

"Maybe you *would've* had time to react if you hadn't been speeding. Am I right?" She turned toward Harper, only to discover her best friend had followed Peter, and the two of them were now both out of earshot.

Declan held up his cell phone. "I'm trying to apologize, okay? You haven't even asked if I'm all right, by the way." He rolled his neck back and forth.

"Oh, don't try to pretend like you're a victim." Lucy focused on the sprawling oak limbs that dipped toward the road.

"Just tell me your number, and we'll work it out."

She took a deep breath. Had he deleted her number from his phone?

Of course he deleted your number, Lucy! That date the two of you went on was over a year ago. His family's elitist perspective toward your own and the all-out war his father declared—mistakenly—against your family can hardly be negated by an evening of cute little shared anecdotes and a love for the same local eateries.

Still, the fact he had deleted her number filled her with the most unexpected ache of disappointment. Where Declan was concerned, she was beginning to get used to the feeling.

The sparks she once felt with him had been smoldering. Intense.

But so had the watery bucket of reality, as it splashed upon the fantasy.

Lucy sighed.

She recited her number again as he fiddled with his phone, then turned on her wooden wedge heel toward the house. Now she was going to have to go car shopping. She hated car shopping. Adjusting to a new dashboard, new mirrors . . . new blind spots. She stopped herself at the porch. She wasn't done with this guy yet.

"Not everything in life can be bought, Declan."

"Wait, Lucy—" He jogged closer, then caught her elbow gently as she started toward the door. She turned, her jaw clenched. He held up one hand. "Can you at least tell me who owns this beat-up old place?" He nodded toward her new home.

Lucy planted her feet on the ground. "You're looking at her."

A flicker of unease passed over his eyes. He lowered his head as he scratched the back of his neck. "Well, this is awkward."

"Why?"

He met her gaze. "Because I want to buy it."

"Of course you do." A determined grin slipped up her lips. "It's not for sale."

"Come on, Lucy," he said. "Everything's for sale."

Oh, not everything. He would find that out soon enough.

Declan didn't know why he'd pretended to have lost Lucy's number.

The truth was, he never deleted it after their date a year ago.

Okay, he did know why. But it was embarrassing.

He still had feelings for her.

He never *stopped* having feelings for her.

But none of that mattered. Not anymore.

And especially not now that he was in this predicament.

Declan had managed to close some pretty challenging property acquisitions, but he had never been in a situation like this before.

"You're really used to getting whatever you want with a flash of your credit card, aren't you?" Lucy asked from the porch of the house on Longitude Lane. "People like you disgust me."

"Okay, I realize we got off on the wrong foot." He cleared his throat. "How about you let me buy you some tea at the shop up the block, and we'll go over what it's going to take to get your car fixed?"

She stared at him in response.

He looked back into her hazel eyes. This woman was relentless, no doubt. And exhausting. But her spunk attracted him, much to his own chagrin.

"You have got to be kidding," she said. "I would sooner have another date of my mother's choosing."

"You think quite highly of yourself, don't you?"

She raised her chin. "Do you have a problem with hearing the truth, Mr. Pinckney?"

"On the contrary." He slid his cell phone back into his pocket. "I have a problem with being rashly judged based on my last name."

Lucy rolled her eyes. "Come on, Declan. You and I both know it's more than just your last name."

"I suppose now's the time you're going to pretend to know nothing about the silver. Maybe even tell me the awful stories about my great-grandfather that have been passed down in your family?"

"He broke my great-grandmother's heart."

"And that's reason to take it out on me?"

"You're all the same." She shook her head in disgust. "You, with your fancy cars, and your look-at-me wardrobe, and your prestigious reputation. You think anyone and everything can be bought—you said it yourself a few moments ago. Well, this house is not for sale." Lucy crossed her arms. "Your money means nothing to me."

"Clearly." He straightened his collar. "And I suppose you think my great-grandfather is to blame for all that history?"

"My great-grandmother's only mistake was falling in love with a Pinckney."

Declan's jaw tightened. "Okay, now you're really starting to make me angry."

"Maybe I can take you up to the corner for a cup of tea to discuss it."

Declan blinked. He was dumbfounded by this woman. Completely dumbfounded.

She took determined steps toward the front door of her house, clearly signaling she was done with this discussion. But before she reached the entry, she turned, and a curl of her hair fell out of place. It was a beautiful curl—a wild curl—and Declan hated himself for thinking it.

"What do you want with this house, anyway?" she asked.

He was done trying to be charming. He'd tell it to her straight. "My company owns the adjacent lot on this side of the alleyway. We need the property for a development." His gaze traveled across the weed-filled garden to the faded siding and the missing shingles. "And we *will* find a way to buy it, Lucy."

"Nobody threatens me, Declan." She reached for the doorknob and threw open the door.

Truth be told, Declan was half scared the whole door might come off. But it didn't. Perhaps the structure was stronger than he realized.

With a final glare, she added, "Just you wait and see."

And maybe it was something in her voice, but for a moment, her resolution shook him. Then the moment passed, and he remembered once more the family to which he belonged.

NINE

"This new painting is striking," William said, coming to stand behind Eliza.

She turned her head and smiled up at him, her nearness captivating.

It was the evening after their walk, and they had decided to meet in the carriage house. The whole thing started innocently enough, at least.

They'd planned it all. He would play the piano to let her know he was nearby, and she would sing over the wall. And then he would climb the wall and she would show him all the artifacts she had recently saved on another one of her preservation outings. His plan had been to use this opportunity to get a better look at her paintings.

But now that he was standing here, so near her, William could not remember wanting anything so badly as he wanted to kiss Eliza. His affections for her were growing, and he knew he needed to protect her from the one thing that might pose the greatest threat. Himself.

Cadigan had been right, of course, about her beauty and charm. But there was more than that. Beneath her onyx-colored bob and her brown eyes and the lines of her lips was a woman who had bewitched him, body and mind. William couldn't sleep at night for all his wondering whether she'd left another note at the wall. He kept waking himself as he'd shuffle his own feet, bumbling about and lost in the memory of her dancing in his arms.

In any other circumstance, he would say he meant to court Eliza Jane. But the very startling reality was, he actually meant to rob her. And every time he woke from his dream, the nightmare of that reality brought a cold sweat down his back.

He intended, of course, to do such a fine job that she never suspected the forgeries. Then the moment his sister and the baby were well enough off, he would simply disappear from Eliza's life, so as not to break her heart.

Because she deserved so much more than the thief he had chosen to become.

So as her nearness intoxicated him—the jasmine smell of her hair and the porcelain of her skin against his fingertips—he dropped his hands from her arms, even as his lips tickled from forbidden anticipation.

Eliza looked up at him. William wondered what she saw: honesty or devotion?

And indeed, which of the two did he see more of within himself? William swallowed hard, tried to think of something else. It was difficult to think with Eliza so near and their almost-kiss so practically tangible. He could still smell the fragrance of jasmine.

Almost imperceptibly, Eliza sighed. Whether relief or disappointment, William may never know. He didn't intend to get so close to her again. He didn't intend to compromise her affections, as his had already been.

He was in love with her, most likely. And yet he couldn't act upon it because he had a duty to his sister and her baby boy, and he would stop at nothing to make sure the two of them stayed fed, for they had no one else in the world upon whom to rely.

William wasn't sure if that made him a bad person.

All he knew was he needed to keep his wits about him as best he could and take these next steps meticulously. Far more carefully than the choices he'd thus made, resulting in the entanglement of his heart.

Eliza had already graciously offered him the painting. He could use it to study her techniques. To be successful, William would have to create forgeries so flawless that no one would know the difference from the originals.

"Penny for your thoughts." Eliza moved her necklace back and forth along her neckline.

"Oh, I'm afraid you'd find them a mere imitation of anything substantive."

Well, it was true, wasn't it?

Eliza turned her head to the side and studied him with a gentle smile. William reached out and tucked her hair behind her ear, though it'd been only moments since he'd resolved not to touch her again. To be honest—that resolution was never going to happen. But he did catch himself, and he did recognize the attraction welling up.

"Soon it will be dark. I'd better get back home."

Eliza watched him another long moment, then blinked.

He tried to remind himself he wasn't hurting anyone by being here. She would likely never even know of the reproductions. His sister needed help, and his best skills were music and art—neither of which could land him much of an income in a city that was still recovering from the aftereffects of the Civil War, no matter how roaring the rest of the country. He believed in art. He believed in its integrity. But he believed in his sister more.

"Good night, Eliza," William murmured.

Having just finished church and then Sunday lunch, Eliza took the turn down Atlantic Street with a little more skip in her step than usual, her drop-waist hem sashaying.

She was skipping to a new tune. William had been working on composing a new piano number. She'd been listening all day yesterday while attempting to paint from the garden beside the carriage house. The flowers were inspiring, as was the afternoon breeze. The heat, not so much. But very well, that was Charleston in the summer for you.

The one antidote to her misery was that song, carried over to her by the breeze.

Eliza was perfectly inspired by having her own personal Cab Calloway just over the bricks.

And yet still, she struggled to paint.

Susan and Alice waved from a walkway in front of the house where Eliza was headed, their conversation framed by an antique window box boasting yellow summer blooms. Both of the women were icons for art and suffrage and preservation.

Eliza checked both ways for automobiles and jaywalked across the street, where her friends met her with open arms in front of the pale pink, black-shuttered, two-story house.

Susan Pringle Frost had become a household name, what with her helping found the Society for the Preservation of Old Dwellings and her presidency over the Charleston Equal Suffrage League.

And Alice. Why, Eliza was certain the name Alice R. Huger Smith would be scrolled along the bottom of paintings that would some-day make their way into the best museums in America. No one commanded color and water and light like Alice. She had a unique way of both remembering and envisioning the Lowcountry.

Susan took Eliza by both arms. "What's gotten into you? Your eyes are even more doe-like than usual." She squinted. "Have you changed your makeup?"

Alice looked on and did nothing to help Eliza avoid the questions.

Eliza's heart spun. She didn't want to admit her affections for William when their romance was more a girlish fancy than anything else. And yet she'd been secretly hoping he would appear as she walked the couple blocks down to Atlantic Street where her friends were waiting. He had not.

Susan released Eliza's arms and brushed the collar of her dress in place. "Whoever he is, he'd better appreciate your art."

"If he knows what's good for him," Alice added with a wink.

Eliza tried to divert their attention toward the little table they'd set up at the gated entry of the house. Each week, artists all along Atlantic Street would set up small displays to show off whatever they'd worked on during the days prior, and sometimes they'd sell the smaller pieces for five dollars. But they never sold on Sunday. Was not fittin' to buy and sell on a Sunday.

When it became clear neither Susan nor Alice was diverting her gaze from Eliza, Eliza waved her hand. "Oh, it's nothing. Just a musician. You know how these things go."

"Do we?" Susan asked. She looked toward Alice. "Do you?"

"Indeed, I do not."

"All right." Eliza pursed her lips in defeat. "He's quite handsome. Does that satisfy you?"

"I have two conditions," Alice said. "First that he, as Susan mentioned, respects your art. And second that he never breaks your heart."

Eliza ran her hand along the sharp edge of her bob. Was she really so obvious in her infatuation? "I will relay the message, should I ever get the chance."

Both friends offered satisfied nods.

"Now, what were you two talking about before I arrived?"

"Oh, Susan was just telling me her plans for that beat-up property on East Bay Street she owns. Well, they're not *plans* in the sense of being imminent—"

"They most certainly are imminent," Susan corrected. "Just as soon as I find an investor." Susan's family had lost a fortune, which caused her to take a job for herself. But the long and short of that led to her becoming a realtor and singlehandedly saving the history of Charleston. Well, singlehandedly, that is, by Eliza's account. Indeed, Eliza thought very highly of them both.

Others may balk at the measures Susan was taking as a single working woman to secure the properties before they could be destroyed. And to secure what Susan deemed "equality" as well. But not Eliza. She thought it was remarkable, and imagined history would look favorably upon the efforts.

Eliza crossed her arms over her dress, tapping her fingers against her elbows. "And what exactly are these plans?"

Susan grinned at Alice, then Eliza, and hesitated, holding up both her hands. "Okay, I'll admit Alice may be right. Truly 'tis a dream at this point. But wouldn't it be lovely if we could buy up the whole street of those old houses—they're pre-Revolutionary, you know?—and paint them each in a different, vibrant pastel? Dorothy Legg helped with the idea. . . . She said she'd live in one of those homes just a block up from the water for the rest of her life, and she plans to live a century."

Eliza wrinkled her forehead, trying to imagine it, then laughing. "You want to paint East Bay Street pastel?"

"Laugh all you want now, my dear. Just wait until you see the lavender one. And the yellow. And the pink. Someday, a hundred years from now, tourists will be flocking to Charleston to see the rainbow of colors."

"A rainbow row?" Eliza grinned, taking a step toward the table to get a better view of Alice's newest work. "That'll be the day, Susan. That'll be the day."

Eliza was sitting on the third-floor balcony when she saw the birds the next morning. She cradled a cup of tea in one hand as the summer wind whipped against her bare shoulders. She'd splurged and poured it into her grandmother's old teacup.

Grandma Clara had always loved bluebirds. Eliza could still hear the elegant drawl of the woman's voice . . .

"One shouldn't be fooled by how quickly they startle. Bluebirds just like open spaces, that's all. Open fields where they're free. And when they find a place, they come in hordes, and they keep coming. They're faithful little settlers. They know when they've found a place of beauty."

Eliza leaned over the chipped railing and watched the birds fly into the oak tree as the sun rose higher and the sky turned shades of pink. She watched every second of its ascent, how it was oh-so-slow in the coming, yet oh-so-fast in the going. And like that, the colors of the sunrise slipped beyond the horizon, and she thought of her mother.

Suddenly, the air felt colder, and Eliza hugged her teacup with both of her hands.

It'd been ten years since the Spanish flu took her mother—and her grandmother too—just when they'd thought the threat from the pandemic was as good as gone.

If she'd only known.

"Oh, Mother," Eliza whispered, looking off toward the huge oak trees at the sides of the garden, stretching their limbs like a canopy. "Grandma Clara . . . if only."

Tears began to roll down her cheeks as her mother's presence suddenly seemed at once near and far. These walls held safety and familiarity. But these walls also needed restoration, and truth be told, Eliza didn't know how to save them. One reason she got so wrapped up in saving other properties was because it provided a distraction from the loss of both these women from her life. Somehow, it felt as though if she could save the structures, maybe she could also save the memories of those she had lost. Memories that rushed to Eliza's mind with every glance at the wooden planks beneath her feet.

For a short while when Eliza was young, they had all lived in a farmhouse together and William's family had owned both the house over the wall and their own. But Grandma Clara, as Grandma Clara was prone to do, had managed to get it back. She was as persuasive and fiercely stubborn as anybody Eliza had known.

Eliza inhabited two spaces here—at once a little girl baking cookies and also a grown woman in mourning. She didn't know which was more real or which she was now becoming.

She closed her eyes and breathed in deep. Everything about the house had seemed more faded and broken since her mother and grandmother passed. Everything, that is, except the smell. Yes, the smell was the same. Earl Grey, a little bookshelf dust, and jasmine that'd caught on the breeze. It smelled like her mother. It smelled like home.

Eyes still closed, she thought of the nights she'd slept here as a child. And how she'd slept peacefully, never once thinking there would be a last night with her mom. More tears rolled down Eliza's face, and she sniffed as she wiped them with the back of her hand.

The bluebirds startled into the trees with a flutter, and the clouds covered the sun. The day had begun. Eliza took another sip from her teacup. She wouldn't wallow in memories.

Her grandmother loved this house.

Her mother did too.

And so Eliza determined to take care of it well.

Grandma Clara had always said the place had a story to tell, and Eliza suspected maybe she meant more than the obvious . . . that it *actually* had a story. Something happened with her grandmother here back during the Civil War—though Grandma Clara would never speak about it. Eliza only knew because her grandmother was supposed to marry a Pinckney but instead fell in love with a Union soldier, and sometimes, late at night, Eliza would have sworn she heard her mother and father use the word *spy*.

That's why the Pinckneys were so convinced Eliza's family had the missing silver . . . because the last place it was seen was in their garden.

But Grandma Clara tried to dig it up before she died, and the silver was gone. No one in Eliza's family knew where it went, so they blamed the Pinckneys right back.

And yet knowing William as she did now, Eliza had begun to

wonder if perhaps her family had it all wrong. Maybe somebody else had the silver. Maybe someone was watching when Grandma Clara hid it all those years ago and stole it for themselves. Any number of things could have happened. But the William she knew would not lie about silver.

The William she knew was as honest as they come.

TEN

Modern Day

Lucy almost forgot about the key.

She made sure Declan was good and gone before she took the steps back down the porch to where Harper and Peter had come out of hiding. She'd asked Harper to hold the key for her earlier while she was slipping the ownership papers into her purse, and she'd never gotten it back.

"I know my cousin comes across a little intense, but give him a chance. He's got a good heart," Peter said. In reality, *Peter* was the one with the heart of gold. Harper looked up at him, glowing. Lucy half expected engagement news from the two of them soon.

But just because Peter saw the good in Declan didn't mean Lucy had to.

"Thanks for holding on to the key for me." She held out her hand toward Harper, purposely avoiding Peter's attempt to make peace.

"Lucy, you are just as stubborn as he is." Peter put his hands into his pockets and leaned back on his shoes. "The two of you are a match made in heaven."

Harper swatted at him. "Peter Perkins, cut it out or else Lucy is never going to invite us back over here."

Lucy slid the old key into the lock. A perfect match. She grinned over her shoulder. "Don't worry, Harper. You're always invited."

She winked toward Peter to soften the joke. Then she opened the door.

Lucy stopped, stunned by the beauty of the house.

Sunlight streamed through a stained-glass archway just past the entry. Very Art Deco and yet startlingly on trend. Lucy had actually just pinned some similar glass to her Dream House board on Pinterest.

The effect was something like a rainbow, only one you could step into, and Lucy craned her neck back and turned in circles to try to take it all in. She felt as though she'd just stepped through the wardrobe.

"Do you think there are vintage shoes in here?" Harper whispered behind Lucy's ear.

Lucy laughed at Harper. "Probably. I promise to share them if I find some."

Harper looked as though she'd be no more thrilled if Lucy had offered her nuggets of gold.

Lucy meandered back toward the entry near the stairs. Single houses like this one were unique in their long, skinny design, constructed to maximize the Charleston breeze in the days before modern air conditioning. Accordingly, the houses were one room wide and typically multiple stories—sometimes even three or four—with long porches running alongside the house and narrow gardens at the side or back. Yes, the gardens in Charleston were iconic, especially on this street.

The architecture here had always fascinated her. It was one of the reasons, along with those Charleston Renaissance watercolors, she'd decided on art school. The play of color and fanciful elements along the wrought-iron fences or the window boxes or the eaves—each piece of creativity coming together to tell a larger story.

Lucy stopped abruptly when she noticed something glittering on a small table beside the curved staircase. She reached for the ring and held it up for inspection.

The oval diamond was framed by a cluster of little diamonds that looked like leaves. Surely the stones weren't real?

She slipped it on her finger and waved her hand back and forth, watching the probably imitation diamonds glitter under the light of the glass mosaic.

She was mesmerized. So mesmerized, in fact, that she almost didn't see the letter beside the ring. The left edge of the paper was rough, as though it'd been ripped from a diary.

The ring belongs to you now.

I admit, leaving it is difficult, but the thought of this ring away from this house is even worse. You could say the two of them belong together. And my own sentimentality is nothing notable—after all, I have always had a difficult time leaving things behind.

But if the house is yours, so is the ring. So also is the story. Take care of it for me?

Eliza

The words quickened Lucy's heart and sank deeper with every beat. She rotated her hand back and forth in the colorful light once more, this time preoccupied by the encircling of the glimmering leaves.

She'd so readily tried it on her finger, so readily accepted the house . . . but she hadn't, until now, considered just what she had inherited and just what she was wearing.

Harper walked into the room as a prism of light scattered from Lucy's ring onto the floor. "Wow. What is that?"

Lucy stepped closer and carefully handed Harper the letter. She watched as her best friend's eyes widened in response until finally Harper offered the crackly paper back to Lucy. "What do you think this means?"

Lucy looked back down at her hand. "I have no idea, but how beautiful is this ring?"

Harper took Lucy's hand and held it up for inspection. "Judging by the shape and condition, I'd say it's from the 1920s. If I were you, I'd be nearly as excited about this as I was about the house. Today has been a really good day for you." She dropped Lucy's hand.

Lucy laughed. "No kidding." She held the ring up to study it herself. "Do you think the diamond is real?"

Harper shrugged, and the little floral embroidery lining her collar pulled upward as if in a smile. "I'm no jeweler, but it doesn't look like a real diamond to me. That said, it probably is an authentic antique. And just think, I imagine there are a good many other things about it that are far more valuable than the diamond anyway. Like its story."

"Yeah, for sure." Lucy straightened the ring on her finger. She hesitated, wondering if she should voice the question that had reverberated in her heart since she first got the news about this estate at the lawyer's office. If she could say it to anyone, she could say it to Harper.

Lucy took a breath. "But why leave it to me?"

"You can't think of any connections you have to this house? Even from childhood?"

Lucy shook her head. "Not unless you count going on some of those popular walking tours back in high school and swooning over all the houses in this area of Charleston." She looked around the well-worn walls, each section of board-and-batten like puzzle pieces coming together, only she was too close to the pieces to see them clearly.

The previous owner had even left some furnishings. Maybe it had functioned as a rental before the mystery angel-of-a-person gave it to Lucy? "I know the house isn't in the best condition, but it's still got to be worth a fortune. Why give it to me? Why give me this gift when I don't even know the story?" She shook her head as elation and shock and even a little guilt settled over her, and it was hard to keep her thoughts straight.

"Well, you know she lived here a hundred years ago and her name was Eliza, so that's a good place to start."

"But I don't know anyone named Eliza," Lucy said.

"Judging by the styles we've seen in the house and even the ring, she was probably not a child in the 1920s, which would mean she's not still living." Harper pulled at a loose thread in her sweater, then adjusted the seam. "I don't know. Maybe someone since then wanted to preserve her legacy, and you seemed like a good candidate for it."

But Lucy wasn't so sure. Why would anyone choose her, a recent college graduate who was still struggling to find a full-time job with her art degree and struggling still with bigger life questions of her career—and bigger life pressures of the sort of man and pedigree her mother wanted her to marry? Her mind spun with all the possibilities. She needed a plan.

This afternoon, once Harper and Peter left, she would go through the house and look for clues Eliza might have left here. Clues about who Eliza was, clues about what she accomplished, and clues about when and why she would leave a house like this.

Lucy didn't even mind that the electricity was shut off. She was too excited to care. She'd open the windows and let in the garden breeze.

Lucy would read this house floor to ceiling, and maybe it would tell her its story.

Lucy stayed in the overgrown garden until daylight slipped into twilight. She had promised herself she would head back to her sister's apartment before nightfall. She wouldn't be able to see inside the house without electricity and was liable to bump into something.

But she couldn't help herself. She had fallen in love with the place and couldn't bring herself to leave.

She'd spent the day enraptured by every nook and cranny of

the space, and had begun looking through the bookshelves and drawers for other little notes from Eliza . . . as though Eliza might have left them for her to find all these years later. But for some reason, Lucy got the sense that the garden was the biggest message Eliza had left behind. Even though it could use some weed-pulling, pruning, and edging, that garden was magical—to think how, long ago, those seeds were planted and how some of them were still growing, still blooming, still becoming something . . . even now.

Lucy fumbled her way over to the bed and patted the tattered quilt with her hand until she discovered where she'd tossed her purse. Maybe she could use her cell phone as a flashlight. But when she reached inside and found the phone, she realized the battery was low. She'd need to use it wisely.

Lucy used the phone to illuminate the room. She sat down on the old wooden floor, and she closed her eyes, breathing in the old-books smell of the space.

A knock at the front door interrupted her thoughts. At least, it sounded like a knock on the door. Who would know she was home?

The only logical explanation was that someone was trying to break in.

Her pulse quickened, and she grabbed an encyclopedia on her way down the stairs. But when she made it to the door and looked through the keyhole, her heart raced even faster as she caught a glimpse of a man illuminated by the streetlight.

Declan?

Much to her chagrin, Lucy found herself obligated to open the door.

He used his own cell phone to see her. "Lucy?"

The single beam streamed into her home and cast a shadow of her against the staircase.

"You sound surprised to see me," she said.

"No, I just didn't expect you to appear from the shadows like the Ghost of Christmas Past." He wore a casual but tailored suit jacket and jeans that probably cost more than her entire savings.

Lucy startled when she noticed the woman standing beside him. The shadow had hidden the other woman initially, but clearly, she intended to be seen. Her stilettos must've been at least four inches, and her blond curls were nearly as long as her legs. The formfitting dress she wore flattered her figure but left little practicality to bend her knees.

"This is Kaitlyn." Declan nodded toward the woman.

"I'm Lucy." She held out her hand. Was it her imagination or did Kaitlyn hesitate to shake it?

"Why are you holding an encyclopedia?" he asked nonchalantly.

"I thought you were breaking into the house."

"So you were going to use trivia to scare me away?"

"I had plans to thrash it against your head."

"Wow." Declan adjusted his tie. "Sounds like you've already thought that one out."

"I didn't realize it was you at the door." Had she realized, she would've brought something heavier.

"Your porch light is out. I saw your car still outside and was worried about you." Declan looked up, then into the house. "But it seems like the rest of the house is also . . ." All at once, he realized what was going on. "You don't have electricity here, do you?"

"Not yet, but I'm going to work on that tomorrow." Lucy moistened her lips. "Thank you for the chivalrous gesture, but I'm perfectly fine in here."

Declan hesitated. "You're not staying all night, are you?"

"I can manage." Lucy had absolutely *no* intention of staying another twenty minutes, let alone the whole evening, but now to prove her point, she felt she had to. Ugh. Sometimes her own willfulness got her into trouble.

"Okay." He swept his hand through his hair. "If you're sure."

"Well, thanks for the concern, but I'm really fine." She put one hand on the doorknob. "You two have a nice date."

Declan caught the door before it closed. Kaitlyn walked down the steps toward the sidewalk.

Lucy soon realized he was nearer than she would've liked, had daylight afforded her the opportunity to see him clearly. So near, in fact, she caught a whiff of his cologne. And it wasn't entirely disagreeable. A pull of attraction threatened her better judgment, and she chided herself for having such a reprehensible impulse.

"Are you sure you're okay alone in here with it being dark? Why don't you just come back first thing in the morning?"

"I am perfectly happy here." She rested her hand against the bookshelf by the door, but it wobbled at the gesture, and several books slid onto the floor. "My family and my house do not need your charity."

"I was just trying to help," he said, rubbing his hand across his face.

Lucy glanced through the open door. "Then maybe you should help your date down the cobblestone street. Looks like she's struggling in those heels."

"You know what . . . forget it." Declan started to leave. "There was a time I thought we understood each other . . . that we *had* something. I guess I was wrong. Seems you're far more concerned with the past than you are with the present."

For a brief moment, he watched her, and Lucy didn't need the light of day to sense the fire in his eyes. She leaned her hand against the doorframe, a more stable structure than the bookshelf, and tried to think of a reply.

Declan stood still but firm in his stance, saying nothing more.

Lucy straightened her shoulders and raised her voice to be sure he could hear. "While I'm sure it's difficult for a person like you to understand, my own family raised me to recognize the value of others' stories beyond the bottom dollar. That's exactly what I'm going to do by restoring this house. You see, Mr. Potter"—would he even get the *It's a Wonderful Life* reference?—"some people are more concerned with a house's story than with the resale value of its bricks."

Declan waited a moment more. "Are you quite done?"

Lucy lifted her chin. This man brought out the worst in her.

"I wonder if you'd use but half the energy you've invested in comparing me to fictional villains and focus on getting your facts straight, Miss Legare."

"You may bristle at their reality, Declan, but I can assure you, my facts are quite straight, thank you."

He took the slightest step forward. "You really don't know, do you?"

She frowned.

He must've taken her silence as confirmation to his question, because he added a final retort. "Your precious great-grandmother broke my great-grandfather's heart."

ELEVEN

1929

Eliza sat out in her garden with her paints and easel and a bluebird for company.

She washed her paper in water, dipped a brush in the cobalt color, and then stopped herself just before the bristles could touch the page.

She was going about this too hurriedly.

She lifted her brush, took a deep breath, and looked over at the bluebird perched on the fence post. Was it looking for a meal to fill its belly for the evening? Or was it simply taking in the day and watching—being fully alive?

She took her cue from the bird and intentionally slowed the stroke of her brush along the page. She heard crickets, the hum of the curious hummingbird past her ears, and noticed the stride of the clouds across the sky. And that same sky showed twilight's blush as the bluebird kept sitting and sitting, and she told herself she'd better sit too.

And her heart felt full, though not for any reasons except the simplest—that she and her paint and this nectar were, for a few moments, all perfectly in tune.

So for now, she'd watch the bluebird. Maybe waiting. Maybe simply sitting, until the night brought it back to the trees.

Eliza smiled as she looked at the paper, watching the colors blur into one another so unexpectedly.

William straightened his tie as he took the steps up to the front door. The ornate home on the Battery had a better view of the water than what even his own father could afford.

The butler greeted him, taking his coat as the gramophone roared a Cole Porter tune from a nearby room. William rubbed his jawline with his thumb. Being here was not a good idea.

Not so long ago, a party like this would've been the highlight of his week. But talking with Eliza had changed him. Now, all the pomp and circumstance—the feathers in the hair and the furs—seemed excessive, empty.

Cadigan had insisted he attend because the party host had recently purchased one of William's fake watercolors, and the boss figured William could get the details about what they'd like in another painting before it conveniently came on the market.

A woman in a sequined green dress whirled past him holding a flute of something that did not smell like it was Prohibition approved. Her eyes lingered on him a moment longer than appropriate, and he offered a tight-lipped smile that discouraged further study.

Cadigan was busy speaking with several men William did not know, so rather than interrupt, he made his way toward the library, which, as it turned out, had a remarkable piano.

William sat, stretching out his elbows and then setting his fingers over the keys. He was about to hit the first chord when a voice behind him purred his name.

The woman gingerly hopped up on the office desk across from the piano and crossed her legs. It was a sight the likes of which had put a spell over his heart in years prior.

"Violet." William removed his fingers from the keys and shifted to look at her. She wore a drop-waist dress with an ornamented headband around her bobbed hair and lipstick so red, a sailor could spot it from a boat in the water.

"I haven't seen you lately." As she smiled, the elongated liner on her eyes seemed to turn upward too. "I've missed you," she crooned.

A year ago, he would have been flattered. Played along in a harmless game of flirtations and asked her to dance with him. But he never thought about her the next day, the way he thought about Eliza.

"I've been busy."

"So I hear. I asked after you the other day, and the girls told me you don't come around to the parties much anymore. Tell me you aren't planning to settle down." She leaned closer, and only then did he notice the skinny cigarette holder she dangled between her fingers. "Tell me you aren't hiding something."

"I'm not hiding something." He grinned, crossing his arms over his chest.

She wagged the cigarette holder toward him. "You're a troublemaker, William Pinckney."

Okay, so that much was probably true. He shifted back toward the piano as Violet hopped off the desk just as quickly as she'd hopped on it. She started toward a painting on the far wall.

"This is beautiful," she said. "I've never seen it here before." She turned to look at him. "They must've purchased it recently. Come have a look."

William gulped. Even from the piano bench, he could tell which painting it was. He stood, slipping his hands into his pockets before she got any ideas and tried to hold one.

His heart began beating faster as he walked toward Violet, and he told himself to calm down, that she didn't suspect anything about the painting and he didn't need to give himself away.

He stood beside her, and she looked up at him, wide-eyed. "What do you think?" she asked. "Why, isn't it divine?"

William nodded slowly, clenching his jaw. "It's something, all right."

She waved her hand back and forth, illustrating her words as she spoke. "I've seen this woman's work before. She's incredible. The way she uses color is so unique because it blends the actual, physical location with something that looks like a dream." Violet sighed, looking up at William. "Isn't it so romantic?"

William simply stared back at her. He certainly couldn't agree. But he also couldn't argue.

"You aren't going to say a word?" Violet placed her gloved hand against her chest. "That's what I get for trying to talk to a man about art like this. You're hopeless, William Pinckney." Her grin was wide as she gently pushed him away.

Yes, hopeless was putting it mildly.

The morning had brought not one but two new notes from William, and Eliza might as well have been the Queen of England for how rich she felt. So when her aunt announced they were having a guest for dinner, Eliza didn't give it any mind. Turned out, she should have.

Because Robert was now sitting beside her and asking for another portion of the chestnut salad because it was oh-so-delicious, but Eliza knew her chestnut salad was nothing to write home about, which clearly meant he had ulterior motives. What she *didn't* know was whether her father or her aunt was responsible for this new attempt at matching her into domestic bliss, and whether her would-be husband had any idea what he'd stepped into.

Eliza smiled and passed him the salad bowl. The girls' school teacher who'd instructed her in manners and the dying art of china painting would be proud. *"We keep ourselves mannerly not for those with whom we engage, but for our own self-respect,"* her teacher was always saying, and though Eliza loathed the sentiment at the time, now that she had grown up a bit she could see some of its merits.

Not that she was particularly keen on being duplicitous, but sometimes femininity did have some innocent falsities bound up in its charms. For instance, the act she was playing now, as though she were interested in the slightest in all Robert's droning on and on about his concerns for the economy. But the economy had never been better. . . . Eliza had a feeling Robert concerned himself with quite a few things he needn't worry himself about.

Oh, he was perfectly fine as a human being, but he was also no William. See, there was practical, and then there was Robert. He was ten years her senior and had helped to secure his family business after it took a hit during the Great War. All of this hard work led to his parents being able to remain in their family home, which previously had been ravaged for many years after it took a cannon ball during the War Between the States. Eliza liked that about him, and she certainly respected it. But none of that made him any less dull of a conversationalist.

Yet in her aunt's mind, and probably in her father's, there was a proper time in life when a young woman ought to marry, to secure her future. Eliza, her aunt, and her father were perfectly comfortable here together financially, but they also by no means retained the old wealth that once went hand-in-hand with the family name . . . wealth that only a few families, including William's, had kept in abundance. Still, her aunt privileged the place in high society that she had—wealth or no—from her family's long presence here in Charleston, stemming all the way back to its days as Charles Town. And part of those high-society expectations included eligible young women being matched into appropriate marriages at appropriate times.

Apparently Robert was what they deemed appropriate.

"What hobbies do you enjoy, Robert?" Eliza thought this question would provide the simplest opportunity for Robert to convey something—anything—about himself that may pique interest and further conversation. She could tell he was shy, and perhaps if she asked him the usual dinner topic questions directly, the rest of dinner may be less uncomfortable.

He spent longer than necessary cutting his roll perfectly even, aligning the two sides of it, before looking up at her and smiling. "To be honest, Eliza, I don't suppose I keep any hobbies."

"None?" Eliza feigned disbelief, though she grew increasingly more concerned the real problem may be that the man truly did not have fun. Or wit. "Surely there must be something."

Robert set his knife down at the edge of his plate. "I do enjoy keeping chickens. Would that suffice as an answer?"

Eliza made every effort in her power not to allow her shock to show on her expression. "Chickens, you said?"

"Yes, I was raised on a farm, and the sound of chickens in the morning makes me feel like I'm home again. I enjoy having them, and all the fresh eggs."

Eliza's mind spun.

Okay, so he actually *had* answered that his favorite hobby was caring for chickens. She wasn't imagining this.

It was one thing that he hadn't thought to ask her about her *own* hobbies—she could overlook that because he was clearly the quiet sort and was probably nervous. But to outright say he preferred the company of livestock . . . well, Eliza didn't know what to do with this information.

"Do tell us, Robert. Why has a handsome man such as yourself never married?" Her aunt smiled, casting a casual glance toward Eliza. Was the glance meant to chide Eliza for not asking the question herself?

Although Eliza did wonder it. Apart from being rather quiet and certainly dull, he was one of the more suitable men her father and aunt had attempted to bring home over the years. He was handsome enough, hardworking, and had a sense of integrity at least. He was the type of person Eliza would welcome the sight of, should, say, a criminal was stealing something from her.

Robert used his fork to move the salad about his plate. The little crow's-feet wrinkles around his brown eyes tightened as he looked up. "There was someone, once." His Adam's apple warbled, and Eliza could tell he truly loved that woman. "We were engaged, but she was unfaithful." He gave a sad smile. "But that was a long time ago."

For the first time in the entire evening, Eliza felt drawn to him, and even ached for him. She could only imagine how she would feel should William break her heart. And she wondered if perhaps she had been too quick to judge poor Robert and that perhaps he was so dull because he was guarded, because he had been hurt deeply in the past. The fact he was here at all said something about his strength, to recover from a broken heart like that and not come out of it with scars. Or maybe, what's perhaps more, to come out of it *with* scars and still keep growing.

"I'm sorry." Eliza held his gaze. He nodded once. It was the most sincere engagement anyone had all evening.

Shortly thereafter, Robert excused himself before any pies could be cut. Though Eliza was relieved the uncomfortable conversation was over, she couldn't help but wonder if Robert had gone home thinking of his almost-wife, and she did feel badly for him about that.

She'd gone and fetched a box of Girl Scout cookies from the pantry when she heard her aunt and father's raised voices from upstairs. So like a good detective, she slunk up the stairwell on her tiptoes, cookie box in hand, and then stood outside the open door eavesdropping.

It was nearly August, and her aunt was folding dresses and stacking them neatly into her luggage. She would leave tomorrow to spend a month in Asheville so as to avoid being considered one of those "August ladies," as her aunt said with derision, who hadn't the income to escape town when temperatures went from hot to hotter.

Eliza supposed she herself was an August lady, but she didn't mind much. Her aunt had begged her father to let Eliza accompany her—because apparently people in town needed to think the family was richer than they actually were, richer than they had been ever since the War Between the States laid waste to their fields. But

Eliza would far rather be an August lady than go anywhere with her aunt, and so her father, to her relief, had said he needed her help around the house.

But that didn't seem to be what the two of them argued over now.

"You have to do something about this." Her aunt made no attempt to hide the agitation from her tone.

"I have the situation under control," her father said.

Eliza chewed her cookie as softly as possible. She didn't want to miss a word.

"You know about the forgery, and you let it happen. How is that having the situation under control?"

A forgery? A forgery of what? Father hadn't said anything to Eliza about this.

"We don't know for certain who is responsible," her father said.

"Pishposh, of course we do. And your idea to instead pique her interest with Robert failed miserably. Could you have possibly found a man more dull? You need to tell Eliza. She hasn't the faintest idea and deserves to know the truth."

Eliza stopped chewing. Well, this was very unusual. It almost sounded as though her aunt was the one sticking up for her. Eliza peeked her head around the doorway just as her aunt forcefully shut her suitcase and came blazing out of the room. She nearly ran clear into Eliza.

All Eliza could do was hold the Girl Scout cookie box tighter and swallow.

"How much did you hear?" Her aunt puffed out a breath.

"Enough to be confused." Very confused. Eliza couldn't make heads or tails of it.

"Keep eating those cookies and you'll be big as a house. You truly care nothing about keeping a man like Robert interested, do you?"

"If I can't eat cookies and keep a man interested, then he's not a man I want around." Feeling brazen after having already been caught eavesdropping, Eliza reached into the box for another cookie. She held it out toward her aunt who, in a surprising move, actually took it from her hand and sighed.

"Oh well. If you can't beat them, join them—isn't that how the saying goes? Besides, if there was ever a night to indulge . . ."

Eliza took another cookie for herself. "What did you mean about my father needing to tell me something?"

"It's not my place to say." Eliza's aunt reached out to brush cookie crumbs from the collar of her dress in a startlingly maternal gesture. "But before I leave for Asheville, I will tell you this much. Don't trust anyone. You wear your heart on your sleeve, and sometimes, people are not who you think they are."

Eliza frowned, shaking her head. "Is this all about Robert?"

"No, sweetheart." Her aunt squeezed both of Eliza's arms. "This is about you. Though I do believe you and Robert would make a good match. Lord knows you're plenty colorful enough to make up for his drab sense of humor. And then some. He's kind, Eliza, and responsible, to boot."

Eliza waited a long moment, mulling this over. Finally, she closed the tab on the cookie box. She wasn't hungry anymore. "I don't even know Robert's last name," she murmured. Things would be so much simpler if only she could feel for Robert the way she felt for William.

"It's Legare."

TWELVE

Modern Day

Obstinate woman.

Declan held the door open for Kaitlyn, but Lucy was the one on his mind. The smell of bruschetta pulled him into the restaurant, but the thought of Lucy on that broken doorstep pulled his attention back out.

He'd never had this problem before. When he was with a woman, he was fully present. And the same applied when he was at work, or reading, or hiking. He lived in the moment and lived moments well. Women did not root themselves in his mind like Lucy had done. And though he was far from charmed, she had captivated him nonetheless, and that fact was more than a little troubling.

Kaitlyn slid into the booth and flashed him a pearl-white smile from behind the small vase of flowers on the table. He sat, and she reached across the table to take his hand. "I thought you'd never ask me out, Declan."

"Oh?" He smiled. Her hand was cold as a glass of iced tea against his own.

"Honestly, I've had a crush on you ever since your dad hired me last month." She turned her head slightly and flipped her hair in the perfect angle for a selfie. Declan had a feeling she'd practiced that pose.

"I hope I'm not being too forward," she added. With looks like hers, Declan imagined men did not mind her being forward at all.

He pulled his hand from under hers and drummed his fingers against the menu. Was this date about to turn into another grab for his family's money? Declan was heir to a small fortune, and that was common knowledge to all the women in his family's social circles.

Declan cleared his throat. "So you're in school for landscape design?"

"Yes. I've always been inspired by the gardens at my family's home."

"Nothing like getting your hands dirty with soil, right? Knowing in time, plants will come."

Kaitlyn laughed. "Oh, I'm not much for dirty work. I draw the designs. I'll hire people for the other parts."

"I see." Declan held up his menu and perused the pasta options.

The waitress arrived, and they ordered the house bruschetta and two iced teas while they decided on their entrees.

Ready to commit to the lasagna, Declan set his menu down and looked straight into Kaitlyn's eyes. The corner of her lips rose slightly as she looked right back.

"Do you know who Mr. Potter is?" he asked.

She tilted her head. "Mr. Potter . . . is he another employee at your dad's office or something?"

"No, like, the fictional character."

The waitress arrived with their teas, and Kaitlyn took a sip of hers. "I'm sorry, Declan. I have no idea what you're talking about."

"*It's a Wonderful Life?*"

"Oh, is he the one who sings that 'What a Wonderful World' song?"

Was this woman joking?

Declan loosened his tie. "Uh, you know what? Don't worry about it. Silly of me to ask."

As the bruschetta arrived, so did the suffocating realization that despite all odds, Lucy was *still* on his mind.

Declan excused himself and left before taking even a bite of the appetizer.

"Mom, where do you keep the plastic baskets?" Declan had emptied the closet, its containers strewn through the marble entryway of his parents' home, and he couldn't help but feel like a child making a mess of things.

Anna Pinckney appeared, wearing a light-knit sweater, her grey-peppered hair in a bun, and a smile on her lips that was as glowing as the Carolina sunset.

"Already back from your date? It's barely eight o'clock. Did you leave before eating?"

"Why don't you sound surprised?" Declan rolled up the sleeves of his button-down. He'd ditched the tie and jacket upon arrival home.

"I watched out the window as you left the house. Why you insist on going out with these women who are so obviously not right for you is beyond me." She fiddled with the costume jewelry around her neck. She always said the real stuff made her feel pompous. And Declan often imagined if she hadn't gotten married, she might be living in some modest cottage out on Edisto Island. Or in one of the homes the preservationists had saved from demolition in the 1920s.

"Thanks for the reminder of why I do not live at home, Mom."

Her grin matched the sparkle in her hazel eyes. "You know you love my meddling."

"I don't know if I'd go that far, but I do love *you*, so that's something."

She seemed to notice the mess for the first time. "Now that we have that settled, you want to tell me why you're wreaking havoc on my closet?"

"I'm looking for plastic baskets—you know, the storage ones."

"At eight o'clock at night?" She stepped forward and reached up to the top shelf of the closet to grab the exact basket he'd been looking for. She'd always had that classic mom way about her. Despite the size of their family home, she could find anything he needed just when he needed it.

And the same generally held true for her advice.

Though, he did not need to hear her evaluation of Kaitlyn right now. He'd already come to that conclusion himself.

And Lord knew he did not want to tell her about Lucy. He could only imagine the meddling that would open up.

"Just working on a project using a few things we've already got around here. No time to get to the store."

She sighed and shook her head. "You're so much like your father. Always preoccupied with projects. Always mysterious. Can't you two ever just come out and say what you're thinking like a normal person?"

Declan smiled.

In this case, no. He could not. "Nice try, Mom. Isn't it enough that you got to spy on my date tonight?"

"I wouldn't call it spying, exactly."

"Oh yeah? What would you call it, then?" He chuckled.

"Using my keen deductive skills for the well-being of my obviously incapable son." She straightened to her full five foot four inches. "Besides, what else am I supposed to do while your dad is working late?"

Declan stood, basket under his arm. "Hey, when I'm done with this, are you in the mood for a little Jimmy Stewart tonight?"

"Honey, I'm always in the mood for Jimmy Stewart. Were you thinking Washington or Bedford Falls?"

"Bedford Falls, but only if you promise not to do the Charleston during the movie. You almost broke your ankle last time."

This was not the first evening Declan had spent watching classic movies with his mother while his father put in long hours at the office, and he suspected it would not be the last. No matter the years that passed, he was always thankful for movie nights with his mom.

But right now, he had another woman on his mind.

The doorbell rang. Startled, Lucy jumped up from her spot rummaging through the books on the bookcase. She'd told herself she would continue looking for little notes or clues Eliza had left behind only so long as her cell phone battery held out. It had lasted far longer than she'd expected.

She loosened the pins in her hair and shook it free as she hurried to the door.

Her heart raced from the abrupt interruption, but she decided to skip the encyclopedia this time. She realized that was probably an overreaction, so instead, she grabbed her phone and creaked the porch door open.

Hmm.

No one in sight.

Then Lucy looked down.

A plastic basket rested on the door stoop. On top was an envelope with the word *Lucy* written on it.

She bent down to retrieve it and used one fingernail to break the seal. Inside, the handwritten script read, *Next time, I hope you take me up on my offer for tea. Truce?*

There was no name, but Lucy didn't need one.

She sighed.

That stubborn, impossible, handsome Pinckney.

This was probably just an attempt to get on her good side so she'd sell him the house. She would not fall for his manipulative schemes.

Lucy lugged the heavy basket inside and glanced over its contents.

The basket held two portable fans, a glass-enclosed candle and matches, two bottles of water, and a large bag of Reese's Pieces.

She reminded herself Declan was only doing this to win the house.

Stay strong, Lucy. Stay strong.

She looked at the Reese's Pieces bag. If she were a weaker woman . . . well, she might let herself believe Declan Pinckney was actually being kind for kindness' sake alone. She might imagine he really *was* as charming as he seemed. And if she were really feeling impulsive, she might even fantasize about accepting his offer for tea.

Lucy raised her chin.

Good thing she was *not* a weaker woman.

She opened the bag of Reese's, ate a handful, and lit the candle.

Immediately, the room filled with warm, soft light. Her cell phone buzzed its warning that her battery was on its last leg, so she turned it off.

She reminded herself the battery dying was supposed to be her cue to return to the apartment she shared with her sister. But thanks to Declan, she had the candle now.

Lucy opened one of the bottles of water. Had Declan guessed her utilities, like her electricity, were also off? Well, whatever his reasoning, she had to admit, the water tasted good right now. She'd already finished the bottle she'd brought over this afternoon in her car.

Lucy flipped on one of the battery-powered fans. Far more powerful than she'd expected, it quickly circulated air around the room.

Shadows danced along the bookshelf, and she imagined Eliza living here, dancing and laughing freely. What had Eliza's life been like? *Had* she known love and romance and dreams? Was she involved with the preservationists, and did the Great Depression take her way of life as it had for so many?

What would Eliza think if she could see Lucy now?

Would she be sad that Lucy's uneventful life had become this house's legacy?

An old, worn Bible on the bookshelf caught her attention, and Lucy pulled it out by the candlelight. The pages had been underlined, and notes filled the margins. When she was a little girl and afraid of the dark, her mother would take out a Bible and read a passage. And when Lucy grew older and afraid of all new sorts of things, her mother's reaction was the same. She wondered if reading this Bible would have the same effect.

But as she flipped through the pages, a letter fluttered out. Lucy pressed the creases that hadn't been touched in ages and began to read the faded, handwritten script.

My dear Eliza,

My heart races as I think of your graceful hands holding this page. Oh, how I wish I were there to sit beside you at the carriage house with the stars as our company. How many evenings have we spent in such enchantment?

You must think me a hopeless fool for how ardently I've come to love you. But there are things about me you do not know.

As I write this letter from the other side of the wall, my suitcase sits beside me, and my stomach churns with remorse. If only there were another way. I've been sprinting from my past, and my past has found me. Secrets long kept are surfacing, despite my greatest attempts to run from them.

I wish I could say more. I wish I could take you into my arms, kiss your delicate lips one last time, and make good on my promises to you.

But all I can say is this.

When I told you I love you, I meant those words. When I told you that you'd never fade from my thoughts, I meant that too. You have changed my life, dearest Eliza, and I will mean it with every breath to come.

I hope when you think of me, you'll remember these words.
Especially when you realize what I must do next.
    Do keep the ring.

                            Yours,
                            William

Lucy stared down at the letter in her hands, reading it again and again and wondering if her mind was playing a trick on her. She squinted as though doing so might help her see things more clearly. It did not.

"William?" she murmured aloud to herself. Who was William?

THIRTEEN

1929

Eliza put one hesitant foot inside the small boat, then looked back up at William.

"Are you sure about this?" She wore her bobbed hair curled, with a pin to hold it behind her ear. The dress her aunt had made for her birthday showed half her knees when the tassels flapped, and the only things keeping the ensemble from perfection were her old shoes.

But maybe we all need something to keep us grounded, even in the beautiful moments.

That's what Eliza had learned this past year as her feelings grew for William. There was a mystery about him, something he wasn't saying. Even now, she had a feeling he was running from something.

Oh, the paradox of a needful, glorious life.

"Eliza, I've got you." He took her hand and steadied her.

The afternoon sun pulled sweat from her back, and it trickled down as Eliza put both feet inside the boat. Why had she agreed to this?

"A *birthday surprise*," he'd insisted.

She watched as the current tugged the water, and she stepped out as boldly as she could manage.

If her father knew about this . . . but William had assured her everything was fine.

Eliza settled into the small boat, careful of her dress, and William climbed in too. Still standing, he pushed from one of the oaks with an oar. His hat wobbled with the movement, and he reached for it. The brown of his suspenders and trousers mirrored the brown in the trees, and he seemed right at home here.

Ahead, the water snaked through what looked like a meadow of tall, green grasses. And though it was—let's face it—a swamp, the sunlight bronzed the horizon, echoing off that grass in the most beautiful way.

Just like a painting.

Eliza sighed.

"Where are we going?" She shot a glance toward William as he rowed slowly.

"You'll see." William looked off in the distance, pretending to be aloof, but a grin spread across his lips.

Eliza turned back to the water in front of her, and her heart warmed with contentment. It didn't matter where, really. As long as William was by her side.

The current pushed the water forward, and their boat followed suit. Eliza couldn't help but feel that this moment was an image of her life. She and William, in their tiny little boat, pulled along by something much deeper and greater than both of them. And the sunlight was turning them golden, and twilight promised even more color.

So long as the night never arrived.

Half an hour later, give or take, William directed their boat toward an island. Eliza felt the pulse of music from a distance, and she glanced up at him.

"What's that?"

"That, my darling"—he took her hand and helped her out of the boat—"is jazz. And more specifically, it's the Charleston."

"You mean, people dancing it?" Somewhere other than her father's garden?

William laughed. He led her along a walkway as the music grew in volume. "Yes. I know how much you like the dance, and this island is where it originated at the turn of the century. Well, at least according to the stories I've heard. It's hard to know for sure."

They ducked under some brush, and the scene came into full view. Eliza's eyes went wide. There must've been at least a hundred people, and the beat was lively. At the front of the group, Eliza caught sight of a piano, two saxophones, drums, a banjo, and some other instruments she didn't recognize.

Blacks and whites—the grandsons and granddaughters of slaves and plantation owners—all jumped together on the beat, arms flailing. Her aunt would be stunned at the sight. Horrified. She would insist such intermingling wasn't proper and that someone should call the authorities.

But Eliza's grandmother, as well as her mother, hadn't raised her that way.

Grandma Clara had been a revolutionary.

And there were others, all among them, it seemed, who also believed that sixty years following the trauma of the Civil War was far too long for segregation to be continuing.

Eliza had heard about dances like this, and music like this, too, being enjoyed by different races in one singular audience—it happened all the time in Harlem—but she had never experienced it herself before.

What a sight it was to see.

Eliza was so mesmerized by the coming-together-ness of it that she realized she could do more, and she *would* do more, she determined, to make this normal in society.

A white man Italian with those dark curls?—and a black woman gether, laughing and beaming at one another in betw and kicks. It took Eliza a moment to realize the woman e family way. Considering the enchantment

113

the couple seemed to have with one another, she assumed this man must be the father.

And Eliza wondered what life must be like for them, what life *would* be like for them, and for their mixed-race baby, outside of rare dances like this one. It was surely a beautiful thing to dance so freely, and she wondered how they accomplished it, what with racism and hate and prejudice abounding beyond the protective cover of this evening. As she watched them, she had the strangest sense of knowing them—as if their story and hers were somehow intertwined even though they were all strangers.

Her mother had taught her long ago that when this unexpected sense of knowing came upon her, it meant God was telling her to pray. And so Eliza said a little prayer for their baby, that the child would grow to dream big dreams that would mend and change the world someday.

A sharp beat in the music drew Eliza back to her surroundings. Real flappers kicked their legs this way and that, and laughter flooded the street. The music pulsed through Eliza. She felt joy. She felt alive. She looked up to William with a grin.

"Happy birthday," he said. She could hardly hear him over the roar of the music. So to thank him, she squeezed his hand and stepped closer to the dancers.

William slid his arm around her waist, standing beside her. He slipped back with his right foot, then kicked it, encouraging her to do the same. Then he kicked the left, and stepped back, hesitating for a beat. With his arm around her waist, Eliza sensed the movement against her body. The steps came easily.

Sweat now covered her whole body, as the heat of the dancers so close together radiated the heat of the sun, and the powder she wore on her face melted clear off.

The pin in her hair slowly slipped downward, and she suspected her curls were victim to the humidity. The music throbbed so loudly, her head ached. And the colors of the dancers' clothing were vibrant as an art piece.

But Eliza was caught in a beautiful dance with William. It was as if the honesty of the music pulled deeper than everything else around them—just like the current along the river.

The music slowed as twilight dimmed, and William pulled her closer.

She fixed the pin in her hair and was sure a ray of light came through her skin for how she beamed. William's nearness awakened her dreams and quickened her pulse.

He leaned a little closer than usual, and Eliza's lips parted. William brushed a stray piece of hair from her sweaty forehead.

He kissed her eyebrow first, then the tip of her nose, and time seemed to still as he leaned down to really kiss her. The dancers continued skipping to the beat around them, but their footsteps seemed to be clapping.

The colors of the twilight sky swirled together, and all Eliza could feel was William's lips against her own as a chill went over her skin and a tickle ran up her spine.

It was the best birthday of her life.

It was the moment she realized she loved him.

William didn't sleep a wink the night after Eliza's birthday.

She had captured him wholly, and there was no question in his mind any longer. He could not deceive her. He simply could not do it.

He never should have done the forgeries in the first place and felt both deep regret and deep shame over the lengths he was willing to go. Regardless of his father's feelings toward his job prospects in the arts, surely he could have found a job to help his sister and the baby boy by some other means. He was desperate, yes, and his heart was in the right place, but none of that justified that he would so much as consider working with a man like Cadigan.

What a fool he had been.

These were the conclusions he'd come to with startling clarity as the full moon slipped behind the clouds, then beneath the horizon, and the sun rose on a new day.

For quite a while now, guilt had ravaged William, tugging him toward the higher path of integrity. The money was good, and seeing what it did for his sister Hannah had kept him going. But each stroke of gentle color only muddled the landscape of his conscience.

Cadigan was already unhappy that William hadn't brought another painting. He'd given William one more week to "*mind his p's and q's*" and get something together.

Yet as William spent more and more time with Eliza, he'd begun to see *her* as someone to take care of too. Oh, Eliza could do perfectly well for herself, that much was true. But he wanted to protect her from loss and from heartbreak, and he couldn't fool himself into denying he was the source of both those things any longer.

He'd tried to sell his own original paintings for weeks, but no one had bought them.

So now he was trying a different, far riskier approach. Well, risky as far as the heart was concerned, because if his parents found out, they would be mortified. If he met with failure, he would be mortified too. But the risks were worth it, because knowing Eliza had awakened him to the nuances of life—the subtle blending of colors during a sunrise and the similar bending of notes in a well-crafted lyric.

He hoped that was what his music could represent, and that it might resonate with others. Clearly he needed to tell her the truth about the forgeries, though he had no idea how—just that it must be done sooner rather than later.

His plan was to take things one step at a time, and this was what he knew:

He was writing a song for her. He would call it "My Dear Eliza."

And if all went well, he would play it as he proposed.

FOURTEEN

Modern Day

"Dad, I'm telling you, this woman is determined." Declan adjusted his suit vest and leaned against the side of his father's desk.

The desk, like his father's expression, was unwavering. For several moments, the only response was the birds' song from the tree just outside the office window.

His father tapped an expensive pen against his portfolio. "You're saying Lucy Legare is singlehandedly such a force to be reckoned with that our entire development group won't be able to sway her?"

Declan bit his bottom lip. He could feel his chest tightening as it always did when his dad adopted this tone. When would his father see him as a regular employee rather than a protégé to be groomed? How was he supposed to live up to his father's expectations when the man would never trust Declan's instincts?

"This is nonnegotiable, Declan. Make the deal." His father's face reddened.

Declan took a deep breath and looked down at his hands. "It's not that simple. She doesn't care about money."

"Doubtful," his father scoffed. "But even so, clearly you haven't made the right offer."

"What's that supposed to mean?"

"If she truly doesn't care about the money, what *does* she care about?"

Declan drummed his fingers against the desk. "I don't know."

"Therein lies your problem."

Declan shook his head.

"How do you expect to make this deal when you know so little about her?" His father settled into the plush chair behind his desk. "Go find out what the woman wants."

"How am I supposed to do that?"

Robert Pinckney shrugged. "You have your ways."

"Are you insinuating I date her?"

Because after the way his last conversation ended with Lucy, that proposition was laughable.

"Now there's an idea." His father began shuffling through the papers on his desk, a clear sign he was nearly done with this conversation. "But not necessarily. Just find a way to get her to open up, one way or another."

"Why do you need her house, anyway? Can't we do the development using the other lots on the block?"

Robert paused. "I hesitated to tell you this in case it didn't pan out, but you're wavering, and you need to understand the importance of the project. This isn't just about the development. The heirloom silver that's caused the longstanding feud with the Legares . . . the silver that thief keeps coming after . . ."

Declan frowned. "The Paul Revere silver spoon?"

"Yes." He rubbed the facial hair on his chin. "It's on her property. Maybe *in* her property. Buried in the ground, I mean."

Declan sat back in the chair across from his father. His pulse raced. He dropped his head into his hands. "Are you sure?"

"Fairly confident, yes. The complete collection could be worth a million dollars."

"Or more." Declan sighed. Now he understood. The only missing item in their family's collection was that spoon.

Declan looked up at his father and was met with a smile for the first time this afternoon. He stood and started toward the office door, then turned around. "And when I uncover what she really wants, what if she still doesn't take the offer?"

"Then you turn the offer into a threat."

Chills ran down Declan's arms because he knew he had no choice in the matter. If he didn't follow through, his father would. And his father's threats were no laughing matter.

Lucy had the day off from working at the museum, so she'd slipped away to her new house as soon as she could manage to get away from wedding central. She'd spent the afternoon with her Swiffer and her detective hat as she searched for more clues about the house and who William might have been.

Once she got inside the house with her cleaning supplies, she'd realized that much of the needed repairs were cosmetic, and she suspected some fresh paint as well as new porch boards would do wonders. The place was by no means turnkey, but her Magic Eraser had taken off many of the minor scuffs.

She was pulling weeds from the garden when her cell phone rang.

"Hello? Lucy Legare speaking." She pinned the phone between her shoulder and ear as she wiggled a rather large weed free.

"Hi, Lucy! This is Anna, the museum director."

Lucy set the weed on the ground, brushed her hands free of dirt, and got a better hold on her phone. "So nice to hear from you."

"We've been investigating the painting you flagged, the watercolor from the Charleston Renaissance." Anna paused. "Turns out, you were right, Lucy. It's a forgery."

"I . . . I don't know what to say." She took a seat on the little wooden bench beside the carriage house. "I mean, I'm not surprised, but at the same time, I didn't actually think I was right, either. . . ."

"I know. It's quite surreal, isn't it? So, Lucy, obviously I am impressed by your eye and expertise. I was wondering if you'd like to curate an exhibit on Charleston Renaissance artists."

Lucy's jaw dropped, and she covered her mouth with her free hand—her mother would be proud she'd managed to recover her manners, even if no one was watching. "That would be an absolute dream."

"Wonderful!" Lucy could hear papers being shuffled on Anna's end of the line. "Meet me on the museum steps tomorrow morning, just before opening, and we'll go over the details then."

"I'm looking forward to it." Lucy made sure she hung up the phone properly before shouting for joy and doing a little jig around the garden. She was going to be employed full-time. By an art museum! And the timing of all this would work perfectly in conjunction with the permanent curator position she had just applied for at the cultural center on Sullivan's Island.

Lucy was so giddy, she thought to walk a few blocks toward King Street to get some ice cream. But then she figured an even better idea would be to call the utilities company. Maybe they could get the water and electricity on by later this afternoon.

Thank God, because she wanted to move in here as soon as possible, and there was only so far she could take her relationship with dry shampoo.

She made the call and decided she'd finish gardening before getting her ice cream. Lucy tugged on a pair of gloves and began pulling thorny weeds from the garden that spanned the side and back of the house. The larger portion, behind the home, was separated into different sections that almost resembled outdoor rooms. That's where she was working now as a mockingbird swooped down into the dry birdbath, then hopped around the yard.

"Don't worry," Lucy said to the bird. "We'll both have running water soon enough." With a smile, she went back to the garden. There was something cathartic about digging up roots that didn't belong.

As she turned the soil, she got an idea. She'd seen several large planters as well as some perlite in the carriage-house-turned-garage. No telling how long that stuff had been in there, but she didn't have potting soil, and it was worth a try.

Lucy opened the rounded door of the carriage house, then hoisted the planters in the air. She couldn't see where she was going and nearly walked into the sprawling oak tree. A couple squirrels looked down at her from tall limbs.

Sweat dripped down her back as the sun ripened into its afternoon prime, and she heaved the planters down onto the ground. Grabbing fistfuls of soil, she mixed the tilled-up dirt with perlite to get the planting mix ready. It'd be nice if she had some rooting medium, but as long as she kept a careful eye on the cuttings, she was pretty sure this would work without it.

Using small cutting shears, Lucy made several slits in the jasmine plant that trailed up the side of Eliza's porch. Lucy imagined the woman sitting near that plant with her morning cup of tea, keeping the door open so the sweet floral fragrance lingered in the hallways throughout the day.

Maybe Lucy could propagate some new cuttings, even grow one inside, next to the sunny window in her bedroom. She was lost in the thought when she reached for the next stem and felt a sharp and sudden sting.

Then the sting began throbbing. And reddening.

"Ouch!" Lucy swatted this way and that, as if it would make a difference that she'd already been stung. The wasp was long gone. She dropped the cuttings to the ground without thinking.

Benadryl. She needed to take some Benadryl. Only, she didn't have any. And this time of day, with traffic, it'd take ages to get back to the apartment.

Drat. This wasn't good.

Lucy turned in a circle, looking around and considering her options. The last time she'd been stung, her throat had swollen up like her mama's hair on a Sunday. She'd taken a Benadryl in time, but not before the word *EpiPen* was thrown around.

Think, Lucy. Think.

Her gaze landed upon the roof of Ms. Beth's house on the other side of Church Street. She had walked home with Ms. Beth many times after their shifts ended at the museum and knew exactly which house was hers. She could be there in no time flat.

Ms. Beth would know how to help, right? If she was home, that is.

Lucy hustled just down the road and across the street, past the blue hydrangea and sprawling rose bushes that lined the walkway, then rang the doorbell.

Please be home. Please be home.

Her arm was beginning to itch.

The floral wreath shook slightly as the door opened, and Ms. Beth appeared.

"Lucy?" She lowered her teal-colored frames to get a better look. "Well, girl, why are you so flushed and sweaty?"

"Thank heavens you're here." Lucy fell into the woman's arms for a hug. "I'm so sorry for the random circumstances, but please tell me you have Benadryl."

"Absolutely, honey. Come with me." She waved Lucy inside, and Lucy gladly followed. She had only been in Ms. Beth's home a few times before, but it had always been beautiful. The wooden floors had been restored to perfection, and antique pieces offered a pop of color against the stairwell. A red bookshelf here. A blue desk there. Lucy loved the vibe of artistic mixed with historical.

Not to mention the roses. Roses everywhere. Every color and variety, in vases large and small. Ms. Beth was the only person Lucy knew who could grow roses like these.

The sweet scent of pure rose flowers was infinitely lighter in the air than perfume, and Lucy took a deep breath of it.

Beth reached up into a cabinet for the medicine, then poured Lucy some water in a cup that looked like Depression-era glass. She leaned closer as Lucy took the glass from her hand. "Sweetheart, what happened?"

Lucy was starting to feel lightheaded, and her throat tingled.

She tossed the pill back and washed it down with a gulp of water before explaining about the plants and the wasp and the sting.

"My! Do come and sit a spell until it passes."

Lucy waved her hand. "Oh, no. I couldn't."

Though the vintage settee Ms. Beth was moving toward looked mighty tempting, with its plush pillows and view of Beth's award-winning garden.

Ms. Beth took her hand and patted gently. "I insist."

Lucy was about to object again, then looked at the empty water glass in her hand. Maybe it wouldn't be so wise to hurry back to a house where she had no electricity or running water. Not to mention the bricks Peter said needed to be replaced. It would all be there when she returned later that day.

She took a deep breath and sat at the edge of the sofa. "I suppose I could stay for just a bit." She rubbed the fabric of the couch with her hand. "Only if you're sure I'm not overstepping."

"Are you kidding?" Ms. Beth swatted the idea away. "It's not as if you're making a ruckus, my dear. You're just lying on the sofa." She fluffed the pillows for Lucy and sat down beside her. "And besides, I love company."

Ms. Beth noticed the empty cup and stood. "Let me get you some more water, and you just rest a bit. I'll be back in a minute."

Lucy's eyes fluttered closed, and her heart warmed with the comfort of hospitality. She'd forgotten how it felt to be taken care of. And she had to admit, the cozy comfort was a pretty good feeling. There were some things about Charleston that perhaps she had missed more than she liked to admit when she was away from home in Savannah.

Lucy slid off her shoes and snuggled one of the pillows against her chest. Maybe she would close her eyes just for a bit longer. Ms. Beth's house felt blessedly chilly.

Lucy breathed in the fragrance of freshly cut roses once more. The itch was beginning to subside. But in its place, she felt the pull of fatigue.

Just a few more moments here . . .

The next thing Lucy knew, she awoke to find the afternoon sun dimming. A mockingbird sang its final song of the day from its perch on a rose bush just beside the window.

How long had she slept?

Lucy pulled off a soft blanket Ms. Beth must've draped over her shoulders and yawned. Beth had turned on a lantern-style reading lamp and was humming from the other room. The smell of freshly baked muffins filled the air.

Lucy stretched her arms above her head and scuffled barefoot into the kitchen to find Beth moving the muffins from a pan to an intricately pattered plate. Beth wiped her hands on her apron. "I made your favorite—banana nut with extra pecans. Go ahead and take one. They're fresh out of the oven."

Lucy needed no arm-twisting. She reached for the plate Ms. Beth offered and took a fork from the counter. None of Beth's antique silverware matched, and Lucy loved the eclectic nature of her kitchen.

Ms. Beth went back to the pan of muffins but held up the knife she was using to loosen them since she couldn't talk with her hands. "Now, you want to tell me why I haven't seen any power on at your house?"

Lucy pinched off a bite of the muffin and blew on it as steam rose. "Well . . ."

"Please tell me you at least have running water."

Lucy's hesitation to answer was all Ms. Beth needed in response.

"Lucy! Why haven't you come over sooner?"

Lucy shrugged. "It's only been an afternoon . . . and I guess yesterday too. But don't worry. I'm having the utilities turned on today." She glanced out the window at the dimming light. "Actually, they probably already came. I didn't want to bother you."

Beth *tsked* under her breath. "Child, that just hurts my feelings."

Lucy smiled. She should've known Ms. Beth would be as hospitable as ever.

"So, what's the scoop with your new home, anyway?"

Home. It was an interesting choice of words. Because, really, was Eliza's house her home?

"I inherited the house."

"That's some kind of inheritance." Ms. Beth put the last of the muffins on her serving plate, then poured two cups of tea. Taking one cup at a time, she moved them to the table and sat across from Lucy. "So, the house is yours." It was more of a statement than a question.

"It is." Lucy brushed the ends of her hair with her fingers and fixed her messy ponytail. It was still so strange saying those words. The house was *hers*.

"Who gave it to you?" Beth dunked her tea bag in and out of the cup, letting it steep.

"I have absolutely no idea. I'm trying to figure that out." Lucy took a bite of her muffin. It was every bit as delicious as she remembered. The pecans added the perfect bit of crunch, and the banana flavor wasn't overpowering. "But I have found some things inside belonging to a woman named Eliza. Do you remember her? Did she live here when you bought your own house?"

Ms. Beth hesitated. "She did." She stirred two tiny spoonfuls of sugar into her tea. "I remember the house was so much more than bricks and walls to Eliza. In a way, it was her legacy. She insisted it had a story to tell, and that she'd preserve it through her watercolors, just as she preserved so much else in this city." Beth took a bite from a muffin. "But of course, you already know all this."

Watercolors.

The word pinged like a marble in Lucy's mind.

"Wait. You don't mean to suggest that the Eliza who once owned my house is the same Eliza who painted the famous watercolors during the Charleston Renaissance?" Lucy's medicated brain fog lifted quite suddenly at this prospect.

"Well, sure." Ms. Beth pinched off a bite of a muffin and dropped it in her mouth. "Didn't you know? The place was one of her greatest preservation projects."

Lucy could hardly believe what she was hearing. The famed watercolorist she'd admired for so long had once owned her house? Excitement fluttered within her at the very thought. But why Lucy, of all people?

"I had no idea *that* Eliza was *my* Eliza."

Ms. Beth smiled. "Well, now you do. And the mystery is all the richer, I suppose."

"Sure is." Lucy took a sip of her tea and straightened the quilted placemat. "You know, I was trying to propagate some cuttings from the jasmine vine when that wasp stung me."

"What a lovely idea," Ms. Beth said. She stood and reached for the teapot to refill their delicate cups. "Do you have any rooting hormone powder?"

"No, ma'am." Lucy held up her cup for Beth to refill. "I thought I'd just stick them in a potting mix."

Ms. Beth chuckled, no doubt from years of gardening experience. "Sugar, you can't just stick something in the ground and expect it to grow." She set the teapot back down and looked Lucy straight in the eyes. "If you want to sprout roots, my dear, then tend them carefully. Roots are fragile before they're strong. It's as true for plants as it is for life."

Lucy smiled and took another sip of her tea. The stones in Eliza's ring glittered from Lucy's hand when she set her cup down. She may not have any roots yet, but at least she had the ground to start.

FIFTEEN

1929

"William." Cadigan startled from the carved mahogany desk where he worked. "You've surprised me. Did we have an appointment?" Always offering the veneer of gentlemanly conduct, Cadigan stood and gestured toward the empty chair across from him. "Please have a seat."

William swallowed past the lump in his throat, adjusting his bow tie. He was prepared for Cadigan to take what he had to say poorly. Well, at least . . . he thought he was prepared. Much as a man could be from playing out the conversation in front of his mirror this morning.

William nodded and sat, careful to keep a strong posture about his shoulders so Cadigan wouldn't notice any slumping and take him for a weaker sort of man.

Cadigan leaned against the side of his desk and pinched his black mustache to a point on both sides. "Just what can I do for you, William?"

Here was his chance.

William cracked his own knuckles, a nervous habit he hadn't indulged in for years for how it grated on his mother. "About Eliza . . ." He cleared his throat. No, that was all wrong. Not how he intended to start. "About Eliza's paintings." William locked

127

eyes with the man and found a mixture of what he deemed to be surprise and mirth in his expression. "I can't do it anymore."

Cadigan walked to the other side of his desk to light a cigar. "Well, truthfully, I can't say I'm surprised. You've lasted longer than all the others."

The thought of *others* made William's gut clench. Both the others who had attempted to steal from Eliza as well as the others who had apparently vied for her heart. The response was new for him. He had never felt a shred of jealousy in the past. But then again, perhaps he'd never had a need to.

And though he knew he was doing the right thing by confronting this now, William also felt the sour regret of having believed these lies . . . that imitation in any form might sustain him, might sustain those he cared about. In the process, he'd made a mockery of all that was true—a mockery, even, of his love for Eliza.

William tossed a large wad of cash down on the desk.

Cadigan popped off the rubber band and unrolled the bills. "What's this about?"

"I want to buy back the paintings. All of them." William folded his hands.

Cadigan simply stared at him, bewildered. Then after a long moment, he began to laugh. "Buy them back?"

William did not allow himself to be fazed by the response. "Yes, the lot of them."

"And I suppose you think it's that simple?" Cadigan tapped his cigar in the tray. "As though your work does not belong to me and I have not already sold it."

"It doesn't belong to you, not truly." William surprised even himself by the boldness of his words. "And have you?"

Cadigan rubbed his eyes with his free hand. "Might I ask what has prompted this sudden turn toward righteousness, hmm? I suppose you now consider yourself altogether grand and valuable to this universe, playing the part of the hero?"

"It's not pride, if that's what you mean. I assure you, I have little pride left. So will you do it? Will you sell them back to me or not?"

Cadigan set his smoldering cigar down in the tray and crossed his arms over his chest. "I'll sell them to you, but not for money. There's something else I'm after."

A warning plucked William's spirit like an off-tune guitar string. And yet he would do near anything to get the paintings back, to make this right.

"I need you to take something that's buried in Eliza's estate. And before you object, don't worry. It doesn't belong to your dearly beloved." The quirk of his smile was wicked. "It's an old family heirloom, is all."

Cadigan picked his cigar back up and puffed.

William was beginning to feel nauseated, whether from the smell of the curling smoke or Cadigan's proposition, he wasn't sure. Most likely, both were causes.

"What kind of an heirloom?"

"A rice spoon. Legend has it, the spoon was buried during the Civil War and hasn't been seen since. It's Paul Revere silver and stems back to the beginnings of America. You could say it's fairly priceless." He drummed his fingers against his desk, looking straight at William. "But I would say, everything has a price."

Chills ran down William's arms at these words.

Of course it was common for folks to bury their family silver as the Yankees were moving in, but most of them had the good sense to come back for it. That said, many people *did* return and couldn't remember where exactly they'd buried it—in their haste to avoid cannon fire, leaving no markers for all sorts of treasures they'd left behind.

But in this case, that was decidedly *not* what had happened.

Because William knew where the silver was. And William knew where the silver was going.

He was the *only* person left who did.

And he was certainly not going to make Cadigan privy to these answers. How did Cadigan even know about it, anyhow? Unless . . .

William tightened his fists. This was all making sense now. Cadigan's insistence that Eliza's paintings were the particular ones he wanted, his lack of interest in any of the other artists in Charleston. The silver was what Cadigan had been after all along.

William collected his bills from the table and shoved them back into his pocket.

Cadigan stood, puffing one more swirl of smoke from the corner of his mouth. "Where are you going?"

"I'm getting out of here, like I should've done in the first place. Keep the paintings, Cadigan. I won't sell my soul to you any longer."

William took determined steps through the doorway, but as he was leaving, Cadigan's voice boomed behind him.

"Mark my words. You will regret this display, William Pinckney!"

No, he certainly would not.

Of that much, he was sure.

Two Weeks Later

Eliza came inside from the garden, her hands full of fragrant flowers, the ones that could withstand the heat of August, the ones she had planted back in June. She was about to put them into a vase when she heard voices from her father's study. One of the voices sounded oddly like . . . William?

Eliza set the flowers down on the table instead and then hurried down the hallway to sneak a quick look. The vase would just have to wait.

She wore a split-sleeve, silken blouse with a sash pinned to her shoulder that swayed like a cape as she moved toward the study. Her heart began to race faster than her feet. Yes, that was definitely William's voice. But what was he doing here?

Eliza wanted to reach for the crystal handle of the door and make her presence known, but she caught herself. If William wanted her to be a part of the conversation, surely he would have told her about it.

She didn't know whether to be offended or excited about the prospect of all this might mean. So she did the only thing she could do. She closed one eye and used the other to try to peer through the slit between the door and its frame.

"My sister . . ." Her father's voice trailed off. What was he saying about her aunt? Eliza moved her ear closer to the door so she could listen rather than watch.

"I know," William said. "There is a long history between our families, but that doesn't matter to me. We have the chance to settle the old feud now."

Her father sighed. Hesitated. Eliza heard a chair scrape against the floor as though one or both of them had just stood. "All right," her father said.

"All right?" William's words skipped with enthusiasm.

"All right." The same words, far less enthusiastic. But nevertheless, he'd agreed. To what, exactly, Eliza wasn't sure . . . but if it made William this happy, it must be good. She was amazed enough that her father had even let William in the house, given the way her aunt had poisoned Father and everyone else's opinions of William's family.

Eliza better get out of the way before she got caught spying. She hurried down the hallway toward the kitchen, holding her hands to her skirt to keep it from flying. By the time she made it back to the flowers on the table, she was slightly out of breath, so she tried to calm herself in case William or her father entered the kitchen.

She was reaching for the vase in the top cabinet when William stepped into the room. Though she expected to see him, her heart still leapt at the sight. He wore a button-down vest, his hair parted sharply to the side, and a bright smile.

"Hello, Eliza." He grinned at her and she smiled back, glad she'd attached the silken scarf to the side of her outfit.

"Come with me." William took her hand and led her through the back door, through the garden, to a step he'd set against the wall beside the carriage house.

Roses from her garden littered the ground and the step with red and pink and yellow, leading all the way up to the top of the brick wall.

Eliza turned to face him. "What's this?"

He brushed the silk scarf behind her shoulder, his eyes twinkling with secrets. "You'll see."

William removed his suit jacket and laid it at the top of the bricks, then climbed up and extended his hand. "I saved you a seat."

Eliza didn't need any convincing. She hitched up the hem of her skirt and reached out to take his hand, letting him steady her as she climbed the step and hopped up on the top of the bricks.

"Now sit here, and I'll be back in a minute." William jumped off the top of the wall onto his side of the fence, as if he had no concerns about ripping his finest trousers.

Eliza settled in, the hum of anticipation growing ever louder from her heart. She was sitting among a blanket of petals from her garden in the very spot they swapped the journal. Call her romantic, but a woman could only hope what this gesture might mean.

William stepped inside. Eliza watched through the widow as he sat behind his piano, his fingers rolling effortlessly over the keys. After the first few measures, she recognized the song. And all the walls within her heart and all her aunt's warnings and all her fears began to crumble down.

He was playing her song. He'd thought to lower the widows so she could hear the lyrics for the first time.

"My dear Eliza," the chorus rang out, and Eliza's heart spun such that she couldn't focus on any of the other words clearly. They were all so beautiful, all blurred together like pigment in a watercolor, and she knew. She knew he was about to ask her to marry him.

William ended the song with a flourish and smiled at her a long moment while still at the bench of the piano. Eliza's tears streamed down.

Then he moved from the bench and stepped back outside, kneeling in front of where she sat along the wall with her feet dangling down. He held up a ring and warmed her heart with his grin.

"I never expected to fall in love when we did, but now, I never expect I'll be the same without you. I'm preoccupied by you when I fall asleep and when I rise. You are my muse, my inspiration, my friend. My dear Eliza, will you also be my wife?" He stood and held out the ring.

Eliza nodded, covering her mouth with her hand as she shamelessly allowed happy tears to stream down. "Yes, William. Yes!"

She jumped into his arms, and the rose petals flew up, then fell in a beautiful scattering of color, of promise. And when William's lips found hers, Eliza thought her feet may never touch the ground.

SIXTEEN

Modern Day

Three knocks sounded at the front door in an almost melodic fashion.

"Coming."

Lucy hopped toward the door as she put her other heel on, then tightened her ponytail. She suspected her visitor was Declan. And she suspected she knew why he was here. After all, a full evening had passed since his last attempt to sweet-talk her into selling him the house.

But when Lucy opened the door, what she didn't expect was how different he would look with a backward baseball cap and jeans on. He handed her a to-go cup that smelled like Earl Grey, as well as a paper pastry bag.

Lucy looked down at the bag and peeked inside. "A croissant?"

"Hope you like the traditional ones. I didn't know how you felt about chocolate." He gestured toward the corner of the street. "The coffee shop up there makes some great pastries."

"You and that coffee shop."

No need to tell him she'd actually ventured there yesterday afternoon after an early morning spent moving her furniture over to the new house. And there was definitely no need to tell him he was right about the place.

Lucy stepped out of the doorway and locked the worn white door. "Thanks for bringing this by." She took a sip from the tea. Her guess was confirmed. Earl Grey. How did he know she liked the flavor? Did something about her scream *bergamot*?

"Oh, I almost forgot." While holding his own drink, Declan used his free hand to pull several sugar packets from his pocket. "I also wasn't sure if you use sugar. I got raw sugar and the fake kind."

She plucked two raw sugar packets from his open hand, careful not to touch his palm, and raised one eyebrow. "What are you doing here, Declan?"

"Isn't it obvious? I'm bringing you breakfast."

And trying to convince me to sell you the house.

"I'm on my way to work."

"No problem." He followed behind her as she headed down the walkway. "I'll walk with you."

She stopped in her tracks and looked straight at him. Unfazed, he stared directly back.

"I know why you're here," she said.

"Do you?" He took a sip of his beverage—did she smell coffee?—and smiled pleasantly. "Then why'd you ask?"

Ugh, this man was impossible.

Was he trying to get credit for the care package he left several nights ago? Or was this breakfast all about the house? Well, he'd be surprised to know she could not be bought with little surprise visits and pastries. No matter how attractive he may be.

Though she did have a weakness for tea.

Lucy took a bite of her croissant. It was delicious. He wasn't exaggerating.

"I've got to tell you, Declan. After thinking more about the house . . ."

"Yes?" He slipped his free hand into his jeans.

A woman walking a fluffy dog passed them on the sidewalk and smiled. "Morning."

"Morning," Declan said.

Lucy echoed the sentiment and took another sip of her tea. She checked both ways before crossing the street, and her heel caught slightly against the cobblestone. Declan steadied her elbow with his hand.

She pulled her elbow free and looked at him. "I've firmly decided to keep the property. I know you want it for your company, but I'm just not budging."

He puffed out a deep breath. "I see."

She held her chin higher as they passed colorful, historic storefronts. "As if I weren't already swooning over the place, I've discovered it once belonged to one of my favorite artists from the Charleston Renaissance. It seems meant to be, you know?" She curled the ends of her ponytail with her finger. "I'm sorry to disappoint you, but I'm not going to change my mind."

Declan held tighter to his cup, though she had to give him credit. He kept a calm appearance, at least. "So you're staying in Charleston long term."

Church bells rang for the eight o'clock hour. She needed to walk faster so she wouldn't be late.

"That's the plan. I've got a temporary curator position here that I'm hoping will become permanent." Lucy pointed toward the museum they approached.

"A curator position . . ." Declan frowned.

Now in front of the art museum, Lucy stopped walking. "Why are you making that face?" She looked past Declan to see Anna open the door behind him.

"Lucy," Anna said. "Welcome!"

Declan groaned as he slowly turned toward Lucy's new boss. Did he know her?

"Mom?" He said the word slowly, as if he couldn't believe this was happening.

"Wait. Anna Pinckney"—*director of this entire museum and wielder of my career's fate*—"is your mother?" Lucy pointed between the two of them. Of course she knew the last names were the same, but how many Pinckneys were there in Charleston? A whole lot.

Then again, Declan did have a knack for standing out.

Anna simply smiled in return. She was confident. She was poised. She didn't seem surprised by this development in the least.

Declan quickly scaled the steps toward the museum, and Lucy followed, holding her satchel close to her hip. What would Lucy's own mom think if she knew *those* Pinckneys were *these* Pinckneys?

"What is going on here?" Declan asked, his gaze shifting between his mother and Lucy. Clearly, he was just as surprised as she was.

"I see you two have met." Anna continued to smile, completely at ease. Her lightweight scarf caught on the morning breeze, and she waved at a well-dressed passerby who held up his newspaper in greeting.

"Lucy is going to run a new exhibit on the Charleston Renaissance. Did she tell you? She's a perfect fit, given her art education and her family's personal history in Charleston. She also has an eye for imitations."

"Did you just say her family's *personal* history in Charleston?" Declan blinked. "I suppose it's a coincidence her family's history just so happens to coincide with our own?"

Anna glared at him with mama-bear eyes. "Declan, I may be the museum director, but I need not remind you I am also your mother, and I will not allow you to address me in such a way—on a city street, no less."

Declan lifted his baseball cap and shoved his hand through his hair. "Oh, Mom—you act as if I have no say in the matter. Don't you think I see what's happening?"

She raised her eyebrows as though asking indignantly. Lucy inched backward on her kitten heels. So *not* how she expected this morning to go.

"Need I spell it out?" Declan continued.

Anna waved at another passerby, then forced a response to Declan through the smile on her lips. "Go ahead, dear. Humor us."

Lucy wanted to laugh at the two of them arguing like siblings. Though they quarreled, she envied the openness of their conversation.

She took a sip of her Earl Grey.

Declan lowered his head and his tone. "You're trying to set me up with Lucy."

Lucy nearly spat out her tea.

His eyes darted toward her.

She covered her mouth. "I'm sorry. What?"

Who would *ever* think Lucy and Declan would make a good match?

Declan tossed his cup into the can nearby and looked at his mother. "Just because Lucy is intelligent and attractive does not mean we would get along. Under any circumstances."

Before Anna could speak up, Lucy interjected. Her ponytail swung as she took a bold step forward.

"Excuse me, but did it ever occur to you that your mother gave me this job because I'm actually qualified for it?" She looked up at his tall stature intently, but she refused to let him look down at her. "Or is it too outlandish to believe someone from my family could work with someone from yours? Maybe you're just struggling with the idea that not everything, Declan, is about you."

He leaned back, dumbstruck.

Anna seemed to be holding back a grin. She acted as if a woman had never spoken up to her son before.

"You're in over your head, Lucy," he said.

In her spunk, she'd stepped mere inches from him, but he made no move to distance himself. His arrogance disgusted her, and yet, the smell of sandalwood drew her in.

Declan watched her, his chest heaving with a sigh. After a few moments, his eyes softened and his lips parted slightly.

She wondered if he were going to apologize, but he said nothing. And yet, his sentiment echoed: *You don't belong here.*

What Declan didn't realize was that the feeling was not an original one. Lucy's mother had been trying to cozy her way into high society since the day she married Lucy's father. And because of it, Lucy had always felt one step behind.

Declan shuffled his feet. "Guess that's my cue." He turned to walk down the steps, getting halfway down them before finally turning and glancing briefly back over his shoulder.

She watched him leave, so sure in his steps. And she decided then that she would respond to his arrogance with grace and determination. Sticks and stones and whatnot.

But two stubborn words skipped through her mind.

Intelligent. Attractive.

Declan found her agreeable, did he? Well, that was just fine. He was probably struggling with the fact she didn't fall at his feet like every other woman in his life.

And though he disgusted her right now, his inadvertent compliment strengthened her confidence and her resolve.

The game was on.

"Lucy?" Anna's voice was gentle. "Ready to go inside?"

Lucy blinked, finding her way back to the moment and the opportunity in front of her. She cleared her throat. "Absolutely."

She loved this woman for completely ignoring what had just transpired.

Anna held open one of the large, wooden doors of the museum. Once inside, Lucy looked up. Though quaint in size, the architecture of the museum was in itself a work of art. Amazing, high-arched ceilings provided a framework for the pieces as natural light streamed down. Lucy marveled every single time she entered this place at the way hope seemed to float in the air.

Anna scanned her badge to enter a second set of glass doors and organized some paper work for Lucy.

"Once you fill that out, let me know, and I'll give you the details about the exhibit."

Lucy took a pen from the container on the desk. She hesitated when she got to the address category, then listed Eliza's home for the very first time. It was her house now, after all.

Anna approached with a framed watercolor, and Lucy handed back the paper work. She reached for the piece.

"This is stunning."

In what was recognizably a Lowcountry sunset, trees and swamp and flowers blended together by watercolors. Rather than detailing the scene, this piece evoked emotion—with literal drips of color blending past with present, the seen with the unseen. Twilight filled the sky, but the dimming sun flooded the piece with unexpected color and illuminated two figures dancing.

"This one, as you can probably tell, was done by Eliza," Anna said. "But the work speaks to the value of art in bringing about change, transcendent of the artist's identity."

Lucy nodded, studying the work.

"I'd love for you to visit the subjects of her pieces, Lucy, to provide photographs we can display alongside the paintings."

"What a great idea." Lucy looked up, smiling. Already, she felt a sense of connection with this piece, and she was desperate to know more about the woman behind the art.

"One more thing." Anna stood beside her, looking with admiration at the painting. "As you create the exhibit, don't shy away from her story."

Lucy stepped closer to the piece and wondered—just what did Anna mean?

SEVENTEEN

1916

After years of her precious house being owned by the Pinckneys, Clara was finally back home. The Pinckneys had agreed to sell it back.

She had been there a grand total of ten minutes before finding an excuse to hurry out to the carriage house, where she and Rose had hidden the family silver decades prior. Her daughter and son-in-law had no idea where the silver was buried before selling the house to the Pinckneys, and by the time Clara had received their letter about selling the home, it was too late. She never would have been able to get a response back to them in time.

And so instead, she had simply waited until the Pinckneys were willing to sell it—filling her time with fulfilling her promise to Rose and hoping beyond all hope the silver would still be where she'd left it when she returned.

She'd figured leaving it there in the carriage house with no one the wiser was the safest place for it, with all the back and forth travel she'd done . . . there were secrets that still followed her, after all, and she couldn't stay in one particular place too long lest those secrets catch up.

But as it turned out, she'd been wrong. She should have told her daughter about the silver. At the time, she thought she was keeping them all safe from the secrets. Now she realized there had been more than one option . . . well, now that the other options were gone.

Clara's heart raced as she kicked the heel of her shoe hard against the wooden slats, then used a hand shovel to dig in the spot where she and Rose had last left the spoon.

Her bronzed shoe buckle loosened at the movement, so in very uncouth fashion she sat down on the floor to tighten it and to more easily rifle through the dirt.

But as she dug up the dirt scoop by scoop, her stomach began to turn like the soil.

There was no silver to be found.

"Balderdash," she mumbled to herself. "It's gone."

"Grandma Clara?"

Clara clambered upward to a standing position to find her precious granddaughter staring, the little girl's eyes as round as quarter dollars.

"What's gone?" Eliza asked, fidgeting so the hem of her youthful skirt moved this way and that. "You seem sad."

Clara set her shovel down and wiped the evidence of dirt from her hands. How much should she tell the girl?

Perhaps—and it was absolutely impulsive to consider—but perhaps she should tell Eliza everything, so the girl would understand. Clara had been caught red-handed here and saw no other option.

Besides, just look where keeping secrets had gotten her.

Clara sighed. "There are some people named the Pinckneys who are angry at me because they think I broke a promise I made. Even though I didn't technically . . ." She fiddled with the long pin at her lacy neckline. "Anyhow, they're angry, you see, and they took some silver that once belonged to me—silver I left here a long time ago."

"You mean the family that lived here before we got the house back?" Eliza asked in disbelief.

Clara nodded. "That's the one." She leaned down and planted a kiss on top of Eliza's forehead. "But don't concern yourself with that now. I'll find a way to get it back . . . eventually."

But little Eliza wasn't so easily convinced. "Can I help?" she asked.

Clara grinned, not expecting the bold offer. She put both hands on Eliza's shoulders and looked gently into her eyes. "Yes, my dear," she said. "You can indeed. Let's have a chat now, just you and me."

September 1929

Dear William,

I must confess—though we see each other often these days, our correspondence journal still holds a special place of fondness in my heart, and I am glad we have continued writing.

Your wife-to-be,
Eliza

My dear Eliza,

I share your fondness, for it is through your notes that I initially came to know you. Perhaps we can continue it in the months to come over our kitchen table. What do you say?

Yours,
William

Dear William,

The kitchen table sounds perfectly pleasant to me, so long as you plan on delivering my notes with a cup of tea.

Eliza

My dear Eliza,

Tea seems a fair exchange, though I wonder that you didn't set your sights higher, like a trip to Paris, where all those writers and artists are holed up these days.

Yours,
William

Dear William,

Had I realized you were hiding a small fortune, enough to send us to Paris after we wed, I assure you, I would've gladly taken that route. However, as it stands, I believe a cup of tea and some flowers from my garden will have to do.

Eliza

My dear Eliza,

Well, at least you've now added the flowers.

Yours,
William

Dear William,

My father says the stocks are fluctuating and he may need to take measures accordingly. I don't know what any of that means, but it sounds serious enough to concern him. There was even talk about him moving back to my grandmother's old farmhouse should the economy decline, even though the cotton's long been dried up. What is your take on the economy? Should I worry? After all, I do so love my watercolors, and paint isn't cheap.

Eliza

My dear Eliza,

From the little I understand of the situation, no one truly knows what the stocks will do. But I wouldn't worry. You have

your father, after all, and myself to help you. One way or an-
other, we will all see it through. And besides, the market was
at an all-time high just a couple weeks ago. Surely that means
something.

Yours,
William

Dear William,
    My aunt returned last week, and I finally found the nerve to
tell her of the engagement. Needless to say, she is less than ap-
proving. She keeps insisting your family took my family's silver.
Do you know anything about this matter, that I might settle it
with her once and for all?

Eliza

Eliza waited days for a reply, but none ever came.
Two full weeks passed before she finally realized . . .
William was gone without a trace.
She finally got so worried about him, she walked over to have
a talk with his landlord, who gave her the update. *"Was a good*
man," he said. *"I'll miss having him around the place"*—as though
he were discussing a worn pair of loafers and not Eliza's every
hope for the future.
And so on one Saturday afternoon that wasn't particularly sig-
nificant except insofar as it was the day she accepted she would
never see William again—insofar, also, as the grief of abandon-
ment reawakened, and insofar as she missed her mother and her
grandma more deeply than perhaps she ever had before—it was
on this Saturday afternoon that a heartbroken Eliza went to the
carriage house once more.
She clutched the journal to her chest and sank down to the grass
in her garden. Tears streamed down her face, like rain blurring the

horizon of a watercolor. And all her hopes and all her plans and all her dreams were ruined in that one colorful storm, as one by one they dripped down to the soil—to water the flowers and the seeds yet to sprout, to fall from the canvas in little mosaics of color.

One Day Prior to His Disappearance

William was debating with himself how to respond to Eliza's most recent note about the silver when three knocks sounded at his front door.

He thought nothing of it at first, that maybe it was Eliza come to fetch him for answers since he'd been avoiding her. So he opened the door wide.

When the man's fist connected with William's cheek—and the sharp, raw pain of a bloody lip seared through his body—that's when he realized. This was not Eliza.

A second man grabbed William by the shirt collar. "Where is it, you bloke?" he demanded. He wore his tweed vest unkempt and his hair ruffled. His breath smelled of moonshine—or was that his companion?

William spat the blood from his mouth. This wasn't the first time he'd been in a fistfight, but it was the first time he didn't know why. "Where is what?"

The first man, the one who threw the punch, stepped closer. His features from under his hat were familiar . . . but from where?

"Don't play a fool. The boss sent us to fetch the silver, and it ain't there. What'd you do with it, you dewdropper?" Another solid punch, this one to the stomach. William doubled over, trying to regain his composure though his entire body groaned to get out of there.

The boss.

Of course. He remembered where he'd seen this man before— his ticket to get into that first garden party where he met Eliza.

146

The men were Cadigan's.

William swallowed hard and righted himself to standing, though he stumbled a bit on his feet. He could do all right for himself in a boxing match one on one, but you'd need the confidence of a peacock to provoke the two of these men together. So he tried to lie low, though everything in him said to swing.

"You forget how to talk or something?" The man laughed and clearly thought himself funny. His buddy bumped him with an elbow, as if to say *good one*.

"I've got nothing to say." William wiped more blood from his lip.

"How'd you even know where to find it, anyway?" the one with the hat asked, and the two of them crowded closer. Did they really think he was going to give them details?

"Cadigan had it all wrong," William said. "It was my family's silver to begin with." That much he could admit, and that much was true.

"*Your* family? Whaddaya mean? Cadigan said it belonged to some doll named Clara back in the Civil War and that we could find it in Eliza's yard, in the carriage house. Only, it wasn't anywhere to be found."

"Clara took it from—" But he shouldn't say that. William's stomach ached in pain, and his fingers itched to throw a punch of his own and get them out of here. But he couldn't do anything stupid. And he wouldn't waste time telling them more.

They didn't need to know that William once lived in Eliza's house as a boy, before her family bought back the property.

They didn't need to know about Clara's initial explosion with his own grandfather, or that every time his family talked, William was listening.

They didn't need to know about Rose and Ashley.

And they *definitely* did not need to know that one day, while William was yet a boy, he'd snuck into the carriage house by the light of the moon, broke the floorboard, and put that silver in his own toy treasure chest. He'd discovered it quite innocently earlier that day, pulling up the boards as a secret hiding spot for his own treasures, and despite his young age, he'd immediately known the impact of his discovery. Back then, he'd thought that maybe if he kept the silver his father was searching for, his father would pay him more attention.

William had kept the silver ever since.

Well, until recently . . .

"Look." William held up both hands. "The point is, the silver is not there any longer. So you can tell Cadigan he best leave well enough alone, because if the silver were still there, you would've found it during your search."

The two men stared at William a long moment as if dumb-founded anyone would have the gall—or maybe the stupidity—to challenge their employer so directly.

But William was a different man than he was a year ago. And while he'd once believed a petty theft could be justified if one was desperate enough, with a little mouth to help feed, he now realized how wrong he'd been.

Except now he'd gotten in too deep, and there was only one way out. One way to protect Eliza from Cadigan.

He would have to hide, find some meager work, and send money to his sister discreetly. He couldn't keep living as though he hadn't penance to pay.

"How do we know you're not keeping it squirreled away some-where in here?" One of the men swept the house floor to ceiling with a long, inquisitive look.

"Do I really seem that stupid?"

The men hesitated. Were they contemplating?

They spent the next ten minutes poking through papers, in desk drawers, and behind paintings until Eliza's voice called, "William?" from the other side of the fence.

She was his saving grace, just as she always seemed to be.

"You'd best get out of here before she catches wind and calls the authorities," William said.

"You're going to regret making this difficult," the man in the hat hissed. "If Cadigan sends us back here again, you will not get off so easily." He punched William once more, square in the jaw, before they both walked away.

William's fist pounded against the closed door, finally with a place to land. He quirked his jaw back and forth, knowing full well he was going to look rough in the morning.

But it didn't matter, not anymore.

Because the only way to feel alive was to love Eliza.

But the only way to protect Eliza was to leave.

EIGHTEEN

Modern Day

Lucy was going for a stroll through Waterfront Park when she spotted Declan and a dog by the Pineapple Fountain. She considered running from him, but it was too late. He waved. She'd been spotted. And she was at that awkward too-near-to-escape-or-to-simply-nod distance, which meant she would have to actually speak to him.

Lucy sighed. She wiped the sweat from her forehead with the back of her hand and fluffed her cotton tank to keep it from sticking to her skin.

As he came closer, she realized the scruffy little dog was actually walking him. Lucy smiled. She loved these scraggly Toto types, and bent down with her hand outstretched as the dog pulled near.

"Oh, I wouldn't do that. She's scared of—"

But the dog had already jumped into Lucy's arms and was licking her nose with its tiny puppy tongue before Declan could finish the thought.

"What were you saying?" Lucy laughed. The puppy pawed at her as if trying to shake hands.

"Amazing," Declan said, holding tightly to the dog's leash. "She usually hates everyone but my mother and me."

Lucy sat down on the walkway around the fountain and let the puppy crawl over her lap as it tried to chew her hands. "She knows a dog person when she meets one. I'd say she's a good judge of character, but . . ."

Declan scrunched his nose and scratched above his eyebrow. "Okay, I deserved that."

That was putting it mildly.

She wouldn't even be talking to him right now were it not for this cute little dog.

Declan sat down beside Lucy, and the puppy hopped from her lap to his. Lucy was surprised at this move on his part, and wondered that he wasn't worried about dirtying his khakis.

Something about him sitting knees bent, eyes sparkling, with a dog in his lap made him seem more approachable. In another circumstance, Lucy would've found him downright attractive. She would've envied the woman sitting beside him.

This was not another circumstance.

"Lucy, listen." He shifted toward her, and the puppy looked at her as well. *So* not fair to bring a dog into this. "I really am sorry for what I said. I can have a temper sometimes."

"No kidding."

He took a deep breath as the Pineapple Fountain trickled behind him. "What I said was ugly."

Lucy avoided looking at the puppy so as not to be weakened in her resolve. "Why do you care?" Did he really still think he had a chance of buying her house by apologizing?

"I care because I hurt you. I saw it in your eyes." His gaze was honest. But then again, it'd also seemed honest when he'd suggested he was the only reason she'd gotten her job.

Lucy watched him for a moment to see if his sentiment wavered. He didn't look away. She had to give that to him, at least.

"Can I make it up to you?" The puppy jumped up and began to growl at a Yorkie passing by.

Lucy laughed. "You weren't kidding about that dog, were you?"

He stroked its furry head. "Bailey thinks Yorkies are particularly ferocious. Apparently one harassed her all day at her former home."

"Oh, she's a rescue?" Elbow against her knee, Lucy rested her chin on her hand.

"She is," Declan said. "She's been through a lot in her five months of life." The puppy put her paws on Declan's shoulders and tried to chew his nose.

"Forgive me, but you don't really strike me as the dog-rescuing type."

"Really?" Declan adjusted his watch and scratched the dog's fur. "Because I'm very much the dog-rescuing type." He looked her straight in the eyes, and for some reason, the words stuck like the humidity in the air.

Okay, so maybe she'd underestimated him.

"Now, I understand if you hate me. But I'd really like a second chance to congratulate you on the new job."

Considering her reply, Lucy watched as a pair of squirrels chased one another around a tree.

"Actually, there is one thing I could use some help with."

"Say the word." His winning grin appeared once more.

The puppy jumped from Declan's lap to Lucy's and tried to chew her ponytail. "I'm doing research for the exhibit at the museum, and your mom asked if I could photograph the locations that might've inspired the watercolors I'm displaying. Most of them I recognize as spots around the city, but one I'm having trouble with. Looks like an island."

"Sounds interesting." Declan leaned closer as Lucy pulled out her phone. The smell of his cologne mingled with his Charleston drawl.

She loved people's accents here—she always had. The way everybody managed to say the word *y'all* in the middle of pronouncing *Charleston.* Slow as the pace of the river but refined as British tea.

"Okay, here's the picture." She enlarged the photo she had taken of the painting so Declan could see it more easily.

He took her phone and studied it closer. "Definitely an island off the coast of Charleston. Maybe Edisto?"

"Edisto? How far is that from here?"

"Depends on how fast we drive. Should we take your car or mine?" There was a dangerous twinkle in his eyes.

"Mine is still in the shop." She gave him a southern smile.

Declan turned the ignition of his BMW and reached his arm around Lucy's seat to look out the rear window. After they dropped Bailey at home, along with her fluffy bone and leash, he'd checked his email and made sure he was good to take the rest of the day off from work.

He came to a stop sign near the historic church on the corner and checked traffic both ways before turning. Lucy had walked a block up to her house while he handled things with Bailey, and she had changed into a colorful embroidered blouse and jeans. Everything about her intrigued him, down to her vintage style and her cloudy hazel eyes. She was beautiful.

But he had to proceed with caution, and he knew getting too close would be dangerous. Not only was this woman beyond stubborn and frustrating, but she was also the key to acquiring that property, which his father had demanded in no uncertain terms.

And Declan had to admit, the kind of money that silver would offer was not negotiable . . . not to mention the security it would bring to know they would never get another visit from that notorious silver thief. Maybe if Declan made this deal, his father would finally respect him and start treating him differently.

Yet as he looked at Lucy in his car, his pulse raced, his stomach turned with unease, and his hands felt cold. He recognized he was beginning to care for this woman, even in a small capacity, and that complicated things. He would hurt her by taking the house.

But he would have to.

He needed to stop thinking about it.

For today, he would help her get some photographs. It was that simple.

Because he really did feel bad about what he said at the museum earlier. He wasn't a monster, though she seemed to think that, and he couldn't say he blamed her.

"Tell me more about what you're wanting to do for the project." Declan's mother had given him an appreciation for the arts, and though his father made it clear he was expected to take over the family business, he'd always appreciated the beauty of a good painting. Guess it was in his genes.

Lucy shifted toward him, the bracelets on her wrist jingling together. "Well, I'm in charge of an exhibit that will feature an artist from the Charleston Renaissance. Her pieces are watercolors, and they are stunning. They tell a story of that unique time in Charleston's history when it found its identity at the interchange between past and present, and the beauty and grief in each. I love watercolor as a medium . . . the way the colors bleed and take on a life of their own. The artist positions them, but the final product, the way it dries, is beyond her control."

She shook her head and continued. "It's frustrating—that loss of control—yet somehow, also liberating. I like to think it mirrors the Charleston Renaissance in that way . . . that the preservationists, and the artists, and the musicians were all trying to frame this larger picture of the city's beauty, but ultimately, the final result was beyond their reach. And I think their efforts ought to be appreciated, and valued, and preserved just as a painting would be. Because in participating, we widen that canvas and bring our own colors to its history." Lucy smiled and looked ahead through the window as they passed sheets of Lowcountry grass and snaking rivers along the side of the road. She turned to him. "Anyway, I'm rambling."

Declan hadn't noticed the rambling.

He was too busy thinking Lucy had been right when she'd called him out on the steps the other day. He never should've assumed she didn't earn her new job at the museum.

She was passionate, qualified, and experienced, and she sounded like his mother when she was talking. This was why his mom had hired her. They shared a common calling, of cultivating and preserving beauty.

He'd really blown it by spouting out all that rude stuff at the museum. Looking back, he'd acted just like his father.

Lucy twisted the thin ring on her finger. The diamonds in its intertwined pattern of leaves and roots caught the sunlight, sparkling radiantly. "So, back to your question. Your mom suggested that I dig into this artist's provenance to learn more about her history, and take photographs of the current locations featured in her paintings. I think I already told you that I recognize many of them—Church Street, Saint Michael's, the City Market, and what is now Rainbow Row—though of course, those buildings weren't painted until the 1930s. But in the particular piece I showed you, I couldn't figure out the location. I was so struck by the blending colors of the Lowcountry sunset, and the figures dancing, and the romance of the thing. What I'd like to do is take the photograph at sunset to capture that same feeling."

Declan glanced at the clock in his car as he turned toward Edisto. Still a good bit before sunset. That gave them plenty of time to find a location to take the picture. That is, if she didn't try to kill him before then.

Old cottage-style homes sat here and there between groves of oak trees and long, grassy lawns. There was a peacefulness about this place, and Declan often drove out here when he needed to get away from the pace of the city and think.

He'd spent many a day dreaming about building a small home along the beach. He'd hang a hammock under an oak tree draped with Spanish moss, and look out over the sea oats as the tide pulled the ocean back and forward melodically.

How many times had he gone fishing along these riverbanks and watched the sun rise over the Lowcountry? How different his life would be if this were his reality.

"I think I know the perfect place for your picture." He drove toward the beach and pulled his car onto the sand along the side of the road. Lucy looked through the window, and he watched her reaction. A small smile slipped up her lips as she took in her surroundings slowly. A short wooden fence sectioned off the sand from the sea oats, and two ropes lined the walkway. Gentle waves hurried to the shore, leaving wet lines in the sand like footprints.

Lucy nodded. "This is perfect."

"And you haven't seen the sunset yet." Declan unbuckled his seat belt and pulled her photography equipment from the back seat. Lucy opened the passenger side door and stepped out of the car. She followed him toward the shore.

He should've thought to grab a couple of lawn chairs from home, but Lucy didn't seem like the type of girl to mind sitting in the sand.

"There's no way to know for certain, of course, which island your painting was supposed to represent. But if you're looking for a place that captures what you described earlier"—he looked around, breathing in the fresh ocean air—"this is it."

Declan took Lucy's hand to help her over a fallen log on the path. She looked at him as though surprised by his touch. And he was equally surprised by the way his stomach jumped abruptly, as if preparing for a roller coaster. He cleared his throat.

"There's a bench this way where we can sit and get your camera set up."

Lucy's flip-flops flapped sand toward him, and she stopped to take them off. Declan did the same. The sand under his feet was soft and warm from the afternoon sun, though thankfully, the heat of the day had passed. Otherwise, it might've felt more like hot concrete.

Declan had never brought anyone else to this bench. In fact, no one else knew about it. But somehow, oddly, he knew Lucy would appreciate his favorite spot.

Lucy sat down and looked out at the water. Her legs swung, inches from touching the ground. He set her photography equipment down and sat beside her.

"Well, we've still got a few minutes until sunset." He ran one hand through his hair. "I hope you can stand my company."

"Guess we'll find out." A sly grin appeared on her face, but she didn't make eye contact. She was teasing him, and he loved it. She wasn't like the other women he knew.

Lucy didn't care the slightest bit about his money. If anything, she held it against him. She was feisty, and he appreciated that about her.

"This place is beautiful." Her gaze swept the beach and the trees beyond.

"There's an interesting cultural history here as well. Did you know that many of the gravestones have stories on their epitaphs?"

"Stories?" Lucy turned to face him, curiosity in her tone. "What do you mean?"

"Of the people's lives. Like a miniature biography."

Lucy tilted her head. "What a neat way to honor the legacy they've left behind."

"I've always thought so."

She tucked one foot under her other knee. "So, tell me. Have you always wanted to work for the money-grabbing, history-destroying development company that is your family's business?"

Declan blinked. After the shock of her question wore off, he started laughing. "By all means, please speak your mind freely."

Lucy held back her grin by biting her bottom lip. "I'm sorry. I promise to be more civil."

"No, no." He looked down at his hands and rubbed the inside of his palm with his thumb. "I'd far prefer you say what you mean."

Declan thought for a moment about her question.

He'd mastered the art of shoving his own dreams back down

inside his heart. He'd done it so long now, he'd nearly convinced himself they'd disappeared. Words his father had spoken flittered through his mind.

Respectable.

Reputation.

Salary.

His father meant well. Declan really believed that. The family business had been their bread and butter, and without his father's hard work, Declan wouldn't have had the education or opportunities that were afforded to him. What was that old saying? Don't bite the hand that feeds you?

At first, Declan's own dream of studying architecture had seemed to complement the family business perfectly. But when his father realized Declan was more interested in the art behind building design than he was with making money, he had quickly thwarted any further investment in Declan's dreams. And he'd begun treating Declan as if all his business decisions needed approval and amending.

Somebody had to take over the business, after all. Declan was as good a candidate as any. And so he'd been chosen to receive this as his inheritance, whether he wanted it or not.

"Declan?" Lucy asked. She stood from the bench to set up her camera.

The sun was teasing the horizon now, but his mind was somewhere else entirely.

He realized he'd kept her waiting.

"Architecture." Declan turned to look at her. "I went to school to study architecture. I've always been fascinated by the art behind beautiful buildings. I guess I get that from my mom."

Lucy stiffened. He wasn't expecting the reaction. What about the word *architecture* put her on edge? Did she share his interest?

They met eyes for a long moment. Then she blinked. "Forgive me, but aren't the buildings your company creates designed for the bottom dollar, not for great architectural feats?"

"Yes." He sighed, looking out at the water as children splashed near the shore. "And therein lies the reason my father and I have never seen eye to eye. He marks the success of the business in terms of profit, and feels our family's reputation depends on the sustenance thereof. I guess I've always had a different dream of building remarkable things."

Declan thought he heard Lucy mumble something under her breath. She watched him closely, waiting for him to say more.

"Long ago, I realized that some dreams require . . . bending."

She glanced into her camera display, and then, clearly satisfied with the photos she'd taken, stood upright to look straight at him. "Do they?"

"Well, of course."

"Or could other aspects of our lives bend to our dreams?" She crossed her arms, coming to sit beside him once more.

"Look, Lucy." He rested his arm over the back of the bench, inches away from her shoulder. The skin on his fingertips danced from the nearness of her. "Not everyone can pack a bag and move into a dilapidated house to chase a dream."

"Is that what you think?" She scooted closer to the edge of the bench and planted her toes in the sand as the remnants of the day slid beyond the waterline and the sky became a watercolor that was true to life. "That I'm here chasing dreams?"

He shrugged. "Well, yeah. I don't mean that derogatively. Aren't you?"

The waves made a gentle sound as they lapped against the sand.

"In a way, maybe."

A shooting star flashed against the beginnings of the twilight sky. Lucy saw it too because she looked at him, her eyes glimmering.

"What did you wish for?" he asked. He knew shooting-star protocol prohibited discussing wishes, but curiosity got the best of him.

"I don't know," Lucy whispered.

"What do you mean, you don't know?" Declan hadn't expected her response. "Doesn't everyone have something they wish for?"

"I mean just that . . . I don't know." Her voice trailed off. Declan's heart tugged for her. She seemed quite suddenly unnerved, and he had no idea why. He dropped his arm so that his hand rested on her shoulder. Though mere inches in distance, the gesture went a long ways in meaning.

He hadn't touched her like this since their date last year.

He'd *wanted* to—man, how he wanted to—but he knew he had to keep himself guarded. His mother was literally the only person who would approve of such a match, and Lucy herself seemed to despise him. Not to mention the whole house issue.

But he did care about her. And he wanted to comfort her, to know more.

Lucy turned to look at him. "For a while, the plan was art school, and that went well. Then the plan was to get a job at a museum, which I now have . . . sort of. I mean, the exhibit has been wonderful to work on, but I'd like it to be full-time, you know? I have this deep-seated feeling that I'm missing something. That I haven't found my calling yet. Hearing you talk about your own dreams— and hearing Harper and Peter for that matter—well, I guess what I mean to say is you already know what you want in life, even if your dad is an obstacle. I wish I had that kind of clarity. Isn't this the time in my life when I'm supposed to just *know*?"

"Not necessarily." Declan shrugged. "Maybe you're still finding your way. And that's okay too."

A sandpiper scurried past.

"I can't figure you out, Declan." She shook her head. "One minute you're crashing into my car, acting arrogant and obnoxious—"

"By all means, please continue." He winked.

She smiled in return, her gaze not moving from his own.

"And the next minute, there's this other side to you. This depth. A man who rescues little dogs and has these big architectural dreams and is actually empathetic." She hesitated. "Which one is the real you?"

Declan felt strangely understood by this woman. And truthfully, that was probably not good. He was letting her too close. He needed to take a step back.

But her hair fell in gentle, wind-tossed waves and smelled like coconut. And her lips had the slightest tint of pink.

And despite every objection—and Lord knew there were many—he just couldn't fight this draw toward her. A draw that was growing stronger every moment.

"You tell me," he murmured.

With one finger, Declan reached to tuck a curl behind her ear. She looked up at him, eyes wild with anticipation. Then her eyes fluttered to a close, and he swallowed, the moment slowing.

His lips tingled with the peppermint smell of her lip gloss and expectancy. He had never felt such a rush of emotion before kissing a woman, and he'd kissed plenty.

In that moment, he *was* the architect she described. He was a man with a blueprint for a custom-designed home on Edisto Island, on this beach. A man who stood up to his father's vision for the company. Who prioritized character and artistry over family obligations.

He was the man he had always wanted to be.

He could've stayed in that moment forever.

Only he couldn't. For so many reasons.

And in his hesitation, her eyes fluttered back wide open, and he wondered if maybe he had imagined it all. Chalked it up to wishful thinking while the moment dimmed, just as a dream fades with every waking blink.

And yet his heart raced—not only from what could have been, but also from what could be.

Deep down he knew that this moment might have just changed everything.

NINETEEN

October 1929

Three weeks after William's departure, Eliza still had no appetite and found that even the simplest unexpected changes to her schedule brought a sense of loss. Yesterday, she'd dropped a teacup—just an ordinary teacup, not even her grandmother's antique—and nearly began crying at the thought she could not piece it back together, could never sip from it again.

She was heartbroken.

When she lay down in the four-poster bed and closed her eyes at night, her thoughts would turn to him. She'd force herself to stop. And then, inevitably, would come thoughts of Eliza's mother and grandmother, who also had left her behind. The same cycle, over and over again. Such had been the hours of three to five a.m., until she'd finally noticed the slightest hint of sunrays sweeping over the floor.

When she was a girl and both Mother and Grandma Clara died, nights were always the hardest. The stillness, and the darkness, and the dreaming took her thoughts to them every time. And there was something beautiful about those first rays of dawn because they meant morning was coming and another night was gone.

As a girl, Eliza would make breakfast and ready herself for school, and all would be right once more. Until another night fell. This continued until, one evening, a slivered moon rested like a chair in the sky. And Eliza watched from the upstairs piazza as her father arrived home from work. And for the first time in such a long time, and for no very good reason, she felt peace again. And she, like the moon, rested all night.

Now grown, Eliza pushed her bare feet against the wooden porch and rocked. Last night had been a full moon, and a bright one, and the only light flooding her room was from moonbeams. She'd lost sight of the hope she'd once felt when she'd look into the silvery night.

She was older now.

She wanted so badly to hold on to hope but hadn't the strength any longer.

No more mornings spent welcoming the dawn in the carriage house, searching for a new note in their correspondence journal.

She would paint for herself now. And her love would be the city of Charleston.

She'd miss the smell of the narrow stairwell most of all, for that was where the jasmine caught when she snuck out late at night to look for William's letters, to listen to his songs.

The jasmine wasn't blooming anymore.

Yesterday, her father had tried going to the bank just to be on the safe side, because the stock market was still fluctuating and he said that was probably very bad. While he was still in line, there was a run.

The bank closed its doors, locked them real tight with an iron bar as if the whole thing weren't already dramatic enough, before her father could get any of his money out. *"That's all right,"* he'd said. *"Don't fret over it, Eliza."* And he'd ruffled her hair just like he had when she was a child.

Only she was different now. She wasn't a child.

And the aunt she'd always scoffed at was now beginning to seem increasingly more level-headed as the days ran on. Why had Eliza always bristled against her aunt's opinions when the woman was simply speaking her mind? Was it wrong for a woman to be so forthright, in this age when women could even vote for the president?

After all, her aunt had told the truth about William, had she not?

A man of character would never have disappeared without a word like that.

And maybe, perhaps, that's what hurt most of all.

Sure, on mornings when Eliza herself was feeling strong, she hoped that William might return, just like he did in her dreams. But evening always came. And by evening time, Eliza always realized he would not.

So when her aunt and her father sat her down in the office as if going over a business exchange, and they explained that miracle of all miracles, Robert Legare was still interested in marrying her, and that given the current state of the world and the security he could offer, they would like her to accept—well, the whole thing happened late in the day when Eliza had lost faith she would ever see William again.

"Yes," Eliza murmured. "I'll agree to it."

For after all, he was nice enough.

Eliza had spent the better part of the day with her friends at the Preservation Society and had taken a long walk with Susan Pringle Frost past buildings in the process of being demolished. Susan kept saying, "Saving Charleston is more important now than it's ever been," or something to that effect, but Eliza had to admit that, at times, the destruction seemed inevitable.

For lately, Eliza felt inexplicably preoccupied with loss . . . not just the losses that had occurred, but those that *might* or *would*. The loss of the could-be's. With every brick bulldozed and every iron railing pulled and then melted down. Each of these structural compromises represented a compromise far greater—that the generations coming would never know the houses' shared histories.

And that maybe in the process, she would lose her own.

At least there were women like Susan to carry on. Perhaps one day she would live in one of Susan's pastel houses on East Bay Street. Eliza nearly giggled at the absurdity of the thought. Maybe she could get in on the ground floor with Dorothy Legg for the purple one. Or was it the pink?

May as well have been pure gold, for the likelihood of that actually happening.

Eliza returned from that walk unsure whether she'd been inspired to save the historic structures that were left, or ready to give up on the whole of it. What with the economy going from bad to worse, how were Susan and all the others going to convince investors to buy and preserve broken old homes?

And even if she *could*, what did it mean to be preserved in that state? Would the people of Charleston ever have the means or the desire to offer these dwelling places new life again? Or would they simply be purchased, only to remain in disrepair?

Such were her thoughts when she looked at herself in the mirror, ran her hand along her bob cut, and moved William's ring from her left to her right hand.

She, just like those buildings, could remain in a state of disrepair—or she could allow all she once considered valuable to be stripped away and simply move forward.

Eliza brushed the little wrinkles from her floral, button-down dress and freshened her poppy pink lipstick. Then she added a string of pearls for good measure.

Robert, her aunt, and her father were already waiting in the foyer when she came down the stairs.

"Eliza." Robert's expression was warm. "You look beautiful tonight."

She nodded toward him and smiled softly. "Thank you, Robert."

Together, the three of them walked into the kitchen, where Eliza and her aunt had laid dinner out. Her aunt was so excited about this new development with Robert that she'd spared no expense in dishes for the meal, even made a pineapple upside down cake with pineapples that were straight from the Caribbean.

If the bank stayed closed, this was the finest they were likely to eat for quite some time. Although Robert had a steady income. Robert had been preparing for the economy to fail. As his future wife, then, she would be okay if the state of things continued worsening like her aunt and her father feared. This security was a large part of why they wanted her married off to him, and yet Eliza kept forgetting this.

Robert passed her the glass dish of mashed potatoes, and as casually as one might ask the time, said, "Eliza, I know we haven't long known one another, but I confess, you caught my interest from the first time we met."

Eliza took the bowl of potatoes from his hands. It felt heavy. Heavier than when she whipped cream into the dish earlier. Her hands were beginning to warm from holding it, but she couldn't seem to move them to put it down.

"I know I will be a committed husband and have always wanted to be a good father." He blinked, his brown eyes by all appearances perfectly earnest. "I know this isn't a storybook romance, but neither is what's happening in the world right now, and I can be steady for you. I can give you that. Will you let me? Will you marry me, Eliza?"

She swallowed, setting the mashed potatoes down and scooping a heaping portion of them onto her plate. Why she did that before answering, she couldn't tell, and to be honest, she sort of regretted it. She wanted this proposal—this proposal that would lead to an actual marriage—to be as beautifully memorable as possible, and yet she could not for the life of her move her attention from the potatoes.

Perhaps it was all simply too much to take in, and that's why.

In any event, she did eventually look up at him, nodding and doing her best to smile. Oh, it wasn't that she dreaded marrying him. On the contrary, he was rather attractive, completely reliable, and perfectly kind.

But he wasn't William. Nor would anyone ever be again.

How would she pretend otherwise?

Robert stood from his chair abruptly, setting his napkin down on his plate. "If you'll excuse me, I actually brought you a little something in hopes you'd say yes."

"Oh?" Eliza watched him hurry off to the other room, only then realizing he hadn't given her a ring. Did he mean to? Had he forgotten? Or with the banks closed, was a ring too hard to come by?

When he came back to the table, Robert passed Eliza a small, thin parcel that was wrapped in brown paper. Interesting. It was just the size of one of her paintings.

Slowly, she unwrapped it—first to find the frame, and then the canvas.

"I don't understand." She shook her head. "What's this?"

"I know how important art is to you, Eliza. So when I saw this, I had to get it as an engagement gift because it reminded me of something you would paint yourself. I know you do not love me, but I think the way you've painted our city is really something fine. Tourists are going to want to come because of these depictions, Eliza. You'll see someday, even if you don't see it now. So take this gift as a token of my respect for you and your work, and my hopes that someday the sentiment may grow into more."

"Oh, Robert." Eliza's heart swelled at his generosity. Yes, she could come to care for this man. She may never love him, but already, he held a place of fondness within her heart, and that was something.

He smiled back at her. "I'm glad you like it."

Eliza gently pulled the rest of the wrapping from the painting to see the piece. And then her heart stopped.

It was the landscape she'd painted after her birthday on Edisto Island with William. Only this piece lacked the signature flower petals she distinctly remembered painting. Besides, her painting was still sitting in the carriage house.

This piece was a forgery.

And only one other person had seen the original . . . which meant only one other person could have done it.

So that's why he left.

Eliza could've doubled over in grief at the thought.

But instead, she set the painting down beside the table and forced herself to smile at Robert. After all, it wasn't his fault.

She would save her tears for later, when the bluebirds were her only audience. When, like the changing leaves of autumn, the tears could freely fall.

Spring 1930

The wind whipped the little white flowers from the pear tree outside Eliza's window, the window overlooking the garden. The flowers would not bloom again this spring.

The racket those branches made was too much to sleep through, so Eliza slipped her wrap around her silken chemise and wandered over toward the window. The garden outside was dark. The garden, once so full of hope and promise, would look different in the morning, after the storm finished ravaging what was left of the February blooms.

But she had already, of course, fallen in love with a different season after her mother and grandmother died in the summer. She had already adopted February over June. So she would simply have to do that again: to tell her heart to see the beauty in March or April or May.

The problem, of course, occurred when the wind roared and the rains flooded everything.

Nothing about this was the way she'd planned.

There was nothing wrong with Robert. There was just nothing

right about him either. But why should she pine for the man who'd left her behind? Why, in such uncertain times, should she cease to keep living . . . so preoccupied by a dream?

Maybe she could find a new dream. And she always had her love for painting, so that was something, at least.

When the nectar fell from the trees, she would paint it by memory.

TWENTY

Modern Day

"What do you mean, you almost kissed him?" Harper's eyes widened, and Lucy took her by the elbow to yank her out of earshot from the other bachelorette party guests. "I thought you hated him."

Lucy's sister, Olivia, wore an oversized pin that read *Bachelorette* tacked onto her white blouse, and she sat on a velvet couch beside their mother, whose curls had been sprayed so thoroughly that even a hurricane wouldn't loosen them.

The guests were enjoying tiny cakes and expensive teas and a typical array of southern brunch foods as Olivia opened the gifts. Probably not the best time for Lucy to make this confession to Harper, but she didn't want to risk her best friend making a scene over it.

"I do hate him . . . *did* hate him . . . I don't know, okay?" Lucy whispered back. "Besides, the whole thing was probably in my imagination. The more I think about it—and I've been thinking about it *a lot*—he probably never had any plan to kiss me at all. Which is a relief, right? Because I'm still not sure I trust him. Even if I did see a side of him that was different when we were out at the beach taking those photographs. Even if he was . . . nice."

Harper waggled her eyebrows. "Should I go ahead and start

sewing you a wedding quilt now, or would you rather wait until you've picked out your china?"

Lucy rolled her eyes, then crammed an entire tea cake into her mouth, thankful her mother was too preoccupied with Olivia to be watching.

"Seriously. You *kissed* him?" Harper hissed, then smiled and waved when Olivia reached for the gift bag Harper had brought. Lucy knew all about the gift, a silk chemise from the 1950s that Olivia was going to swoon over.

Lucy took her time chewing, buying time to think of a response. She covered her mouth as she swallowed. "*Almost* kissed him, Harper. No actual lip touching, okay?"

"Walks like a duck, talks like a duck. That's what I always say."

"I have literally never heard you say that." Lucy took a sip from her teacup.

Harper grinned back. "So I guess he's not so bad after all, just like Peter told us. But why do you say you still don't trust him?"

"Because he's after my house. And speaking of the house—" Lucy cleared her throat—"there have been a few . . . complications. As you know, I've been fixing the place up, and turns out it's worse than I initially realized."

"Needs lots of repairs, you mean?"

"Well, more so that the repairs it needs are expensive." Lucy tucked her long curls behind her ears. "I have a little savings but nothing like what will be needed to take this on. And my job at the museum is part-time."

Olivia pulled the nightgown from the bag and held it close to her chest. "Thank you, Harper!" she called from across the room.

"You're welcome! It's from the 1950s." Harper smiled again. She always knew how to give the best gifts. She turned her attention back to Lucy. "What about that other art job you applied for before Anna offered you the Charleston Renaissance exhibit? The one on Sullivan's Island. Wasn't that a full-time permanent curator role?"

"Yes, but it fell through." Lucy shrugged. "I'm kind of surprised, actually. I thought that would be a done deal since I knew the museum director from our time at Savannah College of Art and Design. She acted very strange too. Just said something had come up." Lucy shook her head. "Anyway, the point here is, I'm starting to get a little nervous."

"Have you considered actually selling it to Declan? I mean, you could probably get a lot of money out of it and buy something else."

"I don't want something else." Lucy took another sip of her tea. "I want this house. I want Eliza's story."

Harper put her hand on Lucy's shoulder. "Then I guess we're going to have to figure something out."

"Lucille Clara Legare!"

Lucy winced at the mention of her full name and set the lace tablecloth she was folding back down on the food table. She held up the tray of mini muffins toward her mother, hoping it might be a peace offering.

"I know we didn't end our conversation last week on the best of terms, but you are still my daughter. And no daughter of mine is going to be living without electricity, for goodness' sakes." Her mother took one of the mini muffins, but it did little in the way of satisfying her passion. She'd managed to temper it so convincingly during the party that Lucy thought she might be off the hook, so to speak.

Apparently she wasn't.

"How did you even know about—"

"The man who turned on your utilities is the son of one of my tea ladies."

"Of course he is." Lucy just stood there, still holding the tray of mini muffins as if they were protective armor, unsure whether she should set them down or start eating more. Ultimately, she decided to put them back on the table, then go around to the other side so she could keep her hands busy by consolidating the mini donuts inside their box. "Mom, it was nothing. Truly. It's not like I slept over there with the electricity off. I just had a couple meals and spent a few hours doing work before they turned on the lights and water. No big deal."

She would conveniently leave out the part where she rushed to Ms. Beth's house to avoid an EpiPen situation after the wasp sting.

Her mother gracefully brushed the muffin crumbs from her hands and threw her wrapper into the trash can. But when she walked back over, Lucy realized she had a smudge of chocolate still on her chin. This sort of faux pas was very unlike her mother, so Lucy handed her a napkin and motioned to her own mouth so her mother would know what to do.

And in that moment, in that everyday sort of chocolate-on-the-face moment, Lucy's mother looked less like a mythical creature and more like a human being. And Lucy wondered if it was possible she had come to see her mom through a lens that was not entirely accurate—if maybe, for all the woman's ridiculous preoccupations with marrying Lucy into the Charleston elite, she was actually compensating for some of her own insecurities.

Lucy probably should have been more transparent about the house instead of assuming what her mother might say.

"Did I get it all off my face?"

Lucy nodded. "Mom, do you forgive me? The truth is, I was just worried you wouldn't approve and would insist on bailing me out. I wanted to pay my own way."

"I can respect that." Her mother straightened her pearls. "I remember feeling that way when I was your age and marrying your father." She sighed, gesturing with her hands as she talked. "Lucy, you've got to understand. I just want what's best for you."

"I know." Lucy pressed the fabric of the tablecloth with her hand. She wanted to say, "*Could you please let me sort that out without Emily-Gilmore-ing me in the process?*" but she knew better than to push this very satisfying conversation any further. Though there was one other question she could ask, since they *were* having a heart-to-heart and all.

"Why does our family have such a longstanding feud with the Pinckneys?" Lucy licked some chocolate frosting that'd been on the donut box from her finger. She was curious if asking the question directly may bring any new information to light. Not that she needed to see *Declan* in a new light or anything . . . that would be ridiculous. Right?

Her mother sighed as though exasperated. "Because they aren't to be trusted, that's why."

"Mom." Lucy bit down on her bottom lip. "Come on."

Her mother waved one hand through the air. "You know the story. Your father's grandmother. That man, William." She shook her head. "Anyway, it's not just about those people long ago. It's about the way the Pinckneys have acted ever since. They stole the family's silver and never gave it back, and they act as though *we're* to blame." She raised her chin. "Besides. When your father and I married, they had the gall to say I didn't belong in a family like his."

Lucy stopped tidying the table. Suddenly this made more sense. All the stories she'd grown up hearing about the Pinckneys and *those kinds of people*. When maybe all along, the Pinckneys had been telling their own stories of *her* kind of people. How far back did this rivalry go? And did they truly steal the heirloom silver? Or did anyone still living even know? Surely there was more to the story.

As Lucy tried to make sense of it, one word her mother had spoken registered with a delay.

William.

Lucy's heart raced her thoughts as recognition buzzed through her body.

William. She knew that name.

"Mom, what was my great-grandmother's name? On dad's side." Her breath came quick. "Elle, right?"

"No, Elle was just a nickname." Her mother smacked her perfectly lined lips as if trying to recall. "Mmm . . . you know how quiet your father is, and not particularly interested in genealogy. Wish I could remember." She hesitated. "I think it was Eliza?"

Eliza.

This could not be happening.

The prominent watercolorist she'd always admired from the Charleston Renaissance was Lucy's great-grandmother?!

"Harper?" Lucy called out, trying hard not to sound frantic even as her fingers rapped against the table. "Harper?"

Her friend appeared from around the corner, carrying several empty food boxes. "Everything okay?"

"Can you handle the rest of the cleanup? I need to get back to my house quickly. I think I've just solved a mystery that's been bothering me."

"What is going on, Lucy? You look as though you've seen a ghost." Lucy's mother closed the lid of the donut box and stacked it on top of the muffin box.

"I think I might have," Lucy said. She reached into her purse for her phone and sent a quick text to Declan.

Lucy sat barefoot on the top step of her house with Eliza's journal in her hands. The ring on her finger glittered as she carefully turned the pages. She reread each of the entries but took particular pause after the final one, which seemed to end abruptly.

She murmured the words aloud to herself.

> *Dear William,*
>
> *My aunt returned last week, and I finally found the nerve to tell her of the engagement. Needless to say, she is less than approving. She keeps insisting your family took my family's silver. Do you know anything about this matter, that I might settle it with her once and for all?*
>
> *Eliza*

Lucy could not believe what was before her very eyes.

The famed watercolorist who'd made huge strides in preserving the history of Charleston was *her* great-grandmother. *Her* Eliza! And this house once belonged to the woman.

What was more, Lucy now wondered . . . were all those long-held family rumors true? *Was* there buried silver from the Civil War, and if so, why had no one found it? Who stole it from whom, and when?

Three knocks sounded against the door, and Lucy stood. She stuck one finger in the diary to hold her place and held the journal against her chest as she hurried down the stairs.

When she opened the door, she found Declan wearing a softly faded blue button-down tucked into khakis. Concern tugged at the lines around his eyes, and he looked generally windswept.

"I came as fast as I could," he said. "Is everything all right? Your text said it was urgent."

She clenched her teeth. "I might have exaggerated the urgency just a tad. I'm sorry to worry you. What I meant was urgent-ish." But nice to know he would drop everything to come to her rescue. Not that she anticipated needing rescuing, but you know, should the situation present itself.

He took a glance inside and caught his breath. "So there's no fire or piazza collapse? Your CO_2 levels are fine?"

"I think you mean carbon monoxide, and yes, as far as I know, my air quality is fine." Lucy smiled. "What I *have* found, however, is rather shattering in an entirely different way."

Declan shut the door behind him. "Go on."

Lucy held the book out, open to the final page of entries. "You should read this." But she cringed when he reached toward it. Maybe this was a bad idea. "Just please be very careful with the pages."

Declan silently read, then flipped back to prior entries. "Son of a gun. That's what he's after," he murmured.

"Come again?" Lucy frowned.

He seemed to suddenly remember her presence. "Oh. Sorry. Just thinking out loud. Obviously I knew about the silver." He looked up at the stained-glass archway, the bookshelves, the stairs. "But I didn't make the connection between this house and our families." Declan pointed toward the journal. "You really think they were our . . ." He pointed between himself and Lucy.

"Great-grandparents." She reached to take back the journal, still feeling both excited and exposed for sharing the sentiments inside. But they were half his, weren't they? It was his own grandfather. Well, great-grandfather. But still.

"I'm kind of in awe of her," Lucy added. "To think she created art that stirred tourist interest in the city during the Great Depression. That is, when she wasn't rifling through torn down buildings and trash heaps for crystal doorknobs and glass panes that would maintain the integrity of the buildings. Oh, and you know, actually saving the properties as well, along with the help of local heroes like Susan Pringle Frost."

"So I have them to thank for the hassle I receive every time I try to help move the city toward progress." Declan pocketed his hands and shifted his weight from one leg to the other.

Lucy scoffed, rolling her eyes. "Progress, my foot. Pretty soon the entire city will be filled with wealthy nomads appropriating Charleston's history for the sake of cute window boxes and a slower way of life. All the dynamic history of the place—its triumphs and its traumas, tales my great-grandmother fought to preserve for future generations—will be reduced to a few plaques about the National Register of Historic Places, like an epitaph to lost stories."

"Yes, I'm painfully aware of the many restrictions upon properties on this side of town. And if I didn't know better, I'd think I were talking to Eliza herself with the way you lit up like a firefly just now." Declan's slow grin sent an unexpected and entirely unwelcome tingle down her spine.

"I will take that as a compliment." Lucy raised her chin and smiled, holding the journal close to her heart. "So will you do me a favor and look to see if you can dig up any old journals or letters from William? I want to use some of this in my exhibit at the museum." Lucy hesitated. Her thoughts were turning so fast, every few minutes brought a new realization. "Wait—do you think your mom knew all this time?"

Declan shrugged. "I wouldn't put it past her. She's clever and curious about history and entirely unpredictable."

"No wonder we get along so well. Too bad her son doesn't share her attributes." Lucy exaggerated her grin.

"You're quite the comedian for someone who's asking for favors." Declan frowned in concentration and reached out, wiping something from just above Lucy's lip with his thumb. She melted at his touch, both with attraction and horror to realize she'd apparently been having this entire conversation with a frosting mouth. Declan glanced down at his thumb. "Looks like chocolate."

"Guilty as charged." Lucy held up her hands and laughed, trying to play it off so he wouldn't see her cheeks beginning to blush with embarrassment. Yes, embarrassment was definitely why she was blushing.

"I've got to get back to the office, but yes, I will take a look at my parents' house." Declan stepped past her and reached toward the door.

"Maybe we should work together."

But as soon as the words left Lucy's lips, the two of them both began laughing at the absurdity of the thought.

TWENTY-ONE

March 1930

The afternoon breeze picked up notes of pollen, dandelions, and the litter of oak trees, and William sneezed. He rolled up the sleeves of his worn linen shirt and chased his nephew through the field, their race hemmed in by two long rows of blooming azalea bushes and the buzz of honeybees.

Hannah pushed her hair back from her forehead and carried an apron full of strawberries back to the little house where she and Franklin lived. Well, suppose William lived there too for the time being. He'd roamed around like a vagabond trying to get good work so he could get money over to his sister. At one point, he'd even hopped a train to see what he could find out there.

Oh, he didn't know where *there* was, exactly, or even if it existed. But he had to try, for his sister's sake. And okay, if he were being honest, also for his own. Because he'd been broken ever since he left Eliza.

Couldn't get his head on straight. Couldn't rub two nickels together to make a dime either, for that matter. But he knew he had to figure out something, especially with the economy like it was these days. His sister's state would go from bad to worse quickly if he didn't. Not to mention, he had to get back to Eliza just as soon as it was safe. He was still working on that part too—how to stay clear of Cadigan—but he'd managed to sidestep the man the past six months already, so that was saying something.

William caught up to his nephew and scooped the boy off the ground, pretending to gobble up Franklin's belly. He shot a glance toward his sister and forced a smile, though she looked back at him quizzically, her bottom lip in a pout.

Franklin kicked his little feet and held his arms out toward the chickens, so William set him down and followed Hannah inside.

She dumped the strawberries from her apron into the sink and watched her son through the open door, her attention bouncing between him and William—not split attention, but somehow she seemed to be fully aware of both people. A unique skill William imagined belonged solely to women, because it certainly didn't belong to him.

She rinsed the strawberries and handed him one. "What were you thinking about just now? You had a far-off look on your face when you were playing with Franklin."

William took a bite of the strawberry. Though red in color, it was still just a tad bit too tart and could stand a day or two in the windowsill to ripen. Still, he savored the taste of the fresh fruit on his tongue.

When he didn't answer straightaway, Hannah prodded. "It's a look I've noticed on you often lately." She stopped her work and put one hand on her hip as the chickens clucked outside the door. "It's the woman, isn't it? Haven't heard you talk about her in ages. And you put on a good show around Franklin, but the sparkle's gone from your eyes."

"My eyes had sparkle?" William plopped the rest of the strawberry into his mouth and chewed. Had he really been so obvious?

Hannah gave a half grin, scooping the strawberries into a large bowl. The chip on the side caught William's attention, and he imagined his cute little nephew may be at fault. "You know what I mean. What is going on?"

William slid his hands into his trousers, looking around the one-room home for anything that may prove a distraction long enough to get him out of this conversation. The search was futile. His sister always did have a knack for digging up secrets he otherwise held close to the vest.

"You want the long or the short explanation?"

Hannah leaned to get a better look out the window. "He could chase those chickens for hours. Give me the long."

William blew out a deep breath. All right. Here went nothing. "I may have gotten involved in something . . . illegal."

Hannah's eyes widened, and she looked ready to swat him dead as a fly with her kitchen towel.

William shook his hands. "Nothing like that. Nothing that would land me jail time. Well . . ." He moved his head to the left, then the right, considering. "Not serious jail time anyway."

"What did you do?" Each word was punctuated such that William empathized with Franklin for having Hannah as a mother whenever the upcoming disciplining years of parenting really set in. She was not messing around.

William uncuffed his shirtsleeves to give himself something to do. "I stole art. Well, technically I just forged it. But the whole thing was a bad idea."

"No kidding." Hannah paced back and forth in her small house. "I can't imagine what possessed you to be so stupid." She untied the strings of her apron and slapped it down on the counter. He imagined she would probably prefer to be slapping him. "Tell me this isn't how you got the money you gave me and Franklin this past year." Her gaze bored holes through him. When he didn't respond, she rubbed her face with her hands. "Oh, of all things."

"I'm sorry, Hannah. I really am. Not that I mean to excuse it, because there is no excuse, but just so you understand . . . it was a last resort. I'd tried all the other means, and I couldn't find honest work quick enough to get the money to you. Art and music, that's what I'm good at. It's no secret to anyone. I knew I could make enough doing this to help you. You had a baby, Hannah, and you were starving. You think I didn't notice how your dresses hung on you? It's not normal, I tell you. Not for a new mother. You were sick from malnutrition."

"And so you decided becoming a criminal would fix things?" Hannah crossed her arms over her chest, but he didn't miss the way her knuckles turned white with the movement.

"Clearly it was shortsighted." William used his hands to slick his hair back down from where it was parted sharply. "You're really not going to like the next part."

"At this point, I can only imagine."

William looked through the window as Franklin reached down with his chubby toddler arms for one of the chickens, then cackled when it flew.

Was William proud of what he did? No. Would he repeat it if he had the chance? Absolutely not. But the issue was also more complex than Hannah made it seem. They *did* need him, whether she wanted to admit it or not.

"I fell in love with her. Eliza. The artist." William slowly moved his gaze to meet his sister's. Her expression softened. He was well aware she had never heard him say this about any woman he had dated in the past. "You can probably guess the rest of the story." He looked down at the cuts and calluses on his hands, hands that hadn't touched a piano in months. "I refused to do any more of the paintings, then realized the forgeries were all part of a bigger scheme to steal her silver."

"Wait. Eliza? You don't mean . . . our ancestors, and the big feud? Their family thinks we stole what rightfully belongs to them, and our family says *they're* the ones with the silver that belongs to us?"

"That would be the same Eliza, yes." William reached for another one of the strawberries and took a bite. This one was far sweeter. "Her aunt forbade me to speak with her at first. But the months went on, and love blossomed rather unexpectedly between us. They say love makes you blind, but in my case, my vision became suddenly clear. I had to put an end to all of it." William wiped a trickle of strawberry juice from his lip. "Then Cadigan sent his hooligans after me to rough me up, and I knew she wasn't safe so long as I was there. So I left a letter."

"You didn't." Hannah took a step closer. "The poor woman was probably heartbroken." Yes, if she had felt even a fraction of the heartache he had, that was true.

"It was the only way to protect her from what I'd done."

Hannah's attention wandered around the room, and she drummed her fingers against her arms.

"What is it?" William asked. She appeared to be deep in thought about something.

"Cadigan, did you say?"

William's heart began to race. Why would his sister recognize the name?

"It's just . . ." She looked directly into his eyes. "Before Franklin was born and they cut me off, I could swear I remember a man of that name working with our father."

William's gut sank, and it wasn't from the unripe strawberry. "Are you sure?" Hannah had still been living at home while William, who was older, had been out on his own for years. If Cadigan had visited or worked with their father, she was far more likely to know it.

She nodded slowly. "Quite. I remember him as smarmy."

Unbelievable.

William felt as though the entire room had been spun like a top on the floor. To think that his father was in cahoots with Cadigan—perhaps even employed him—*perhaps* even knew what William was doing . . . well, this just beat all.

He reached for his hat from the counter and planted a kiss on his sister's cheek.

She lifted her chin and gave him another look that said *don't mess around*. "William, you had better be careful."

"Careful is my middle name." He gave his hat a tap and grinned, though smiling was the last thing he felt like doing. "Oh, and did I mention I'd proposed to her?"

"I hope it works out for you," Hannah said. "I really do."

William had a feeling it would work out just as it was supposed to. He only hoped when he arrived, nothing had changed.

William looked up at the three-story house that was not quite considered "on the Battery" but was waterfront and highly envied all the same. He took a deep breath, telling the pattering in his chest to subside, as he removed his hat and knocked loudly against the door of his family's estate.

The housemaid was the first to greet him. She registered surprise with the little inhale and the half step she took backward before she composed herself. "Mr. Pinckney." She nodded, gesturing toward the hallway that was covered in scrolling, luxurious wallpaper. "Right this way."

"Good to see you, Dot." William winked at her, and her cheeks flushed with her smile. She was always all business, fittingly formal, but the two of them had gotten along swimmingly for the past ten years.

"Are you here for Mr. Pinckney?" she asked. "Can I get you some tea?"

"Yes and yes." William followed her into the study and waited there while she left to notify his father of his sudden arrival. The truth was, hot tea sounded downright dreadful after that endless walk here from Hannah's, and though only spring, the humidity just about did William in. He pulled his sweat-drenched shirt from his stomach, hoping his father wouldn't notice.

But speak of the devil, his father chose then to enter. "William." The man clasped his son's hand and patted his opposite shoulder. "Good to see you, my boy. Where have you been all these months? You're quite the enigma, you know. You worry your mother sick, but I keep assuring her you're only sowing wild oats and will come to your good senses soon enough."

"I'm not sowing . . ." But there was no use getting distracted or

184

rambling on. He needed to get on with it. William raised his fist to his mouth as he cleared his throat. "Let's just cut the idle chatter and face the issue directly." He never would've been this forthright with his father before, but all that'd happened with Hannah had made him stronger, and all that'd happened with Eliza had made him wiser. And he needed an answer right now, for both of them. "Why are you in business with Cadigan?"

His father raised his bushy eyebrows, then came to sit behind the desk, lighting a cigar before answering even though William knew for a fact his mother hated the smell of them on his father's clothing. Maybe that's one reason William hated it so much too. "Better sit down."

"I prefer to stand." William rested his cupped fingers against the table.

"Feisty, my boy—I don't know whether to reprimand you or consider myself relieved you finally found your gumption. It's taken you long enough."

William waited. He would not be distracted by the petty insult.

His father glanced toward the door, clearly satisfied to find it fully shut. Then he leaned forward. "The truth is, I've dealt with Cadigan for ages. Your mother doesn't know. But she's accustomed to fine things, William. . . ." His visible swallow looked painful.

"And you took to acquiring them illegally." He finished the sentence, looking his father square in the eyes.

"Some position you're in to lecture me. Why, several months ago, I purchased a charming watercolor by a certain acclaimed Charleston painter, only the brush strokes reminded me of someone else's work. Someone who should've been taking over the family business rather than wasting his time dabbling in finer arts better suited for women."

William had heard this insult before, of course—for this very sentiment had been the driving force behind leaving his parents' home, long before they turned Hannah out onto the streets. But still, it stung.

He focused his attention on the long, dark draperies to distract himself from his reeling offense.

William breathed in deeply. He needed to get past the diversions and get on with it. "What are you after?"

"Surely you're not that daft."

William crossed his arms over his chest. "The silver?"

"You know I haven't got it. I don't like games." His father stood, pounding one fist against the desk.

"Neither do I, Father." William didn't budge. "So call Cadigan and have him back off Eliza. Maybe then I can help you."

"I don't respond to blackmail, especially from my own flesh and blood." His father twisted the cigar into the sooty ashes. "And besides, I don't see why you care, what with your precious Eliza engaged to be married. Or is she already married? I can't keep track of the date."

The room around them came to a sudden standstill. William struggled to find any air, much less find any appropriate words.

He was too late.

Either she hadn't believed he'd come back for her, or she'd fallen for some other man. Either way, his worst fear had just been confirmed.

"The silver is no longer in Eliza's ground." William's voice was hoarse. But this was the least he could do now to secure Eliza's safety after all he'd done to jeopardize it. "Call off Cadigan."

"On one condition." The corners of his father's wicked grin curled upward, his face stout and his cheeks reddening on account of the quarrel.

William knew his father was capable of a good many things, but this beat them all.

"What's that?" William would probably regret asking, but at this point he'd do anything just to see Eliza safe and secure.

"Your mother and I have a marriage prospect for you. We chose her weeks ago. I think you'll find her perfectly agreeable, and quite interested in protecting the family fortune—a lesson you could do well to learn from."

"What do you mean, you picked her out weeks ago? How did you know I'd come here?"

His father fussed with the hem of his vest. "Oh, William. Be sensible. You were bound to return eventually. Took you longer than I expected to put the pieces about Cadigan together, I'll be honest. But the important thing is, you're here now."

"No." William shook his head, his stomach turning so dramatically that he thought he might empty it. "I won't do it. I refuse to marry under duress."

"Such a pity for Eliza. To think how she's already struggling, what with the economic turn. The value of her paintings is sure to plummet when buyers see yours publicly."

William studied the man a long moment and finally decided he was monstrous enough to follow through with it. "When do I meet the woman?"

"Thursday for supper. Don't be late." His father shuffled some papers on his desk as though this conversation were business as usual and not dismaying coercion.

William stepped toward the door, ready to get out of this stifling room even though he had nowhere else to go. "Did you know they roughed me up good?" He turned to face his father, not entirely sure he wanted to hear the answer.

"You needed to learn a lesson."

And William knew then that he had to go through with it. Because if this man was capable of doing *that* to his own flesh and blood, William could only imagine how his father might destroy Eliza and all she loved.

Besides, it was William's fault for involving her in the first place.

TWENTY-TWO

Modern Day

Lucy's sister made a beautiful bride, and the reception venue glowed nearly as much as she did. Olivia had chosen to rent the garden courtyard of one of the historic houses on King Street. Historic mansion was more like it. This place was incredible. Twinkling white lights were draped from the iron gates, from the archways, from the oak trees. And the florist, a friend named Alice, had come all the way from New Orleans to help Olivia put together an unpredictable, colorful assortment of flowers that even Lucy's mother approved of. Tonight, Alice sat unaccompanied at the same table as Lucy, Harper, Peter, Declan, and Peter's grandmother, Millie.

As the bride and groom waltzed through their first dance, Lucy put her elbows on the dark teal tablecloth and leaned closer to Alice. "These arrangements are incredible. You said you own a store?"

"I do!" Alice's smile was bright and her loose auburn curls whimsical. She had a dainty look about her, slightly bohemian, or maybe Lucy was just picking that up from the cat pattern on her purse. "My aunt and I own a place on Magazine Street. It's technically a flower shop that specializes in highly customizable bouquets, but if you've ever been to Magazine Street you know that none of the shops there can decide on just one thing." She tucked her shawl over her shoulder. "So we also do a few antiques, old books, even vintage clothing."

Harper leaned closer from the other side of Lucy and pointed toward Alice. "She's actually going to stop by Second Story tomorrow morning before she heads back. You should come too. We can get her all set up with a new outfit *and* send biscuit mix."

Lucy laughed, although her shapewear prohibited her from breathing deeply. "Only if they're from Callie's."

"You know I wouldn't offer anything else." Harper drummed her fingers against the tablecloth, and Lucy couldn't help but wonder how long it would be before her best friend wore a ring on that left hand.

"I'm looking forward to it. And to the biscuits. Although y'all know we do eat our fair share of biscuits in New Orleans, right? They don't only belong to Charleston." Alice straightened her multi-strand necklace, which glimmered in the candlelight.

"Oh, I'd beg to differ. You'll change your mind about that when you eat Callie's." Harper laughed. "Besides, I thought New Orleans had mostly French and Creole recipes, not traditionally southern."

"Depends on who raised you. As it stands, my aunt who runs the flower shop with me is from Shreveport." Alice grinned. "She's got the strongest southern accent on our side of Magazine Street."

A chorus of clapping brought Lucy's attention to the dance floor and the live jazz band Olivia hired. They were set to play all sorts of old-fashioned tunes, although Olivia favored music they could swing dance to, because that's how she and her husband first met.

It was so cute it was almost unbelievable. Who finds a man at a swing dancing lesson? Doesn't everyone who goes to those things already have a date? Apparently not. All this time, there was a whole world of eligible, perfectly charming men out there who Lucy could have been dancing with. The fact she did not know this until recently made her doubt the vibrancy of her college experience. Maybe she'd spent too much time with her books and canvases and paints.

Her mother certainly thought so.

"Would you like to dance?"

Lucy snapped out of her mental wanderings at the sound of Declan's voice. He'd slid closer when Harper and Peter stood to get in line for the buffet. Her heart nearly leapt out of her chest at the request. Was this really happening?

"Absolut—" Lucy stopped midway through the word when she looked up and realized Declan had meant the question for Millie.

Declan winked at Lucy. He clearly didn't miss her misinterpretation.

Oh. My. Word.

How humiliating. If she crawled under the teal tablecloth for the duration of the reception, would that be an option? Lucy was sure that Harper would sneak her a slice of cake, so she had that much covered.

Millie smiled at Declan. "Well, aren't you cute as a button, with your slicked-back hair and suspenders. It'd be a delight to dance with you, if you think you can keep up with me."

Lucy caught herself halfway waving at the two of them as Declan took Millie's hand and led her toward the dance floor. Then she tucked her hands under her dress like an elementary schooler who couldn't be trusted to stop fidgeting.

Why was she waving at them? She nearly groaned. Declan should absolutely not be making her this nervous. And on top of that, she was jealous of Peter's *grandmother*! Surely there was some rule of etiquette about being jealous of grandmothers at weddings. Did Emily Post write anything? Did people besides Lucy's own mother even care about Emily Post anymore?

Lucy decided to take a sip of her tea so the glass would give her something to hold. But two stuck-together ice cubes kept falling inconveniently against her front teeth, freezing them and blocking the flow of liquid. Why was she having so much trouble functioning tonight? She did finally manage to get a few sips in before the song ended and Declan and Millie came back to the table.

She'd decided her strategy would be to completely ignore that awkward little interaction earlier. Yes, denial was always a good route. But she did not expect for Millie to settle into a chair beside Harper and Peter, who had just returned, or for Declan to hold out his hand toward her.

She also did not expect the cozy glow she felt as Declan led her out toward the dance floor. And she *really* did not expect the next song to be a slow one.

"Figured I better get you out here before you elbowed past someone else's grandmother." Declan slid his hand toward the middle of her back, remarkably confident in a formal dancing posture, and Lucy wondered if he had taken ballroom lessons or maybe if he, too, was one of those guys who went swing dancing.

Leave it to Declan to bring up her moment of humiliation just as the song was starting. But what did she expect? A romantic waltz? This wasn't a date. She wasn't even sure she liked him.

He was after her house, he was far too preoccupied with his wealth, and she—most likely—could not trust him. So what if she'd Googled him? And maybe possibly dreamt about him. And was looking for him every time she turned the corner on Church Street. None of that meant anything in actual, real life. Right?

But real life aside, the man knew how to dance.

Lucy rested her hand on his arm as the band began to croon. Her heart skipped twice as fast as the meandering beat, and she told herself she would not, under any circumstances, do anything else embarrassing around this man.

Declan met her eyes. A breeze ruffled the edges of the table-cloths, but his nearness kept Lucy warm. "I think I found something. About William."

Lucy looked back into his eyes. "What about him?"

"I found some old letters. I think he might be the one who forged Eliza's painting. Possibly plural."

Lucy stopped mid-step. "What? You mean the painting I came across recently?"

"That's the one." Declan shook his head. "But it's not as simple as it sounds. Lucy, I think he loved her. I think he never stopped loving her. Remember, when you first got the house, how I told you she broke my great-grandfather's heart? Well, I knew that from hearsay, but looking at these letters . . ."

Declan pivoted her into a spin by his hand at her waist, and she realized, quite startlingly, he was indeed a very good lead—his hold the perfect strength.

The lamplight cast a glow, and she thought of her great-grandmother and William dancing. And for a moment, she was enraptured by this man and his history. And in that moment, all else simply fell away.

"So he did break her heart, but maybe she broke his too," Lucy whispered.

Declan nodded.

"Then where's the silver that was mentioned in the letter?" she asked. "Does your family have it?"

"No." Declan righted her back into his arms. "Does yours?"

"Do you think I would've asked that if we did?" Lucy grinned at him, awakened just by the smell of his cologne.

Declan pulled her closer for a small dip as the song ended, and the softness of his button-down brushed her arms. When he drew back, she felt his breath just inches from her own.

"I almost forgot," he murmured. He made sure both her feet were good and steady on the ground before reaching into his pocket for something. Gently, he tucked a stray piece of hair behind her ear, then placed something into her open palms. It took a long moment before she realized what he'd done.

He had returned her silver crown, as he'd called it the night of their first date. Only now, the headband was repaired and felt light as air as she slid it into her ornate wedding curls.

Lucy looked up at him and couldn't help but feel mesmerized— by the gesture, by this moment . . . by him.

"You kept it all this time," she whispered.

He touched her chin with his thumb and raised it almost imperceptibly. "I told you I would." Declan cleared his throat. "Lucy, there's something I need to tell you. . . ."

She was dizzy from the way her thoughts spun as she looked up at him.

But before he could say anything else, the band announced it was time to cut the cake, and reality ended the dance.

Lucy and Declan both grew busy with bridal party duties. Giving toasts and blowing bubbles. Before she left the wedding that night, she planned to ask him just what he was going to tell her. But he disappeared before she had the chance.

Just like a Pinckney.

One person did catch Lucy's arm as she was gathering her beaded clutch, though. Her mother.

"Lucy, who was that man I saw you dancing with?" Her mom's eyes sparkled.

"Handsome, isn't he?" Lucy tried to adjust the shapewear now digging into her sides. But wiggling was no use. She suspected she would have elastic indentations for the rest of her life.

"He sure is." Somehow, her mother's hair hadn't budged an inch, nor frizzed from the humidity. How many hair products had she used to accomplish this feat? "Looked to me like there may be a spark between the two of you. Where do you know him from?"

"Oh, but don't you recognize him? That's Declan." Lucy's smile grew wider. "Pinckney." She shouldn't do this, she really shouldn't, but the look on her mother's face was priceless.

If looks could kill, Declan would've been deader than the crustaceans in this evening's she-crab soup.

TWENTY-THREE

1931

She was painting again, so at least there was that.

Eliza had been married half a year when fall returned once again to Charleston and brought with it the colors of the season, namely reds and oranges and browns that were unexpectedly lovely. And Eliza was working on a new watercolor, turning the canvas so the paints blended with the same rhythm as the water snaking through the tall grasses of the Lowcountry.

Being wed to Robert had been similar—something unexpectedly pleasant despite the sudden change of seasons. Charleston as a city had struggled after the War Between the States, and the decade prior was far from an exception to the rule. Many families spent the time pretending they were richer than they actually were. Pretending trauma had not come to the city through slavery and racism. Pretending brokenness did not abound through the streets in more ways than one.

Grandma Clara had never been one to pretend. And maybe because of her, Eliza valued honesty.

But ever since all that happened with the stock market, well, let's just say few people were still pretending. Few people were able to. Marriage to Robert had brought along with it a certain measure of financial security, and Eliza was better off than most. Not wealthy by any measure, but stable.

And yet she was still afraid. She watched more and more houses fall into disrepair as the months went on. More and more people trying to get work. Her father might soon be among them. Her aunt had gone for an extended stay in Asheville now that she'd seen Eliza married and settled. Eliza and Robert had purchased a home on Atlantic Street, just up the corner from her father, but with the way things were going, she wondered if her father would soon be living with them under one roof.

She worried for him. Even from the time she spent visiting, she'd noticed how he'd become particular about things, like the hours he kept in the office and his insistence upon retrieving the mail himself. Seemed as though he was trying to control the little things, as he had no control over the big ones.

Banks were failing, and fear crept its tendrils so deeply that sometimes, when she awoke in the night or the morning, Eliza would almost swear she could see those spindly arms. She wondered why God in His sovereignty would allow it, and then the tendrils would grip her for having the heretical thought in the first place. If God was truly good, why wouldn't He sustain them? Why hadn't He sustained her mother, her grandmother? Again the tendrils would twist, round and around.

And yet she forced herself to rise early in the morning, to make a proper cup of tea in her Grandma Clara's heirloom porcelain, hoping if she steeped it long enough that she, too, would be stronger.

Sometimes it worked. Sometimes it didn't. And some days— make that every day—she thought of William, wondering why he would leave her.

Still, she was struck every time she stepped outside by the many ways that nature continued to bloom.

That the bluebirds still nested, and the songbirds remembered how to sing.

That the God who cared for the sparrows had fed them another day. This probably should not surprise her, and yet it often did. Faithfulness, provision, and beauty enduring.

Maybe the world was stronger than it seemed.

Today, Eliza had set up her painting supplies beside the piazza that ran along the side of the house, just in front of the gate, so that any passersby who were interested could stop and look and maybe even purchase one of the little paintings she'd set out on a table.

Several looked, a few stopped, and none bought her work, but she appreciated the company all the same. She was watching the warm colors blend into layers of the horizon in her painting when a family approached, a couple with a baby girl of maybe one or two years old.

Eliza smudged one section of color with her finger before she turned from her work to greet them. Their baby was a little thing but already steady on her feet, and she made a beeline toward Eliza's painting. Or at least that's what Eliza thought until the little girl kept going, straight for Eliza.

"Millie, baby." Her father reached out and scooped her up, tickling her so she started laughing. But the baby still reached for Eliza.

"I think she likes your red hat," the mother said. Though the fabric of her dress was modest, it'd been expertly crafted, and the pleats at the collar were so intricate, Eliza would have painted them. The shimmering cream color laid beautifully against the mother's skin tone and brought out the warmth of her grin.

A grin she had seen before. Eliza hesitated, trying to place it.

And then the man slid his other arm around the woman's waist, still holding the baby, and it all came back to Eliza at once. This was the couple she'd seen dancing the night of her birthday, the night she and William went to Edisto and danced the Charleston.

A night that seemed a lifetime ago now.

"I've seen you before." Eliza unpinned her hat from her own pin curls and held it out for the baby to get a better look. The mother took the hat from Eliza, and Millie tried to grab it with her chubby fingers. "Both of you," Eliza added. "Dancing on Edisto, while you were still in the family way with this little one."

The woman brushed Millie's tiny hand along Eliza's red cloche.

"Sounds like the two of us." She grinned at the man. "Sorry I don't remember your name," she was quick to add.

"Eliza." She pointed toward the baby. "And might I add, you have one exceptionally gorgeous child."

The baby cooed as though she understood.

"Do you like pretty fabrics, my dear?" Eliza asked the little girl.

"She sure does," the mother said. "I've already caught her eyeing my best buttons. Maybe someday she'll be a seamstress. That right, Millie?" The woman gently took the cloche to hand back to Eliza, but the baby reached for it again.

Seeing the child so happy over such a little thing brought joy like sunbeams into Eliza's heart. "You know what? You keep it." Eliza closed Millie's tiny palms back over the hat. "You remember me someday whenever you've got your own dress shop."

"Are you sure?" the father asked. "Times are hard, and we wouldn't want to take anything from you. Can we pay you?"

Eliza shook her head, smiling. "Truly, it would be my pleasure." She stepped back over toward her easel to check how the paint was drying. Good. Just the right effect.

"Thank you, signora." The man gently tossed the baby into the air, sending her into a fit of giggles. "We are much obliged, yes, Millie?" The little girl laughed some more. Was there any sweeter sound than a gleeful child?

"God bless you." The mother cradled the red cloche in her hands, as Millie reached for it again. "When she grows up, we'll tell her about the woman painter who gave her the hat."

Eliza picked up her paintbrush and laughed. "I'd be honored to be remembered by such a story." She dipped her brush back into the water as the three of them left but was surprised when the woman stopped and turned.

"You like sweetgrass? Baskets, I mean."

"Sure I do." Truth was, Eliza didn't know much about them besides that her grandmother used to have a little one she kept her jewelry in every night. Said it was a precious gift and the things took hours and hours to make, that she'd rather stick to painting porcelain herself.

"This your house?" the woman asked. "I'll bring you one next week. My sister makes 'em, dime a dozen. She won't even notice one missing."

Eliza laughed. "Well, tell your sister I said thank you. And same to you too. You have a beautiful family."

The woman smiled and dipped her chin, and then she was gone. And Eliza was alone with her painting once more.

Robert combed his wavy hair at its part and looked over toward Eliza as she fastened the imitation pearls he'd given her as a wedding gift. Real pearls were, of course, far too luxurious for the times, and Eliza never would have expected them anyhow. Though sometimes she did wonder how they sat against a woman's neck, if they were light or heavy, cool or easily warmed by the sun. She'd never worn them, even with all her father's social parties. Maybe someday in years to come. Perhaps when she was older, and Robert too, and all this nonsense with the economy settled down. Her father predicted stocks would rise and jobs would return within the year. How Eliza hoped he was right. Robert said it would take much longer.

"I like your dress." He said it with a gentle kindness the same way he said everything else. "What time is your father arriving for dinner?"

"He should be here any minute."

As though their conversation had been broadcast, three knocks sounded against the front door. Eliza quickly slid a beaded hairpin onto the side of her bob and hurried, surefooted, down the steps toward the door. Not one to ever tarry, Robert followed close behind, adjusting his fedora.

"Hello, Father!" She greeted him with a hug.

"Looking lovely tonight, as always." He released her and turned toward Robert. "And how are you, son?"

"Doing well." Robert clasped his hand. "Come in, come in."

Robert shut the door behind them.

"Any further word on the imitations?" Robert's insensible question was clearly a misstep meant for her father. Judging from the increasing pallor of his cheeks, he seemed to regret saying it immediately. Had he forgotten she was in the room?

A quick glance toward her father proved what Eliza expected, that he was staring at Robert.

The *imitations*? What did Robert mean by that? What were the two of them trying to hide? Was *that* why Eliza's father had been so particular about who retrieved the mail when she visited his house?

Eliza thought to ask these questions, but she knew her father would dodge the questions just as he always had, and that Robert, in turn, would take cues from her father. Instead, she would do some snooping later tonight to see if she could find any evidence among Robert's own items.

She thought back to a conversation she'd overheard between her aunt and her father. Could these be the same imitations of which they spoke too?

Dinner dragged on and on so long that Eliza nearly excused herself on account of a headache, which wouldn't have been entirely untruthful, seeing as how the stress the two men were putting her through became downright painful. But her aunt had said she deserved the answers, so very well, for once she would actually trust that woman.

When her father finally left and Robert mentioned listening to a radio program, Eliza knew she had her chance. She felt a spike of nervous energy as she tiptoed toward Robert's drawers, beginning with the bedside table he usually kept to himself.

She reached into the back of it—because isn't that where you would hide something if you were trying?—and touched something. A folded piece of paper. She pulled it out.

But when she looked at the script and the simple name *Eliza* penned along the back, the paper nearly fell from her fingertips.

Her heart fluttered faster than a hummingbird's wings, and she sat on the bed so she could ground herself.

William.

Why was a letter from William—a letter she had never seen before—hidden away in Robert's bedside drawer? Eliza's stomach lurched clear into her throat as she unfolded the two pleats in the letter with a date from months prior.

My dear Eliza,

My heart races as I think of your graceful hands holding this page. Oh, how I wish I were there to sit beside you at the carriage house with the stars as our company. How many evenings have we spent in such enchantment?

You must think me a hopeless fool for how ardently I've come to love you. But there are things about me you do not know.

As I write this letter from the other side of the wall, my suitcase sits beside me, and my stomach churns with remorse. If only there were another way. I've been sprinting from my past, and my past has found me. Secrets long kept are surfacing, despite my greatest attempts to run from them.

I wish I could say more. I wish I could take you into my arms, kiss your delicate lips one last time, and make good on my promises to you.

But all I can say is this.

When I told you I love you, I meant those words. When I told you that you'd never fade from my thoughts, I meant that too. You have changed my life, dearest Eliza, and I will mean it with every breath to come.

I hope when you think of me, you'll remember these words. Especially when you realize what I must do next.

Do keep the ring.

Yours,
William

Eliza struggled to swallow.

Then she realized there was another page . . . another letter, dated months later.

My dear Eliza,

I thought I could do it—living without you—but I can't. I will explain everything when I return. That may be a matter of months, or it may be far longer, but I can't come until I know you'll be safe. Right now, my arms would only endanger you. There are secrets you don't know I've kept. Wait for me.

Yours,
William

Eliza read the words again and again and again.

Each time she read, she felt the sentiment resonate more deeply.

He had told her he would come for her.

She had not been abandoned.

Hope bobbed gently within her heart at this knowledge, only to be tugged down forcibly by the tide of grief. For really, this changed nothing. She was married. She had *not* waited for him . . . because someone had hidden his message.

And now it was too late.

A shadow eventually appeared in the doorway, and she realized it was human, and then she recognized Robert. He must have known immediately the merit of what she'd found because he came and knelt beside her, told her how sorry he was and what an awful thing he'd done.

"After I purchased the painting for our engagement, some men I work with told me about William. They said he's mixed up with some bad people, or at least he was, and that he probably only pretended to care about you so he could get your money. He'd been forging your paintings, Eliza. *That's* what I meant by my question to your father earlier. He wanted to protect you from the truth about the imitations. So you see, I couldn't give you that letter because you wouldn't have gone through with our wedding, and you would've been waiting on a ghost for the rest of your life."

Eliza blinked several times, the sudden surge of all this information slamming into her like a wave against the rocks of the Battery. She just kept shaking her head until finally she murmured, "It was the silver."

"The what?" Robert frowned.

"William's family and my own have long feuded over silver that went missing during the Civil War—arguing over who has proper rights to it and where it disappeared to. If he was after anything, he was after that." Eliza tried her best to look at him, but all she could see was betrayal. "I already know about the counterfeit paintings, Robert. The painting you got for me upon our engagement was one of them."

"What?" His eyes widened.

"You should have told me." She held up the letters.

Robert hung his head and rubbed his hand against the back of his neck. "I know. I'm sorry." He stood, placing his hand on her shoulder. "I really am, Eliza. I'll give you a moment." He left then, and closed the door behind him.

Letters in hand, Eliza walked toward her drawing table. She sat down, rested her head on the table, and began to weep. The sort of shoulders-trembling, mascara-running type of weeping she hadn't allowed herself until now. Not only for William but also for all she'd lost along with him. That he'd come after her inheritance. That she'd been driven from her garden because of it.

She wept because she wouldn't see the February blooms, and she wept because she wouldn't see the March ones either. She wept for the empty spaces that hope had hollowed out within her heart.

She had become someone else these last months. Stronger, perhaps. A better preservationist and certainly a better artist too. Where for years she had been afraid to let the colors of her paintings bleed, now she did so fearlessly. Where she had hesitated to salvage certain materials with Susan—glass window panes and heavy doorframes, lest the sharp edges cut her or become too weighty—now she relentlessly dug through piles for them.

But the cost had been high. She had lost that which she never thought to lose and, through it, had found a fear of losing more. That's why she fought to save the old buildings and to capture the character of her home and her city through her art. Because she was scared if she lost any more of these things, she may not come out of it stronger. She may not come out of it at all.

Eliza wiped her messy tears and sat upright, pulling William's ring out of the drawer and setting it beside the letters. She traced William's script with her hand.

Did he truly have an explanation? Though she was furious, she knew deep inside that she would forgive him if ever he asked. She knew him well enough back then to assume he wouldn't have done all this if he didn't have a compelling reason. Or at least she'd thought she knew him. . . .

Not that any of that mattered now.

If he'd truly loved her, he would have found another way. Would've come to her in person, thrown a rock against her window, begged and pleaded for her to understand why he must go away.

Emotion tugged so strongly her physical heart ached, and she knew stirring up all of this was hopeless. William was gone, either way. And she, married.

Eliza opened up the drawer and set the items back where they belonged. There was no use in thinking about what might have been when she'd made a commitment to the here and now.

She stood from her desk, intent on making things right with Robert. Trying to ignore the tug on her heart from the items in the drawer, items from another time. But the pain in her chest reminded her she was still capable of feeling deeply, deeper than she was comfortable feeling. And she was doing a rather poor job of ignoring the heartache.

TWENTY-FOUR

Modern Day

Just past dawn on the morning after the wedding, Lucy's phone announced a text message as she pushed her bare feet against the wooden porch and rocked.

> Dad, I already told you. Lucy Legare does not want to sell, and I get the impression no one can make that woman do something she doesn't want to do for herself. I know you want the silver and all, but I just don't see it happening.

Lucy reread the text message and frowned. Had Declan meant to send this to her? What was he talking about? Seemed like he accidentally sent a text intended for his father. She responded and asked him as much. Moments later, his reply came.

> Yikes. Meant to send that to my dad. Sorry.

But he had just alluded to his father wanting *her* silver, and that being the motive behind buying her house. Eliza's house. Did they think it was here? Hidden inside the house? Buried in the ground? Yeah, "sorry" wasn't going to cut it.

Her heart plummeted with disappointment that it'd come to this. After that moment she'd shared with Declan at the wedding, she'd begun to believe he was worth a second chance. But really, should she be surprised?

Lucy hurried down the steps of the porch barefoot and hopped from the garden stones. She opened the gate of her yard and stepped out onto the cobblestone street. Her feet wobbled as she walked on the smooth, rounded stones. She didn't have time to waste on finding shoes. She needed to talk to Declan right now.

In no time at all, Lucy made it to the house. She squinted to see the church clock that rose above the line of houses from a couple blocks up.

It wasn't until that point that she regretted not putting shoes on. What seemed very bohemian at the time now seemed unsanitary. She'd blame it on the early hour. And the shock of that text message.

Lucy stepped toward the front door, but a sound stopped her in her tracks.

She heard murmuring from the other side. She recognized Declan's voice, but who was the other man? Could it be his father?

A pedestrian made his way across the street at the corner. Lucy looked down at her vintage dress and bare feet. He would certainly wonder what she was doing at the Pinckneys' house dressed this way, and especially at this early time of morning.

She needed a cover, so she slipped her feet behind a large planter, grabbed *The Post and Courier* on their stoop, and opened it quickly.

He had already waved and bid her good morning when she realized she was holding the paper upside down.

Oh well. She fought the urge to laugh. They would definitely hear her if she made a sound. But as she folded the newspaper back up and bent to set it down, she heard a few muted words.

"Progress . . . Lucy . . . house."

Her eyes went wide. From a crouched position, she pushed her ear against the door to better hear the conversation.

"Give me more time," Declan said.

"We don't have it."

A bee buzzed past Lucy's face, and she shook her head while flapping her hands. She would not be stung again. Not now.

"We need that silver, Declan. You and I both know it's somewhere at that woman's house."

Lucy's jaw dropped, and she covered her mouth with her hand. They were talking about the silver right now! She knew it. Good thing she hadn't stopped long enough to put shoes on. She might've missed this by the time she buckled her Mary Janes.

"And you're sure it's in her ground?" Declan asked.

The bee flew past once more. It didn't seem to appreciate Lucy's proximity to the planter full of flowers. This time, she stood still as a statue.

"Certain as one can be, given the circumstances," the man replied.

"But I've already told you," Declan said. "She won't budge about the house."

"Oh, I wouldn't be so sure of that."

"What does that mean?" Declan asked.

Lucy's calves began to burn, but she didn't dare move a step. She pressed her ear a little harder against the door.

"I've taken steps to encourage her to sell."

"What kind of steps, Dad?" Declan's voice was low.

"Let's just say there's a new curator at the museum where Lucy recently applied for a job. I used one of your mother's contacts."

What?

Declan's father was the reason she didn't get that full-time curator job? So she was qualified after all. Lucy felt nauseated.

A long pause followed.

Finally, Declan spoke.

"You mean you knocked her out of the running for the position?"

"Sure. You're the one who said she was insistent."

"Well, yeah, but I never said to ruin—"

"Look, Declan." The man huffed. "If you hadn't told me how badly she wanted that job, I never would've thought of it. See, this way, we've created a financial crisis for her. She'll have no choice but to sell us the house—for a generous amount, of course—and in turn, we will give her financial security. Everyone wins." Someone tapped against the door, and Lucy tried to lean even farther back behind the planter. "It's just business. Nothing personal."

This man was a monster! She couldn't believe Declan would be involved in his scheming. Though really, why should she be surprised?

To think, she'd almost played directly into their hands.

Fuming, Lucy stood up from the door stoop and brushed off the skirt of her great-grandmother's dress, which she'd found in the closet upstairs. She hurried along and only glanced back once—though she could've sworn she saw Anna Pinckney peering through the blinds.

She was halfway down the block before the thought struck her.

The sunlight filtered through the cascading branches of the oak trees, and a new hope dawned.

The silver was in her ground.

Declan had no idea she was aware of that little fact. So she would pull information from him, just as he had from her. Two could play that game.

She would dig in the name of tending the weed-wrought lawn, if anyone even asked. And she would, quite simply, find the silver herself.

With her head held high, Lucy strode straight through her front door, twisted her hair into a bun, and slipped her shoes on. Now all she needed was to find that shovel.

Sweat drenched the back of Lucy's dress. Her skirt swung with every heave of the shovel, and large dirt holes littered her yard.

She'd been digging for hours and had found absolutely nothing. But every time she was tempted to stop, she thought of Declan and all he'd done.

And she kept digging.

She didn't know what made her angrier.

That he'd turned out to be exactly the man she'd expected, or that she was fool enough to fall for him. To think, this whole time, he was after her silver. *Her* silver. Or really, even, Eliza's.

As if he didn't already have enough wealth to feed the entire city of Charleston for a month, he had to go and acquire her house to get his grubby little hands on even more.

Yes, his father was the one responsible for Lucy's dream job falling through. That much was clear. But Declan hadn't done much in the way of stopping it, had he?

He'd proven family obligations ruled over propriety, and morality, and compassion, and good manners. His family obligations ruled over all. He'd do anything to follow his father's bidding. She realized that now.

She'd been captivated by his dreams of architecture, his passion and eloquence, and the man she thought she saw in him. And all of those things were a real part of him, though sadly, only a part.

His decisions showed his deeper character. Which was unforgivably lacking. But oh, she could teach him a lesson. That wealth and social prestige could not buy everything in life. And no matter his father's determination or Declan's own willingness to play into that plan, he could certainly not have her house.

Or her silver, for that matter.

Lucy struck the shovel hard into the ground, unearthing only dirt yet again.

She spent another hour digging without results, then decided to go inside for a lunch break. She spooned leftover macaroni and cheese from Beth's house into a bowl and put it in the microwave, then poured herself a tall glass of water.

The microwave beeped, and she stirred the macaroni. She

hadn't realized how hungry she'd become. As Lucy carried her bowl to the table, she looked out upon her yard where she'd up-turned the sod. Going forward, she would have to be intentional. Strategic. But for now, she needed to eat.

Each spoonful warmed her stomach and calmed her nerves as only homemade mac and cheese can. As she ate and thought of Beth's hospitality, for some reason, this house really felt like her own.

She would get through this.

She would find a way.

She was a Legare, after all.

"Still not speaking to me, I see." Declan's father reached across Declan toward the butter dish on the formal dinner table. He daubed the butter on his slice of fresh Italian bread and twirled a spoonful of pasta on his fork.

"Surely you can see why." Declan leaned back against the hard dining room chair, arms crossed.

"Go ahead and have a little fit like a child, but someone has to run the company."

"*Run the company*? Are you kidding me?"

"I most certainly am not." His father's face reddened. "To be frank, Declan, your ignorance toward the ugly side of success-ful business practices concerns me. You have become idealistic to a fault. I wonder sometimes what will become of the family business when you take the reins someday—if experience will be your teacher in my absence, or if you will drive our family's long-held reputation into the dust." His father took several visible deep breaths, as he always did when short of breath.

"And *I'm* the one throwing the childish fit?"

Declan's father hesitated before eating the pasta. "What I did is for your own good, Declan."

"I hardly see how."

"Because the good of the company works for the good of our family. You are a member of our family, are you not?"

"It's one thing to go after her house, Dad. That's business. I get that. But to jeopardize the woman's job to intentionally put her in a financial crisis?" He glared toward his father and leaned forward. "Did you really have so little faith I might convince her to sell?"

The man put his drink down and looked Declan straight in the eyes. "You're compromised."

"Compromised?" Declan shook his head, baffled. "What is that supposed to mean?"

His father took another bite of his pasta. "Oh, come on, son. You think I don't recognize when you have feelings for a woman?"

Declan fiddled with the napkin on his lap. "I hardly see how that's relevant."

"Don't you?" His father took another drink of sparkling water. "Ought I trust this entire challenging acquisition to a man in love with Lucy?"

Declan froze. "You think I'm in love with her?"

"Aren't you?"

The word *hardly* almost escaped Declan's mouth, but he stopped himself. He couldn't say it truthfully. He'd certainly developed feelings for her. He'd admit that much. But in love with Lucy Legare?

It was, of course, a completely ridiculous thought. A relationship with her would be impractical, infuriating, unlikely, and . . . captivating.

Declan took a deep breath. He wasn't sure what to make of his father's assertion.

The man broke off a piece of bread and looked toward the kitchen door. "Well, no matter the case, Declan, would you do me a favor and stop this foolishness before your mother comes back? She needn't know of our squabble. Can we at least agree to that much?"

Slowly, Declan nodded. They'd troubled his mother with many an argument over the years, and his father was right. She didn't need to know about this one. She didn't need to know Dad had cost Lucy her next job.

Or that Declan had inadvertently been involved.

And she *definitely* didn't need to know the troubled state of his heart.

His mother pushed through the kitchen door with her back and carried a tray of tiramisu to the table.

She glanced between Declan and his father. "What's going on between you two?"

Declan jabbed his fork into his spaghetti, then stabbed a sliver of parmesan. "Just another stressful day at the office, Mom." He forced a smile.

She raised one eyebrow and shook her head, then set the tiramisu down while they finished eating. "I don't know why I even ask."

Declan's father shot him a look that said he'd better hush, so Declan changed the subject. "How are things at the museum?"

"Oh, wonderful." His mother spooned extra parmesan onto her pasta. "Lucy has been doing a wonderful job with the exhibit." She broke off another piece of bread. "And how is Lucy today?"

"How should I know? Didn't you see her at work?"

She frowned. "No need to get defensive, honey. I was simply asking." She dipped her bread in olive oil. "Lucy had the day off. Though, knowing her, I'm sure she's probably working on some project. She never stops, that woman. She's got the determination of a saint."

Declan pushed the pasta on his plate around with his fork.

His mother was right.

That was exactly what worried him.

TWENTY-FIVE

Modern Day

Lucy was boiling water for her Saturday morning tea when she heard someone pounding on her front door. She'd pulled all the books from the large shelf in the entryway in hopes one of them contained secret information about the silver. None had.

"Just a minute." She dropped the tea bag into the delicate cup in her hand, then set both on the counter and hurried to the door. The stack of books against her entryway provided a bit of an obstacle course, but she managed to successfully step around them.

Several more knocks sounded.

Lucy looked through the privacy hole to see Ms. Beth's worried face peering at the door. When she opened it, Ms. Beth flung her purse down and took Lucy by the arms.

"Thank heavens, you're still alive."

Beth let herself inside and moved her purse to Eliza's antique sofa.

Lucy laughed at her antics. "What are you talking about?"

"Well, with all the giant holes in your yard, I thought Declan might've dug your grave and tossed you in it when he learned you'd been colluding with me at the Preservation Society meeting last week."

Lucy rolled her eyes and laughed.

But Beth wasn't done. "So obviously you have a giant mole living in the yard."

"Beth Bennett!" Lucy swatted at her arm and headed back toward the kitchen to finish making her tea.

"Seriously, Lucy." Beth followed her into the kitchen. "What is going on? You *are* planning to tell me what's going on?" The sentiment was half question, half statement.

Lucy shrugged. "I'm gardening."

Beth raised both eyebrows and leaned against the sink. Clearly, she wasn't buying it. She waited for Lucy to say more. But was telling Beth really a good idea? Lucy had hardly processed all this herself. Though maybe her dear friend could add some much-needed perspective. Lucy wouldn't mind being able to talk through everything.

Except her feelings for Declan.

Lucy cleared her throat.

Yes, her feelings for Declan were crystal clear already. She had none.

A twinge pulled her heart.

Okay, so she had some, but that was to be expected, considering the situation. And soon enough, she was certain, her lingering attraction would give way to the heartbreak he'd caused.

And what a devastating heartbreak it was.

Stupid Pinckneys.

She bit her bottom lip. Ms. Beth *had* known Eliza in some capacity. Maybe in addition to being a sounding board, she could give Lucy practical advice on where to look for the silver? Maybe she even knew where Eliza might've kept her most precious items?

"Would you like a cup of tea?" Lucy reached into the cabinet to grab another cup and tore open a tea bag before Ms. Beth could answer.

"Let me try that again. You are going to tell me what's going on here, young lady."

"I'm not so sure that's a good idea." Lucy poured water into her cup and dunked her tea bag inside.

"I'm worried." Ms. Beth crossed her arms. "Why, you nearly uprooted one of those lovely rose bushes I helped you plant."

Lucy spooned in some sugar and swirled it around. "I just . . ."

Ms. Beth took the kettle and poured water into her own cup, letting the tea steep as though she had all the time in the world. The woman was patient enough to grow flowers from seeds. Trying to hold out was probably a losing battle.

Lucy took a deep breath. "If you really want to know . . ." She pulled out a chair, and it skidded against the floor. "Then we'd better sit down."

She explained about Declan wanting to buy the house, about the watercolor paintings, and the accidental text. She left out the part about the not-so-accidental almost-kiss.

"You're telling me he said the silver is in your ground?" Ms. Beth's eyes were wide. "And he's sure?"

"Yes and yes." Lucy took a sip from her teacup. "Although there's one thing in particular that keeps tripping me up."

"What's that, sweetheart?"

Lucy shook her head. "I know it sounds unlikely, but I keep thinking if I could just find out why someone would give me this house, maybe that person would help me understand where the silver went. *Maybe* the silver is even the reason they gave me the house. You know, so I would look after it? Or even solve the mystery for them?"

Ms. Beth took a sip and looked up at Lucy over the rim of her teacup. "Maybe," she said.

Declan traced the faded script of William's old journal as he read the entry one more time. His room was dim with twilight, and he flipped on the lamp that sat on top of his bedside table.

Why had his great-grandfather been so obscure? Declan's father was convinced this entry was a clue to the silver's whereabouts under a tree, but Declan himself wasn't so confident.

> *My heart burns within me—with the fire of fear and passion— but at least I have succeeded with the silver. I shouldn't still love Eliza, and yet I suspect I always will. I wonder what would be better, to tell her everything or to keep running.*
>
> *I try to remind myself I've kept these secrets in the best way I know how, and I pray she will be safe from them. Not from the secrets, that is, but from those who chase them. I have returned the silver to its roots—for silver roots draw beautiful wings.*

Declan sighed. William would have, no doubt, objected to what his father was doing. Though his father always said the family business was everything, as far as Declan was concerned, nothing could excuse his father's behavior toward Lucy.

William's love for Eliza had clearly been stronger than his desire for the silver their families still feuded over. Now *that* was an example worth following. Though Declan did wonder what had gone wrong between them. Had William faced a quandary like the one Declan did, the choice between family obligations and love?

Declan felt sick to his stomach for the plans his father had put into action. For his own growing feelings toward Lucy. And sicker still because he knew he had to find that silver for the sake of the company. Attraction was an emotional privilege he simply couldn't afford to indulge in.

Though in the quiet of his room, as the reading lamp cast a shadowy glow upon his great-grandfather's journal, he couldn't help the whispers in his heart saying something deeper was at play here. He wasn't simply attracted to Lucy.

He was in love with her.

The more he'd thought about his father's words, the more the wild idea had begun to tame him. He hadn't been sleeping at night, and when he did, he saw her in his dreams. And he wondered for the slightest moment if love was strong enough to beat out all the rest of the things he faced.

If he and Lucy could finish Eliza and William's story.

Lucy pulled a lightweight scarf over her shoulders should her dress provide insufficient warmth now that the sun was setting. She locked the front door of her home and twisted her hair into a loose bun as she took the steps toward the cobblestone street.

The streetlamps were already glowing, and her bag bounced against her hip as she hurried along. She'd normally take her car to get to the museum more quickly, but the body shop was still waiting for her new bumper to come in. She'd finally arranged for repairs rather than replacement.

If only she'd known at the time that her car wasn't the only thing Declan would break. He'd also cost her a dream job, albeit indirectly.

And then there was the small matter of her stubborn heart, which raced even stronger at the thought of him than it ever had before. But he would not—under any circumstances—take Eliza's home. She was determined on that account.

Knowing her great-grandmother was the same artist she'd long admired opened up a new world of possibilities. So she'd decided to get out of the house and take in all the paintings at the museum with a fresh perspective. The exhibit would open soon, and she wanted to make sure she'd really captured the spirit of the Charleston Renaissance.

She also wanted to avoid the fact she still hadn't found the silver in her house. . . .

"Lucy!"

She jolted to a stop. Lost in her thoughts, she hadn't been paying attention to her surroundings. Lucy recognized the voice instantly.

Slowly, she turned. She took a deep breath to steady herself, as her slow jog down the road had left her nearly breathless. Though that wasn't the only thing that flustered her.

Declan.

She was as close to hating him as Jesus would permit her.

Declan cleared his throat. He wore a lightweight caramel sweater, his signature chinos, and the slightest hint of sandalwood cologne. His dark hair was parted sharply, his hands were hidden in his pockets, and he'd donned the chestnut reading glasses she'd only seen him wear once before.

She was furious with him. Absolutely furious. Yet he'd never looked so attractive. He was equal parts Cary Grant and Mr. Darcy, and she despised—*despised*—herself for thinking it.

"I'm glad I ran into you. I was just"—he kicked at a pebble under his feet—"on a walk."

She frowned. "Directly past my house?"

He laughed softly, and his eyes caught the glimmer of the street-lamp.

She was acting paranoid. She needed to stop, or he might suspect something. But she was a bundle of nerves around him right now for so many reasons, and she just wanted to get out of here.

"I haven't seen you in a few days."

"Yeah, I've been busy." She adjusted the bag draped over her shoulder. It was getting heavy.

He slid up and down on the heels of his suede loafers. "I have to admit, I was a little concerned when I saw your yard all torn up. Everything okay?"

"I'm working on a big gardening project."

That was one way of putting it.

"I see." He nodded. After pausing a moment, he added, "From the looks of it, your renovations to the house are coming along nicely."

What a joke. He expected her to buy into his act, didn't he? She ran her tongue along her teeth, willing herself not to say what she was thinking.

"So, listen," he said, looking down the street. "I was actually planning to make some dinner at home now that my own renovations are in a better state." His gaze traveled toward her. "I don't suppose you'd want to join me?"

Breathe, Lucy. Breathe.

Dinner with Declan would be an opportunity to probe for information about the silver. How much did he know, aside from the fact it was buried on her property? Maybe she could even "sneak off to the bathroom" and do a little snooping.

But when she glanced up at him and met his gaze, her instincts seemed to scream *Danger!* His nearness stirred her emotions in the most unwelcome way. Not to mention, the last time she'd seen him was at the wedding, when . . .

Lucy swallowed.

He didn't know she'd overheard his conversation with his father. That she knew the truth, including the part he played in the schemes. He didn't know she was furious. All he knew was the dance at the wedding.

So he would never expect she was up to something.

Oh, if only Declan weren't involved in this whole thing. But Lucy could be strong, no matter the pull of her heart.

She'd been strong plenty of times before.

Lucy planted her feet firmly on the ground and put on a smile that was Golden Globe–worthy. "I'd love to."

TWENTY-SIX

1917

A nervous little Eliza hid her blue-dyed fingers under the pleats of her dress, only making the problem worse.

Her mother turned from pouring kettle water into her teacup and, for the first time, noticed what Eliza had done.

Eliza's palms began to moisten from embarrassment, and she frowned. "I'm sorry, Mother."

"Goodness me," her mother said, setting down the cup on the counter and hurrying over toward the kitchen table. "Why, Eliza, I thought you promised to either lay a protective cloth down or to do your painting outside from now on." Mother looked down at her dainty new wristwatch, smoothing the fabric of her waistline as though it may loosen her corset. Mother was always complaining about that corset. Eliza was determined she herself would never wear one when she came of age. Mother would be mortified by the lack of decorum, but she would accept it eventually.

Her mother sighed. "Your Grandma Clara is set to arrive back by carriage any moment now, and not only do I have a blue-dyed kitchen, but I also have a blue-dyed child."

Slowly, Eliza pulled her hands out from where she'd hidden them under her skirts. "How did you know about my hands?"

"Didn't you know? I can see straight through objects. It's a special ability God gives to us mothers. Someday you'll see what I mean."

Eliza smiled, feeling rather silly for having worried her mother might be angry about the innocent mishap. Mother never got angry. And Eliza had a lot of mishaps. Yet Mother never made her feel inferior, or as though she should act a mirror image to the other girls her age. She always accepted Eliza and took these things in her graceful stride.

Mother sat down at a chair beside the painting-gone-wrong and motioned for Eliza to come sit on her lap. Eliza gladly obliged, relieved for her mother's understanding.

"Want to tell me how this happened?" Mother asked. "Why, it seems you've dyed a six-inch portion of my lacy tablecloth the grey-blue hue of storm clouds."

"I was trying to make blue." It was an innocent answer, and an honest one. Eliza tilted her chin to get a better view of her mother. "It's more challenging than I thought."

"And why did you need more blue, Eliza? You've ruined the indigo you did have by pursuing more." Mother softened the truth with a gentle smile.

Eliza returned the gesture. "You're right. I'm sorry."

Her mother took a slow breath, holding Eliza tight with her arms and then resting her chin on top of Eliza's curls. "You know, this indigo we've got isn't synthetic . . . so it isn't colorfast. Over time, especially when the beautiful sunbeams stream through the windows and fall upon it, the indigo will fade, turning into another color entirely."

Eliza bit down on her bottom lip. "I didn't know that."

Mother swept a spray of hair from Eliza's forehead. "You thought you could create more indigo, and I understand why you wished it, Eliza, for indigo is the color of bluebirds, the color of the twilight sky. Newton insisted it be added to the colors of the rainbow, and once upon a time, its cousin true blue was such a rare pigment, its price rivaled gold. People have fought wars over indigo crops and used it to bolster and brag of their wealth. Why? All in an attempt to make beauty lasting."

Eliza looked down at her blue-stained fingertips, wondering if *they* would be lasting as well. But if she hadn't enough indigo pigment for the bluebirds in her painting, a little stained on her fingertips wasn't the worst thing in the world. Indeed, it was quite akin to the dust of fairies, like in her stories, and she wondered for a moment if her stained fingertips may prove to others she was a real painter, or at least she would be, once she practiced more. If that were the case, she would gladly keep blue fingers forever.

But something about her mother's words had struck a chord within her heart. "Why are you telling me all this, Mother?"

"Because, my sweet daughter, much as we try, we cannot make the bluebirds stay forever. And though that fact may grieve us, and we may be tempted to despair, we must always remember this power—that in accepting the comings and goings of the beautiful from our lives, we cannot change their temporality, but we *can* be changed by them. We can allow beauty to point us toward the God who made it. And so we paint them, my dear Eliza, not to save them forever, but by them to remember. By them, to become more beautiful in our own hearts. And *that* my girl, is the reason behind preservation, and why it's so important."

Mother stood, removing the lacy tablecloth from the table and wiping at the streaks of blue with a cloth she kept handy. "People go wrong two ways in life. They either save all their blue paint until it's dried up and gone, or they waste it upon futile attempts at perpetuity. Promise me, Eliza, that you will use your indigo, and use it well."

Eliza fidgeted her blue-stained fingers. "I promise, Mama."

Her mother nodded once, seemingly satisfied that this promise was strong enough to carry Eliza from her youthful naivety into a more mature sense of responsibility. A realization of what, exactly, she'd agreed to in the years to come.

1931

With every heave of her shovel, Eliza's pin curls loosened and the sequins of her dress flew. She was furious, and she was heartbroken, and no matter her formal attire, it seemed the perfect time for gardening. And by gardening, of course, she meant searching for the silver.

She'd managed to keep her wits about her during an entire lunch spent with her aunt at her family's house. But as soon as the woman left to purchase a new pair of shoes on King Street, Eliza could not pretend any longer.

She was alone here—truly alone here—and she had every intention of finding the truth. She would search through the flowers, and if she didn't find it, she would search through the roots too. No telling how deep the inheritance ran.

She'd been allowing summer's flowers to showcase their final blooms before uprooting them. But the leaves were brown, most of the blooms dead, and she was tired of it. Tired, tired, tired of it all.

Shovelfuls of dirt flew behind her into the grass, toward the oak tree and the carriage house where she'd gotten engaged. And when she struck a deep root, she shoveled harder, but it wouldn't come up. So she jabbed and jabbed at the thing, trying to get the flowers up. Trying to make room for new growth.

But nothing.

Finally, she gave up.

She sat down inside the carriage house, dirt all over her face and through her hat and her hair, and her anger gave way to tears.

She'd seen William this morning in an automobile with a woman named Mary Gibbes. Her neighbor had filled her in on the news. The two of them had married, a match more acceptable to both Eliza's aunt and William's own family than the ill-fated notion that he and she could ever reconcile their family's feud.

Had Eliza been a fool to love him back then? Had her aunt been right all along, and if she'd only listened, could she have avoided this shattered hope that now sat within her—these colored shards she daily tried to piece into something more beautiful? A picture of Christ or a rainbow or sparrow. A mosaic that, put back together, meant even more than it did before.

Every time she tried to preserve that part of her story, she came away cut and bleeding, the sting of it fresh and never healing. Not just because of William himself, but because of her hope. Because of the person she was back then, before he deserted her and the economy crashed and the whole world fractured.

She didn't fault William for marrying the woman. She'd married Robert, hadn't she? And she refused to pine after someone to whom she wasn't wed. But she did mourn what might have been.

Help me put these pieces back together. Eliza murmured the prayer.

The words stuck to the roof of Eliza's mouth like an Oh Henry chocolate bar.

Outside the window, a light rain shook the trees. Eliza thought of her wedding to Robert—how it had also rained that day. And she thought of how fickle the rain can be, to water the ground with life and then flood the same roots with catastrophic strength.

And she was seized by the sudden need to save something.

So she stood and brushed the dirt off her knees.

She walked all the way to Susan's house, never minding the rain. And together, the two of them set out to see what they could preserve.

TWENTY-SEVEN

Modern Day

Puffy, white clouds—the type you make into shapes when you're a kid—settled over top of Declan's yard as Lucy watched from the kitchen window. His house was two rooms wide with a covered front porch. Not a single house like her own, and yet surprisingly historic for someone so interested in property development.

A long hallway split the house in two, with a study and guest bedroom on one side, and on the other, a stairwell and what must have once been a formal sitting room. At the back of the house was the kitchen, which had been built as a far-later addition to the original square footage and was apparently the reason for his recent renovations.

Declan stirred cheese into a large pan of grits and dunked hush puppies into the fryer, careful not to splatter hot oil all over his fancy new kitchen.

He'd explained Bailey was still showing her puppy ways, despite several weeks of expensive dog-training lessons. She was currently chewing at the hem of Lucy's dress from where they both sat on the wood floor.

"Bailey, cut it out." Declan continued to stir, turning his attention toward Lucy. "Don't let her snag your clothes. She may look innocent, but those puppy teeth are fierce."

"I don't care if she does snag them. Puppy snuggles are worth the sacrifice." Lucy tossed Bailey's tiny tennis ball into the air. The little pup came prancing back with the ball in her mouth as if it were her finest possession.

"She loves that little ball," he said. "Chasing it is her favorite pastime, closely followed by shredding paper."

"Do you like to shred paper?" Lucy asked the dog, scratching her little belly. "I don't believe you would be such a troublemaker."

The oven timer beeped, and Declan turned it off. "Oh, believe it." He checked the shrimp. Apparently not quite done because he kept them cooking. "So far, she's ripped up several receipts for items I was planning to return, my insurance policy, and—oh—my birth certificate."

Lucy started laughing, then covered her mouth. "I'm sorry. Not funny."

A half grin slipped up his lips. "It's kind of funny." He stirred the grits once more and looked down at her. "I do have furniture, you know."

Lucy leaned against the cabinet doors, her knees tucked under the hem of her dress. "I'd rather play with Bailey."

"Well, it's probably just as well, because I'm almost done here."

Dark blue cabinets contrasted with a white backsplash and stainless steel appliances in a look that was screaming for a magazine cover. Lucy wanted to know more about what went into the design. "So you built this kitchen separate from the rest of the house?" she asked.

"Sure did." Declan wiped his hands on a kitchen towel. "I designed it myself. It's called a hyphen. Have you heard the term?"

Lucy scratched the puppy's soft fur and shook her head. "I haven't."

Declan pulled two glasses that looked like goblets from the cabinets, a far step up from the plastic cups she'd been using at her own house anytime she wasn't drinking tea. "Basically it means a brand-new extension that's added on to a historical property.

Many houses this age, of course, were originally built with bathrooms and kitchens separate from the main structure. This way, everyone wins. The historical aspects are maintained, but things like kitchens can be modernized."

"Hmm." Now that was an idea. "And you designed it yourself, you said?"

Declan nodded. "I'm really into this kind of thing." He pulled out the salt and pepper, then turned to her. "Actually, if I'm being honest, Lucy, I wish I could do more of it with the family business, but . . ."

"Not your dad's cup of tea?"

Declan shrugged.

Interesting. He wouldn't have struck her as someone so interested in a building's history. She thought back to their conversation on Edisto. Was all of this wall-leveling his father's doing, then? And if so, why did Declan allow the man to go to such extremes? Their business was known for being ruthless and constantly at odds with the Preservation Society.

"I've always been interested in it too. Architecture." Lucy blurted out the words before she could think better of it.

Declan turned his head. "Really?" He seemed genuinely surprised. She was as well, honestly. The only person she'd admitted that to was Harper. She'd almost told him about the secret dream back when they were at the beach, and she'd wondered if he'd noticed her hesitation. She hadn't meant to hide her interest, necessarily, but the truth was she just wasn't sure she could make it in the business. Architecture was *hard*, and so was all art, really, but paintings and history and the like were kind of her thing. She'd never really considered that she might actually be capable of studying something different. She always had been Lucy, the artist. Lucy, the free spirit.

Never Lucy, the architect.

Declan held her gaze. "So it seems we have something in common after all."

His attention sent an unexpected and unwelcome jolt of nervous energy through her, and she felt as though they were connecting on a deeper level she didn't entirely know how to put into words. Maybe because she didn't entirely understand it.

But he was still the man planning to take her silver, along with his father. She would do well to remember it. She decided to change the subject.

"Are you sure you don't want help with dinner?" Lucy straightened the scarf along her shoulders. "I'm not used to people cooking for me."

"And risk you ruining my famous cheddar grits? No, thanks." He grinned, but his attention never wavered from her. What did he see there? Had he noticed he had touched upon the lightly held dream of a young girl, made long before she decided it was unrealistic?

And why did part of her still want him to ask more about it?

Lucy sprinkled salt over her second helping of hush puppies. The man could *cook*.

She took another bite as the kitchen timer beeped. Declan set his cloth napkin down on the farmhouse-style table, which she was pretty sure she recognized from Restoration Hardware, and went to pull a pie out of the oven. As he opened the oven door, the smell of chocolate chips and pecans wafted toward her. She took another glance at her hush puppies and determined not to eat another. She needed to save room. Because if his pie was anything like the rest of this meal, she'd dream about it later.

He set it down on top of the oven and walked back toward the table. "The pie will need to cool a few minutes."

Lucy's stomach turned, and it *wasn't* from the hush puppies.

This was her chance. She knew it. Yet she couldn't get her feet to move. She'd come into this evening determined to uncover the Pinckney family secrets, just as they'd attempted against her. But

Declan had been so . . . well . . . charming . . . that she found her heart softening.

Maybe his father was primarily to blame.

Maybe it wasn't fair to use him in this way.

Maybe it's okay to fall for him after all.

She chided herself for the thought. No, she needed to be strong. If she wanted to save Eliza's house, she needed to find the silver before the Pinckneys got their hands on it. And she needed to do it quickly.

Lucy took a sip from her glass and then stood, pressing the wrinkles from her outfit. "Could you point me in the direction of the restroom?"

"Sure." Declan gestured with his hand toward the hallway just past the fireplace. "You'll want to take a right, then pass my office. It'll be on the left. You can't miss it."

Straight past his office? Maybe this would be easier than she'd thought.

"Thanks." She flashed him a quick smile, then hurried in the direction he'd explained before she lost her nerve.

He walked back toward the kitchen. "Take your time," he said. "I'm just going to clean up a bit. I can't cook without making an epic mess, or I'd do it more often."

Lucy laughed nervously, then turned the corner and immediately saw the office to which he'd referred. The glass-paned door creaked as she eased it open, and she glanced over her shoulder to be sure he hadn't heard.

Her pulse raced.

She'd never snooped like this before.

Just past his office window stood a grand oak tree, and the streetlamp cast a magical sort of glow through its branches to the ground below. Inside the room, floor-to-ceiling bookshelves that had been painted the same color as the kitchen cabinets gave a modern yet dignified feel. She was surprised how cozy his house seemed. She'd half expected a marble entryway and crystal candlesticks.

One lamp had been left on beside the bookshelves, sending just enough light toward the desk that she immediately noticed an open journal. She stepped toward it. The pages were worn and fragile.

Careful not to leave any indication she'd been in the room, she used one finger to mark where the journal had been open and gently flipped the pages.

Eliza.

She gasped when she saw the word, then immediately shot a glance toward the door. Was this journal William's?

Was this how Declan and his father knew about the silver?

She turned back to the pages marked by her finger and skimmed them.

> *My engagement is ruined. I've left Eliza for her own safety, though I can't tell her that. Not until the men coming after her silver cease looking, at least, and that will be no time soon. I told my father I would marry the woman of my parents' choosing, and in exchange, he will ensure Eliza's safety. According to him, Eliza has already wed another, so if I cannot have my beloved, what difference does it make?*
>
> *I never should have entwined myself with these people in the first place.*
>
> *What have I done?*
>
> *If only I'd known from the start where this would lead me. If only I'd known it was about the silver. That it was always about the silver.*
>
> *If only.*

As if she were using a loom, Lucy wove the missing pieces of the story in and out of what she already knew to form a fabric she could use. Honestly, Lucy had doubted the famed silver ever existed—at least, until she'd overheard Declan's father a couple days ago.

But according to this journal entry, the silver did indeed exist, and perhaps it was no far stretch to say the Pinckneys were the reason it was missing. But if that were the case, why were Declan and his father seeking it on her property? Something didn't add up. Clearly they didn't know where to find it, or they would've found it already.

So what exactly had William done? And why?

She knew him to be the man who broke her great-grandmother's heart. But could there, maybe, be more to their love story? Lucy continued to skim through the entries, looking for more clues. Her eyes caught on the next line.

I have returned the silver to its roots—for silver roots draw beautiful wings.

She frowned, trying to make sense of it. Silver roots . . . beautiful wings . . . why did that sound familiar?

Of course! The painting she was currently working on for her museum exhibit was entitled *The Silver Tree*. Had Eliza known about this tree to which William referred? Did she ever uncover the rest of the story?

Footsteps came from around the corner.

She jumped to her feet, set the journal back, and hurried off into the bathroom. Quietly but quickly, she shut the bathroom door and leaned against it, trying to catch her breath.

Had she just discovered something of significance? Had Eliza given a clue in her portrayal of that tree? Why else would she refer to it in the same way William had in his journal entry?

Declan tapped against the bathroom door. "Lucy? You okay?"

She closed her eyes and steadied her voice. "Just fine, thanks."

Fine was putting it mildly. But she couldn't give him any indication she'd just made this discovery. She needed to play it cool. Normal Lucy, doing normal Lucy things. She would say nothing about the silver or William and Eliza or that painting at the museum. She'd get her tea from the shop down the road fifteen minutes early in the morning so she could be there first thing.

230

"Good," he said, oblivious to her racing pulse on the other side of the doorway. "Because dessert is ready."

She turned on the water to wash her hands—he was listening, after all—and scrubbed off a smear of dirt caught under her ring from her earlier work on Eliza's house. As she towel-dried her hands, she smiled at Declan's words.

Yes, this was all about to get far sweeter.

TWENTY-EIGHT

1932

Eliza returned home that night covered in the dust and dirt that comes from salvaging old things. Susan was in the middle of a key preservation project near East Bay Street and had insisted no one else had Eliza's eye for what could be saved and restored. When Eliza had mentioned it to Robert last week, he graciously offered to keep watch over their little daughter so that Eliza could work with Susan.

Eliza had acted nonchalant about the opportunity, but secretly she had been counting the hours.

Oh, she loved being a mother. And she was not entirely bad at being a wife, either. Robert was steady and kind to her, and her affections for him were steady and kind as well.

But it'd been a long time since she'd painted anything—in fact, she'd sold off the remainder of her paintings. People kept buying them as souvenirs of their trips to Charleston and saying that every time they saw the paintings, they wanted to come back. She felt good about knowing she had—in some capacity—helped to redefine the city by her art. Maybe someday she would paint again.

And it'd been a long time since she'd saved anything, and doing that work felt good as well. Keeping items from being thrown out always made her feel as though she was saving someone's story. And every story had value.

So on this particular night, she and Susan comically raided a trash heap near the property in hopes of finding doorknobs, ironwork, or fixtures.

"I've got something! Someone threw away a fur stole," Susan had exclaimed. But when she pulled it out of the heap, a raccoon made the most ungodly hissing sound before Susan shrieked and jumped out of the way.

Eliza and Susan were laughing so hard, neither of them had any idea where the raccoon scurried next.

By the time Eliza arrived home, Robert had made sure Bea was freshly bathed. He was in the middle of trying to comb her hair when Eliza walked in the door.

"Mommy, Mommy!" Bea came running, her arms up in the air.

Eliza picked her up and planted a kiss on her forehead. "Hello, my sweet girl."

Robert handed her the comb. "She's insistent only you know how to comb her hair."

Eliza smiled. It had been good to get out of the house with Susan for a while, but it was also good to come back home. Simple as they may be, tasks like being the best hair brusher were like badges of honor, sweet acknowledgments of all the day in, day out things mothers do when no one else is looking. Until Eliza had become a mother, she had no idea just how many of those day in, day out things she would need to do. And yet still, all of it—the kissing bruises and preparing snacks and organizing the same spaces over and over—was all worth this life she lived.

"Princess story, Mommy?" Bea asked, smiling sweetly.

With one arm holding on to her daughter, Eliza used the other hand to comb her hair. "Sure, sweetheart." Bea asked for this same fairy tale over and over.

Several minutes later, she and Bea were snuggled beneath the covers of the little girl's bed. Eliza reached for the book and read it by the light of the lamp in the room. Bea's expression lit up as it always did when Eliza got to the part about the glass shoes. But tiredness hit her, and she was asleep before the carriage turned back into a pumpkin.

Just as well, Eliza supposed.

She kissed Bea's soft hair and turned off the lamp.

She stopped short when the little girl turned over in bed and said sweetly, "Mommy, did you ever live in a fairy tale like the princess?"

The question rumbled through her, and Eliza closed her eyes a moment to take a breath before she turned and stepped back toward her daughter's bed.

Her mind flashed memories of dancing with William, of walking through the streets of Charleston near her garden and talking about paint and preservation.

But she knew she shouldn't think these things, even as a reflex. She forced herself to stop, or at least she tried to.

"Mommy's never been a princess, sweet girl," she said. "But who knows? Maybe you will be. And maybe you'll get your own mice and glass slippers and castle someday—but the best way for that to happen, right now, is to find them in your dreams."

A giddy smile rose from Bea's lips, like the two points of a silvery half-moon, and Eliza's own words came back to her in an echo within her heart.

Find them in your dreams.

She'd meant the statement to fill her daughter with cozy wonder before drifting off to sleep, but now she wondered if there weren't a deeper resonance and if maybe, actually, the opposite was true—if dreams shouldn't stay in slumber and if the real power of them was in the waking.

Eliza gently shut Bea's door behind her.

Robert waited for her in the sitting room. He set his novel down on the side table and stood when she approached, eager to wrap her in a hug. His arms were warm, familiar, and predictable. He was strong, and she loved that about him too.

But she wouldn't tell him the fur-stole-gone-wrong story. He wouldn't appreciate the humor. And maybe that was okay. Maybe happily ever afters didn't only come from fairy tales but also from the day in and day outs, and *maybe* someday she could grow to love him as much as he loved her.

"How was your time with Susan?" he asked, kissing the tip of her nose so it tickled.

"Perfectly pleasant," she said.

1941

The men on the radio said a war with Germany would solve the Depression. Depression—such an interesting word choice. A word Eliza couldn't help but feel downplayed the significance of what she had seen, of what she had felt. People starving, homeless, jumping trains with the hope the next stop may provide a meal.

Through it all, Eliza had begun to paint again.

Well, maybe, actually *because* of it. Because she needed something beautiful in all this mess, and if she couldn't find it, she'd make it from her memories. From her mother's memories. From her grandmother's too. And she would help to build a better story for Charleston than the brokenness, than the trauma that so many people in its past still faced—whether from slavery and its systems, from poverty, or from despair.

From the moment rumors first began stirring that Americans might enter the war, Eliza knew Robert would find a way to be a part of it. Over these past ten years of their marriage, she had grown to know him—respect him and his quiet strength. The love they shared might not be the youthful fire she had with William, but it was still an altogether good thing.

She'd always marveled how birds or wind could carry unexpected seeds into broken-up ground, and in due time, they might turn into the most beautiful blooms if the weather cooperated. That's how she felt about her marriage to Robert. There was an unexpected grace that had developed between them, and she hoped she might someday pass that on to their daughter, Bea.

She never expected he wouldn't come home.

First came the letter telling her he had been injured. Then nothing. No word for weeks. Only the sleepless nights and the brave smiles for her daughter's sake and the hidden ways she sneaked off to the pantry, busied herself making tea so no one would hear her weep.

Strange how she never pictured herself the type of person to weep alone in the pantry. But perhaps no one ever pictures themself in these ways; they simply become them, with hope they may someday grow beautiful blooms from the unexpected soil in which they landed.

Such was the state of things when three knocks sounded against her door. Bea was off with a friend, collecting books and blankets for soldiers. Eliza's father had gone to the grocery.

Eliza was left alone to answer. She opened the door to discover a boy who couldn't be much more than Bea's age wearing a Western Union courier's uniform and leaning his bicycle up against the porch. He handed Eliza the standard yellow envelope. The envelope she'd known was coming and yet had not, until this very moment, the audacity to actually receive.

"Thank you." Eliza took the envelope, her blood pumping so fast she thought she might faint. Everyone knew what a yellow envelope meant.

"You're welcome, ma'am." The boy straightened his cap and, wearing suit and tie, climbed back on his bicycle, and all Eliza could think was where was that boy's mother and why was he working a grown man's job? But she knew. She knew why. Because the men were gone and many of the women too. Because the men were dying and leaving spaces all over this city, reminders how they were needed not only overseas but also in their homes. In their jobs. In their families.

She twisted the crystal door handle until she heard the click, then leaned back against it. She watched the sunlight stream through the stained-glass archway beyond the entry, the one Robert had patterned after her old house. Light sent a chorus of color through each one of the broken pieces so that they glowed like little rainbows everywhere, like the earth does after an especially hard rain.

And the light and the color made her want to paint, but she couldn't seem to get up from the doorway. She couldn't seem to stand or even to stop shaking. And when she finally made her trembling fingers open the telegraph, she couldn't seem to make out the words.

She didn't know how long she sat like that against the doorway, but it must have been hours, because when she finally came to, daylight had nearly turned to darkness as Bea's singing voice from the piazza outside roused her and her father's voice did too.

"Eliza," he said. "Why have you locked the door? Are you okay?"

No.

No, she was not. Robert was dead. Had probably been dead for weeks, only they couldn't find the body to bring back for burial, which meant Eliza had to mark an empty grave, an empty grief. She had known when he left this could happen, but she hadn't imagined it actually would.

And so in shock she'd locked the door. She'd locked it because she couldn't let anything else in.

1946

It took twenty years, but Dorothy Legg really did paint that house on East Bay Street pastel pink. And the others liked it so much, they painted their adjoining homes pastel too. Who would have thought all those years ago that there really would be such a thing as a Rainbow Row?

On this particular night, Eliza had been invited to a party in the courtyard of one of these homes. Susan had saved the row. She had actually saved the row. And a whole lot of other places in Charleston as well, despite having to go at a snail's pace for the repairs and despite the economic depression and despite everything up against her. Together, the group of them had created an image of Charleston that made folks want to visit in lieu of expensive trips to Europe. And as more visitors came, so came more money. As more money came, more of the city was restored, and over time it began to resemble the Charleston Eliza had once imagined as a little girl: the art became so beautiful that the real thing grew into its colors.

Her daughter, Bea, was at home on a telephone call with a boy from Edisto, the girl's grandfather within earshot should he be needed. So Eliza walked the path to East Bay Street that summer evening alone, wearing a scoop-neck black dress and her hair in Victory Rolls so that she felt like a dark-haired Ingrid Bergman in that new movie *Notorious.*

Peggy Louise, the host of the gathering and Eliza's friend from the Preservation Society meetings, greeted her with a warm smile as Eliza nearly skipped toward the doorway. "Welcome, my dear." She gestured toward the entry. "You're looking stunning tonight. So glad you could come." Then she took Eliza's arm to pull her closer and whispered, "There's someone I want you to meet."

Eliza stepped inside, turning her head. "Oh?" Peggy Louise, herself happily married, was perpetually taken by the hobby of matchmaking. "Reading *Emma* again, are you?"

"You know I love my Austen, and I will take that as a compliment." Peggy Louise held on to Eliza's arm and navigated her through the maze of people. Men in suits and women in dresses laughed and smoked and carried on as though the war had not taken anything from them years prior. Or maybe they were just pretending. Eliza did that sometimes too. But she always remembered her garden eventually, and how there was something oddly hopeful, oddly poetic about the harshest day of winter because it meant the worst was over and spring was coming.

She shook her head slightly, hoping to scatter the thoughts from her mind and just enjoy this charming evening. And it was charming.

Someone was playing "Boogie Woogie Bugle Boy" on the grand piano in the other room, and folks began dancing. One woman in a white dress held on to her hat as her partner spun her in what looked to Eliza like the Lindy Hop.

And she thought of William, and her heart swelled.

All these years later, she still thought of William.

Eliza sighed. Perhaps she needed to socialize more, aside from her regular meetings with the Preservation Society. She had clearly turned into a Scrooge, that an event so upbeat would render her so suddenly melancholy. She leaned closer to Peggy Louise so the woman could hear her speak. "Are you really taking me to meet a man?"

Peggy Louise looked her up and down as they continued meandering through the crowd, into an even busier room. "We can't let a dress like that go to waste, can we? Besides, it's time for you to get out and meet people. And by *people*, yes, I mean men. Handsome ones. You're still plenty young, you know, but you won't be that way forever."

Eliza rolled her eyes and grinned widely. "Thanks so much for that, Peggy."

Peggy Louise winked. "A woman needs a reminder every so often about these things. Those paints of yours may obey your every command, and I know you love the company of your canvases, but neither of those can replace a good kiss, now, can they?"

"I paint watercolor on paper, not canvas."

Peggy Louise stopped mid-step. "See? This is why you can't keep a man, despite all the ones I've sent your way. You're ornery."

Eliza raised her chin. "I'm not ornery." And she *could* keep a man if she wanted to. Problem was, she got bored with them. Inevitably, she'd remember how William had once made her feel, and maybe she was just chasing ghosts, but no other men lived up. And on the days she was *really* being honest, the truth was that Robert—God bless his soul—had never excited her or challenged her like her first love, and she did not want another marriage where she had to try so hard to pretend. She was faithful to Robert, of course she was, and if she'd had her way there would've been no war and she could've continued being faithful to him forever, in all the ways one remains true. But she didn't have her way, did she? So for now, she would enjoy her own company. It was far simpler that way and involved far less pretending.

Besides, there was no point in idealizing William and all he once meant to her. His wife had died, just like Robert did, only of tuberculosis two years ago. She probably caught it working for the Red Cross in the war, or at least that's what Eliza heard from her hairdresser.

All that to say, he could have come for Eliza. He could have come and at least explained, like he said he would all those years ago.

But he didn't.

And so now Eliza was here. Smiling at Peggy Louise, who maybe was right about her being ornery, and she didn't love that about herself, but life had sort of made her that way lately. She would work on it.

"Doll, you know I'm just poking fun, don't you? You know I think you're a catch for any man." Peggy Louise nudged her back to the present with her elbow.

"Of course, Peggy." Eliza patted her Victory Rolls, making sure no strands of hair had escaped her careful twirl. "Tell me more about this guy."

Peggy led her farther still through the crowd, and the piano music grew louder as the two of them stepped past more dancers. Apparently this was the dancing room. Peggy leaned closer toward Eliza's ear. "He's handsome, a widower, and he's got a wit that's only matched by yours. I think the two of you would hit it off with sparks."

Eliza tried not to audibly sigh. She did, after all, appreciate a man with a good wit about him. But she really didn't want to talk with him. At some point, she'd simply lost the nerve to try.

Still, Peggy Louise had been extraordinarily kind and Eliza *had* worn the Ingrid Bergman dress, so there was that. She should probably try and be nice to the guy, for Peggy's sake if nothing else.

"All right. Where is this attractive, exceedingly witty man?" Eliza scanned the room, the men smoking cigarettes, and the women laughing with glee as though they'd never heard jokes before, and the beautiful vases full of flowers she assumed Peggy had cut from her own garden.

"At the piano." Peggy Louise wiggled her eyebrows as though proud of herself for keeping this little tidbit to herself.

Eliza fussed with the pearls around her neck and rubbed her lips together to ensure an even spread of color, which was a shade deeper than the red she'd worn during the war.

The pianist ended the song and began another as Eliza's gaze moved toward him, and she wasn't sure which registered her recognition first, his face or the notes of the song. It all sort of captured her, body and heart, in one sweeping moment so that the room blurred all around her and she couldn't think but only feel the rise and fall of her heart, the rise and fall of her breath, the rise and fall of the song.

"I forget the name of this one," Peggy Louise said in Eliza's ear. "Though I've heard he plays it at every party he attends. Susan told me it once had lyrics too, but for whatever reason he doesn't sing those anymore. Beautiful still. He's quite a remarkable talent."

"*It's called 'My Dear Eliza,'*" she wanted to reply, but of course Peggy Louise wouldn't understand, and explaining was the last thing she wanted to do right now.

Eliza couldn't pull her attention from him any easier than she'd been able to pull her affections, and as his fingers nimbly traveled over the notes she felt as though she'd gone back in time.

She was the girl in the garden again.

She was falling in love with the man who wrote her letters, the man her aunt had forbidden, the man who would inspire a thousand paintings though none of them compared to what she felt the night she sat on the wall between their houses and he told her he wanted to marry her, and he played this very song.

Eliza remained entranced this way as the world around them swirled and the dancers spun and the merry couples laughed, simply staring at William and watching him and imagining what might have been had promises not been broken, had he never left.

He finished the song, after what felt like a lifetime and a blink all at once, and before Eliza could think through what was happening, Peggy Louise was leading her toward the piano and it was too late, far too late to go back now.

William ended the song with a flourish and looked up at her. He met her gaze, that same fire still in his eyes. Did he know how he held her there, how he held her still?

"Eliza."

She imagined he'd whispered her name, but no, that couldn't be right because the party here was roaring about them even though she paid it no mind. Yet it felt like a whisper, for it was so gentle, and Eliza wasn't sure exactly what she might do next.

"Hello." The word was taffy on her lips, sweet and sticking within the space between them. She wanted to say so many things to him. To tell him she still cared for him and always would, to rage at him, perhaps, and to ask him why. Where was the silver and what had he done with it? Now was her chance. And yet in such a twist, *hello* seemed to be the only word she could get out.

Eliza shook her head and looked at Peggy Louise before she could cry. "I'm sorry," she mumbled, or at least she thought she said it out loud. Then she hurried down the sidewalk and down the cobblestone, down all the paths that led her back.

She could have sworn she heard someone calling out.

"Eliza, Eliza, Eliza—hold on."

But she never looked back. She was too scared what ghost she might find chasing her into the night.

TWENTY-NINE

Modern Day

Declan's father sat behind his mahogany desk, his hand on the computer mouse and books sprawled out in front of him. He looked up when Declan opened the office door.

"Excellent. You got my memo."

Declan stepped inside.

"Be sure you shut the door." His father peered behind him as if checking that no one else was listening.

Declan sat in the chair, the huge antique one that sat low to the ground and always made him feel small. "What's going on?"

His father folded both his hands and rested them on one of the large books. "I've made a breakthrough."

"A breakthrough?"

"With Lucy."

Declan crossed his suede loafer over his left knee, trying to get comfortable, but his foot wouldn't stop shaking. He covered it with his hand to stop it before his father noticed. "She's agreed to sell you the house?"

His father cawed. "I said a breakthrough, Declan, not a miracle."

"So what exactly have you stumbled across?"

"As you know, I've been racking my brain trying to think of a strategy since Lucy isn't interested in the typical motivators we offer in these situations."

"Meaning money."

Declan's father glared. "Financial opportunities are only one of several motivators, Declan."

"Financial opportunities? Is that what we're calling it now when we try to buy out someone's family history?"

"Do you or do you not wish to be a part of this business, young man? Because I would caution you to watch your tone."

Declan was about one push away from leaving the family business after that dinner with Lucy last night. Surely she wouldn't have rushed home so quickly had his loyalties not been divided.

And she only knew the half of it. If she ever found out how his father had spoken of her family, and the real reason she didn't get that job . . . he nearly groaned just thinking about it. He was fed up. And he'd decided it was time to choose a side.

He chose Lucy's.

So whatever his father was about to say, it had better be good.

His father cleared his throat, drawing Declan's attention back to him. "Last night, as I was lying in bed and thinking—you know my insomnia—it hit me. I've been going about this thing all wrong." A smile slid up his lips, the kind of smile that made Declan cringe, like that snake in *The Jungle Book* who was always up to something. "I need to play by her rules. Beat her at her own game, so to speak."

Declan shifted in the expensive chair. It was hard against his back. "What's that supposed to mean?"

"I found a clause in the documents these historical groups put out. All repairs of homes in our zone must adhere to certain regulations to maintain the integrity of the properties." His smile widened. "Ironically, we can thank Lucy's great-grandmother for this surprising turn of events, because she was one of the initial forces who pushed for these sorts of laws."

"What do you mean—*regulations*?" Declan leaned forward.

"Repairs must be consistent with period-specific materials. So the door handles need to be taken from other old houses, the doors themselves should be authentic, and so on. But the real kicker is the bricks. You know all those bricks Lucy replaced on the side of the house and the chimney?"

"Yeah?" Declan rested his hand against his forehead. He could feel a headache coming.

"She bought cheap ones. I presume that's all she could afford. If I told you how much the appropriate bricks would cost, or at the very least, their likeness, you would fall out of that chair, Declan."

"I don't understand." Declan shook his head. "She's already had the brickwork done, right?"

"Exactly." His father leaned back in his orthopedic chair, bumping the fake palmetto behind him. "So we put in a complaint and insist she rework it to period standards."

Declan's stomach sank. "There's no way she could afford to do that."

His father opened his palms. "And therein lies the answer to our troubles."

Declan swallowed. Hard. "Dad, I can't let you do it."

His father stared back, not expecting to be questioned. "Excuse me? You will not *let* me? I was unaware I was asking your permission, son." His cheeks began to redden. "Besides, it's already done. The grievance has been filed, and I suspect she'll be forced to sell to us within a week."

Declan stood.

That was it. He'd had enough.

"I will not sit idly by any longer while you concoct these truly awful plans to destroy the woman I love. You're acting like a monstrous fool."

His father crossed his arms over his chest, continuing to lean back in his chair. "Well, look who's suddenly become the hero."

Declan took a deep breath to calm his rage.

"Don't you realize your princess doesn't need saving, Declan? She's playing you, and it's painfully obvious to everyone watching. She wants that house just as much as I want that silver, and she'll stop at nothing to keep it, even if that means wooing you. Which is obviously working, so I have to give her credit for that much."

"Do you hear yourself right now?"

His father's chest heaved with quick breaths.

"Why do you even care so much, Dad? Why can't you just let this go?"

Robert Pinckney grabbed the edge of his desk with both hands and leaned forward. Something wasn't right about his eyes.

"Because I need to be sure . . ." He visibly swallowed. "The thief doesn't come after you and your mother if something happens to me. . . ."

Declan hurried over to the desk. "What's that supposed to mean?"

"I've kept a secret. . . ." He struggled for breath. "Health . . . problems."

His face reddened even more as he grabbed his chest.

"Dad?"

As his father slumped down, Declan knelt by his side. "Dad!" He put his ear to his father's chest, relieved to hear him still breathing. "You got too worked up. Take some deep breaths."

But his father's eyes looked past him, and his breaths were shallow now.

"My heart," he whispered, struggling.

"You're going to be all right, Dad." Declan tried to sound assuring. But as he rushed out of the office, panic pulsed through his veins.

"Help!" he yelled. "My father's having a heart attack! Someone call 911!" Fumbling with his phone, he was too panicked to push the buttons.

Fear had left him helpless.

Lucy stood in front of *The Silver Tree* and studied it for what must've been the thousandth time. Still, she could see nothing in the way of a clue about the silver.

In the piece, light rain caused fog to roll about as it hit what Lucy imagined to be hot ground. Sunlight lit the branches with a glow. Bluebirds dotted the landscape, and she smiled when she noticed them, having a new appreciation for these sorts of details now that she knew the artist was her own great-grandmother and that she too had seen the birds—or at least their ancestors.

Two figures held on to one another beneath the tree, and though the watercolor blurred their forms, Lucy imagined them dancing and thought of Declan.

She stared at the painting and swallowed hard.

Every time that almost-kiss came to mind, her heart fluttered as a heap of leaves in autumn. And every time, she chided herself for the feelings that had grown for him. She never should've indulged them. But if that passion were really deceitful, why did it feel so very honest? Why did it feel more was spoken in that moment than all the words they'd ever exchanged?

Why did it seem that the Declan from the wedding was the Declan she'd seen on Edisto, and why did she so readily forget the conversation she'd overheard with his father?

Lucy sighed. She tucked her hands into the pockets of her skirt and looked at the artwork once more. She had to be missing something. The painting certainly resembled the sprawling oak tree on her property, the one by the carriage house, but all oak trees looked similar, did they not?

Perhaps this whole thing was nothing but a treasure hunt and there was no silver at all. Was that diary entry the sole clue Declan's family was using to guide them? Did they not have any other context? And who was to say the silver hadn't already been found?

Any number of things could have happened to it between then

and now. Yet still, the prospect of locating the silver was Lucy's hope for saving Eliza's home. If she could find it and sell it, she would have enough money to keep the property and hire someone for all the increasingly costly repairs that needed to be done.

So she looked back up at the painting and tried to examine it with fresh eyes.

She was studying the pattern of the ground, trying to make something from the wash of brown and green hues, when she heard heels clattering against the tile floor.

A woman from the ticket desk rushed into the room.

"Where's Anna?" She was terribly out of breath.

Lucy glanced behind her shoulder, toward the small hallway. "Last I saw, she was in her office just past that doorway." She pointed.

The woman hurried as fast as her heels would take her, nearly tripping. She threw open the door.

Lucy frowned. Something was wrong.

Declan's mother had become a dear friend, and although she hadn't gotten a chance to mention it yet, Lucy suspected Anna might've known all along that the artist Eliza and her great-grandmother Eliza were one and the same.

Lucy left the painting and followed the desk clerk. She caught herself against the wall as the woman stopped suddenly.

Anna turned toward the open door, wide-eyed. "Whatever is the matter?"

"Ma'am, your husband had a heart attack. You need to come now."

Anna grabbed her purse and ran. Lucy was close behind.

THIRTY

As twilight fell, Lucy balanced the warm Pyrex in one arm and reached for the Pinckneys' front doorbell with the other. Beth had helped her make the dish. The potted flowers she'd hid behind just weeks ago brushed against her legs, and she tugged the hem of her skirt to keep the stems from scratching her.

Declan opened the door. She hadn't seen him since the first night at the hospital. She'd wanted to give them time to process everything that had happened.

He wore a screen-printed T-shirt and jeans that were thread-bare. He looked as if he hadn't shaved in days, and his scruff was approaching beard status.

"Good to see you." Declan ran one hand through the wavy ends of his hair and gestured her inside with the other.

She stepped in and hugged him from the side, but she was still holding the Pyrex, and it was awkward. Did Declan feel it too?

A grand chandelier draped above them in the foyer.

"How are you doing?" She moved the warm dish from one arm to the other. "I'm sorry. That's probably the wrong question."

Declan crossed his arms over his chest. He looked more tan than she remembered.

"We're holding up." He hesitated, looking into her eyes. "What am I saying? We're miserable."

She reached for his arm. "I'm so sorry."

"Thank you." He sighed. "We're getting through."

"How is he doing? Any updates?"

Declan's eyes were bloodshot. "I'm not sure the last you heard, so I'll start from the beginning." He nodded toward the living area. "Let's sit down first, and I'll take that dish from you."

"Be careful. It's warm." She transferred it to his arms, and their hands brushed. She looked away, toward the fancy sofa in the other room. "I'll go ahead and sit down."

"Please do." He disappeared behind the corner. Stacks of laundry littered the floor of the living room, and several plates were stacked up on a glass coffee table. Sunflowers dropped dry petals from their crystal vase.

Lucy set her purse on the floor and sat as Declan entered the room.

He picked up a throw pillow and hugged it to his chest as he slouched on the couch beside her. "Forgive the mess."

"You know I don't care." She tucked her foot behind her ankle. "So what happened?"

He clutched the pillow. "We were arguing, and he just started turning red and having trouble breathing. He grabbed at his heart and slumped over, and that's when I knew." Declan looked off toward the French doors leading to their garden. "Thankfully, someone at the office had aspirin that we gave him right away. The paramedics said that made a huge difference." Declan shook his head. "He got quick treatment for the heart attack, but the clots led to a stroke a couple days later."

Lucy's eyes widened. "I didn't know that."

"Yeah, it was pretty awful. Now his speech is really slurred, and they don't know how well he will recover. They're optimistic, and he's got the best doctors, but still . . ."

"Declan, I'm so sorry."

He turned to look at her. "I appreciate that. I really do."

"So, is your dad close to being discharged soon? What are the next steps?"

Declan shook his head. "No, he's going to need a stent put in, and they're planning to do that tomorrow. And after the morning's surgery, I'll have to return to work, because in his current state, Dad can't run the company." He rubbed his palm with his thumb. "Which means it falls to yours truly."

"Wow." Lucy blinked. "That's got to be overwhelming."

"I'm taking it one step at a time." He straightened the hem of his T-shirt and stood. "Nice weather today. Want to sit in the garden and get out of this stuffy room?"

"Sure."

He reached out his hand and helped her from the sofa. The touch did a number on her heart. "Hey, I've been wanting to tell you thanks for all you've done at the museum so my mom can stay at the hospital." He hesitated. "She really trusts you to run things, and let's just say she doesn't feel that way about everyone."

Lucy laughed and stepped through the French door he held open. Outside, rows of hydrangeas bloomed along the walkway, and garden stones were lined with grass cover. They sat together on an iron bench and looked out at the flowers by the light of the lanterns hanging from the courtyard. "Well, I understand her passion," she said. "Both the artworks as well as the customers need to be treated with a particular kind of care. Not everyone can see that, nor appreciate the need. But for a museum to work well, the two must operate in tandem."

So many stars twinkled from above, Lucy's neck ached when she tried to see them all.

"You should hear how she speaks about you. Yesterday, she was telling me your exhibit is almost complete, and she was nearly gushing." He smiled.

"Yeah, it's almost done." She bit her lip. *And I still haven't found a full-time job or the silver.*

All the so-called clues had turned out to be dead ends, and she needed to discover something quickly if she was going to keep putting the development company off. Not to mention, her temporary job at the museum would soon be over too. She hated to admit it, but she may be forced to consider selling if she couldn't find a better source of income. The chimney repairs had taken out the last of her savings. She'd really thought she would have a full-time job by now.

A mixture of emotions flooded her. On the one hand, she had loved working with Eliza's art, and she couldn't imagine having the same level of investment in other art pieces. But on the other, she couldn't live in this limbo forever. Something had to give.

Declan's voice broke through her rambling thoughts. "Thanks for bringing dinner." It seemed to be a genuine expression of appreciation rather than a casual suggestion she leave.

"You're welcome. The dish is a casserole your mom likes. Ms. Beth's recipe."

Declan tapped against the bench where they sat. A half grin slipped up his lips. "Oh, good old Beth. She is always giving me grief about whatever development project I'm working on in any particular week. I see her often in my delightful conversations with the Preservation Society."

Lucy chuckled.

"I assume she's told you as much," he added.

"Oh, she's told me, all right." Lucy scratched the back of her neck and returned his grin with her own. A long moment followed. Crickets chirped from the brush behind Declan.

He reached his arm up, his fingers grazing her shoulder. "I've missed you," he murmured.

His words sent her heart into a flurry. She swallowed.

Though she'd had plenty of time to process, she was feeling more confused than ever. His father's intentions to acquire her house were ever clear, and yet her attraction to Declan was never stronger.

With her job at the museum drawing to a close, the stakes of her decisions seemed higher than ever. But when she looked into his eyes, she knew she was falling for him.

And falling hard.

It took all of Declan's willpower not to run his fingers through Lucy's hair.

But she was so hard to read. He had really thought something romantic was developing between them after their time on Edisto, and the wedding, then that dinner at his house. But maybe he was just caught up in the allure of uncovering William and Eliza's love story. One minute, Lucy seemed interested, and the next, she was acting . . . strange. Even aloof.

At first, he'd just assumed she was giving him space after the emergency with his father. He was certainly in no shape for visitors initially. But as the days went on, he couldn't help but think about Lucy.

His father would be appalled.

But his mother, on the other hand, would be thrilled. Which terrified him in an entirely different way. Because when had his mother's advice ever been wrong?

The problem now was whether Lucy shared any interest in him. Regardless, he kept dreaming of her like a heartsick teenager.

Had she avoided him because she thought so little of his family? Not that he could blame her, after all he'd done. After all his father had done. And she didn't even know the half of it.

Oh, how the thought of his father plagued him.

The sight of his larger-than-life father in a hospital gown had been nearly too much to take. He'd tried to be brave for his mother and act as though he were confident his father would make a full recovery.

But the truth was, every night since that day, he'd awakened from nightmares. That is, if he could get any sleep. He saw his father's face turning red all over again. The man struggling to breathe.

His mother had sensed it was all taking a toll on him, and she was worried. But he certainly couldn't talk to her about how he was feeling, or the argument with his father that might've caused this whole thing. She had enough to deal with as it was. Her husband was lying in a hospital bed, his speech hardly understandable.

He had never seen his father so humbled, so human.

How many times had he wished the man would come down from his pedestal and show genuine emotion, even empathy? Yet, seeing his father so weak was Declan's undoing. And he had no idea how he was going to run the company. Suddenly all his father's advice—even the condescension—felt so wanted, so needed. His father had been right. Declan was in no shape to lead things. Why, he was scarcely able to think straight.

The employees would see straight through him. They'd all vie for his position or leave to work for someone more competent. His father was authoritative in his leadership. And Declan . . . well, Declan wasn't.

He couldn't believe this was happening.

This was never the plan for the business.

This was never the plan for his life.

"Declan?" Lucy's voice was soft and pulled his attention away from the trauma. "Are you okay? You seem lost in your thoughts."

He rolled a small stick back and forth under his shoe. "Yeah, I guess I just keep reliving it, you know?"

"Reliving what? The heart attack?"

He nodded. "I can't help thinking it was my fault. I mean, we were arguing, and I said some pretty harsh things. I keep wondering . . ."

Declan looked up at the night sky as the full moon cast a spotlight into the evening.

Lord, what have I done? Can all these broken places be restored? Are you a God of broken people? Broken things?

The stars seemed to twinkle from the sky, and he studied them, waiting for answers.

"Declan." Lucy reached up to rest her hand on his arm. The gesture brought comfort yet stirred him to want her closer. "I don't know what was said, but I'm confident your father wouldn't want you having those thoughts."

"I called him a fool." He closed his eyes and shook his head. "Lucy, I called my own father a fool."

She waited for him to open his eyes before responding. "I'm sure he knows you didn't mean it."

"But that's the thing." He swallowed hard. "I did mean it."

Lucy held tighter to his arm. "You know something I've long admired about your relationships with both your mother and father? The three of you fight things out. And maybe it gets ugly. But you don't leave. You're faithful to your family." She shifted on the bench and straightened her sweater.

A stray strand of hair fell onto her forehead, and he considered brushing it away. "I understand your regret," she said. "But your father loves you. He loved you then, and he loves you now. He's just a very passionate man. I'm sure he said things he would like to take back too. He wouldn't want you to feel responsible for what happened. You were just doing what you guys always do. Working through it."

Declan shoved his free hand into the pocket of his jeans. "This was different. I lost my temper."

"You're human. It happens."

Her hair cascaded down her shoulders in natural waves, and Declan wanted to pull her to him right then and tell her the truth—he was in love with her. But he was wearing yesterday's T-shirt, he hadn't slept a wink, and he wasn't confident in his ability to articulate a coherent thought right now, much less a confession of his feelings. So he waited. He didn't want to, but he waited.

Together, they sat and looked at the stars, and Declan wondered if she was wishing as much as he. After a while, she stood. She brushed her skirt with her hands. "It's getting late. I'd better get going."

"I'll walk you out." He started toward the courtyard gate.

"Oh, there's no need." She waved as though dismissing the idea. "I can find my way."

They stood inches from each other, and Declan watched her, trying to read any signals she may be sending. Maybe it was the fatigue, but he couldn't make out anything. He didn't want to pressure her or embarrass himself. But oh, how he wanted to kiss her. After several moments, he broke the silence.

"Well, uh—thanks again for the casserole."

"My pleasure." She looked up at him, waiting.

"I guess I'll see you."

"I'll see you." She nodded, hesitating. "I'll be spending a lot of time outside tomorrow, photographing my oak tree and the carriage house beside it. I need one more picture to display with the final painting. So if you need anything . . ."

"I'll let you know." He stood there, his hand on the gate, his eyes full of wanting. Could she see it? He was typically confident around women and wasn't sure what to do with this newfound sense of nerves.

"Well . . . I'll see you. Good night, then."

She was repeating herself. She was nervous too.

This had to bode well.

He smiled, and his shirt caught in the evening breeze. "Good night."

She raised her hand in a wave, and he returned the gesture.

When he turned back toward the house, it took every ounce of his determination not to run after her down the street. He was ready to tell her everything.

THIRTY-ONE

1946

Eliza's heart had been fluttering like hummingbird wings since the party last night. Peggy Louise had tried to phone her to get an explanation—Bea took the message—but Eliza didn't trust herself to make any sense of it right now, let alone to explain the whole of it to somebody else.

She'd managed to hide her preoccupation with last night's events from both Bea and her father—or at least so she assumed, though they were acting rather odd themselves. She didn't know why the sight of William Pinckney had made her so *very* fluttery when if anything, shouldn't it make her sad?

Yet she fetched the post from the porch with an unusual pep in her step. She opened up the tin box affixed to the wall beside the door, not really expecting any mail today, when her fingers wrapped around something akin to the size of a letter, and all the fluttering came to a sudden stop.

Quickly, Eliza pulled the letter from the mailbox, flipping it front and back as her eyes scanned the words.

She recognized his handwriting immediately.

My dear Eliza,
*   I owe you an explanation. Should we be frank, I owe you far*

more than that. I've been a fool to keep this to myself so long, but you never returned my last letter, and I was afraid if I showed up at your door you wouldn't have me inside. Perhaps you wouldn't have. Perhaps I was right in that, but still, I should have tried.

When I saw you last night, I became quite suddenly undone. Forgive my rash decision to write you now. I hope I won't regret that as well, for I certainly have no wish to cause you any upheaval or harm. But with my son now moved out, I have the house alone to myself and my thoughts—and I find you often occupy them. So much more now, after last night and seeing you in that dress.

Surely when you heard the song, you must have known. The truth is, I still love you, Eliza. I would really like to offer you a sincere apology. Come to my house. It's 5 Zig Zag Alley, just off Atlantic Street. I'll be waiting with an explanation for you this afternoon in the garden. On the contrary, if you choose not to come, I will understand why and will not trouble you again.

Yours still,
William

Eliza closed her eyes and pressed the letter first to her lips, then to her heart. How suddenly the world had shifted. For so long, she had felt like a broken longhand in a clock, tick-tick-ticking but never reaching the top. And now with this swift tap, she could keep step again. Time had been restored to her.

The fragrance of the gardenias along the porch carried on the breeze. The blooms were always sweetest from freshly opened buds. But they had to fall, they had to change, for the roots to grow. So that next season, more buds would open, and the fragrance would spread even farther.

Gardenias. She had never painted gardenias before.

But they bloomed all at once as she'd never noticed them blooming years prior, and the fragrance was so alluring that the smell of it matched the delicate strokes of her smallest paintbrush, and it was the first of May and the first of so many other things, she was sure.

She would paint them tonight, by moonlight, after she returned from William's.

Eliza tucked the letter into her pocket, not yet ready for anyone else to see, and stepped inside from the porch.

Her father and daughter were standing side by side in the entry, alternatively looking at one another and then at her.

Instinctually, Eliza slid her hands into the pockets of her skirt so she could hold on to the hidden letter. "What's going on? Why do the two of you look so demure?"

Bea clutched her hands together and rolled back and forth from the heels of her shoes to her toes. Heels, toes, heels, toes, as if somewhere in this back-and-forth movement Eliza was supposed to understand what was being said.

"You may as well come out with it." Eliza's father put a protective hand on Bea's shoulder. She looked up at him as if searching for confirmation.

Eliza cleared her throat, her pitter-pattering heart suddenly sobered by mothering duty. "Bea?" She couldn't imagine what her daughter—her very graceful, not-at-all-rebellious daughter— needed to explain.

Bea wrung her hands, looked down at them, then looked back up at Eliza. "Donald proposed to me, and I"—she glanced at her grandfather, who nodded once—"I've accepted, if you'll allow it. I know we're young, but girls my age marry all the time. He's just gotten a promotion where he'll earn enough to provide a modest rent, so you needn't worry about that, and you're always saying I've got a good head on my shoulders like my father had, and anyway, surely you don't object?"

Eliza stared at her. She kept blinking, but all she could see was wide-eyed Bea as a little girl, and nothing seemed to jolt her back into the present moment—a moment that, it would merit adding, Eliza's father appeared not at all surprised by.

"Did you know about this?" Eliza asked him.

"Yes." He wiped his hand over his mouth and beard. "The boy asked my permission last week."

Outrage seized Eliza. "He asked—"

"Mother, don't be angry with Donald. He's old-fashioned that way and wanted to ask the man of the house. It's an honor thing. You know we both care about your blessing as well."

Not enough to ask for it, apparently.

Oh, precious Bea. Was she sure? Eliza thought back to the heartbreak she'd experienced after William left, how she never really recovered. Did she want to subject her sweet daughter to that sort of fragmentation? And yet conversely, she thought of William's letter in her pocket, and the way her heart hovered midair at its arrival, and she knew she couldn't prohibit Bea from that sort of joy.

"Just so we are clear, I will need to speak with him about this modest rent payment to which you refer. Can't have my girl living without sufficient funds for Girl Scout cookies."

Bea rushed over to her mother in a fit of happiness, near squeezing the life out of her and squealing too. Eliza grinned, squeezing her in return, and though it was senseless, the two of them began bouncing up and down like two happy little bunnies at the onset of spring.

When the moment had passed, Eliza slid her hands back into her pockets, gently tracing her fingers along the letter she had hidden there. Her heart pulled two ways, tugged at once by her past and by her future, so hard she was tired from the strain.

In the most basic terms, she wanted nothing more than to scurry away to William's house this afternoon. To hear his explanation, accept his apology, and kiss him square on the lips. She'd waited long enough, hadn't she?

But how would she slip away with Bea nearly floating with excitement, and really, was that even a good decision? What made now the right *now* when, for years, William hadn't been ready?

Eliza excused herself and hurried up the stairs, opening her drawer and setting the letter inside with the others. Then she took William's ring and held it up as the sunlight streamed through the window, and a prism of colors as rich as her garden hit the floor with a promise so great it nearly stole her breath away.

William tightened the knot of his tie using the mirror by the back door as a guide, straightened his suspenders, and then snapped a little rhythm with both hands before skipping down the porch steps into his yard.

His garden was hardly Eliza's, but it was hard finding anything in Charleston that wasn't beautiful in May.

Surely by now she had received his letter.

He hesitated.

This morning, ferrying a letter over to her house like some kind of courier had seemed like a grand, romantic gesture, but now, he felt nearly sick at the thought. Did he do the right thing by reaching out? Or should he have left well enough alone? At some point in his life, he would have to stop pursuing her, wouldn't he? But he had tried that before and had never managed to keep his fondness for her far from his heart. When he married Mary, he had purposely avoided streets and walking patterns he knew Eliza would be taking, in hopes he might forget about her. And that worked for a while—he did love and faithfully respect his wife, but after he mourned her, the forgetting stopped, and the memories of Eliza returned with a vengeance. For the memory of her was a song, the most beautiful song in his life.

Surely enough time had passed by now, enough life too, that he'd paid his dues to his father. Surely this might be their second chance to live the life they could have started nearly two decades prior had his own father not blackmailed him with Eliza's safety.

William sat on the wrought-iron bench beside the carefully edged shrubs of his garden and waited, practicing what he might say when Eliza came.

But afternoon turned to twilight. And oh so slowly, darkness fell. With it came the moon, and the night breeze made him shiver.

William never moved from that bench.

She wasn't coming.

She must not love him anymore. Perhaps she never had.

He was a fool to imagine she would forgive him after the way he left her. After all this time.

He had left the ring, of course, but how was she to know the sincerity of that gesture beyond a symbol of broken promises? How was she to know the sacrifices he had made on her behalf? She wouldn't. And he wouldn't blame her.

William was making shapes out of the stars when he heard the iron gate creak open. By the light of the moon, he turned, and there she was, glowing like some kind of angel.

"Eliza."

"William." She stepped closer. The hem of her fancy coat seemed to float behind her. She'd melted him then, and she melted him now.

But she stopped short.

"You left me."

Those three words hollowed him. Wrecked him from the inside out.

"*I'm so sorry*," he wanted to say, but it wouldn't be sufficient. Nothing would.

"You made me promises you didn't keep. You *forged* my paintings." She crossed her arms over her chest.

William's mind raced. He knew this would be difficult. He knew they needed to have this conversation and he had *longed* to have this conversation, but now that the time had come . . . well, he couldn't think straight.

He rubbed his face with his hands. "I know." It was all he could manage to say. "I did it for my sister, Hannah. She had a baby at the time and needed the money. . . ."

"So you thought imitating my *own* creative work was the solution? I put my heart into those pieces!" Her voice rose.

"Of course it wasn't the solution! That poor decision cost me everything."

Eliza shook her head. "I was a fool to ever let you in."

"A fool? What are you saying?"

Eliza hesitated, looking long and straight into his eyes. "I'm saying I loved you, William, as I've never loved anyone else in my life."

William swallowed past the lump in his throat, his hands trembling. He braved a step closer. "Do you still love me?" The words carried a boldness that betrayed his fear she might deny them.

Eliza lifted her thumb to her lips, saying nothing.

Passion pushed through his veins, and he couldn't betray it any longer. He took two steps closer. "Eliza?"

He was near her now, so near he could smell the floral fragrance of her shampoo.

His fingers dared to touch her hair, her shoulders, coming to rest on her arms, and she looked up at him, wild-eyed, as he wondered what she might say. But for this perfect moment, hope was suspended in his heart like a hot air balloon.

"Eliza," he whispered.

And that's when he saw it. She was wearing the ring.

His breath stopped as he reached for her hand. "Surely you don't think I left you of my own volition."

"What else was I to think?" Her gaze at him was unwavering.

"My dear Eliza," he said, his heart quickening. "My father had plans to come after you for your silver and your paintings. He was going to tell everyone about the forgeries and ruin your career. The only way to protect you was to leave. He said he would relent if I left and followed his bidding."

William moved toward a bench under an old oak tree. Eliza followed. He removed his hat and smoothed his hair from the part, stretching his arm along the top of the bench as he waited for her to settle in beside him.

She sat down and they looked at each other, their noses just inches away. And she captured him, enraptured him, with her nearness.

"Why did you marry him?" he asked her.

She rubbed her temples, shaking her head. "I didn't get your letters until it was too late. Either of them."

William sucked in air as though he'd been punched in the gut. He'd never considered the prospect she hadn't read his words. Panic and grief overwhelmed his senses until his ears rang.

He held on to her gaze. "You must've thought . . ."

"That you left me." She bit down on her bottom lip.

"Eliza, I would never—" He brushed a wisp of hair from her forehead behind her ear, and his fingers lingered there. His lips tingled, begging to kiss her.

He inched closer, so ready to pull her near, but first there was more he needed to say.

Eliza nodded, slowly. "I know. Well, now I do. . . . At the time, I was sure you'd abandoned me. I couldn't make sense of why." Pain seemed to tug at the little wrinkles around her eyes. "But I still don't understand one thing," she whispered. "You said you stole the silver . . . but if you've had it all this time, why didn't you give it to your father and end this?"

"Because I haven't had it all this time." William reached for her hand, running his fingertips over the ring. "It was your inheritance, so I gave it back to you."

Eliza frowned her berry-colored lips. "But I don't have it."

"Sure you do. You're wearing it, aren't you?"

Eliza gasped, her eyes widening. "The *ring*?"

"I thought I was being romantic." William shrugged. "Turning it into a promise." He set her hand down but didn't let go. His stomach floated with the anticipation of what could be. "I also thought it would keep my father and Cadigan away, but that's neither here nor there. . . ."

Eliza stared intently at the ring on her hand. "Like a silver tree," she murmured to herself. "You mean all this time, you loved me?"

"All this time." William didn't hesitate, for there was no hesitation within him.

"You once told me, William, that I see beauty everywhere." Eliza took off her shoes and brushed her feet against the grass. "And I have to confess to you, you were wrong." She looked at him, as the bluebirds landed in the tree. "I didn't see beauty in what became of us for the longest time."

He watched her earnestly, waiting for more.

She shifted toward him and rested her other hand on his own. "But I don't regret any of it, William. Not one moment of loving you. And even though I was heartbroken when you left and I didn't understand, I'd fallen in love—pure and wild and beautiful love—and really, having that just once is enough for life."

William dropped his hat to the ground. He leaned close, and he reached for her. And then, as if no time had passed, he swept his fingers through her hair and finally—finally—his lips found her own.

Eliza kissed him back, and she was that girl again, dancing.

And the moonlight became glitter, and the oak leaves, butterflies, as a night breeze rustled those leaves to the ground. And she kissed him as she never expected to kiss someone again, and she felt something then she never had.

The kiss flooded her soul with color, as pigment in a watercolor. And she felt alive. And when he ended the kiss, he still held her close, and he brushed her cheek with his thumb.

"Marry me, Eliza." The words were gentle, the hope sincere. William looked up at the tree branches above them. "I told you I'd come back for you." There was a merriment in his eyes that she'd forgotten, except for when she dreamed of him.

"You sure took your time." She gave him a half grin and crossed her legs at the knees. Her mind spun with possibilities. So much had passed, but so much was yet to come. Forget what might have been. Eliza determined she would focus on what they might become, and on giving her heart back to William.

Though, who was she kidding? Her heart had always been William's.

She looked up at him. He was as handsome now as he had ever been—more handsome, maybe—and vibrant color swept her heart like one perfect pigment blending with another on the page. "Yes," she said, nodding. "Absolutely, yes. Let's set a date."

"How does tomorrow sound?" William placed his hat back on his head, his grin widening.

"Like far too long."

He took her hand then, and she leaned against him, and though time had bruised them as it's prone to doing, it had also made them strong. She gently rested her head on his shoulder and felt his heart beating fast.

William stood and began humming the song he'd written for her. And together, they danced.

THIRTY-TWO

Modern Day

Lucy was on her hands and knees polishing the hardwood floors of the kitchen when the doorbell rang. She wore an antique handkerchief tied around her hair like a bandana, and she set the old polishing cloth down to get to the front door before the bell rang again.

She was making progress on the house, and it was finally beginning to resemble the home she imagined it'd been when Eliza lived here. The home she caught abstract glimpses of in the paintings.

But still, she needed a long-term solution—and a full-time income—if she was going to manage the upkeep.

Lucy pinched her cheeks for color and swept a stray piece of hair behind her ear. Declan had clearly accepted her subtle invitation to come over, and even though she knew she was supposed to hate him, her heart fluttered at the thought of seeing him again today.

She smiled as she opened the door. But instead of Declan, she found Ms. Beth standing there. Beth's face lacked any trace of makeup, and she wore a floral bathrobe over fuzzy plaid pajama pants.

As far as manners go, for a southern woman of Beth's age, wearing such an ensemble out the front door fell somewhere between refusing a grandmother's biscuit and serving party guests stale, unsweetened tea.

"You look as pale as a sheet," Lucy said.

"I guarantee, I feel paler."

"Mercy, come inside." Lucy opened the door wider and gestured with her hand. "Get comfortable, and I'll pour you a drink."

"I'm the one who should be pouring *you* a drink, I'm afraid." Beth sat down on the sofa and crossed her flip-flopped feet.

Lucy stopped on her way toward the kitchen and turned. "What's that supposed to mean?"

Ms. Beth looked down at her hands and picked at her fuchsia nail color—another bad habit reserved for only the direst circumstances. "Maybe you should go ahead and get the tea. In fact, I'll pour."

She followed Lucy into the kitchen and stepped around the newly polished part of the floor to pour water into an electric kettle.

Lucy tore open two bags of peach tea and put them inside teacups. She moved the canister of sugar and a bag of shortbread cookies to the table as her nerves heightened. She'd never seen Ms. Beth like this before.

She took a seat at the table, and Ms. Beth followed. "Tell me they didn't find the silver," Lucy said.

Ms. Beth poured the water into the cups, dunked some sugar into hers, and clinked her tiny spoon against the teacup. She took a slow sip. "They didn't find the silver."

Lucy breathed a deep sigh of relief. As long as the silver was still on her property, untouched, any other problem could be remedied. "Then why are you over here with a panicked look on your face, wearing a British garden bathrobe over your pajamas?"

Ms. Beth smirked. "Very funny." She stood to get an ice cube and then sat back down, dunking it into her steaming tea. "Because something has happened. Something very bad." She took a longer sip from her teacup.

Lucy leaned forward, her elbows against the table. "Well, you may as well tell me so I can get on with fixing whatever has gone wrong."

Ms. Beth looked up at the ceiling she'd recently helped Lucy repair and took a deep breath. "Oh, how do I say this?"

Lucy waited. She realized she was absentmindedly chipping her own grey nail polish. The bad habit must be catching.

Ms. Beth tapped her fingers against the 1920s table they'd found at an estate sale last week after a tip from Peter and Harper. "You know how you hired those repairmen to replace the bricks?"

Lucy straightened the handkerchief in her hair. "Yeah?"

"Well, I noticed immediately afterwards but I hadn't planned on saying anything. But apparently I wasn't the only one who spotted it. . . ."

"Spotted what, Ms. Beth?" Lucy shook her head. "I don't understand. Did I do something wrong?"

"Very wrong, I'm afraid. The bricks you used were not the right grade."

Lucy held her cup tightly. "The right grade? What does that mean?"

"It means that since the house is on a certain block, in a certain neighborhood, and was built at a certain time in history, all the repairs made to it must be consistent with the period. No one can see what you're doing inside, so you could say there's less accountability there. But the bricks . . ."

"The bricks were the cheapest I could find."

"I know."

"They were the only ones I could afford."

Ms. Beth bit her bottom lip. "I know that too."

"You're telling me I was expected to find bricks that were two hundred years old to make the repairs?"

Ms. Beth sighed and took another drink from her teacup. "Or their closest likeness."

Lucy shook her head. "I still don't understand. What am I supposed to do now?"

"Well, according to regulations, you're supposed to replace the bricks."

"I can't even imagine how much that would cost." Lucy took a sip of her own tea, as if the peach flavor could sweeten this bitter moment. All it did was scald her tongue with its heat.

"And you don't want to. Trust me when I say it's well out of your budget. Or mine, for that matter." She swirled her cup. "Otherwise, I'd buy them for you."

Lucy choked back the emotion caught in the back of her throat. Surely—surely—she wasn't going to come this far, only to lose Eliza's house on account of such a trivial thing? "And what happens if I don't do it?"

"Fines." Ms. Beth set her cup down on the table. "Fines that are also out of your budget."

She sat still and looked off at the rosemary plant growing up the window as she tried to make sense of everything. "Who would do this to me? And why? I mean, everyone knows I'm trying to restore Eliza's home to its integrity. It was in much worse shape before I arrived."

"Yes, of course. But no one complained then." Beth looked at her as if she was missing something. And then it hit her. Like a glass wall that you walk into full-speed because you're looking past it and don't want to acknowledge what's right in front of you.

Declan.

Pinckney.

Suddenly Lucy felt sick to her stomach and wished she'd opted for peppermint tea instead. Though truthfully, there wasn't enough peppermint tea in the world.

Ms. Beth reached out and took her hand like a mother would. "You're going to be okay, Lucy."

She knew her gaze was wild-eyed.

"You're going to be okay."

"But the house . . ." Lucy looked around her—at the floor she'd just polished, the grooves made by generations prior, and the stairwell just beyond them. Jasmine caught on the breeze at the open window, and the sun shone through the voile curtains, and she thought of Eliza. If Eliza could protect this property back then, could Lucy manage it now?

She still hadn't figured out who left her the house in the first place, or why they left the letter and ring. This home was Lucy's last link to that part of her own history.

Ms. Beth squeezed her hand so tightly it hurt. "Lucy, I don't know if we can save it from the Pinckneys."

"You've never said that before."

"I've never believed it before."

"What are they going to do? Cite me on some code violation only to tear up the place in search of the silver?"

"I don't know, sweetheart." Beth released her hand. "But I can promise you I will do everything in my power to keep it from happening. And you know what a promise from me means."

Lucy thought of Ms. Beth standing in front of demolition equipment several months ago to save a huge oak tree. Of all the efforts Beth took to fundraise for the museum. Of the patience and persistence Beth showed in her garden. Lucy smiled, even as she held back the tears that were forming.

"So you think I should just give up? Admit defeat?"

Ms. Beth looked her straight in the eyes. "Lucy, it's not defeat to admit you've exhausted all possibilities. Sometimes life prohibits opportunities. Giving up too early is defeat. Holding on too long is denial. But admitting it, at the proper time—that is maturity."

"Eliza never gave up on anything."

Ms. Beth reached for the bag of shortbread cookies. "She gave up on William Pinckney."

"No, she didn't. William broke her heart." Lucy frowned. "That's what everyone always told me."

"There may be more to their story than you think."

Seemed that was the Pinckney way.

Lucy took a cautious sip of her tea, but something didn't sit well with her, and it wasn't the shortbread cookies. She hesitated. "Beth?"

"Hmm?" She covered her mouth while she chewed.

"How do you know all this about William and Eliza's story?"

Beth used the dainty corners of a napkin to wipe cookie crumbs from her mouth. She reached out toward Lucy and covered Lucy's glittering, imitation-gem ring with her own wrinkled hand. "Lucy, I knew them a little better than I may have let on."

THIRTY-THREE

1946

Funny how a young woman spends so much of her youth day-dreaming about being a bride—hope chests and wedding dresses and all the little details.

Eliza never really gave much thought to the possibility of getting married a second time. She wore a dress of her own making, tea-length with an eyelet *V* shape at the back and plenty of volume in the skirt. She and William decided to marry under that old oak tree—the silver tree, as they called it—with her father holding the rings and with Bea as her maid of honor. They took their vows right beside the gardenias, which were wilder and purer and more abundant than any bouquet she could have imagined. When she closed her eyes, she could smell them now, seven months later. Now it was nearly January first, nearly a new year upon them.

Eliza laughed as William led her by the hand through what felt beneath her feet to be a grassy yard. He'd told her he had a surprise, a late wedding present, but she had to go blindfolded. So she'd tied one of her old silk hair scarves around her eyes with a bow in the back for good measure. She held her other hand out in front just in case she was about to run into something.

"And stop." William let go of her hand and slowly lifted the scarf from her eyes. "You can look now."

Eliza gasped. She couldn't believe what she saw. What must have been a dozen paintings, watercolors she'd worked on years ago, were displayed on easels arranged in a half moon. But that wasn't even the best part.

Somehow, William had managed to set them all up in her old garden, right in front of the carriage house.

"Happy wedding." He grinned from ear to ear and slid his hands into his slacks, clearly quite proud of himself for pulling this off, as he right well should be. "I'm sorry my gift is a little late, but I hope you like it."

"But . . . how?" Eliza whispered, afraid using a normal volume might scatter the fog of this dream and reveal reality once more. "You didn't break in, did you?"

William scoffed, pointing toward himself. "Me? Do something illegal? Why, I'm offended." He winked at her, sliding his arm around her waist as they took in the paintings together. "You know I left my criminal activity behind in my youth."

Eliza laughed once more. "Well, forgive a woman if she's apt to ask questions. You've stolen from me once before, haven't you?" She looked up at him, right into his eyes, which seemed to be dancing—or maybe that was just the reflection of her own.

"Not nearly as much as you stole from me, my dear Eliza. How was I to think straight with you around?"

Now it was her turn to grin.

"As far as the paintings go, I've been slowly buying and collecting them for years. My plan had always been to return them to their rightful owner. I knew it wouldn't make up for what I'd done, but still, I had to make things right. I've destroyed all my imitations—or at least, all the ones that I could find." William adjusted his hat.

"How long?" Eliza stepped toward the first of the easels. The watercolor it displayed was one of her favorite works, and she felt as though it'd been painted in another lifetime. "How long did it take you to collect them all?"

"Goodness, how long has it been?" William walked closer, rubbing his five-o'clock shadow with his thumb. "Nearly twenty years, I suppose."

Eliza shook her head, tears welling up. "I can't believe you did this for me."

William took her hand and kissed it. "They were always yours, Eliza. I simply returned them. I hardly get credit for that."

She shook her head, looking around the garden as one recalls the familiar shapes and impressions of a beautiful dream. "And what of the garden? The house? Why are we here?"

"That's the part I'm particularly keen to tell you." He bit down on his bottom lip and watched her. Did he feel the fullness of the moment as she did? "The house is yours, Eliza."

A winter monarch swooped over the red-brick fence by the carriage house, taking its fill of nectar as it migrated onward to the next pot of flowers, and the next after that.

"Mine?" Eliza couldn't make sense of his words. Surely this was all too good to be true. Surely after all these years of dry dirt, such beautiful blooms were a mirage.

"Yours." William nodded back toward the house. "I heard it was going back on the market and bought it." William looked at the garden, and Eliza followed his gaze over the blooming flowers and the overgrown weeds alike. "I get the distinct impression this place missed you as much as you missed it," he said.

Eliza smiled. Now would be a great opportunity to tell him the secret she'd been keeping, and her heart began to quicken at the thought of it. She pointed toward the iron bench near the carriage house where she'd spent so many afternoons pining for William. "Could we sit a moment?"

"Of course." A look of concern tightened the corners of William's eyes, and he took her hand again as the two of them walked over and sat. "Everything all right?"

Eliza nodded. "Quite." She held on to his hand. "I have a surprise for you as well. I'm pregnant."

For a long moment, he sat wide-eyed and stunned. Neither of them expected she would get pregnant, as they both had grown children of their own, though she was apparently still well within childbearing age, so Lord only knew why not. She'd given birth to Bea when she was so very young that it felt like a lifetime ago . . . but Eliza had been thrilled as soon as she'd sorted it out, and she hoped once the surprise wore off that William would be as well.

"You're . . . you're . . ." he stammered. "I mean . . ."

Eliza chuckled and decided to help him with the words. "Going to have a baby." She leaned closer. "Are you happy about it?"

The question seemed to snap him from his stupor. He stood to his feet and picked her up as well, and twirled her so the hem of her dress skirted along the breeze. "I couldn't be happier. And you? Are you feeling all right?"

"Quite." Eliza grinned from his arms as the butterfly flitted toward the next yard and the breeze sent oak leaves one after another scattering down to the ground. A moment she would have to paint sometime, a moment she would treasure, a moment she would commit to memory for the rest of her life.

1948

Eliza had cozied into patterns of behavior that brought joy and structure to her days: little moments to watch the beautiful fly in and out of sight, back and forth between the tree limbs, scattering browning oak leaves to the ground below.

The bluebirds were preparing for this pre-twilight flight as Eliza crossed her arms over her chenille camisole-and-cardigan set, looking up toward the sky. Her little daughter Beth toddled around among the nearby blooms.

They were supposed to swoop down any moment. They were supposed to come with beauty on their wings—after all, they did so every day, their patterns of flight as structured as the veins of the leaves.

But the winds shifted.

Rain was coming.

Eliza knelt down toward her daughter and hoisted Beth up onto her hip. Her daughter began to cry, having been interrupted from her late-afternoon play among the zinnias.

"Hush now, little one." Eliza tapped Beth's nose with the tip of her finger. "A storm's coming. Truth is, I'd like to stay here a while longer too."

Beth quieted, turning her head to study Eliza, then moving her gaze up toward the greying clouds.

William was finishing his work for the day as the screen door screeched behind Eliza and Beth.

"Weather's looking angry," Eliza said. As though on cue, the wind sent a branch scraping against the window.

William frowned. He moved closer to the window as the winds continued growing like a monster just outside the walls. Eliza heard a loud snap and startled with Beth still in her arms. William turned toward them. "You two find an interior room, and I'll get something for supper."

"Supper's already done—I just need you to put it in bowls and get the drinks. Don't forget Beth's cup." Beth wouldn't drink a thing if it wasn't in that cup.

"Got it." William nodded, beginning to turn as the winds howled. He waved toward Eliza and Beth. "Hurry now and get away from these windows."

But Eliza was distracted, watching for the sudden storm. William stepped closer, putting two gentle hands on her arms. "My dear Eliza," he murmured, rousing her from her stupor.

Eliza blinked, then nodded. "Yes. Yes, of course." She bounced Beth on her hip, trying for her daughter's sake to seem as calm as possible. "Who wants to have a picnic tonight, hmm?" she asked

Beth. "Now, won't that be fun? Daddy is getting your special cup now."

"Yum yum yum." Beth's current favorite word.

Rain pushed hard against the house, and Eliza fidgeted the hand that wasn't holding Beth. Should she have done something to prepare her garden for the storm? But there was hardly time for that now.

She felt a sudden and striking disappointment she hadn't seen where the bluebirds were going to land tonight.

But she sighed to herself and kept going, whispering a prayer God would keep the birds safe through the storm.

Soon, William had followed them into the interior bedroom with bowls of soup and grilled cheese sandwiches, as well as two slices of chocolate cake on plates that were balanced against his arm.

Eliza laughed at him, reaching for a couple of the plates. "How on earth did you manage to carry all this?"

"I have a few tricks up my sleeve," he said with a wink toward Eliza.

"Always teasing me. You're lucky I didn't have you sent to jail, you know. You little lawbreaker."

"Jail?" William feigned surprise. "Why, I have no idea what you're talking about."

"Hmm, don't you?" Eliza offered a sly half grin. "You're dangerous."

"Perhaps." He kissed the top of her head. "But let's not forget I'm also the one who returned that silver to its beautiful, rightful owner."

"Whatever you need to tell yourself." Eliza shot a look at him.

Beth made a play for the chocolate cake, abruptly ending their exchange, so Eliza and William simply smiled at one another with the unspoken promise to continue this later.

But the storm outside grew louder still, and Eliza remembered how scared she really felt.

She huddled together with her sweet family and waited for it to pass.

Several hours later, it finally did. But not before knocking out the power, the wind blowing through the fences and alleys around Longitude Lane like a freight train.

None of them expected the damage it would leave behind.

After putting Beth in her little bed upstairs, Eliza tiptoed down the steps and joined William outside.

She gasped, covering her mouth with her hand as she took in the rubble of bricks and iron that had crumbled and fallen near the carriage house. The main house would need a new roof and some repairs, but her garden . . . her garden was destroyed.

Eliza fell to her knees as the realization of this loss settled deep into her bones.

Her mind immediately flashed back to the destruction of the break-in they had a year ago. Thieves, assumably looking for her silver.

And then came another realization: without the wall, anyone might walk onto their property in the night. Without the wall, they had no protection from would-be inheritance stealers. Silver thieves and bandits, trying to take an inheritance that didn't belong to them.

William slowly knelt beside her, reaching his arm around her shoulders. "We'll fix it, Eliza. We will make sure everything is secure and that none of them come to steal from us."

But Eliza looked down at all the places the fallen sticks had scraped across the ground, wounding the roots and the blooms as well. Slowly, she shook her head. It all made sense now—this feeling of deep nostalgia she'd sensed every time she looked at the bluebirds, sneaking in another day and hour, another glimpse of beauty that belonged to another time.

She had known. She had known for a while. Not about the storm, obviously. She couldn't tell the future like that. But maybe in some way, in some depth of her heart, she *had* known she was out of season in these spaces and that sometime—as it turned out—sometime soon—she was going to have to leave home.

Because they hadn't come yet tonight. The thieves, that is. But they had come before. And it was only a matter of time—every hour was one hour closer until they arrived.

"We've been lying to ourselves, William." She bravely looked into his eyes under the light of the stars. "We both know they will come back for the silver. Whether it's now or later, what difference does that make? We're living under a curse here, can't you see that?"

"Then I'll tell them," William assured her. "I'll tell them I've taken the silver out of the ground, and they'll stop searching for it."

"And you really think they'll believe your words?" Eliza asked.

"It's the truth, isn't it?"

Eliza looked down at the silver ring on her hand. "It may be the truth, but what they're after isn't the truth at all. Sometimes, imitation drives our hearts into a deception that is far more persuasive than the truth that would free us. They will believe a lie every time you try to righten this, and they will continue tearing up my garden." She stood and brushed the dirt from her hemline. "For Beth's sake . . . and even for my garden's . . . the only choice we have is to leave."

"Leave?" William slowly enunciated the word, clearly in shock.

"Yes, William." Eliza wiped the tears streaming from her eyes. "I'll contact Susan about renting the property. Maybe then my garden can come back to life, even if I can't be part of it any longer."

"Where will we go?" William asked.

"I don't know," Eliza said, as the feeling of being lost spun her into sadness. "New Orleans, perhaps? All I know is, the sooner, the better. We can't pretend here any longer."

Eliza took one more lingering look over the garden she'd always loved so dearly—her grandmother's garden—determined to paint it again and again until maybe a little part of it would seed and spring back to life in season, even if only within her own heart.

THIRTY-FOUR

Modern Day

The morning after her gut-wrenching conversation with Ms. Beth about the bricks, there was an extraordinary amount of bluebird activity in Lucy's garden.

She knew, of course, that this beautiful, single-house dream was a fleeting one, and like a star disappearing beyond a cloud or like Cinderella's infamous slippers, she could only enjoy it a little while longer. Yet this knowledge did little in the way of keeping the joy flutters, as Lucy liked to call them, from her heart when the breeze brought the fragrance of the new day's blooms.

And so she'd pretend a little longer that this all, the grand sum of it, might *not* be some elaborate dream she was never meant to keep and that instead, she would magically and suddenly solve the silver mystery before it was too late.

She was sitting outside in a rocking chair, enjoying said breeze and waiting for Harper and Millie, when they rounded the corner from Church Street with a third figure walking behind them. The woman wore a straw hat with thick red trim and a coordinating red sundress that looked like the matronly version of Reese Witherspoon's clothing line, Draper James.

"Mom?" Lucy stood from the rocker and immediately cataloged what she was wearing. She was on day two of dry shampoo and had eaten a donut and a half for breakfast, but she didn't *think* she had reached the snowy-scalp stage that usually comes with pushing three days without a real wash. Not that anyone would use dry shampoo that many days in a row. Right? Ahem.

As for the donuts, her mother would inevitably know about that part. How? Lucy had no idea. But she would. Some mothers have a sense for carrying Band-Aids before skinned knees are ever scraped, or a hunch their child needs a warm hug and just the right episode of *Mister Rogers' Neighborhood*. For Lucy's mom, it was pastry clairvoyance.

But too late now. Her saving grace would have to be the presence of Harper and Millie. Her mother would be on her best behavior around Millie, whom she considered an elder and a feisty one to boot.

Lucy's mom waved as though in a passing parade as the three of them drew closer, opening the garden gate and walking over to where Lucy stood on the porch.

"Welcome, everybody," Lucy said.

"I bumped into the two of them on Church Street, so I decided to tag along and see your house." Her mother was looking up at the place, taking it all in. Lucy felt bad she hadn't invited her over until now, but the house had been like a bubble for her to discover more about Eliza, and really, the only person she wanted around was Beth. Well, and Harper, but Harper had been so busy at the store lately.

"The house is lovely, Lucy." Her mother took the steps up the porch slowly, offering Millie a hand of assistance that Millie politely turned down. She seemed to actually mean the compliment, and Lucy felt a pang of guilt for assuming the worst of her. Maybe she'd been too guarded. Not that it mattered now . . . the house wouldn't be hers for too much longer.

Lucy reached for the door and held it open so the three of them could come inside. Her mother and Millie were both oohing and aahing over the archway in the entry when Harper came up beside her.

"Any updates?" Harper whispered.

Lucy shook her head. "I fear the brick situation will be my fatal flaw."

"I'm so sorry, friend." Harper put her hand on Lucy's shoulder. "But don't give up hope. There's still time for you to figure something out."

Lucy forced a smile for her friend's sake and nodded. Yes, there was time, but it was running out fast.

Lucy's mother clapped her hands together. "I'm on my way to a luncheon so I can't stay long, but, sweetheart, I am so proud of you." She planted an air kiss on Lucy's cheek so as not to smear her red lipstick.

Lucy gave her an eager hug. The vote of confidence felt so good, even if disaster in the form of Declan was imminent. "Thanks, Mom."

Her mother smiled. "I know I can be a little"—she rubbed her lips together as though summoning the right word—"well, *opinionated* sometimes, but I really am proud of you, Lucy."

"That means a lot." Lucy smiled back. For now, she would take the compliment and enjoy the fuzzy feelings. "Have a nice luncheon."

"Thank you." Her mother looked toward Harper and Millie with a little wave. "Good to see you both." And the red lipstick, Lucy noticed, really went far in the way of complementing her smile.

Lucy closed the door, still buzzing from her mother's encouragement when she turned to realize Millie was holding a photograph and studying it.

"What is it, Millie?" Harper asked.

Millie held up the picture and looked over toward Lucy. "Do you know who this is?"

"Sure." Lucy shrugged. "That's Eliza Legare. She's my great-grandmother and one of the previous owners of this house. That's why it means so much to me. My own grandmother Bea was her daughter, born back in the 1930s. Although I don't know if she lived here then. I haven't found much evidence of my grandmother's childhood around."

Millie frowned. "Are you sure about that?"

"Which part?" Lucy stepped forward and took a look at the photograph Millie was holding, one of Eliza with the words *New Orleans, 1959* scribbled across the back. She'd found it with a stack of postcards.

Millie straightened her red cloche and stood tall. "See, the thing is, I've met this woman before. She stayed at the boardinghouse I ran with my husband, Franklin. But her last name was not Legare, and the daughter she brought along was still quite young. Definitely not born in the thirties. Why, that'd make her close to my age."

"Are you positive, Millie?" Harper asked, taking a look at the picture herself. "Maybe it could be another Eliza?"

"Quite sure, my dear." Millie looked to Lucy and smiled. "She's the one who gave me my hat, and a person doesn't forget a woman like that. You're fortunate to be her relation."

If there was one thing Lucy knew about Millie, aside from her tenacity and her spunk, it was the fact she could beat them all at trivia. She was sharp as a tack, and Lucy did not doubt her account.

But the timeline did not make sense. Unless . . . did Eliza remarry at some point and have another child? Could *that* person know about the silver, or the house, or maybe even be the one who gave it to Lucy?

Lucy's heart raced at the thought. She was still completely at a loss for answers, but this was new information, at least. Thanks to Millie, she now had a thread of hope to hold on to.

Several hours after Harper and Millie left for afternoon tea as part of their day off, Lucy set out to tackle the invasive ivy climbing up the bricks near the gate of the garden. A neighbor had explained the difference between creeping fig, which was apparently quite safe and lovely, and the ivy Lucy had, which was . . . well . . . not.

She had made sweaty progress and was thinking about a nice shower when she heard footsteps from the other side of the iron gate and looked up to see Declan.

"Hi, Lucy." He was so casual, with his boat shoes and his perfect hair and obnoxious smile. Lucy couldn't play this game with him, not today. She looked back down, ripping ivy that had sunk its splintery little tendrils into cracks in the brick walls.

Lucy shifted. Her thighs were burning from all the squats, but she had more ivy to pull. Twigs crunched under her feet. "You still haven't the slightest idea, do you?"

He put both hands in the air as if at a loss.

"Does the word *bricks* ring a bell?" She nodded back toward her house.

The color washed from his face.

Lucy stood. She on one side of the gate, he on the other.

"You know, Peter is always droning on and on about what a great guy you are. Well, let's talk about that, shall we?" She slowed her speech, making sure he caught every word. "Pretending to care about someone, then ripping her home away. Sabotaging a job she'd worked hard to earn. Am I leaving anything out?" She held one finger up to her chin as if in consideration. "Oh yes. Having a moment . . . whatever that was . . . with her at her sister's wedding before pulling the proverbial rug out from under her. I'm afraid Peter's glasses may be rose-colored, because those things don't scream *integrity* to me. I can tell you a few things they do scream. . . ."

Declan rubbed the bridge of his nose. "Lucy, I swear to you, I did not know about the bricks until it was too late."

She shook her head, brandishing an uprooted strand of ivy in her hands. "You don't get it, do you?" The breeze sent oak leaves scuttling down from the branches above. "How dare you act like you care about me when your actions have shown nothing but disrespect toward me and my family?"

He stood there, his hands in his pockets, just staring at her like he didn't know what to say. Well, at least she'd shut him up.

But she wasn't done yet. "I was kind to you. I forgave you for ruining my car, for those ugly words you spoke outside the museum, and for your general pompousness. How expensive are your jeans, anyway?"

"Pompous—"

She held up one hand. "But I will *not* forgive you for ruining my great-grandmother's home, Declan Pinckney. And you know what? You may be wealthy, but if you can't understand the value of a home—if you don't have the empathy to lend a helping hand instead of a swift kick when someone is trying to restore something precious . . ." She looked him straight in the eyes with a fiery gaze. "Well, then, let me put it this way. You'll fit right in running your father's company."

Still, he said nothing.

She didn't know what to make of that, so the next words slipped out entirely on their own accord, and she wasn't even sorry about it. "By the way, I know about the silver."

Declan's eyes widened.

"Surprised?" she asked. "I have ears, you know. You really thought you could keep a secret like that from me? To think that all this time, what you were really after was some kind of buried treasure."

She set the strand of ivy down and reached to rip out another. "Well, guess what? You're the one who's in for a surprise, because I dug up the whole yard, searched my great-grandmother's journals, and turned the house upside down looking for it. I haven't found a thing. I'm not even convinced the silver exists. So this"—she waved her hand—"the lengths you've gone to may've all been for nothing."

His lips parted briefly, but he didn't speak.

"You want to say something?" she dared.

"Yeah, actually." He crunched several acorns as he shifted his feet. "I came here to tell you about the bricks and apologize. But if this is how you feel about me, I guess you've made your point loud and clear." A squirrel raced up the tree. Probably furious about the perfectly good acorns he'd just wasted.

"Oh, don't act like I should feel sorry for you. You are an arrogant man who hides behind the prestigious name of his family. You can't even follow your own dreams of architecture because you're so busy people pleasing."

"Thanks for the thorough assessment of my character." He pushed up his sleeves. "You want to know what I think? I think you're scared."

She guffawed. "Oh, now I've heard everything."

"You can commit to a car, or a house, Lucy—but you can't commit to changing or imperfect things. Challenging things. Like your *own* dream of architecture or falling for me because my last name happens to be Pinckney." Declan looked at her with a piercing gaze, and in that moment, she realized her mistake. Somewhere along the line she'd granted him access to her heart, and as furious as it made her, in this case he was completely right in this assertion.

He continued, oblivious to how his words shook her. "Life is messy. And change keeps coming. I may undervalue the past, but at least I'm not blissfully unaware of the present, living with my head in the clouds. You hide behind your great-grandmother's paintings as if they can protect you, but they're keeping you from your own life, your own dreams. You get so wrapped up fighting for an old house that you're too busy to even see—"

Lucy stopped him with a wave of her hand. She didn't want to hear any more.

A bluebird flitted into the safety of the oak tree. Lucy bit her bottom lip and tried with all her might to keep from crying. She sniffled and hoped he didn't see the moisture stinging at the corners of her eyes. How could he, this handsome and frustrating man, know her so accurately?

Declan took a small step toward her, his tone softening but his message no less sincere. "Who are *you*, Lucy Legare? Don't you see? The one thing time does faithfully is keep moving." He was still, his posture sure. "You can't save everything."

"Maybe not, but that won't keep me from trying." She trembled, wrapping her arms around her waist to keep him from seeing. "Maybe I do have trouble committing to people and places, and maybe nothing measures up to my memories." The breeze caught the ends of her hair, and she brushed it back from her face. "But at least I honor my own family's history. And my city's. At least I believe in happy endings."

"What more of a fairy tale do you need?" Declan tapped against the bricks with his fingertips. He looked her in the eyes once more, and sparks flew between them—sparks of all sorts of things.

"Good-bye, Lucy," he murmured.

The bluebird hopped out toward the edge of the branches, at home in the tree. It perched there as the breeze blew, so that the whole thing seemed to sing with melody.

Lucy thought about those bluebirds, and what Eliza wrote in her journal about beauty and roots and wings. And she ripped another strand of ivy from the wall as she wondered for a moment if Declan was right about everything.

THIRTY-FIVE

1948

William gave his brown fedora a nudge and reached into the back seat of his automobile for the paper-wrapped paintings. He gathered several of them in his arms and shut the car door with his foot, then hurried up the walkway leading to Susan's front door. The hour was early, but Eliza had telephoned even earlier, and Susan was expecting him.

She opened the door for him, running a hand under the curl of her greying hair as he stepped inside and set the paintings in the entry.

"I'll get the rest." He tipped his hat to her and headed back toward the car, unloading several paintings at a time and being mindful not to scratch or damage any. These paintings represented Eliza's heart, and he would handle them carefully.

Susan had already set to work unwrapping each of the pieces and lining them along a prominent hallway when William finished unloading. He pulled off a few scraps of paper that had stuck to his trousers and rolled his shoulders. Those paintings were heavy.

Susan had crossed her arms and was now studying him. There was nothing fussy about her, no jewelry or ornaments in her hair, but she radiated the confidence of a person doing all they could to make the world better. For Susan, that looked like saving structures. For Eliza, that betterment looked like painting them.

William, frankly, was inspired by such a tenacious pursuit of betterment in all its forms. He'd fallen into a good bit of despair following the war and the Depression, and he marveled at the way Eliza had continued painting and Susan had continued preserving the city, even in the bleakest hours.

He ran his thumb along his freshly shaven jawline, not entirely sure what to do with himself under the scrutiny.

"You broke her heart, you know." Susan let her arms fall, then took to straightening the paintings. She picked one up and directed her glance sideways toward William. "Alice and I distinctly told Eliza if she insisted upon falling in love, she mustn't come away heartbroken. Yet that's exactly what you accomplished." Susan lifted one of the paintings up toward the picture railing along the wall. "Why should I trust you now?"

William raised his hat from his head and held it over his chest. He didn't know why he did it, really, except that Susan scared him a little and this seemed a natural way of expressing respect. "Because this time, I've got enough self-respect to see she needs me as much as I need her. I know it doesn't excuse what I did years ago." He shook his head. "But I left because I thought I was keeping her safe."

Susan hooked the painting to the picture molding, then looked at him. "I can respect that."

That was enough for him. William nodded once.

"I'll wire you the money for the house once we get the papers sorted out and a renter set up. If the two of you ever want to move back, you just say the words." Her smile was kind, her features unfettered by makeup. "What about the paintings? Should I keep them all until you've got a forwarding address ready in New Orleans?"

William resituated his hat upon his head. "No, Eliza's already gone through the pieces she wants to keep. She said if there's anything you don't want for yourself, please donate it to the art museum, and she'll be greatly indebted."

Susan moved toward the next painting and searched for a spot to place it on the picture railing. "You tell Eliza I would be happy to honor her request. And again, my door is always open if ever Charleston calls you back home."

"Thank you, Susan. I'll do that." William grinned, tipping his hat as he headed toward the door.

Fairhope, Alabama

William's car sputtered to a stop in front of the inn. He shifted the gear into park and squinted to read the sign. *Millie's Boardinghouse.* This was the place, all right. And he'd been right about the wife's name too.

He reached for his suitcase from the passenger seat of the car and headed toward the front porch. It was a pretty place to sit, as far as porches go, although he imagined very little compared to the piazzas in Charleston.

He was tired from the long drive, but the thought of seeing Eliza and Beth energized him like a tall cup of coffee. He knocked solidly against the door until his nephew, Franklin, opened it.

"Uncle William!" Franklin had grown into an impressive young man, and if his wide grin were any indication, he was happy as a lark here.

William grabbed his nephew for a hug, then held him by the arms and took a good look at him. "Franklin, you are as effervescent as ever. Alabama has been good to you. I'm so thankful you and your mother aren't out there riding the rails any longer. Wish I could've kept it from happening in the first place."

"Uncle William, you couldn't stop an economic depression. You did everything you could to help us out when I was a kid. And then some." He added this next part with a wink, holding the door open wider for William to step through.

"Just how much do you know?" William clenched his jaw.

"All of it." Franklin kept grinning. He took a step backward as the women came down the hallway.

"William!" Eliza made haste, throwing her arms around his neck. William dropped his suitcase to the ground so he could wrap his arms around her. Beth toddled closer, raising both of her hands.

"There's my girl." William leaned down to scoop her up, and she rewarded him with a toothy grin. "Da da da da," she repeated, looking toward Eliza as if to make sure everyone had seen him. William snuggled her closer. Though it'd only been a few days, he felt as though he hadn't seen his family in weeks or longer.

"Uncle William, meet Millie. My wife." Franklin tucked his arm around Millie's waist. She wore a red hat that looked vaguely familiar. Perhaps Eliza owned a similar one.

"Pleasure to meet you." William held out his hand.

Millie shook it with her own gloved fingers and offered a generous smile. Her olive complexion was offset by the green color of her fashionable dress.

"Likewise. Welcome to our boardinghouse." She looked up at Franklin, then back toward William. "I've heard you're his favorite uncle."

William laughed. Beth wiggled from his arms, and he set her back down. "I'm his only uncle."

"Well, there's that." Franklin clapped him on the back. He and Millie shared a smile.

"Haven't seen that look in your eyes since you were a boy chasing chickens," William said. "Wonder none of them ever tried to poke your eye out."

Franklin cackled. "Oh, they tried, all right. I just ran faster."

"Why does that not surprise me?" Millie shook her head, looking back toward William. She had a warmth about her, and the most beautiful eyes. "Eliza tells me you're headed to New Orleans next. I've always heard it's such a vibrant city."

"Both of our grown children have recently married with their own plans to move, so we're trying to talk them into coming . . . so far, with little success, but maybe eventually . . ." William reached out to take Eliza's hand in his own. He threaded their fingers together and ran his thumb back and forth along the silver roots of her ring.

"Well, the two of you can stay here as long as you need." Millie adjusted her red hat and lowered her voice. "Eliza told me you had to leave Charleston because you had secrets someone was after. I'm so sorry." She shook her head, the empathy in her expression startling. Then she hesitated. "I know what it's like to leave Charleston behind."

William turned his head. "You know, Franklin never said much about your background. How did the two of you meet, anyhow?"

"On the train leaving South Carolina." Franklin tugged her closer. "Millie was a paying customer, and I was riding the rails. That was my last time jumpin'."

Millie looked up at him, all but glowing. "I saw him from the window and wondered about him all the way 'til Savannah."

William frowned. "What happened in Savannah?"

Franklin shrugged. "I snuck on. Sat next to her and shamelessly struck up a chat about her red hat. I told her I was starved for conversation, but the real truth of it is that Millie was the prettiest girl I'd ever seen and if I let her get all the way to Alabama without taking my chance, I knew I'd regret it for the rest of my life."

Eliza beamed. She always had loved a good romance. "What happened next?"

Millie stepped toward the record player and started a jazzy tune in the background. "Franklin offered to accompany me until I could find a safe place to stay, and the owner of this boardinghouse assumed we were husband and wife."

Eliza's eyes widened. "Now *this* is getting interesting." William had to agree.

"Oh, it was all perfectly honorable," Franklin was quick to add. He looked back at Millie and grinned. "Until the woman realized we weren't actually married."

"And then what happened?" William asked.

"We got hitched." Franklin shrugged. "Didn't you hear the part where I said she's the prettiest girl I've ever seen? Turned out she was plenty charming as well. I couldn't let a woman like that get away, could I?"

Millie fiddled with the trim of her gloves. "That's leaving out a few details, but I like this version." Her eyes twinkled like the twilight sky, and when she looked at Franklin that way, William could tell just how much she loved him. And he was so glad his nephew had found a woman like that, a woman just like Eliza.

Millie set her hand on Eliza's shoulder. "I know it likely feels as though you're leaving a lot behind. And you probably are. But if my own experience is any teacher, our past never really leaves us. The houses and the gardens and the experiences are like a long piece of fabric that wraps around us, sheltering our dreams for the next thing in our lives. Your legacy is *within* you, both of you, like roots under the soil, and so long as those roots are growing, the stories they hold will continue growing as well."

Eliza wiped two little tears that had begun to fall from her eyes. "Garden to garden," she whispered.

Millie nodded. "Garden to garden."

THIRTY-SIX

Modern Day

Declan approached the old brick walkway with the afternoon sun at his back, its heat warming his shoulders. The house before him had been perfectly restored. The garden outside, stunning. His stomach was in knots as he reached toward the doorbell and waited on the stoop. He was actually about to do this, Lord help him.

Ring. He pushed again. *Ring.*

He pulled a loose thread on his shirt and looked up at the lanterns affixed to the entry, their little fires forming the perfect maple leaf shape that all Charlestonians aspired to achieve. His mother would be envious.

What was taking so long?

Declan blew out a slow sigh.

Was she home?

Finally, he heard the lock unlatch on the other side of the door. She opened it mere inches at first, then peeked out and opened it more.

"Declan?"

"Hello, Ms. Beth." He hadn't seen her since last Friday, her most recent attempt to keep his company from tearing down some ancient carriage posts in front of a property they'd recently acquired.

She hesitated for a moment, as though considering her options.

He couldn't say he blamed her. "Why don't you come inside?" Slowly, she stepped out of the way.

"Thanks." When he entered the house, he understood why Lucy would be comfortable here. The place was an array of cozy floral fabrics in every pattern and color. His own mother would love it. And he meant that in the best way possible.

Beth brushed the back of her palm against her forehead, smearing dirt. She wore a woven sunhat and tennis shoes. Declan put two and two together.

"Were you gardening?" He noticed vases of fresh flowers all over the room, and the sweet fragrance reminded him of Lucy. "No need to stop on my account."

"Are you certain?" she asked. "I would sure like to get these flowers finished before sundown."

"Absolutely." He followed her to the patio door, which she held open. The courtyard looked like something from an issue of *Southern Living*. Flowers in every type of color lined the winding pathway, and behind them, rows of rose bushes met blooming hydrangeas. He suspected the other green bushes might be azaleas, and could only imagine how they must look come spring.

"It's beautiful back here," he said. "Very quaint."

Beth smiled and tugged on her gardening gloves. "Thank you. I like to sit here with a cup of tea in the early mornings, when the birds are fluttering about."

"I imagine that would be tranquil."

Beth gestured toward an iron bench under a trellis of jasmine. "Why don't you have a seat?"

"Gladly." Declan lowered himself onto the bench and set his hands in his lap. He felt like a child. It was silly, but he did.

Beth reached for her red wheelbarrow and the garden spade that rested on top of it. She studied him a moment, unflinching. Then, she spoke. "Declan, let's stop this charade and get down to it, shall we?" She motioned with the spade as she talked. "Why in heaven's name are you here?"

He took a deep breath and rubbed his palms against his jeans. "I've done something terrible."

"Why am I not surprised?"

Declan looked up at her. "I need your help."

"*My* help?" She pointed the spade toward herself.

"Yes, your expertise."

"Go on." Beth knelt down and placed a petunia inside a hole she must've dug just before he showed up. She scattered the dirt and patted it down with her spade.

"Before my father had his heart attack, he filed a grievance with the historical society about Lucy's bricks." A yellow flower fluttered down to Declan's lap, and he brushed it away. "I'm sure she's told you. It was kind of a big deal."

Beth simply raised her eyebrows in response. "Go on."

"What Lucy doesn't realize is that I fought with my father on this issue. A fight that might've . . ." He cleared his throat and rubbed the palm of his hand. "Well, it might've contributed to the heart attack." Declan shook his head. "I can't get that out of my mind, Ms. Beth. I called him a fool for what he was doing to Lucy, for what he's done with the company." He looked toward Beth, panic flooding him all over again. "But what if I'm the reason . . ."

Beth came to sit beside him and rested her arm on his shoulders. The gesture reminded him of his mother. Her gentle expression urged him on.

Declan's eyes stung. "He's improving each day, but he can still hardly talk." He dropped his face into his hands. "I drove him to that."

"No, you didn't." She squeezed his shoulder and pulled him up by the chin to look him straight in the eyes. "This is not your fault."

He nodded slowly. She was right. He knew that. He just couldn't seem to shake this feeling of responsibility.

"You're saying you stood up for Lucy?"

He looked back into her eyes. "Of course I stood up for Lucy. I'm in love with her."

Beth's eyes widened.

"She didn't tell you?"

"You mean she knows?" Beth covered her mouth with her hand.

"I assumed so." He raked his foot back and forth against the ground.

"You *assumed* so? Now, how does one assume a thing like that? Well. This is a startling development." Beth bent toward him. "So now what?"

Declan hesitated, looking for the right words. "Beth, I want to save her house."

"Can you just have the company buy it?"

He shook his head. "It's not that simple. My dad has already put all these wheels in motion."

"But aren't you in charge now?"

"Yeah, but my best hope at this point is if the house stays in Lucy's name." Declan looked off at a mockingbird hopping around the hydrangeas.

Beth *tsked* her heavy disapproval, then rested her chin on her hand. "So why do you need my help?"

His foot on his knee, he shifted toward her. "I was hoping you know of some Preservation Society bylaw that can get Lucy out of the grievance."

Beth stood and picked up her spade. "I'm sorry, sweetheart." She pulled another flower from its pot and stuck it in the ground. "If I did, I already would've played that card."

Beth patted the dirt, then grabbed her watering can. She looked back at Declan. "There's nothing that can be done."

Declan stood from the bench and brushed off his jeans. "That's what I thought. But I had to try."

"Leaving so soon?" she asked.

He nodded toward the cobblestone road. "Yeah, I've got to get back to work." He pushed his hands into his pockets. "Do me a favor, okay? Make sure she's doing all right? I'm the last person she wants to talk with right now."

Beth smiled. "You bet."

"Thanks." Declan opened the gate at the side of the garden and let himself out. He would think of something, a way to solve this conundrum. He just needed to think like William.

With dirt under her fingernails, Lucy raised her hand to knock three solid times on Ms. Beth's door.

She'd been pulling up the garden all day long. Pulling vines had turned into pulling weeds and then into pulling shrubs and flowers, in a desperate attempt to find that silver. Without it, Lucy would never be able to save the house. Without it, Declan was liable to clear the structure and all its history to the ground.

It wasn't until Lucy had practically bulldozed the garden with her own two hands that she realized what her desperation had done. She'd tried replanting what she could, though she wasn't sure the roots would take after being so disturbed.

She had, in her search for an inheritance, laid waste to Eliza's garden.

So now she stood at Ms. Beth's door wearing an old pair of jean shorts, a tank top, and a scrunchie with a fabric bow on the back, because the least she could do was that, right? She probably had leaves stuck to her hair. But the bow forgave all sorts of disgraces.

Maybe she was frantic. Maybe she was just now seeing clearly. Either way, Lucy had finally given up. She had nowhere left to search. Nowhere left to dig. No money or inheritance to be found.

Ms. Beth opened the door, and—bless that woman—kept her composure despite Lucy's rather unseemly appearance. Though, don't think for a second Lucy didn't catch the raised eyebrows when Ms. Beth first laid eyes on her.

"Lucy, what a surprise." She opened the door wider. "Please, come in. Seems I'm quite popular today."

Lucy followed her inside, taking in the sight and smell of the vases full of roses that were all around the house. Ms. Beth led

Lucy into the kitchen, where she poured two tall glasses of tea, the ice clanking against the porcelain and into the cups. She handed one to Lucy.

Lucy didn't have to ask whether it was sweetened or not. She took a sip. The tea was brewed well with just the right amount of sugar and did its magic soothing her broken heart.

Lucy looked down at the ice in her glass. "I've decided I'm going to sell the house to Declan." She met with a worrisome look in Ms. Beth's eyes. "You think it's a mistake?"

Ms. Beth reached for her own tea. "I didn't say that."

"Should I see if I can take out a line of credit for new bricks? Maybe I could just buy some time—"

"I didn't say that either." Ms. Beth set her glass down on the bar. "It's some kind of position you're in, Lucy, and I don't envy you a bit."

Lucy nodded. She got situated on one of the barstools, balancing her weight from up high. Then she looked down at her filthy fingernails. Her mother would have a conniption if she saw them.

"I destroyed Eliza's garden." Lucy shook her head. "The place she painted all those watercolors. I don't even know how it happened. One minute I was pulling vines, and the next, I'd uprooted a whole heap of flowers."

Ms. Beth reached across the bar to cover Lucy's hand with her own. That's when Lucy began to cry. The truth was, she'd really believed she was about to find the silver.

The secret that would sustain her. The thing she'd been missing out on.

She kept pulling. And pulling. And pulling. Thinking she was searching for silver, she was actually pulling a different kind of inheritance straight out of the ground.

She never found the silver. And now time had run out, and with it, so had her options.

"This isn't how things were supposed to go." Lucy shook her head, and as she did, the kitchen lights made the stones of the ring on her left hand glimmer. "The house . . . and then the garden. I feel like a fool. I'm given my dream home, and I can't even manage to hold on to it. What's even worse is the history. I find out one of the great artists of the Charleston Renaissance is my own ancestor, and I can't manage to save it for her sake either. Now I just have to watch my dream disappearing from my hands."

Ms. Beth frowned.

Lucy tapped the side of her glass. "I should have been able to save the house, Ms. Beth. Eliza helped to save houses all over Charleston, and now all these years later, I can't even manage to save the one that probably meant the most to her of all."

Ms. Beth studied her a long moment. Lucy had no idea what went through the woman's mind, but whatever it was seemed serious. Finally, Beth sighed. "All right," she said. "Come with me."

She picked up a framed photograph as she led Lucy through the living space and then the sunroom and then outside. A trellis filled with roses arched above the patio, leading to a winding garden path made out of stones that Lucy wanted to skip along. Flowers in reds and pinks and whites and purples bloomed from the curved edges of the yard, so beautiful they reminded Lucy of something out of Eliza's paintings.

"I wasn't planning to tell you this because I wasn't sure it would help matters." Ms. Beth handed the frame to Lucy and pointed to the photograph.

In the picture, a man and a woman stood in front of Eliza's house and smiled at one another. They were holding a baby, whose features bore a resemblance to them.

"The baby is my grandson, Sullivan."

Lucy looked up. "Your grandson? But who are these people holding him?"

"That's William and Eliza." Ms. Beth's grin hummed. "My parents."

Lucy nearly dropped the photograph and scattered glass all over the stepping-stones. She managed to keep her grip on it, though, and pointed toward the picture. "So, they . . . Eliza and William . . ."

"Ended up together after all. Yes. And had a child. An exceptionally charming child, if I do say so myself."

Lucy sat down on the iron bench overlooking a little fountain in the center of the fragrant garden, and Ms. Beth did the same. "What happened?"

"All those dramatic stories you've heard about silver and feuds? Those are true. Well, for the most part. When my parents first fell in love, neither of their extended families took a liking to the idea of their romance. The families continued feuding over the silver to the extent both William and Eliza married other people. But times were difficult back then, and when they both lost their spouses during World War II, their lives once again intersected."

Lucy's eyes widened.

"You could say they lived happily ever after. And I've been happy as well—managing the family properties and volunteering at the art museum, working with my mother's watercolors." Ms. Beth tucked a stray strand of hair behind her ear. "Most of the people who were after the silver have been dead for decades, but it didn't surprise me when Declan's father took up the quest. It was never found, you know."

A bumblebee buzzed past them, shimmying into the cave of an open flower in its search for nectar. Everything made sense now—the reason Ms. Beth worked at the museum, the bits and pieces Lucy knew of William and Eliza's story, and the legends that'd been told about the silver. Everything, that is, except . . .

Lucy traced the ambling curves of the silver frame around the photo. "How did I end up with Eliza's house?"

Ms. Beth waved away a gnat. "I gave it to you."

Lucy's mouth dropped open. "You *what*?"

Ms. Beth shifted to face Lucy directly, the fountain just behind them trickling with a stream of water that lured a little sparrow closer. "Who else was I going to give it to? My son travels all over the place, and the upkeep of having two houses has become too much for me to manage alone. Your eyes were glittering that day at the gallery as you talked about your hope of owning a Charleston single house. I didn't tell you it was me because I knew you wouldn't accept the gift."

Ms. Beth was the reason she had Eliza's house?

This knowledge was almost too much to process. Lucy stammered as she tried to make sense of such a gift. "But we're hardly even related. How could you give me something so extravagant?"

"I want someone to preserve Eliza's stories and her art after I'm gone. That's far more important to me than any money I could've received by selling the house." Ms. Beth breathed in the garden air, and Lucy did as well.

She looked off toward an old oak. "See that tree over there? That's where William proposed to Eliza. Well, I suppose that's where he proposed a second time. The first time was under the tree limbs that span the wall behind your carriage house. The ring he gave her—the ring you're wearing—is a representation of those roots and wings that depend on one another in life."

"The silver tree," Lucy whispered in reverence to the moment. So *that's* why Eliza had painted it. Lucy felt as though she'd had single pots of color, separate pieces of the story, and for the first time, they were all blending into something more akin to the horizon. "Are you saying I've been wearing Eliza's engagement ring?"

Ms. Beth nodded.

Tears began to sting Lucy's eyes. "I failed you. I'm so, so sorry."

Ms. Beth reached out and placed her hands on Lucy's shoulders, looking straight into her eyes. "No, sweetheart. That's where you misunderstand. See, Eliza—she loved that garden. And the house too. You're right. But she spent most of her life driven out of it, just as you've been," Beth paused. "Do you remember the story where Adam and Eve sin in the garden?"

Lucy shifted on the bench, puzzled by this apparent change in subject. "Well, sure. They eat from the tree of the knowledge of good and evil and ruin everything. Then they gather fig leaves to cover their shame, blame the serpent, and get themselves kicked out of the garden."

"More or less." Ms. Beth grinned, patting the rounded curls of her hairstyle. "Here's the thing. Look closer at the story, and you'll notice God says He can't let them eat from the tree of life now, because they'll live forever in that state. Now why do you suppose He says that?"

Lucy shrugged. "My Sunday school teacher always said it was a punishment for disobedience."

Ms. Beth leaned closer once again, holding Lucy's gaze with her own. "Okay. But what if there's something else as well?"

Lucy's breath caught on the in-between of that moment as she waited for Ms. Beth to say more, somehow sensing in her spirit that the words would change her. "Something else?" she asked.

"What if even then, God had plans for a second garden? Another tree, and another chance to reach out and accept the abundance of life? What if in Eden, God was planning for Gethsemane?"

The question echoed through Lucy, growing in power with each reverberation within her soul.

She held a flower in her hands. The sweet, exotic perfume floated deep into Lucy's heart—carrying Ms. Beth's words right along beside it. Lucy hesitated, allowing the words to take effect. "Are you circling a closed Eden, or have you chosen to step into Gethsemane, through the open gate?"

Lucy blinked. She had never thought of it like that.

"Maybe what you thought was a closed gate meant to punish you is actually God's way of protecting you from remaining in a place where you won't and can't receive His life."

The truth washed Lucy's heart with color. As it brushed over the harsh edges with water, watercolor blooms began to blend one into the other, filling her with understanding.

Lucy's heart swelled as the long-dry soil soaked up this water.

"Where you're preoccupied with your failures and your fears

and the desire to preserve all you might lose, God has a plan to preserve something else. To root you in a place where life can grow within you once more, freely and abundantly. A garden of death for a garden of life, where through His own resurrection Jesus returns all that was stolen." Ms. Beth squeezed Lucy's hands. "So I'll say it once more—what would happen, my dear girl, if instead of returning to Eden over and over, you stepped into Gethsemane?"

Lucy didn't know.

But Ms. Beth wasn't done. She carefully placed the bud into Lucy's open palm. "You're an expert in imitation, are you not? You recognized that painting once attributed to Eliza was a fraud, even when everyone else had accepted it as an original."

Lucy shrugged. "I guess you could say that."

"So let me ask you this, Lucy. What imitations have you accepted as originals in your own life?"

Lucy sighed. She thought of all the many reasons she had considered herself a failure, choosing to carry a sense of shame—whether it was Eliza's house or not living up to her mother's expectations . . . or even not living up to her own.

"In a way, all art is an imitation of a real, living experience. Think of Eliza's garden and the many times she painted it. We love those paintings. They're beautiful and evocative." Ms. Beth took the blossom from Lucy's palm and held it up to her own nose to smell. "But the fragrance is unique to *life*. And it's life that deserves preserving. Abundant life."

Ms. Beth stood, walking several steps over to an organizer filled with gardening tools. She took a pair of cutters and some rooting powder from her bag and began to clip, then plant. Each one received its own small pot. First jasmine, then roses, and camellias. "These are for you," she said. "They're Eliza's. What you didn't realize is that I had taken cuttings from them all along—with plans to preserve them."

Lucy walked over to Ms. Beth and knelt on the winding path

beside her, helping to righten the plants and to prepare the soil. "Thank you." Lucy meant it with all her heart.

"Take care of them for me," Ms. Beth said. "If we don't tend our ground, something else will grow there. The choice is up to us."

Ms. Beth was right. Lucy would be passive no longer. Even if she couldn't save the house, and even if things failed miserably with Declan, she would choose beauty—in her garden, in her art, in her life.

And maybe, over time, choosing beauty would mean growing beauty—beauty that might outlast the rise and fall of blooms and seasons and circumstance.

Because no matter what else failed, she could always do that.

THIRTY-SEVEN

1957
New Orleans, Louisiana

For the past decade or so, Eliza and William had lived a beautiful life among the walls of their Garden District cottage in New Orleans.

William had begun playing with the band at Preservation Hall—quite the distinction—while Eliza had taught art with a specialization in watercolor. Beth loved her school.

Everything had been going so well until, suddenly, everything wasn't.

Funding had run out at the school where Eliza taught, and she no longer had a job. William's work would keep them afloat, but for how long, and how comfortably?

Now, as Eliza set a pumpkin on the porch of their cottage, her stomach knotted just thinking of their predicament and the letter they'd received last week from Susan. Eliza had read it so many times, she could quote it from memory.

Dearest William and Eliza,
   Greetings from Charleston. The work here is never ending, but in the last years I have seen such progress being made. With

each centuries-old dwelling that is saved from demolition, the city retains a little more of its skyline. I am also thankful for the efforts of so many like you, Eliza, who have, in a way, re-defined the city by their art and through their dedication. Many are continuing to visit Charleston as a vacation destination, and it's my hope they will continue to do so for years—and decades!—to come.

I also wanted to mention that I know you've no interest in selling your home on Longitude Lane, but the most curious thing happened the other day. A man came to me expressing interest in the property and offered to pay handsomely. Again, I know you wanted to retain ownership and understandably, but do call me if anything has changed.

I was over on Sullivan's Island last week and bumped into Bea. She's as much a delight as ever. I know you're looking forward to seeing her on your next trip to Charleston.

Best to you and yours, always.

> *Your friend,*
> *Susan*

Leaving the pumpkin on the porch, Eliza reached for the gardening tools she'd set beside the porch steps and began clipping several still-blooming roses from the trellises along the sidewalk. She had brought the rooted rose all the way from Charleston, and it had flourished here.

With a lump in her throat, Eliza carried the fragrant roses inside the cottage and arranged them in a vase at the center of her table.

She stared at the flowers as though they could speak, offering her an answer.

When they didn't offer anything but their beauty, she decided to do the talking.

"Of course I don't want to sell it." She threw her hands in the air. "I can't even fathom selling it." A slow sigh. "But it seems as though we have no option." Eliza looked around the room, taking in the ornate baseboards and the vintage light fixtures. "But I don't want to lose this place either . . . and if we don't sell, finances may force us to move out of the Garden District."

She stared at the roses a long moment. "I don't have a choice at all, do I?" Eliza swallowed past the lump in her throat. "We have to do it. I have to tell William."

And so she did. She called him into the room, and he stood next to the flowers, and he simply listened, as quiet as the petals.

He watched her closely, as though waiting for her to change her mind at any moment. "You're certain about this?" he asked. "We kept the house so that someday we could return."

"Yes . . ." Eliza wrung her hands. "Yes, I'm aware." She shook her head. "But, William, we're running out of options."

His sigh was deep, and his hesitation long, as he seemed to come to terms with it. "I suppose you're right."

"I usually am." She tried a smile to add some levity, but she knew William could see right through it.

He stepped toward her, reached out, and held her tightly in his arms. Then he rested his chin on the top of her head. "My dear Eliza," was all he said. But that was all it took. One tear turned to many, which turned into a shoulders-trembling sort of grief that spun her, disoriented her, until she didn't know which direction to run. Didn't know how to help the lost feeling that echoed through her being. Didn't know where to plant her heart, not any longer.

She began to weep for the good-byes she never had, the deceitful farewells she *did* experience, and for some reason, all of this made her think of her mother, and she wept even harder. She wept for the past, yes, but she wept for the would-not's, mostly. The wouldn't-be's. She wept for all she was missing. For all the finality.

That was the day she lost her home on Longitude Lane.

1976
Charleston

Nearly twenty years had passed since they sold Eliza's beloved home for good.

And in the meantime, William had learned something.

The buyer was his father.

He could only imagine what that man had done to Eliza's garden in search of the silver—attempts that were bound to fail, as the treasure wasn't there to begin with.

So when his mother called and explained his father was likely on his deathbed, William knew he had to say something.

Do something.

Not for his own sake, but for Eliza's.

What if he never again had the opportunity?

What if they were shut out of her home, her garden, forever? His mother had been clear on the phone: his father—whether out of vindication or indifference or plain stubbornness, William may never know—had already made plans to sell Eliza's house to the highest bidder. And William knew he was not going to be the highest bidder.

Though Eliza had already grieved as though her house was gone, William knew deep in his heart there was another way. And only he could make it happen.

By the time William arrived in Charleston that evening, the roads and walkways had received too much rain and were in danger of flooding. A leftover fog hovered all around him, and he tugged his jacket a little closer as he stepped through the gates of his family's estate, toward the door. The February evening was cold, but the weather wasn't the only reason for his chill.

The entire drive over, he had been playing and replaying in his mind what he might say to his father. His heart grieved for their broken relationship, but his mind warned him not to fall for his father's manipulation.

There was a time William had believed he could make his father proud *and* follow his own calling all at once. Then, over time, he began to realize he would never be good enough. So while he had gladly chosen to make his own path in life along with Eliza, he also knew he would probably never fully heal from the throbbing disappointment that his father would always want him to be something he was not. He only hoped he could find some closure now.

William knocked three times at the door. His mother opened it, then embraced him. Her face was flushed save the dark circles under her eyes, and her frame was weak as she held onto him.

"Son, I'm so glad you're home. He's still having many moments of lucidity, if you'd like to talk with him. The doctor said this could linger for some time, or it could all happen fast. There's no way to know for sure."

William took a deep breath but found the oxygen insufficient, so he breathed deeper still. He nodded slowly. "Thanks, Mom." He set a gentle hand on his mother's shoulder and sincerely hoped it would convey a sense of comfort to her weary bones.

Moments later, he was sitting at his father's bedside. His mind spun. He had wondered through many sleepless nights what he might feel when this scene was upon him. Would his emotion be apathy? Rage? Or something else?

As it turned out, he was heartbroken. Heartbroken, very simply, over the loss of his father. Heartbroken for a future without him—but heartbroken for a past without him too. Could William have done more to bridge the gap between them? But how could he have a relationship with a father he couldn't trust?

"You came," his father said, his head propped up by two pillows.

William reached out for his hand. "Of course I came. I'm your son."

His father's hesitation was long. "I never found it, you know. The silver. So I guess you won."

William closed his eyes and sighed. "Dad, you say that as though it were a game. The silver was always Eliza's."

"Her family promised it to ours." His voice was a rasp.

"A century ago, maybe." William opened his eyes. The fog outside muted the sunlight streaming through the little window beside the bed.

"A promise is a promise."

"Promises are broken all the time." William shifted in his seat beside his father. His father looked at him and held on to his gaze. "Is there anything I can do . . . to buy the house back?"

A sarcastic laugh sputtered from his father's mouth. Even in this state, he retained his spunk. But William hoped he might find a way to convince the man.

"What about my inheritance?" William blurted out the words.

His father's expression went blank from shock. "You would trade the inheritance you'll rightly own for that shabby little house on Longitude Lane with the overrun garden and the broken porch steps? Is that what you're telling me?"

"Yes." William need not hesitate at all. He would gladly give it up—gladly do anything for Eliza.

His father shook his head and lowered back onto the pillows, looking up toward the ceiling. "You're a fool, William. But at least you're a lovestruck one."

William's heart skipped a beat, for the insult implied a softening in his father's approach. "You'll agree, then?"

"Yes." His father coughed into his fist. "But I won't play games about the inheritance. If you choose to continue living as though ashamed of this family, you can have the house, but you won't get a dime of the money."

"I don't need the money. I just need the garden." William squeezed his father's hand. "Thank you, Dad."

His father tried to nod once more. "William?"

William swallowed hard. "Yes, sir?"

"I do love you."

Comfort and closure swirled fast with grief, seizing William's heart, so at first, he dared not speak at all. He tried to compose himself, but his voice broke when he finally did say the words out loud.

"I love you too, Dad. I always have."

The next morning, William carefully pulled one of Eliza's watercolors from the back seat of his car, which was parked in Susan's driveway.

Susan met him on the sidewalk, taking one side of the artwork and helping him carry it so it wouldn't be damaged in transit. "You're really committed to this, aren't you?" she asked him. "I have to say, I am finally impressed by you."

William chuckled under his breath. "Happy to hear that after all these years I've gained your approval."

Susan nodded once, smiling as they stepped through the door. Together, they propped the watercolor against the hallway wall. "What can I say? I have high standards for Eliza."

William and Susan stood side by side, looking at the painting.

"It's something else, isn't it? She's still so talented." He slid his hands into the pockets of his trousers. Eliza had painted this stunning depiction of her old garden just last month. Though the garden no longer looked like that—the garden had been ravaged in the search for the silver—she had preserved its beauty exquisitely through her art.

"You still think we can pull it off?" he asked Susan.

"Do you know who I am?" she teased. "Of course we can pull it off. All it will take is some careful planning *and* careful planting. I'll keep working on it after you return to New Orleans. Eliza is going to be so surprised."

"I sure hope so." William shifted his weight on his shoes. "I really want to give her this garden."

"You already have."

And Susan put her finger to her chin as she and William began planning what to do next.

THIRTY-EIGHT

1976
Charleston, South Carolina
Three Months Later

William wouldn't tell her where they were going. Eliza was dying to know why he'd brought her to Charleston and the reason he tapped his loafer against the interior of the taxi cab as though keeping time with a song.

He smiled a mischievous grin, and Eliza felt like a girl again.

She put her gloved hand out the window for the first time in her life and suddenly understood why people did this—for the draw of the air against her hand offered not only resistance but also the sensation of flying.

And she wondered . . . what does it mean to return, really?

It'd been so long since Eliza had come to Charleston. Honestly, she'd imagined she might never return. Years had turned into decades, and time showed Susan's prediction to be correct—even more visitors had begun coming as Charleston's reputation for being a hospitable destination grew.

The driver reached a stop sign, and a bluebird perched above, then raced their vehicle to the next corner, until the daubs of blue and brown on its feathers blurred into the limbs of a tree and it took a rest, having finally returned home.

Eliza peered through the open window. She recognized these streets, and her heart began to thump faster than William's foot against the seat.

She looked toward William and raised an eyebrow, questioning.

He simply shrugged in reply, still with that ever-widening grin.

And Eliza wondered for a moment if they were headed . . .

But surely not.

Long ago, that cursed silver had driven her from her garden, and the property didn't belong to them any longer.

Surely William had something else in mind. Something lovely, no doubt. Perhaps a reunion with Dorothy or Alice or some of her other friends from the Charleston Renaissance.

Eliza chided herself for hoping for her garden.

She tried so hard to get rid of that longing, but as the taxi drew closer and closer to her old house, Eliza found the impulse increasingly harder to ignore.

"William?" she finally asked. *What have you done now?*

"My dear Eliza?" he replied, as though he hadn't the faintest idea what she truly asked of him. He could be such a troublemaker sometimes.

The taxi slowed to a stop in front of the house. The driver got out, then opened the door for Eliza. William fetched their small suitcase and paid the man before coming to stand beside her.

"William." It wasn't a question this time. She looked up at him, too overwhelmed to cry, her eyes wide. "What have you done?"

He took her by the hand and led her through the gate at the side of the house to her garden.

And she wasn't sure if she actually skipped along or if that was just how she remembered it later, but the point was, the moment blurred the spaces between time so that she found she just kept blinking, as though doing so might bring her heart into focus.

She heard the twitter of the bluebirds whose families had lived here for decades and longer, and she saw one out-of-season, beautifully pure gardenia. And the fragrance of it was so sweet, so innocent, that it was fairy dust to her senses. Smelling it sent her tumbling back and forth through time.

And she was at once a young woman dancing in William's arms and an older woman returning to Eden with a new appreciation for its hard-won innocence.

"Welcome home, Eliza." William held out his hand as though asking for a dance.

She looked at him, bewildered—it must be too good to be true. But still, she took his hand.

"I negotiated a deal with my family," he added, as though this would fill in the wide gaps of her understanding.

William spun her into a twirl, grinning, and Eliza's heart spun faster still.

"What kind of a deal?"

"That doesn't matter." He took her other hand as well.

Eliza hesitated. "On the contrary, it matters quite a lot."

"If you must know, I traded my inheritance for it." William never stopped dancing for a moment.

Eliza followed his lead, but struggled to follow his words. "Surely you don't mean what I think you mean."

"That depends." He drew her closer, his hand on her back. "If you think I mean I am no longer heir to a small fortune because I leveraged it to get your house back, then yes, you have the whole picture quite right."

Camellia petals fluttered down in their own beautiful dance, as though they were welcoming her home. And in that moment—so rich with life—a miracle happened.

All she had dreamed and all she had painted and all she had lost came alive.

"William Pinckney." She whispered the words, looking up into his eyes as her heart leapt in their light. "I can't believe you would do that. And somehow"—she shook her head—"somehow you made the garden look just like my painting. Only real." She marveled with absolute wonder at the feeling of her watercolor come to life.

"I love you, don't I?" He turned her again, this time swirling her so fast her hat nearly came off. Her hands flew to catch it as he lowered her to a dip, laughing. "And I may've had some help from Susan with the flower-planting part."

He righted her balance on the old garden stones. "Eliza, listen," he said. "You're my inheritance. You're my fortune. You're worth more to me than any of that other stuff combined. Now we can live here together without the past chasing after us. The house and the garden belong to you now. I've paid the price. It's yours, free and clear."

At this, Eliza did begin to cry.

"If we'd stayed before, those generational squabbles would have followed us and ruined us. Just like you said after the storm. And then when my father bought the property—honestly, I wondered at times whether all hope was lost."

"But it wasn't," Eliza said.

"I would've spent the rest of my life finding a way to get you back into your garden, so it's good, really, that I've already had the chance."

She wiped her tears and smirked up at him. "So you're saying now I'll spend the rest of my life trying to pay you back?"

"That is precisely what I'm saying."

Eliza chuckled and shook her head. "You're impossible."

He winked at her. "You're welcome."

Eliza fell closer into his arms, and the two of them kept dancing through the garden, as the new blooms from the old plants sent a beautiful fragrance into the space between them, and the late afternoon turned into a sunset, and the birds chirped all around.

So this was what it meant to come home again.

William began to sing "My Dear Eliza," and they danced the Charleston as the sunset slipped into twilight.

And Eliza's heart warmed as though covered with blankets on an autumn day—not because she thought of that young girl in the garden, but because she'd become that girl again. Only better—

having loved William for half a lifetime, with the promise of more to come.

For so long, she had painted this fragrant garden—lovely paintings but an imitation of the garden's true enchantment—but now, a miracle had happened. The inanimate, the lost, had come to life. Yesterday's blooms resurrected by William's sacrifice. And her watercolors became their own kind of inheritance in an all new way, as though life had been breathed back into them, and the silver curse broken.

The beauty of the garden had inspired her art, her attempts to revitalize and preserve the city and redefine it for new generations. But she never imagined the inverse may also hold true. That her art might come to life.

And paint became nectar in a new, beautiful promise.

She danced through it as she danced through time, better for having returned to the garden once more.

2007

Rain dropped gently from a violet-blurred sky as Eliza and Juliet, Millie's daughter, stood in the long hallway full of artwork in Eliza's home on Longitude Lane. They had come to the end of it, where the hallway met the windows that overlooked the garden. And as they talked, a hummingbird buzzed up to the window, looking for nectar. It hovered there a long moment, suspended between where it'd been before and where it was headed in its search. Its wings blurring color and flight like watercolor paint.

Charleston had changed substantially over the years, but two things had remained—the flowers and the fences.

In Charleston, folks put wrought-iron gates around their gardens. In New Orleans, on their doors. But Eliza had come to find home in both, albeit in different ways.

Fences and gardens, at once keeping out and growing within.

ough most striking, perhaps, were the gardens growing along fence lines, scattering their petals to the brick walkways below and to the paved ones too. And the little swallows zipping in and out through the turning curves of the ironwork, a fluid and beautiful movement through the otherwise-steady gates.

A movement that can be summed up in this—that redemption, like sunlight, always reaches through the gates, and that we, like flowers, bend toward what grows us. So that the imitations and likenesses we have accepted as originals are exposed as deception, and we are left with the hope of a truer inheritance, a truer promise: a second garden, where all the dead things come alive and all that was forfeited is restored and all that is fractured becomes a mosaic of color.

Juliet pinned a ribbon around the waistline of the dress she'd made for Eliza. With its sheer cape and flowing silhouette, the gown looked like it'd waltzed straight from the Jazz Age.

She and William had kept in touch with Franklin's family over the years, visiting that charming inn of theirs any time they had the occasion. Both Eliza and Millie enjoyed the sense of family the visits brought, and Eliza had developed a sweet relationship with Millie's daughter Juliet, who was close in age to Beth. Before returning to Charleston, she and William had helped Juliet get settled in New Orleans, which Juliet had chosen as the location for her dress shop. They had even lived as neighbors for a short time in the Garden District.

And now, Juliet had traveled all the way here to Eliza's home in Charleston, making a dress for the party honoring her one hundredth birthday. As it turned out, Dorothy Legg wasn't the only one who could live a century.

Juliet took a pin from between her teeth and tacked the final corner of the ribbon waistline, looking beside Eliza into the mirror in front of them. "Well?" she asked.

Eliza smiled. She met Juliet's gaze from their reflection, leaning her head so it touched her friend's. "It's beautiful." But Eliza's mood turned melancholy as she looked in the mirror.

Her life had been rich and full in all the ways living a century brought wealth. She had seen the blooms in every season and planted roots in more gardens than one. Along the way, she had grown strong.

But despite the vibrancy of her life—maybe because of it— Eliza ached for all the spaces where too much water had flooded the paper, or too little kept the colors from blending. She ached because arthritis kept her from painting anymore, or at least painting well.

As she'd lost dexterity, she'd grown more sensitive to nuance, and she couldn't help but repeat a prayer she'd prayed all those years prior—only this time, as a question. *Can you put these pieces back together?* For she wondered what might happen to her home when she passed from this earth, whether her garden on Longitude Lane was in danger of being lost as the generations after hers moved on.

"Are you okay, Eliza?" Juliet asked. "You seem caught up in another world."

Perhaps she was.

Eliza reached up and patted Juliet's hand with her own. She didn't know what to say, because she didn't know if she was all right or not.

She loved this beautiful new gown. She loved her *now*. But she loved her *then* as well.

Juliet fiddled with the ribbon she'd just tacked on to the dress. "This ribbon isn't just for show, you know. It supports the more delicate parts." She locked eyes with Eliza once more. "There's purpose in the design."

That one phrase echoed as a refrain through Eliza's mind, and she felt the answer to her prayer so deeply within her heart that it may as well have been audible.

What you thought was bound for destruction, I will recover for future generations. I am the God of endless hope, and I will restore the life in these walls. You won't have to look beyond my provision for you. My

*provision is sufficient. It's beauty and resurrection—a second garden
as my resurrection makes way for your own.*

With a start, she recognized what was right in front of her—like
figures forming unexpectedly from the blurring together of paint
strokes—and she knew what she needed to do next.

"Juliet." Eliza held her hand a little tighter.

Juliet stilled. "Eliza?"

Eliza shifted to face her and looked directly into her eyes.
"Thank you for all you've done to make this birthday special. Thank
you for all you've done to look after me these past years."

Juliet shook her head. "Eliza, don't—"

But Eliza just took hold of her other hand. "No, you listen to me,
sweetheart. There's something I need to tell you. I've been doing
some research about my family history, and I think there may be
a connection between your ancestors and mine."

Juliet's eyes widened.

"I've bundled up some family heirlooms, and I want you to take
them with you on your journey back to New Orleans."

Juliet slowly blew out a deep breath. "If you're sure." She
squinted at Eliza as though that may help her see the situation
more clearly. "But shouldn't you be giving these things to Beth?"

Eliza raised her chin. "I've already given Beth the house. She
just doesn't know it yet. And the ring too." Eliza turned it several
times around her finger. "I'll write a letter or something equally
dramatic."

Juliet rolled her eyes and gave a half grin. "You're trouble. You're
just like that rose bush you gave me."

"Beautiful and fragrant?" Eliza batted her eyes.

"Hardy and hard to get rid of. No matter what you're up against,
you just keep coming back."

"I'll take that as a compliment." Eliza hooked her arm in the
crook of Juliet's elbow. "Meanwhile, you'll take the heirlooms.
Figure out their story." She met Juliet's gaze, unblinking. "Promise
me you'll pick up where I left off."

Juliet nodded slowly. "I promise, Eliza."

"Good." Eliza patted her hand once more. "Now that we have matters settled, would you mind letting out this ribbon by half an inch? There's a box of Girl Scout cookies in the pantry that are calling my name."

Juliet laughed and reached to free Eliza from the pins. The ribbon was the color of a bluebird's wings.

Contentment and joy and grief all blurred together—and in a way, Eliza had become the color. And the world, the water, so that all the pieces of her blended in unexpected ways as the canvas was turned a little to the left, a little to the right, and the pink dripped down into the blue, down into the yellow, down into the brown, and so on; life and loss and harvest from season to season. A garden's blooms, continually returning for another encore until the circularity of it all becomes in itself a promise through the winter and the spring and the summer and the fall. Always turning, always returning color to the ground and color to the sky.

Like paint and nectar, always fading, always pointing toward a lasting promise of the beauty that is to come: the beauty that already encircles us if we will only spread our wings once in a while.

THIRTY-NINE

Modern Day

One week after Lucy signed the papers for her house over to Declan, she was boxing up Eliza's journals and some old hats and clothes when her cell phone rang.

Her heart jumped. She chided herself for the impulse. Apparently a week was not enough for reality to set in, because she was still hoping Declan would call at any moment, having changed his mind.

She was devastated, of course, about the house, but she was devastated about Declan as well. She had teased him incessantly but in her heart of hearts had really believed he would pull through at the last minute. He hadn't.

So here she was, jobless and soon-to-be houseless as well. Harper had offered her spare room, which Lucy gladly accepted, but Lucy needed a long-term plan. How, after all of this, had she still not made a long-term plan?

Lucy swiped her phone to unlock it, not recognizing the number. "Hello?"

"Lucy? It's Peter. Do you have a moment?"

Her pulse raced. "Is something wrong with Harper?"

"Why would something be wrong with—oh. No, Harper is fine. I should've led with that. Harper is actually the reason I'm calling.

I'm at a little antique shop on King Street and was hoping you could meet me down here."

Lucy's gaze swept over the boxes littering the wooden floor. She'd welcome a break, however odd this one was. "Sure. I can be there in about ten minutes."

Peter proceeded to give more detailed directions to a store Lucy had passed many times but never stopped to look inside. She slipped her feet into her most comfortable flats and slung her purse over her shoulder.

Lucy arrived at the antique shop even sooner than she'd expected, and from the glass door she saw Peter holding something tiny up toward the light.

"Peter?" The bell above the door chimed as she entered. "Want to tell me why you're acting so strangely?"

His grin could've lit up the sky. "Thank you for coming, Lucy." He stepped closer toward her, being careful not to knock anything off the cluttered aisle of knickknacks. "I'm good with houses and old tile, but this is new territory. What do you think?" He held a ring out toward her, and it glimmered with a thousand rainbows.

Lucy gasped as it all sank in. "You're engaged!" She started jumping up and down. She couldn't help herself. The woman behind the counter gave her a look that said *you break anything, you're buying*, so she forced herself to a standstill position and grabbed Peter's hands to get a better look at the ring he held.

"Well, technically I'm not engaged yet."

Lucy waved one hand in the air. "Oh, you know she'll say yes. What does Millie think? Is Millie thrilled? What am I saying? Of course Millie's thrilled."

"Millie doesn't know yet." He set the ring in her hands, and it was her turn to hold it up toward the light. This thing had some impressive sparkle.

"You think Harper will like it?" he asked. "I want to be sure it's something she would pick out for herself, and you know her style better than I do."

Lucy nodded emphatically. "Any woman would love this ring, Peter." Delicate swirls stemmed out from the diamond at the center of an intricate pattern that was dainty but not fussy. The oval-shaped diamond glittered with the intensity of the promise it held.

If it was possible, Peter's grin widened even more. Lucy couldn't blame him. She was about to scream news of their engagement down King Street, and he hadn't even asked Harper yet.

Lucy held the ring closer for inspection. "You know, it almost looks like the ring Beth gave me with the house. Eliza's."

"Makes sense, because this one is from the 1920s." Peter shrugged. "That's around the time yours was made, right?"

Lucy handed the ring back to him and looked down at her own. She took note of the similarities between them—though Harper's ring held a promise for the future, whereas Lucy's ring held a hidden past. Perhaps, actually, they weren't that similar at all. But still, something within her felt as though she was on to something. . . .

"Peter, you said that ring is authentic, right? A hundred years old."

"Yes, it's authentic. Just like yours." He took a closer look at Harper's engagement ring. "I guess I should ask what the materials are. I don't even know. What did they use in the 1920s? White gold? Silver?"

Silver.

The word spun through Lucy's mind, twinkling like tinsel. She held her hand up and rotated it back and forth, looking from every angle at the ring that encircled her finger.

Of course! Why hadn't she seen this before?

William gave this ring to Eliza in the midst of the he-took-it-she-took-it feud. What if the ring itself was the missing silver, and Lucy had been wearing it all along?

She hurried over toward the counter and caught the attention of the jeweler, who'd shot her a snarky glance just moments prior.

"Yes, ma'am?" the woman asked. "How can I help you?"

Lucy removed the ring from her finger and set it down on the counter. "I inherited this ring. I was hoping you could tell me more about it, particularly about the materials."

The jeweler looked toward Peter. Maybe she was evaluating whether another darting glance toward Lucy would hurt her chances of getting Peter's sale.

She pulled out a small magnifying glass all on her own accord.

"Now that's interesting." She looked at Lucy, then back down at the ring, suddenly serious. "*Very* interesting. Do you see this little mark on the inside of the ring?"

Lucy nodded. She'd wondered what that was ever since she first noticed it weeks ago. She'd assumed it was some sort of inscription. "What does it mean?"

"That's called a hallmark, and this particular emblem is something we only see on very old silver. We're talking Revolutionary War and earlier. This is quite remarkable." Her eyes widened, a considerable change from her chastising glance moments ago. "This ring would have originally been a different, functional piece. Most likely a spoon, if my guess is correct. But whoever transformed it was very careful not to melt it down and, instead, preserved the stamp." The woman held it out to her. "This is Paul Revere silver."

Peter stepped closer to the counter. The little lines around his eyes wrinkled with curiosity. The man loved a good story, didn't he? "You're saying she has been walking around wearing antique silver on her hand?" He turned to Lucy then. "Do you realize what this means?"

Did she? The dynamics were only beginning to reverberate in her heart.

A centuries-old treasure, passed down. Its promise preserved despite—perhaps even because of—its transformation.

All those years prior, William must have known Eliza would be in danger so long as his family was after her inheritance, her history. He transformed it, not only as a token of his own promise, but also to keep her inheritance secure. So long as she wore it, no one would ever be able to take that from her.

And Lucy wore it now. In fact, Lucy had been wearing it all along.

Lucy grinned as she slipped the ring back on her finger. She appreciated the monetary value—which was a not-so-small fortune—but she would never sell it now. She would wear it for the rest of her life.

This was the garden promise Ms. Beth had talked about. For the areas she'd failed, for the areas she was inadequate, for the areas she was striving: this was her second garden. Provision she needed only recognize, bringing dry areas back to life. Transforming a past into a promise for abundant blooms to come.

Lucy took the porch steps by two and opened her front door that led to the piazza spanning the length of the house. At the second door of her single house, she closed her eyes and breathed in the fragrance of Eliza's garden.

Her time here at Eliza's house was coming to an end, but maybe that was okay. She had the ring now. She'd solved the mystery of the silver, discovered Eliza's story, and maybe also discovered her own.

She was storing up this full-hearted contentment when she opened her eyes and saw the thesaurus that'd been set beside the door.

Hmm. Now that was odd.

Lucy bent down and pulled a note from inside the pages.

Thought I'd beat you to the punch this time.—Declan

Lucy grinned and rolled her eyes. She would forgive the fact he obviously entered the house without her permission. Especially considering the house was technically his now.

The sound of music startled her.

Lucy scrunched her nose, trying to better hear the tune, then followed the sound. When she stepped inside, she nearly dropped the thesaurus.

Declan was standing in her foyer, framed by the stained-glass archway above his head. He held on to an old cassette player as a song that resembled a Cab Calloway tune continued to play.

Lucy stepped closer. Declan set the cassette player down as she neared. That's when she recognized the chorus.

"My Dear Eliza."

Even for Declan, this was smooth. Lucy stopped a half step closer to him than she probably should've. Declan took a half step closer still.

"Would you like to dance?"

Lucy looked up at him in a stupor. He smelled like the fancy espresso at that coffee shop up the road, and bergamot, and for some reason, the flowers from Eliza's garden. She swallowed around the lump in her throat. "I probably shouldn't. The last time I danced with you did not end well."

One corner of Declan's lips pulled into a grin. "I beg to differ." He brushed a stray strand of hair from her forehead. There was a gentle quietness in his eyes she hadn't seen since that day in Edisto. Or maybe it was simply peace. Would she recognize that in him if she saw it?

"Lucy." Her name on his lips was spellbinding, and she wondered for a moment where she'd be without him, even though he'd made things impossibly difficult. "Before you turn me down, you may want to hear my new business plan."

She raised her chin, hoping to hide the flickers of attraction she still felt every time she looked at him. "Business plan, you said?"

He nodded ever so slightly. "I've taken full charge over the company, and we're going in a new direction. Sustainable architecture and historical sensitivity."

This couldn't be happening.

"Historical sensitivity?" Lucy spun the ring two times around her finger. Her gaze swept the walls around them, finally landing on Declan. "And may I ask what brought about this sudden change of heart?"

"I met someone." When his eyes met hers, their gazes locked. He didn't look away. He didn't have a reason to any longer. "She taught me that while we can't live in the past, we *can* preserve its structure, and that's a worthy endeavor. Because if no one preserves their homes, who will preserve their stories? And if no one preserves *their* stories, who will preserve our own?"

"Sounds like a wise woman."

"She is." His eyes held warmth, and Lucy found herself inching toward him. "I was rather hoping she might consider staying here, in this house. I have a plan to replant the gardens in the back according to an old photograph of this property that I found among William's journals. I'd like to open the garden for visitors, and obviously this would all work better if someone was living here."

Lucy blinked. "I thought you said I had two weeks."

"I never signed the papers." Declan slid his hands into the pockets of his khakis. "I waited as long as possible. Until my father forced my hand. So I told him I'd made my decision. I would take over the business, but under no circumstance would I take Eliza's house."

"You did that for me?"

"It's something I should have done all along. You gave me the courage. We're going to specialize in offering hyphens for people with historic properties. We've been going about it all wrong. Our goal should've never been to replicate the walls and floors in our house extensions, nor should it have been to destroy them. But rather to create a distinct difference between past and present, history and future, where even something so simple as a wooden floor can tell a story. The story of the in-between."

Lucy shook her head. "I don't understand—what are you actually saying?"

"The house is yours, Lucy. I won't take your silver. The feud ends here and now."

Her heart fluttered as she processed all he'd just said. "You want to make the garden a historical attraction?"

He nodded, smiling. "What do you think?"

She could have leapt into his arms. "That sounds wonderful."

Declan let out a long sigh. "Good, because there's one more thing I wanted to ask you. I've decided to make better use of my architecture degree, and I need to hire an art consultant. Included in the position would be funding should the employee want to further their education by attending architecture school. You know, hypothetically, of course. Do you know anyone who'd be interested?" His gaze danced with charm.

"Do I ever!" Lucy laughed, her curls falling around her face in wild abandon.

The music continued to build as Declan reached his arm around Lucy's waist and pulled her closer. "Be honest. Do you think my great-grandfather would mind me ripping off his moves? I mean, it's quite a song. And he did record it, so I feel like that's fair game."

Lucy looked back at him, so close she could feel his breath mingling with her own. "I don't know. Do you think my great-grandmother would mind me reproducing her watercolors?"

Declan bit down on his bottom lip as he watched her. "I suppose we'd better make this good, then. After all, you do already have their ring."

Her lips parted, and anticipation built higher and higher, until her heart spun so fast she thought she may very likely lift off from the ground. "Now kiss me already, Pinckney."

His grin widened as his lips inched to brush her own. "I do like a woman who speaks her mind."

As he kissed her, every part of her washed with color and she continued to hear the chorus of that moment long after the cassette ended. And just for good measure, she kissed him again.

She imagined living here in the coming months and welcoming guests to the garden. She could even display some of Eliza's watercolors in the setting she'd originally painted them. Eliza may be gone from this place, but her art and her heritage never would be.

Maybe maintaining these spaces really just meant living well. In and out of wars, in and out of summers and winters and falls. Preserving the beautiful parts to pass on as stories and flowers and walls. Maybe people can't always return to the physical spaces or even to the years, but they can return to the spaces of that same feeling, that same joy, and live it in new ways. Because when beauty changes people, the changes are fundamental and continue on.

Lucy grinned, reaching up to twirl a lock of Declan's hair around her finger, and his hair caught against her ring. She would tell him the story about the silver eventually. But really, what was the rush?

For now, she would dance among the garden.

When azaleas bloom in winter.

When hurricanes come in fall.

Maybe the point was not so much these out-of-season moments, but more what was growing in between them. The clumsy grasp to keep summer's blooms in winter would inevitably fail. And yet hope always came rising up, resurrected from frozen ground.

For as garden turns to garden, flowers turn to dust, and glory goes to glory, the changes are within us.

And maybe beauty's greatest achievement isn't in the staying . . . but that in its return, again and again, it paints the eternal—all the beautiful things that will never fade.

A NOTE ON
HISTORICAL ACCURACY

While it may seem unlikely that any family would leave heirloom silver buried underground for decades, the reality is that many people did just that. During the Civil War, homeowners all over Charleston rushed to hide their family silver from the approaching Union troops just as Clara does in the prologue. Many of these people were driven from their houses by the war—a city under siege and wrought with cannon fire. Most of them returned. Some of them did not. But returning was only the first step. These families also had to remember where they'd buried their inheritances, and on more than one occasion, the silver wasn't found until decades later.

Eliza is completely fictional, but her friends Susan Pringle Frost and Alice Ravenel Huger Smith are not. Both of these women, and others like them, were highly instrumental in not only saving the historical integrity of Charleston but also in reimagining it as a city where others may like to come. Their efforts led to a nationwide movement to preserve historic structures, and we have them to thank for the beautiful city Charleston is today. At the same time a preservation movement was rising up, a group of artists and musicians created what is now known as the Charleston Renaissance. Through artwork like Eliza's, these men and women envisioned a whole new image for the city of Charleston—an image that inspired tourism and redefined the culture of the city. In a way, through their artwork, the city itself changed to become more like these beautiful depictions of the Lowcountry. The one caveat to this accomplishment is it came at a time when society as a whole did not yet value Black cultural artifacts—like the satchel we saw in *The Dress Shop on King Street*—and tragically, most of those artifacts and homes were lost. Still, their efforts had fundamental and long-lasting effects on the way we view preservation today.

Eliza's garden is also inspired by a real-life counterpart called Mrs. Whaley's Garden that you can visit on your next trip to Charleston. It is an absolutely magical place that I can't recommend highly enough. While you're at it, take a look at Mrs. Whaley's memoir as well, *Mrs. Whaley and Her Charleston Garden*. I like to think had Eliza been a real person, she and Mrs. Whaley might have been friends.

One final note I will add is that Charleston really is a city of gardens. Many of its residents have beautifully planned outdoor spaces that span the length of their sometimes-petite downtown yards. Plan to take a tour of them if you're ever in Charleston, and you'll immediately understand why Eliza is so caught up in the beauty of all that's growing within.

AUTHOR'S NOTE

Dear reader,

I hope you've enjoyed reading Lucy and Eliza's story as much as I've enjoyed writing it. What a journey this story has been for me. I first wrote this manuscript five years ago, prior to writing what became *The Dress Shop on King Street*. Lucy's story line is mostly the same as that early draft, but Eliza's was completely rewritten in the spring of 2020, as a pandemic changed everyone's patterns of life. In a world that seemed so overwhelming, it was a joy to escape into the worlds of these characters, but I did find myself asking a different set of questions than I had when I first wrote the novel. Somewhere along the way, *Paint and Nectar* was no longer just about the importance of history, but more largely about the incredible hope that beauty offers us—hope of a better world, both this side of heaven and beyond.

In the process of editing this novel, I moved from my dearly beloved first home into my dearly beloved dream house. The themes of memories, and the value of preservation as well, were deep within my heart as I made that transition.

As I tried to figure out what the larger message of the novel had become, I realized that along the way it had changed, and I had too. There is an incredible power in beauty not only to uplift our spirits but also to point us toward heaven if we only pay attention.

I believe that every time we stop to see the beauty of God's creation, we have the ability to be transformed through the comings and goings of all the "bluebirds" in our lives. I hope you'll take the time to do that today.

I'm looking forward to sharing Alice and Clara's story with you in the next HEIRLOOM SECRETS novel!

—Ashley

ACKNOWLEDGMENTS

Eliza's story has been with me in some form since my first trip to Charleston seven years ago. So many people have influenced it for the better over the years, and I am grateful for you all.

A huge thank you, first of all, to you—my readers! What a privilege it has been after pursuing publication so long to have each and every one of you invested in these stories. Thank you for all the kind reviews, the words of encouragement, and the efforts you've taken to share the HEIRLOOM SECRETS novels. My prayer is that God would touch your hearts through these stories as He's touched mine through writing them.

Thank you to everyone at Bethany House for being downright incredible.

Raela Schoenherr, you are the best of the best, and I will forever be grateful you are my acquisitions editor. I'm also grateful to have you as a friend.

Elizabeth Frazier, I have no idea how you do what you do! Without you, my stories would be a jumbled-up mess. Thank you for everything you've graciously put into this book and this series.

Thank you also to everyone who read the early draft of this story and offered editorial feedback. Your early reads are invaluable to me.

Amy Lokkesmoe, Noelle Chew, Rachael Wing, Brooke Vikla,

and Serena Hanson, as well as everyone else in marketing and publicity—you are amazing. I am so grateful for your investment in me and in these stories. You're also all absolutely delightful.

Karen Solem, your expertise, your wisdom, and your kindness humble me, and I can't imagine these books would be here without you.

Ed Grimball and Sue Bennett, you are the two finest tour guides around. Your passion for Charleston and your hospitality largely inspired this novel. I can't wait to see you both again.

Thank you to my parents, Steve and Laurie Young, for your unwavering support, excitement, and friendship.

To my husband, Matthew, and son, Nathanael—you two make my life beautiful. Thank you for supporting my dreams, for celebrating with me when they come true, and for being really flexible about random Zoom calls and "necessary" research trips to Charleston.

I am beyond grateful for my friendships within the writing community and for all of you who have supported the launch of this series. I can't wait to share the final HEIRLOOM SECRETS novel with you soon!

BOOK CLUB QUESTIONS

1. Which character did you most identify with and why?

2. Many times throughout the novel, Eliza finds herself unable to do the thing she loves most—paint. Why do you think she struggles this way, and how does she overcome it? Have you ever found yourself in a similar situation? What did you do about it?

3. *Paint* and *nectar* aren't two words you would typically put together. What is their relation through this novel? How does paint become nectar, and vice versa?

4. Ms. Beth was a favorite character of mine to write. Why do you think she is so interested in her work at the art museum and her garden?

5. Did any of William and Eliza's decisions surprise you? Which ones? How does the time period in which they live affect their choices?

6. Why do you think Lucy is so invested in saving the house, beyond her spite for Declan's plan? What need is she trying to satisfy?

7. Preservation and progress are often hard to maintain side by side. What is important about each of them?

8. Did you know about the Charleston Renaissance prior to reading this novel? It's fascinating how many women were involved in those first preservation meetings. How might Charleston look different today were it not for their efforts?

9. Did you expect what happens to the silver? How does this transformation reflect key themes in the novel?

10. Clara is clearly up to something. Any guesses what might happen with her story in the next HEIRLOOM SECRETS novel?

11. Peter and Harper are getting married! Did you read their story in *The Dress Shop on King Street*? What do you think their wedding will be like?

12. The story touches upon two biblical gardens: Eden and Gethsemane. What is the significance of these two gardens, and why does it matter that one essentially begins the Old Testament and one the New Testament?

Ashley Clark writes romantic women's fiction set in the South and is the acclaimed author of *The Dress Shop on King Street* and *Paint and Nectar*. With a master's degree in creative writing, Ashley teaches literature and writing courses at the University of West Florida. Ashley has been an active member of American Christian Fiction Writers for over a decade. She lives with her husband, son, and two rescued cocker spaniels off Florida's Gulf Coast. When she's not writing, she's rescuing stray animals, dreaming of Charleston, and drinking all the English breakfast tea she can get her hands on. Be sure to visit her website at www.ashleyclark books.com.

Sign Up for Ashley's Newsletter

Keep up to date with Ashley's news on book releases and events by signing up for her email list at ashleyclarkbooks.com.

More from Ashley Clark

In 1946, Millie Middleton left home to keep her heritage hidden, carrying the dream of owning a dress store. Decades later, when Harper Dupree's future in fashion falls apart, she visits her mentor, Millie. As the revelation of a family secret leads them to Charleston and a rare opportunity, can they overcome doubts and failures for a chance at their dreams?

The Dress Shop on King Street • Heirloom Secrets

You May Also Like . . .

Mireilles finds her world rocked when the Great War comes crashing into the idyllic home she has always known, taking much from her. When Platoon Sergeant Matthew Petticrew discovers her in the Forest of Argonne, three things are clear: she is alone in the world, she cannot stay, and he and his two companions might be the only ones who can get her to safety.

Yours Is the Night by Amanda Dykes
amandadykes.com

When a stranger appears in India with news that Ottilie Russell's brother must travel to England to take his place as a nobleman, she is shattered by the secrets that come to light. But betrayal and loss lurk in England too, and soon Ottilie must fight to ensure her brother doesn't forget who he is, as well as stitch a place for herself in this foreign land.

A Tapestry of Light by Kimberly Duffy
kimberlyduffy.com

After her dreams of mission work are dashed, Darcy has no choice but to move in with the little sister of a man who she's distrusted for years. Searching for purpose, she jumps at the chance to rescue a group of dogs. But it's Darcy herself who'll encounter a surprising rescue in the form of unexpected love, forgiveness, and the power of letting go.

Love and the Silver Lining by Tammy L. Gray
STATE OF GRACE
tammylgray.com

❖ BETHANYHOUSE

More from Bethany House

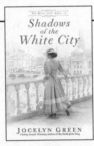

When Sylvie Townsend's Polish ward, Rose, goes missing at the World's Fair, her life unravels. Brushed off by the authorities, Sylvie turns to her boarder and Rose's violin instructor, Kristof Bartok, for help searching the immigrant communities. When the unexpected happens, will Sylvie be able to accept the change that comes her way?

Shadows of the White City by Jocelyn Green
THE WINDY CITY SAGA #2
jocelyngreen.com

Zara Mahoney was enjoying newlywed bliss until her life is upended by her estranged sister, Eve, and Zara must take custody of her children. Eve's struggles lead her to Tiff Bradley, who's determined to help despite the past hurts the relationship triggers. Can these women find the hope they—and those they love—desperately need?

The Way It Should Be by Christina Suzann Nelson
christinasuzannnelson.com

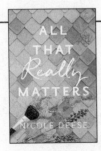

Molly McKenzie has made social media influencing a lucrative career, but nailing a TV show means proving she's as good in real life as she is online. So she volunteers with a youth program. Challenged at every turn by the program director, Silas, and the kids' struggles, she's surprised by her growing attachment. Has her perfect life been imperfectly built?

All That Really Matters by Nicole Deese
nicoledeese.com

BETHANYHOUSE